The Charlotte Armstrong Treasury

The Charlotte

Armstrong Treasury

COWARD, McCANN & GEOGHEGAN, Inc.
New York

Contents

PREFACE BY ALICE CROMIE   7

THE WITCH'S HOUSE   13

MISCHIEF   179

THE DREAM WALKER   303

Preface

A few years ago at a rather motley award dinner, Charlotte Armstrong found herself seated near such film celebrities as Debbie Reynolds and Jeanne Crain, while her husband, advertising man Jack Lewi, had a well-known Hollywood columnist for table partner.

Lewi politely mentioned that his wife was a writer, too, and introduced her. Miss Armstrong, recognizing the blank look and the vacuum behind it, said helpfully, "I write mysteries."

"Oh, well!" said the gossip writer, both relieved and reassuring. "I don't even have time to read *good* books!"

Charlotte Armstrong merrily, wickedly, and typically ever after began her speeches with this great and gratuitous put-down.

In 1957 Anthony Boucher wrote in the New York *Times:* "The festival of Halloween ten days ago was, I trust, celebrated with peculiarly fitting rites in Glendale, Calif.; for there dwells one of the few authentic spell-casting witches of modern times: Charlotte Armstrong. . . ."

Timeless the statement and the lady! She was indeed writing about spells and spooky goings-on and, best of all, *explaining* them, as in *The Dream Walker,* long before sorcerers, shamans, and demonists of almost any denomination had chased the reluctant spies off the best seller lists.

She used botulism, for example, as a sure means of cutting down some of the population well before it became a dreadfully oft-used word in newspaper headlines. (The novel was *Catch as Catch Can,* 1953, and her idea grew from her own home-canning efforts after a harvest of her onetime victory garden. Whether or not her tomatoes or peaches were preservable, her plots remain as fresh as—one hopes —tomorrow's breakfast egg.)

She wrote *The Witch's House* in 1963 and not only created one of
the most memorable and pitiable "witches" in suspense fiction but
took a vivid and unsentimental look at school systems, administrators,
professors, and students, in a day when their problems were not quite
so much the general concern. Who can forget the Provost? "Miles
Drinkwater was gallant with chair, cigarette, ashtray. Anabel endured these ceremonies, but as soon as he had put his rump solidly
into his chair she said brightly, 'Well? What have you done?' . . . 'I
. . . er . . . am inclined to think,' said the Provost, working at a
modified twinkle as best he could, 'that your husband might be rather
disconcerted, on his return, if too much of a fuss were to be raised.'"
And once Anabel O'Shea has assured him she will hold him responsible for not having started the search earlier: ". . . He was not pleased
with himself. He was having a glimpse—very upsetting. A classical
idea. Death was better than dishonor? What? In this year of Our
Lord?"

Mischief, in 1950, which began as a play, aptly titled *Little Nell,*
and became a movie starring Marilyn Monroe, *Don't Bother to
Knock,* must have improved the quality of baby-sitters, if not hotel
detection or easy romancers, giving parents pause to think before
they selected.

The opening of *The Dream Walker* states a case that recurs as
miserably often as hayfever and far more fatally, that of damaging a
statesman's reputation by association:

"It was the old power of the Big Lie. Even now, when you don't
have to believe the lie anymore, it's hard enough, isn't it, to believe
that anyone would have gone to so much trouble? . . . I hear people
still saying, 'Oh, I never believed that stuff *but.* . . .' They are still
talking."

Ellery Queen, introducing one of her prizewinning stories, "The
Enemy," in an anthology, declares that it is far more than a detective
story and "is, unfortunately, as desperately needed today as it was
19 years ago when the story was first published." It dealt with the
meaning and purpose of truth and the power of truth's enemies.

But enough, as almost any one of her heroines might say (those
liberated invincible girls, velvet to the touch, with stainless steel-trap
minds and iron thoughts when needed). The author, above all, would
be impatient with too much talk of messages, although her fan mail
continues in volume with grateful readers giving thanks for her in-

sights, philosophy, and ways of dealing with pesky or major problems.

Nowadays, particularly in England, where many of those who come the closest to being her peers, ask, "What was this smashing Charlotte Armstrong like?" I begin eagerly to answer, usually forgetting that I never really knew her. Except in each of her works.

Take an Anabel O'Shea, hunting for her vanished husband, refusing to be comforted because the police have finally issued an all points bulletin ("some marvelous cure-all, called an APB"): "They won't help me. I'll have to find Pat by myself." And Armstrong fans know it's time to fasten the seat belts.

Or in *Mischief,* when the hopelessly twisted Nell comes "hopping, tottering, kicking . . . and her hands clawed for Ruth's face, hunting Ruth's eyes. *OK,* thought Ruth. *All right.* . . . She was wilder than the tomboy she used to be. She was more vicious than the girl athlete." She was a mother fighting for her child and she was "easily able to be absolutely ruthless. . . . She said to herself, *OK. All right.* And she was not afraid."

I would bet a bottom dollar that this is just about what Charlotte Armstrong said to life or the ever after. She was a storyteller, first and last.

Once, poking at this keyboard, trying to strike the perfect note to describe her latest novel, I had to settle for: "Charlotte Armstrong is a lady who has already used up all the superlatives in this typewriter, but evokes them all again."

And again.

—Alice Cromie
January, 1972

To A. B.

The Witch's House

Monday

HE HAPPENED to be standing perfectly still, considering what, if anything, he ought to take home. Papers to grade? Class statistics to bring up to date? He was a young mathematics instructor named Elihu (but mercifully nicknamed Pat) O'Shea; he was accustomed to using his mind and not his fingers. Therefore, he did not paw his desk or flip his calendar, but, standing still, he marshaled and reviewed his obligations.

His cubicle, all done in gray metal and something less than cozy, looked east; it was dim, at this hour in early March. When the door of the office directly across the corridor opened, the band of late sunlight did not reach all the way to Pat's open door. Pat could physically see his fellow faculty member, Professor Everett Adams (Biology) also preparing to leave at the end of Monday, but Everett did not notice him, and Pat did not move or speak. He was no pal of Everett's, whom he considered a dull old bunny. Nor did he think about the other man, particularly, until sight suddenly connected with brain, and Pat came to startled attention.

Everett Adams was a pace within his own place. No one else could see him at all as he took an object out of his right-hand jacket pocket, transferred it to his left and adjusted his left arm, and the briefcase it held, so as to minimize the bulge of the object. Then Everett stepped into the corridor, pulled his door shut, and locked it.

A sound came out of Pat O'Shea, a growl of angry astonishment. Everett swiveled his thatch of gray. He had very large brown eyes, set abnormally far apart, so that his temples looked thin and flat. The eyes flashed, seeming to reveal a moment of anguished shock. Then they veiled themselves. Everett hunched his narrow shoulders and strode off.

Pat O'Shea yanked open his top desk drawer, swept papers within, shut it, locked it, snatched his brown raincoat from the gray metal clothes tree, and whirled out of his office.

He was furious! *So?* But was it so?

Everett, scurrying toward the intersecting corridor, was detouring now around a knot of students in front of a bulletin board. Pat went after him. When he was angry, his amiable rugged face became another face. Now, as he walked fast, just without running, one of the students detached himself from the group to stare curiously at him. Pat checked himself.

If he had seen what he thought he had seen, *then* he was very angry indeed. But could he be absolutely sure? No. So he would not run, shout, or make a fuss. And he had better not let this particular student suspect that anything was up.

This Parsons boy was neither an athlete nor a brain and not gifted with any particular charm. Nevertheless, he had constituted himself the college gossip and, as such, he had power. It was best not to stir him up, because he was not scrupulous about what tales he told, but relished the exercise of his imagination, in which might lie all the power Mike Parsons would ever have. So Pat slowed down, dismissed as best he could the black look that anger put on his face, murmured a hail and farewell, and strolled by, knowing that Everett Adams had made it to the next wing, down which he would go to the left where, at the end, a flight of stairs led to a lower-level exit to the faculty parking lot. This was Pat's own natural route and he pursued it.

At the intersection of corridors, there was a glass-enclosed place where Joanne Knowles was on the department switchboard. Turning the corner, Pat waved to her, since she was supposed to know what faculty members were in or not in the Science Building. Then he drove his long legs to go faster than he appeared to be going.

Ahead of him, and moving fast, Everett Adams ducked downward. Pat reached the stairs and went bonging down their metal treads. Everett was at the door, at the bottom. Pat hit the glass while it still swung and as he came out into the shaded spot, he shouted, "Adams!"

But Everett was into his car, a 1960 Chevrolet Bel Air, and putting it into motion very quickly. Pat was just leaping down the two broad stone steps to the pavement when Everett backed out of his slot, reversed, and went sailing away. As he did so Pat saw a form, draped in flowered cotton, rise from the coping of a low stone wall that held back the plantings across this sunken court. But he was running to his own '61 tan Rambler, and he pretended not to see the girl, although he knew, at once, who she was and why she was there. She was Vee Adams, Everett's daughter, and she must have been waiting, over there on the sunny side, to ride home with her father.

But Everett had "forgotten" her. Oh-ho, had he, though?

Guilty, thought Pat. By golly, he *is* guilty and he knows I know it. So Pat felt furious all over again.

It certainly looked as if the thing in Everett's jacket pocket was that ultraviolet-reflecting objective for a microscope, an attachment so delicate and fine as to be very expensive, indeed. Just such a small precious piece of laboratory equipment had disappeared, ten days ago, from the university's Science Building. Presumed stolen.

What was making Pat O'Shea so furious was the fact that although there was no proof of the thief's identity, and no open accusation, nevertheless there was suspicion. And the continuance in the university of a second-year student named Rossi was being made not only miserable, but almost impossible. He was the only student known to have been alone in the laboratory on the morning the theft had been discovered. Only that. But it was enough.

This Rossi was a boy whom Pat had wished to encourage. Pat had wanted him to believe that he was free to move from the background of his kin to the company of his kind. The boy came of uneducated people who did not fully understand his urge toward knowledge, but the boy had the qualities that lift a teacher's tired heart. How could the poor kid keep his mind on his studies, or believe in his opportunity, in the shadow of this doubt, so cruel—if he were innocent?

Now, if this . . . this . . . this . . . (Pat couldn't find a word dirty enough for Everett Adams) . . . this highly respected, pompous old *bunny*—who had even called a meeting and spoken high-minded words about basic honesty—if he himself was just now making off with the *loot . . . !*

The man must be crazy! But, crazy or not, Everett Adams wasn't going to watch, from his cozy burrow of privilege, a valuable boy's life-chance snuff out. Not now. Not if Pat had seen what he thought he had seen. Pat would take care of that. *If.* So Pat's car jumped.

Everett had not turned upgrade, to his right, toward the Main Gate as he normally would, but to his left. OK, thought Pat, suddenly jubilant. Follow that car! Wherever the dickens Everett thought he was going, Pat O'Shea was going too. He intended to catch up with and confront the man while the thing was still in his pocket. If the thing was Everett's property, Pat could apologize. Natural mistake. So sorry. But he would have to find out.

And he thought he would find out. After all, the driver ahead could hardly throw a thing out of the car without the driver behind detecting such a movement. And if Everett dropped it quietly overboard, Pat would see it hit the road. Oh no, no, Everett was not going to get away with a thing. Pat turned gleefully left, to follow.

Strict rules prevailed against speed on the campus so the two cars proceeded with dignified obedience past the Library and the Administration Building and bent away to go around the gymnasium, past the tennis courts, to an exit at the southwest corner of the campus. Here, where Everett might have turned left to regain the main road into town, again he chose the other way.

Pat nosed into traffic behind him. This street pertained to nothing significant that he could imagine but, about a mile farther on, it would cross another popular route into the heart of the town. Pat trundled along behind, angry, but holding to the fair doubt, knowing very well that "to see something with your own eyes" is not always reliable evidence.

At the junction Everett did not turn toward town but to his right, which way would lead him out into the country. Pat, suddenly impatient, came up to the intersection rapping his horn button, in the swift *toot-toot-toot* which means "Give me your attention. I want to speak to you." Everett must have heard it, bu he did not even hesitate. On the contrary, his car picked up its heels.

Pat whipped around the corner in his wake, thinking, Guilty, all right! The guilty flee and I pursueth.

(There was a gas station on that corner. Far in upon the concrete, a lad named Dick Green was hosing off a car. He looked up, at the horn blasts, and saw Mr. O'Shea, from whom he took calculus at the university. Dick half raised a hand in greeting. But Mr. O'Shea had not seen him—just went busting around the corner. Funny.)

Now, they were going north and it was becoming country. Pat did not attempt to speed and pass and block Everett's way. Dangerous and unnecessary. Wherever he can go, I can go, Pat thought, and when he stops, there I'll be. His Nemesis is what I am. He grinned to himself, thinking how he would tell Anabel about this cops-and-robbers adventure. The street had become a highway which ran straight. There was home-going traffic on it, but Pat hung on the Chevy's heels. Let the guilty suffer.

Up ahead a red light bloomed. As Everett slid up to the stop, four cars were already motionless there. Everett, with Pat behind him, was in the middle lane. To their left, the left-turn slot was being entered by the car behind them. Everett suddenly yanked his wheel, nipped around the cars that waited, flashed through the left-turn slot, and ran the light. The car entering the slot squealed and braked, and hemmed Pat in.

Well, well, well! Pat rolled to his own legal position and stopped there. Everything he does says he's guilty, the fool! Or why does he run away from me? Which he has just successfully done, by the way. OK. Even so. All *I* have to do is turn the suspicion on him, which I can do with many hedges, from a position of noble doubt and humility before the truth, and so on . . . and he will have had it. And Rossi will be all right. So . . . why don't I just go on home?

But Pat didn't want to go on home. He was not only furious about the theft, the injustice, but miffed on his own account. He had been tricked, caught napping, and he didn't like it. Furthermore, the position of noble doubt and humble inquiry did not fall in anything like as well with his mood as to catch Everett personally and tell him a thing or two. Right now.

But Everett's car had slipped over a small rise, and Pat was stuck here.

When the light changed, Pat came up over the rise, surveyed the scene and saw, a mile away, perhaps, the right-turn blinker of some car flashing. But it was only a glimpse. The road was streaming. The moving ribbons were multicolored. He could not spot the blue Chevy. He began to work his way into the right lane and look for a place to stop a moment. Think a moment. Have some sense, maybe.

By the time he had switched lanes he was nearly upon a side road. On the near corner there was a little grocery store which displayed the sign of the bell. Then he must stop here, use the public phone, and call Anabel. Pat would normally have been home five or ten minutes ago. It would take a good while to get back to town, and then on home, from where he was now. He would be very late. Better call. Confess this chase and his defeat. Well? Pat turned into the side road, whose sign read OLEANDER STREET. A delivery boy was busily backing his panel truck into a slot behind the grocery store.

Pat called out on impulse, "Hey, did a car turn in here just now?"

"What's that?" The boy had a red head, a long, thin freckled nose, and a stupefied expression.

Pat repeated his question and the boy said, "Sure did. And left rubber." He began to look interested. "Can I do anything—?"

"Was it a Chevy? Blue?"

"It was blue. I'll tell you that much. But see, I was watching my left rear—"

"Where does this road lead?"

"No place."

"Dead end, you mean?"

"That's right."

"Any crossroads?"

"Nope. Not one."

"Oh," said Pat. "Thanks a lot."

"You bet," said the grocery boy.

Pat stepped on the gas joyfully. If a car, a *blue* car, had squealed around this corner, it might very well have been Everett, who was in a hurry all right. Pat had seen a signal blinking. By golly, from habit —and law-abiding habit, at that—had the fox signaled the hound? If so, if so, then Everett was trapped on a dead-end street with no crossroads. Get him yet, Pat thought.

Oleander Street was paved, but narrow and meandering. Far ahead rose some of Southern California's sudden hills, barren and dry, uninhabited. Oleander Street would not lead up into them. It twisted along the level, no thoroughfare, simply an access road for the small truck farms that were hardly more than garden patches, and the small chicken "ranches" that were staggered along on either side, each with its small house, erratically placed.

What was Everett Adams doing here? *If* here.

Proceeding slowly, now, and watching on all sides for any glimpse of the car he hunted, Pat came drifting around a curve and stopped, because there was a knot of chattering people in the road. He was directly opposite a picket gate, beside which there stood a wooden platform about four feet high on which there had been bolted a wooden armchair. Pat looked at this structure and saw a boy, about nine years old, sitting in the elevated chair with his thin unevenly developed legs stretched before him in their metal braces. Pat felt a quick pang for whatever father had built this contraption.

But the little boy was not having anybody's pity. His big brown eyes were blazing. "Mister? Mister?"

"What happened, old-timer?" Pat leaned out.

"A hit and run! A killer!" shouted the little boy. "Killed my mother's chicken. Didn't stop!"

"What kind of car?"

"Blue, 1960, Bel Air," shouted the boy with the sure knowledge of little boys. "Four-door, two-tone, didn't get the license. Sticker on the rear window, yellow and blue—"

"Right you are," Pat said. (The university's parking stickers were yellow and blue.) "Where did he go?"

The boy pointed on along Oleander.

"This street goes where?"

"Nowhere," cried the boy. "Just to the witch's. Catch him, mister. Please catch him?" He leaned out of the chair almost to the point of falling. "Take me."

"I'll catch him," said Pat cheerfully. "You sit tight."

He saluted and let the car move gently. The half dozen women and children did not speak to him. Now he could see the mangled bird, a patch of blood and feathers, and he was careful to avoid it. In his rearview mirror he saw the people beginning to disperse.

Jamie Montero's mother lifted her son down from his perch. Jamie cried, "No, Mama. No, Mama. Wait, Mama. He is going to catch the killer. The nice man! Mama, the bad man killed your chicken and he didn't stop. But the nice man will catch him."

"Hush-hush-hush," his mother said. "Suppertime. Hush, we are rich. It don't bother us that much."

Pat went, warily, farther along the meandering road. He had not caught the word the boy had used. *Just to the . . .* WHAT? No matter. The houses were thinning. Not far ahead, the terrain was beginning to roughen. On this flat land there were a few live oaks, a stand of lemon eucalyptus ahead, and one square of darker trees over there, which usually meant that someone had planted them. Was there one more house within that square?

Ah, now—the final curve to the right and suddenly, on a fan-shaped flat of dust, the end of the road.

Within the trees directly ahead of him there was, indeed, a dilapidated old California bungalow, gray from the weather—a slightly crooked house within a crooked fence. There was no garage, no driveway. But to his left, where the eucalyptus grove stood, Pat could see in the waning light far in among the barkless trunks a glimpse of blue. A car.

He cut his motor, set his brake, and stepped out.

Got him! Pat thought.

Everett Adams leaned over the brink, staring down at the heap of trash. This arroyo was, or had been, an unauthorized dump, used by those who wanted to be rid of garden clippings without paying the fee at the legal place. Everett had gardened for fun in other days, long ago, when Lillian was alive. Since then, the city fathers had posted the place. The heaps below were moldering. Everett was running his straining gaze over the humps and surfaces to be sure the bright metal that he had just cast over had gone deep enough into the confusion.

He was thinking, Damn O'Shea, never closes his door! Didn't occur to me . . . What did he see? Foolish to panic. Could have simply stared him down. Or could have said "I did it for money." They'd boot me out. Twenty years of teaching. Ah, but the risk. . . . No. Let it alone now. Shaken him off. Rid of it. No one will ever know. . . .

He felt sick. He was a sick man. His brain flipped and flopped and flubbed. He looked behind him and saw O'Shea's figure coming, in the greenish gloom, between the slim and pale and naked trunks of the trees. The short twilight seemed upon them. The sky was strange. The light was yellow-green and O'Shea's figure, a bright gray, came on, not fast but steadily. It was like doom.

Everett took four steps to his car. O'Shea didn't understand. Didn't know. Even if he knew, would he understand? No, no, the risk. . . . Stare him down.

"Are you following me, O'Shea?" he cried out angrily. "May I ask what the idea is?"

O'Shea kept coming. "May I ask what you've got in your pocket?" He was cold, hard. He was doom.

"I beg your pardon?" Everett pulled in his chin, tried to look haughtily outraged, but he had to keep his hand on the sill of the open door of his car to steady his knees.

O'Shea seemed to study the hang of his jacket. Then O'Shea walked to the brink and glanced over. "I see," he said contemptuously. "Got rid of it, did you?"

Everett stood and strove to hide his trembling. Even the car trembled. He hadn't cut his motor, that was it. He licked his mouth and tried for words appropriate to outraged innocence. He couldn't think. Flip, flop, flub. . . . Rage took him and its strength shook him and he shouted, "No, you don't see! I'm trying to save a human soul. You wouldn't understand that. You don't know and you don't see. . . ."

O'Shea wasn't even listening. He began to shout. "Look out, you idiot!"

Everett was forced to stagger because his car was moving. It crept. It was too close to the brink. What was happening must not happen. He threw his weight against the door, grasping the metal with both hands. The car was gaining momentum. He should have tried to get around and at the brakes. His feet were slipping.

Then O'Shea's hard hands grabbed him and pulled at him and Everett was torn away to fall on the ground, all tangled with O'Shea, and from there to see his car go down with a crunch as its front wheels slid over the edge. It slid another foot or two. Then it lifted its hindquarters slowly up, it tottered, it slid again. It described a stately, fated, heels-over-head, down into the arroyo.

O'Shea was making a moaning sound. Everett himself was crying, in high-pitched squeals, from far up in the middle of his skull. Neither could rise nor run nor see over. They caught breath, with a single impulse to listen. Nothing came to their ears. No explosion. Not even engine sound. Nor to their eyes any gush of black smoke and hot flame out of the gulch. Everett's car had simply disappeared.

Everett squirmed and ground one knee into the slippery leaf-strewn soil. He turned his furious face downward. "Now you did it! Now everything is going to happen. You wouldn't wait! You wouldn't listen! You wouldn't even try to understand!"

O'Shea lay on his back with his face white. He said quietly, "I think my ankle or my leg is busted."

"Good!" cried Everett, frothing. "Good! Because by what right do *you* judge? By what self-righteous ignorance do *you* destroy!"

It didn't occur to him that he might have gone over the brink and been crushed himself, or that O'Shea had been trying to save his life. He thought he had been attacked. Into his mind were sifting patchy visions of the consequences. Never get the car out without a crane. Without people, who would find out. Couldn't lose a car and say nothing. It would be found. And prove to be his. Ought to have burned. No, fire would have brought people. But there were no people here . . . not yet.

Suppose the car were never found? Or, he could say it had been stolen. Ah, no, stupid! Here was O'Shea, to tell the whole story. And the stolen object would be found, too, because O'Shea knew it was there.

Damn O'Shea!

"Oh, damn you!" croaked Everett. "You know absolutely nothing about the real problem. You think it matters to me anymore? You think it weighs in the scale against a human soul?" A final outrage. O'Shea wasn't even listening now. In O'Shea's eyes Everett read himself dismissed as incomprehensible. As probably quite mad. So Everett's right hand found a stone. His right hand went high, of itself. O'Shea jerked his head but the stone came crashing down. The head turned bloody at the side. Very bloody. Everett raised the stone again. Had to finish it now. A point of no return. No other way. He brought the stone down a second time.

His arm went weak. All his limbs turned soft. He began to pant— great gasps for air that were like sobs. O'Shea was out of it. Bloody, limp, and silent upon the ground. O'Shea was dead.

Well, then, at least he couldn't tell.

Everett's breath sawed. He got to his feet and staggered to the brink. The drop-over was twenty-five or thirty feet. There lay his car, upside down, on a slant, helpless as a turtle, its wheels still turning. But no sound. The motor had stalled? Or what? No matter. Nothing could be done about the car.

What could be done at all? At all? Now he had sacrificed, indeed. Must this, too, be for nothing? Tried to think.

Could he switch the story around, say it was O'Shea who had the stolen thing and Everett who had pursued him and here, at the end of the road, fought with a criminal at bay? In self-defense? Did Everett have the cold nerve to tell that story and keep to it? No, no, impossible. The cars in themselves told the order of their going. Or someone must have seen them, along the way. The pursuer doesn't go first. No, *think.*

Hide the body? He had an instinct to hide the body, put it over the brink into the dump and simply leave it. And go home. Say that his car had been stolen. Know nothing.

But how to go home or even back into town? Why, in O'Shea's car, of course. Get away from here. Keys? Everett went down on one knee and began to pry into O'Shea's pockets. Eyes shut. Fingers would do. Couldn't look. No keys?

Everett turned his back and bent to weep. He couldn't. He was finished. It was all over, all up with her, and with him too. He'd never meant to come to this. All so stupid, so incredibly stupid. And so inevitable.

Kneeling in the grove, with the dark thickening, Everett could feel a cool trickle of truth seeping into his understanding. He had been dominated for a long time by something that had simply wiped out his intelligence. Now, he was destroyed.

But as he knelt there, the oldest instinct stirred and it was cool, like truth. Run, then.

Maybe the keys were in the car. Money? He walked on his knees, he pushed at the limpness, got O'Shea's wallet. Take it. Too late for scruples. A long time too late. He had sacrificed them. *Now,* should he hide the body? Yes, of course, hide it. Smooth out the tracks, the gashes in the ground. Bury the blood. Confuse the signs. Run. Hide.

And give her up—which was the one thing demanded of him from the beginning. Now he could see clearly that it was accomplished.

He rose. His breath was coming more slowly. There was something of comfort, something almost delicious, about having it all over. So to simplicity. To eat, to drink, to sleep, and rise again to eat, to drink. . . . A dog was barking.

Everett tingled with the shock. No, no, he had to think this out. Had to have more time. Could not be caught now and taken, irrevocably, to the drama of cops and courts and fame and shame. Not before he had thought!

His trouser knees were stained with dirt. He had O'Shea's wallet in his hand. He put his head down and went stumbling and sometimes sliding to O'Shea's Rambler. He had the terror of the hunted on him already. But the keys were in the car. An omen, surely! Everett got in and started the motor.

He didn't have to reverse, he could circle here. He circled, holding the wheel as far as he could to the left with a suspicion that he could never move it again, that he would just go around and around and around until the gasoline was gone. It had become very dark. The sky rumbled. Storm? Well, yes, the weather report. . . . That yellowish light had been warning. The car had come around half circle. His mind was going around again. Everett bit his teeth together and wrenched at the wheel. The car bounced upon Oleander Street's worn pavement.

Headlights? Fumbling for the switch, his icy fingers found it. He was really quite clever. But what was behind?

He looked into the rearview mirror. All he could see, against what light there was left in the sky, were the moving trunks of the trees as they swished their tall tops in a sudden wind. Then lightning flashed and in the flash Everett saw behind him the figure of a woman, all in black, and he saw beside her a huge black dog.

The fiend: It was the fiend!

He shuddered, head to toe. His toe shook on the accelerator. He made the curve. His scalp crept. The sky cracked.

When the sky cracked, it was as if the film had been jolted back upon the sprockets; the pictures of consciousness began to run in Pat's mind. His lids lifted to a darkish world. He could hear, he could sense, the beast coming. He could smell, he could feel, the breath upon his skin, the snuffling; the muttering threat in the throat was loud to him.

"Nice doggie?" Pat murmured. His head shifted; the pain cracked. Light flashed and went out.

The sound of thunder roused Anabel O'Shea from her book. Ah, the predicted storm. Listening, she could hear no tinny drumming sound where the house gutter ought to have been fixed. Not raining yet, then. Pat had his raincoat. She had reminded him.

But, sitting in her favorite corner of the living room, she felt uneasy. Why? All her duties had been done, little Sue abed, dinner ready—"held back" in the oven—table set, house and herself neatened, the whole ménage ready for Pat to come home. She must feel guilty for having been reading so long, going with the novel, absorbed by the characters. Was it so long?

She looked at the time. Pat was a little late, but half an hour was nothing. He would come in a minute.

Anabel chewed her lip. Had she apologized? Yes, as she remembered, they had both apologized—well enough. Pat for making the date with the Provost and his wife for some stupid party on Saturday night when Anabel had wanted to go to the concert. And Anabel for blowing off almost all of her disappointment and disapproval. She had a temper; this was understood by both of them. Yes, they had given each other the pecks and the pats that signified "I'll get over it." And Anabel had sputtered around the house for twenty minutes more and then had been over it. Hadn't given it another thought, until now.

It wasn't worth another thought. She got up and went around to all the windows. It was going to rain and she might as well batten down the hatches. When she had made the complete round of their neat modern house, all on one floor and on its way to being furnished, although still on the bare side, Anabel worried briefly for the seeds she had put in hopefully along the garden wall. Rain would be wonderful—if it didn't wash them out. Anabel liked her house and garden very much and was in the midst of many projects. Why didn't Pat come?

She sighed and loosened her shoulders, took a couple of dance steps, considered music. But she did not turn on the FM. She went back to her chair and her book, wishing, for some reason, to keep her ear on the state of the universe.

The book was losing her or she was losing the book. She kept listening for the car, for the phone, for the rain.

At a quarter of seven, she leaped up, ran to the kitchen, and turned everything all the way off. Dinner wasn't going to be very good, she thought ruefully.

Then, moving slowly on her long, handsome legs, holding her honey-colored head to one side, pushing her lower lip out in the expression of the stubborn child who "doesn't care," Anabel went to the phone and dialed the university's number. No answer. She dialed the night number, asked to be connected with Pat's extension. No answer. Anabel hung up and scolded herself for such female carryings-on as this. But it was seven o'clock, so she found and dialed another number.

"Joanne? This is Anabel O'Shea."

"Oh, hi."

"Say, did Pat leave late, or something, do you know?"

"He left about his usual time," said Joanne Knowles. "Why, Anabel?"

"Well, he hasn't gotten here and I'm wondering what to do with some pretty sad-looking lamb chops."

"But it's after seven!"

"That's what I mean. Well, he's been detained someplace, that's all. I didn't know but what the Provost had everybody locked up in a meeting, and Pat was stuck."

"No, no. He left . . . it must have been just a bit after five thirty. I'm sorry I can't tell you anything more. I'm sorry if you're worried," worried Joanne.

"Oh, I'm not, really. Just wondering." Anabel chatted a few minutes more. When she hung up she heard the rain beginning.

The storm had been a long time breaking, but when it broke it was a deluge. The drumming of the drops lasted only a moment. Then the rain fell in a solid, relentlessly total rush. "Wow!" said Anabel aloud.

She moved the draperies in the living room. Even the streetlights were nothing but a yellow shimmer behind silver. Nobody could drive in this. Wherever Pat was, he would have to stay, now, and wait this out. No use expecting him. He could not come in this rain. The house felt like a locked box, shut up to only its own supply of air. It was hard to breathe. Anabel hoped that Sue, who was only four, wouldn't wake up and be frightened. There was nothing to be afraid of, was there?

The rain fell on the plain and on the mountains.

Partway up the mountain, within the pass, there was a diner, a place called Hamburger Haven. Ten minutes after the storm began, the place was packed. For one thing, a transcontinental bus driver had come early, thankfully shepherding his flock. Then one motorist after another had crept gratefully off the road into the parking space and he, and whatever passengers he carried, had come running through the wall of water. Now the place steamed with damp people, and the help scurried desperately to serve everyone, for people were stimulated to great hunger and thirst by the adventure of it. But they were genial and patient with each other, safe here from the weather and all of them, in a manner of speaking, in the same boat. They were noisy. Hamburger Haven was doing a business that literally roared.

When the rain had been coming down some twenty-five minutes, the door opened once more. "Mule" Mueller, behind the counter, saw a plump man, dashing water from his hat brim, zigzagging between groups of people, talking to himself.

He reached the counter and a customer moved obligingly to give the newcomer room. "Great night for ducks, eh?" said the customer. "I dunno how we ever made it," said the plump man earnestly, fearfully, triumphantly. "I tell you, it's a miracle. Got a cup of coffee there, Mac? What'll *you* have?"

The plump man's head turned far to his left and slowly his whole torso began to twist left. Then he turned back and said to Mule, "Where's the fellow that came in with me?"

Mule shook his head slightly.

"Wait a minute," said the plump one. "You saw us come in."

"Saw *you,* mister."

"Huh?" The plump one pulled away from the counter and went weaving his way back to the door. Mule had a few floodlights out there, but they were helpless. The plump man opened the door and peered out. There was just this silver brightness. He stood there in the open door, a fine mist blowing in past him, until somebody shouted, "Hey, shut the door. Do you mind?"

Whereupon the plump man shut the door. He came back to the counter and leaned upon it heavily. Damp and pale.

"Coffee, you said?" Mule inquired.

"Right. Yeah. Thanks."

The plump man's excitement had leaked out of him entirely. He was silent and subdued. He rubbed his chin, his cheeks. He took off his glasses suddenly and rubbed his eyes with stiff fingers.

The rain roared upon the old roof and it rushed down all around. Within the room dust seemed to be shaken out of the walls and ceiling. The place was dry and dusty. Pat O'Shea blamed his own sense at first. He thought the roaring was in his own head and the acrid air a dryness in his own nostrils.

He knew that he was hurt. When he tried to open his eyes his head ached violently. There was light from some source, here where he was, and the light hit his pupils like a knife cut. So he held his lids against pain and tried to guess where he was. He was lying on something soft and he was covered. He could listen. . . .

"Ah, now. Ah, now. They couldn't and I knew they couldn't. Never, never keep him. Not Johnny Pryde. Eh, Rex? Eh? Eh?"

A woman's voice, was it? A dog barked. Not loudly. It was just as if the dog had understood her words and was answering them. The dog was saying, "That's right."

The woman said, "That's right. Johnny's home. Eh, Rex? Ah, now. Johnny Pryde. Them cops, never going to get you. Not you. No more. No fear," she said.

Pat forced his eyes open. He was lying on a bed, an old-fashioned double bed with a high carved wooden headboard curving above him. The room was very small and perfectly square. It was wallpapered; the paper was much faded. There was a chest of drawers, a wooden chair, a small table with a marble top, and one lamp burning. It really was a lamp, with a wick burning.

All this Pat saw but did not even list in his mind yet, because he was looking at the old woman in the black dress.

Her hair was white and cut in short wild locks that tumbled in confusion on her head. Her eyes were black and bright. Her face was seamed with a thousand wrinkles and it was the color of a brown eggshell. Her lips had a blue and gummy look. She was thin, bent. She had a staff in her hand—a stout stick it was, but straight and much handled, as smooth as if it had been polished. Her hands were claws and they were folded around the staff.

Now she began to laugh. A cackling sound, with a small shriek running in and out of the sound to give an effect of high and malicious glee. "You're home," she cackled. "Johnny Pryde."

Pat put aside the consideration of his injuries and swallowed hard. He lifted himself on an elbow. "What happened?"

"I knew you'd come home. I've been waiting. Me and Rex. Waiting a long time. But we knew. Eh, Rex?"

The dog answered. Pat's startled eyes saw the black fierce head, the teeth, the dog's lip beginning to curl.

"Good dog. Good Rex. Here's Johnny. Good Johnny. Mind, Rex." The old woman's voice became sharp. "Go, Rex. Guard. Guard the door."

The dog protested, in a small mutter, but then it obeyed. It turned away and padded into another room.

Pat had caught his lower lip in his teeth. Now he released it. "I'm glad you speak his language," he said. "Have you a telephone, ma'am?"

"No fear," she said. "Nobody'll get you now. Never. No more."

Pat shut his eyes, because the light hurt so much. He cleared his throat. "My name is O'Shea," he said politely. "I teach at the university. I've had a little trouble, it seems. What time is it?" He knew he could not focus on his watch. "Could you please call my wife?"

He began to struggle to sit higher up against the headboard. She came to help him. Her old hands were hard and strong. She put them under his arms and helped him. But now there was a drag upon his right foot and Pat clenched his teeth.

He remembered his knowledge of something breaking when he fell with Everett Adams. He remembered, and saw in a vision upon his eyelids, that face in an extremity of rage and fear.

"My leg . . ." he began.

"Never go back there. Never. No more," the old woman was crooning. "You've come home and I'll take care. No fear."

"I'm very sorry," Pat said, tightening against pain, opening his eyes. The long staff had fallen against her shoulder and she was holding it with her chin. Her black eyes were shining. "But I am not anybody named Johnny, ma'am," Pat went on. "My name is O'Shea. I am a teacher at the university. If you have a telephone, would you please call. . . . What's the time?" Now he felt anxious. "Anabel will be worried sick."

"Ah, now," the old woman said, "nobody bothers me. You'll see, Johnny Pryde." She put her hands on her staff and the end of it against her leathery cheek.

He thought, Where's her hat? She was almost comically the witch in the fairy tales. She lacked only the high black conical hat. And the cat. Pat caught his mind slipping off toward nonsense. "What goes on here?" he muttered, and began to shift his legs.

Something pretty drastic was wrong with his right leg, just above the anklebone. He wasn't sure that he could walk, but he could hop, he supposed. Now he realized that the continuing rush and roar was out-of-doors. "Is that rain?" he exclaimed.

"Rain," said the old woman. "Good rain. You remember Pa putting the new roof on? You was too little, Johnny? Your grandpa, he didn't want it, but your pa, he put the good roof on and no rain gets in. No more. No more."

Pat squinted at her and said, "Mrs. Whatever-your-name-is, I am grateful to you for bringing me in out of the rain. But I have to get back to town and to my wife and little girl. So if you please—"

"No girls," she said severely. "None of them. None of them. Them girls, them damned mean and sneaking, lying girls. I knew they was lying. I knew it. And I knew you'd come home, Johnny Pryde, and no girls. No more. No more."

"Ma'am," said Pat grimly, "if you don't mind, please try to stop talking like Poe's raven. . . ." He was not quite fully aware of the almost total lack of communication here. He had a notion that the old woman was deaf. Then he must speak slowly and with more volume, and be very patient. Straining to be loud and clear, he said, "Help me to your telephone."

"No telephone," she answered.

"Neighbors?"

"No neighbors. You'll see, Johnny Pryde." She cackled suddenly.

"Then, will you please. . . ." Pat leaned back. Not in this rain. She couldn't go anywhere to get help until the cloudburst was over. Pat felt confused. He murmured, "How long has it been raining like this? How long was I out, away?"

"Ten years," she said. "Ten, pretty near eleven. But I knew. *They* couldn't keep you. I knew you'd come. I waited. Didn't I? But no more."

She wasn't deaf. Pat thought, Then she's mad as a hatter. He let himself back against the pillow. He moved his right foot and the pain stabbed. He looked at his right hand. It was scraped and lacerated and something had punctured it, deep, there along the edge of his palm. The wounds were dirty. He put his left hand to his head. The left side of his head was encrusted with a dried something. Could it be blood? He said, "I think I'd better get to a doctor."

"No doctor," she said. "Nobody. I'll take care. I know more than them doctors. None of them."

"Can you boil some water?" he snapped. "I'd like to be clean."

Her black eyes sparkled. "I brought water." Letting the staff lean on the wall, she turned to the marble-topped table and he saw that there was a crockery bowl on it and an old rag that she picked up in her claws. She dipped the rag. She wrung it out.

He said sharply, "Let me see that."

But she was leaning very close now. He could smell something sourish. She began to mop gently at the side of his head with the wet rag, which was cold. He winced away. "Let that alone, please. Never mind. It's my leg. May need setting."

"I know what to do," she said. "No fear." Her eyes shone. Pat realized that she was happy and that this was very frightening to him. He didn't yet understand why.

She pulled the blanket away from his body. He was still in his clothing, which was, he sensed, very dirty. But his shoes were gone. He pulled himself up to look at his right leg. The old woman put her hands on it.

Pat yelled. His back arched. He yelled again. The dog barked. But her hands worked. The pain sickened him. He began to black out. He fainted.

The old woman poked and pried at the bones with her small strong fingers. Then she went off to another part of the house and came back with more rags. She began to bind up the leg, winding and pulling, crooning to herself.

"Johnny's come home. And I'll take care. Nobody knows and nobody shall know. No more. No more."

Out in the front room of the old bungalow the dog let go and flopped suddenly, and put his black nose on his paws.

After the rain stopped, Vee Adams listened to the dripping and the trickling and the soft shifting of the water all around the house and yard. She sat at the dining-room table, with her books spread out under the center light, just as she usually did on a week night. As usual, half the time she sat dreaming.

Her father had not come home for dinner. He had not yet come home at all. Vee was hanging a dream or two upon his unexplained absence, resigned to having the dream shattered and Everett come in, wet, and anxious lest Celia have been troubled. As if Celia cared.

Her young stepmother was lying on the couch in the den, nibbling and sipping and watching TV, just as usual. She claimed not to be feeling well, all day long, but Vee wasn't worried about her health. Celia had these spells of total lethargy and, on the whole, they were somewhat easier to bear than her spells of restlessness. Vee had done, as usual, what she conceived to be her duty, bringing Celia what food she asked for, being polite.

When her father had married two years ago, Vee had been enchanted. Celia was so darling, so beautiful, so mysterious and sad. Vee had tried to imitate her, speak as Celia spoke, wear her hair as Celia wore hers. But when Celia's health had improved and she was no longer quite so limp about everything, Celia had simply lost interest. She had never been mean or cross, particularly. She had just begun not to see, not to hear, not to notice a teen-aged girl in the house. And of course, since the day Everett Adams had first seen Celia Wahl, *he* had lost interest altogether. Vee had sensed that from the beginning.

So she had done her best to guide herself by clinging to what she could remember of her own mother, Lillian. The only thing she had kept from the first six months of Celia was the new version of her name. Celia had hooted at "Violet" and dismissed "Vi" as just too, too old-fashioned. So "Vee" it was. But in all else, Vee tried to be what her own mother had been and had wanted her to be—a little lady.

She chose and wore dainty dresses, in tiny prints and pastel colors and made with tight bodices and full skirts. She wore the daintiest little flat slippers she could find. Not for Vee the tight wool skirts, the big sloppy sweaters, the sneakers or the saddle shoes that were the current campus uniform. Or the sheaths and spike heels and the glitter.

She was a bit of an odd-body on the campus. A professor's daughter had a count against her in the first place. A town girl, living at home—that made another. Vee had never been a joiner. She hadn't been asked much.

She went her own way, a way that was so lonely and miserable that it had to have the compensation of these dreams. A prince would come, who would see at once that there was only one real princess. Celia would die and her father would take a sabbatical, and he would take Vee abroad, where she would be an American princess, mysterious and sad. Mrs. O'Shea would die, and Mr. O'Shea would be devastated; only one heart would have the gentle understanding that would bring him back to life. Vee would die . . . or almost die . . . and everyone would be very very sorry.

To Vee, death was romantic.

When her mother had died, her father had romanticized it and canonized a meek and colorless woman. He and his little girl would go on, courageously, sustained by her memory. That was before he had gone to Los Angeles one weekend and there, somehow, somewhere, encountered Celia Wahl.

Celia had been a waif, or she had seemed to be. It had been almost a year before her brother had turned up. Vee tried never to think about Cecil Wahl at all. He was too much for her and she could fit him into no dream whatsoever.

But where was Dad? After all! Now that the storm was long over, and it was getting late, a shaft of true anxiety pierced through.

Vee began to close up her books and notebooks and pile them neatly, ready for tomorrow. (Lillian had been very neat.) Then she went through the long living room of this conventional and Lillianish house, which was not modern but not really old, either, and very little touched or changed by Celia.

Celia was in a long blue garment, a kind of housecoat that zipped all the way up the front. She was propped up upon many pillows, smoking, watching the screen through half-closed green eyes. Her feet were hidden under a bright afghan. Her ash-colored hair was loose and unkempt. Her face was not made up, nor was it even clean. Celia was still beautiful. The air was close in here, full of smoke and perfume and the mysterious fragrance of Celia's flesh.

On the coffee table were some dirty plates, a cup half full of cold tea, a telephone, a big ashtray heaped to overflowing, some magazines, a dish of hard candy, and three bottles of nail polish.

Vee knew better than to speak while the program was on. She stepped quietly and picked up the dirty dishes, dumped the cigarette butts on one of the plates, carried these to the kitchen, washed the dishes. She went back to stand in the door of the den and wait for a commercial. When it came on, she said, "I'm going to bed now. Did you want anything more?"

"I guess not," said Celia. She didn't turn her head. Her feet twitched under the afghan.

"Are you going to wait up for Dad?"

"Hm?" Celia's eyes squinted against smoke. "Oh, I don't know. Where is he?" Her fair brow puckered. It was as if the question had only now occurred to her.

"I saw him leaving school," said Vee. "I told you." Celia said nothing. "He forgot I was supposed to ride home with him." Celia's shoulder made a tiny shrug. "Mr. O'Shea left right after him," said Vee with a small bursting out of her need to be noticed. (The rest was in a dream; she wouldn't tell the rest.) "He might know."

"Pray who," said Celia coldly, "is Mr. O'Shea?"

"He's on the faculty. You've met him." Celia just looked at her. "I know you have," said Vee stubbornly. "He's the one in the office right across from Dad's."

Celia's eyes simply left Vee's face and turned back to the TV screen.

Vee turned her back and went away. She crossed the living room and went upstairs. She had locked no doors, turned off no lights. Sometimes she got so tired of being the one to think of everything. She hurried to her bed because there the dreams come easily. She would phone Mr. O'Shea who would come, saying "Poor brave. . . ." No, Mrs. O'Shea wouldn't let him. But he'd be sorry. Her father would die: Celia would be sorry. Then Vee could say what she could not now, loyally, say to anybody.

Downstairs, in a few minutes, Celia reached for the phone and dialed a long number. She was smiling faintly.

"Yes?"

"C?"

The man's voice said, aside, "It's only my sister, honey." Then it said, "Yeah, C? I wish you wouldn't call here."

"Something's funny."

"What?"

"He hasn't come home tonight."

"Well?"

"I don't know."

"What do you think?" said her brother sharply. "He's baring his little soul?"

"Probably he's drowning his little troubles. Maybe he got rolled." She giggled.

Her brother made a sound of exasperation. "Anybody been there?" She didn't answer. "They'd have come by now," he said. "Does he . . . write things down, C? Is there anything around?"

"How would I know?"

"Look."

"I wouldn't know where to look," she said with a sultry stubbornness. "Or what you've touched in this house, either," she added and heard his breath catch.

"Nobody's been there?" he said in a moment. "Maybe I'd better come by, C?"

"Do," she said on a soft pure note.

The wire carried nothing for a second—but something, just the same. "I'll see you, C," he sighed and hung up. She hung up and hugged herself.

Upstairs in her room, which was as neat and dainty and beruffled as Lillian had thought a little girl's room ought to be, Vee lay on her bed and dreamed with her eyes open. After a while, she began to wish her father would come home. There were some dreams that might be too exciting and too terrible if they ever were to come true.

An hour later, Vee sighed, got up, and went softly downstairs, where the lights still burned, the TV still ran, pouring forth some late late show. Vee, feeling prim and in Lillian's skin, went into the den and turned off the TV. She took up the afghan and pulled it higher to cover the sleeping form of her stepmother. No use trying to rouse her and get her properly to bed. Celia didn't care. She had no idea of propriety, no order, no routine, nor any sense of time or duty. Just was. Was Celia. Everett Adams might be enchanted still. His daughter was not enchanted anymore.

Vee put out the light in the den, left one light on in the living room, in case her father came, locked the front door, went back to her own place. She crept under the covers, thinking with honest pain that she was probably the loneliest person in the whole world. Quickly, she wove the healing dream. If anything terrible *had* happened, then she would just go away somewhere. Alone. Mysterious and sad. Somebody would notice. . . .

On the dot of midnight, Anabel O'Shea uncramped her legs from their huddled position, went to the phone, and called the police.

"I would like to report that my husband hasn't come home," she said, "and I am afraid something's happened to him."

"May I have your name, ma'am?"

"Anabel O'Shea. My husband is Elihu O'Shea, but everybody calls him—"

"Address?"

"3407 Pine."

"Does he drive a car, ma'am?"

"Yes. A Rambler."

"Can you give me the model, color, and license number?"

Anabel gave him this information precisely, in the same order, visualizing a paper before him, some kind of form to fill out.

"What was his destination?"

"His what?"

"Destination? Where was he going?"

"Why, he should have been coming home," she said, feeling a ripple of exasperation. She could understand the four-syllable word. It had just seemed an odd word to choose.

"Where was his point of departure, ma'am?"

"The university. The Science Building. He is an instructor—"

"When and where was he last seen?"

"Listen, I don't know. The point is, I haven't seen him. I'm afraid that he's had an accident or he's hurt—"

"He had identification on him, ma'am?"

"Well, I suppose so. Of course he did."

"We'll check the jail, ma'am."

"The jail?"

"Yes, ma'am."

"But why?"

"If he has been booked for some traffic violation, such as drunk driving, he might not be able to get in touch."

"He was not drunk-driving," she cried. "He is *missing*. He isn't where he should be, where he was expected." (All right, she could condescend, too.)

"You'll have to come down to the station, ma'am, and make out a report on that."

"Report?"

"Yes, ma'am. Missing Person report."

"Come *down* there?"

"Yes, ma'am."

"But it's midnight. I have a small child. I have no car. I can't—"

"In the morning, ma'am—that is, if he hasn't gotten in touch by then." It was obvious that the voice assumed her problem would vanish with the dawn.

"But there was that terrible storm," she cried. "And he would have called me."

"We'll check the jail, ma'am," the voice repeated patiently. "And you come down in the morning."

"Thank you," she said dubiously. They hung up. Then she was suddenly very very angry.

Jail! Anabel had been astonished by the word. Now she was angry at the very thought. Angry with the policeman. Angry with Pat, too. How could he do this to her?

Anabel yanked herself around. All right. He *couldn't*. And she was getting angry so as not to be afraid.

She got out the phone book that had the yellow pages and began to call every hospital in town. Had they a patient, brought in this evening, named O'Shea? No? Then had they an unidentified man about thirty? No? Finally there was no number left to call and she perceived that, in the middle of the night, with Sue asleep, with no friend living close by, or even, in fact, a friend in this town that was, in any sense, close enough, there was nothing more that Anabel could do except see to her own state.

Anabel King had been a normal, happy, all-American girl. Raised in comfort (if not luxury), sent to good schools, always popular, always successful (at least in middle terms). Been wooed and won, had a lovely wedding, a wonderful honeymoon, a darling baby girl, this cute house, and many projects for a good happy future . . . with, all along the way, the usual "problems" to give life spice. . . .

She left the light in the bleak emptiness of the living room, went into their bedroom, crept into their cool bed, resolved to go to sleep. After all, Sue would be up and shining very early, and Sue must be taken care of. That was something that Anabel, all-American young mother, could and must do.

But with her hands tight on the edge of her pillow and her nose buried, Anabel King O'Shea, female person, prayed as hard as she knew how to pray. Let him be all right. Let it be something silly that I haven't thought of. Just let him be all right and let him come home.

Then she lay, groping for what could not sustain her, and thought, Up to now, nothing—not even Daddy's death—nothing really bad has ever happened to me.

Tuesday

TUESDAY HAD a gray dawn. The storm had washed the land. In the hard light, everything was startlingly clear. Yet there was no sunshine.

Anabel lifted little Sue out of the taxi, paid the man, and taking her child by her soft little hand, led her into the police station. Even in her anxious weariness, it struck her that this was a strange thing to be doing, early on a Tuesday morning.

When she stated her business, she was sent to a room and to a desk within the room, where a very young man in an ordinary suit gave her the paper and pen. In her own writing, Anabel put down all she had said on the phone last night, and a description of Pat besides. Age: 31. Height: 6 feet. Weight: 180. Hair: brown. Eyes: blue. Scars: none. How meaningless! she thought. How perfectly undistinguished! Shouldn't I put down "Very intelligent. But lighthearted. A gay and loving man"?

She kept her head down and asked, "What else?"

"Has he ever been in any trouble? Any misdemeanors? Traffic violations? Drunk driving?"

She said stiffly, her tears staunched, "I have never known him to be drunk." (Were the police *obsessed* with drunk driving?)

"Doesn't drink at all?"

"Of course he drinks," she said a little impatiently. "Socially, moderately. But he does not 'get drunk' and he is a good and conscientious driver."

"He is not wanted by the police, ma'am?"

She said stonily, "Why should he be wanted? He is not a criminal." Anabel's heart was beginning to pound. "Why do you ask me these things?" she demanded. Little Sue, sensing the gravity of this expedition, was being very good, quiet as a mouse, standing in the shelter of her mother's left arm. Anabel thought, She is only four. She won't remember, will she, these insulting questions about her Daddy?

"Has he any known enemies?"

"Any what?"

"Is there any reason to suppose," said the young man with just a trace of weary patience, "that he has met with foul play?"

She said, staccato, "Yes. There is. He didn't come home."

The young man went on, blandly, "Was he in an emotional state, Mrs. O'Shea? For instance, had there been some dissension between you?"

"Nothing important," said Anabel in a moment, trying to remember that he must have been trained, he must only be doing what he was supposed to do. His face did not change but his mind closed. She seemed to see it close. She said sharply, "Nothing like that."

"Is he in debt?" the young man continued impassively.

She stared at him. She couldn't even answer.

"Is he happy with his job? Or is he restless, would you say?"

Anabel said, forcefully, "What are you talking about? Do you think he might have run away? Leaving me to just wonder?"

The young man said coolly, "I'm sorry, ma'am. Could there be, do you think, some other woman?"

Anabel leaned toward him. He had very smooth, clean-looking young skin. He was a good-looking lad, a type she knew—the young buck, arrogant of his youth and strength. To such, she, aged twenty-eight, was already an old *bag*.

She said, speaking very distinctly, "If you will listen to me, I'll tell you what kind of man you must look for. A highly intelligent, highly educated, highly respected, successful, happily married, devoted. . . ." She had to stop before her voice broke.

The young man had waited for her to stop. Now he smiled at her and she could have hit him for the pity in his smile.

"But I suppose," she said, "you have your statistics, don't you?"

"Yes, ma'am," he said. He picked up the paper that she had signed. It was a gesture of dismissal.

"What will you do now?" asked Anabel.

"We'll hold this for twenty-four hours."

"Hold it!"

"After that, we'll probably put out an APB on his car."

"A what?"

"An all-points bulletin, ma'am."

"But for twenty-four hours, did you say? You'll do *nothing*?"

"That's right, ma'am."

"Don't you understand?" she cried. "Or don't you believe me?"

"Yes, ma'am." His young face was cold.

"What is your name?"

"Carlson, ma'am."

"Who is your superior?"

"That's Captain Murch, ma'am."

"Where is *he?*" If he called her "ma'am" once more, Anabel might scream.

The young man said smoothly, "Unless we have some reason to believe that there may have been foul play, it is the policy of the department—"

"I told you the reasons," Anabel stood up.

"Captain Murch isn't in the building, ma'am," he said lightly as he rose. He was watching her.

She hung on to her control. She could read in his eyes his expectation of hysterics, for the handling of which no doubt he had also been trained. It was the child who suddenly began to cry.

Anabel gathered her daughter up into her arms. "May I phone for a cab, please?"

"Yes, ma'am. Certainly." Oh, he was just as glad she wasn't going to have hysterics. He didn't want to have to bother with them.

Anabel thought to herself an iron thought. They won't help me. I'll have to find Pat by myself.

Once at home, Anabel put Sue down among her dolls and phoned her mother in San Diego, "So will you come, Mom? And will you drive? Because I'll need a car."

Susan King, in San Diego said, "Of course I'll come, dear. I can be on my way in about twenty minutes. I should get there by noon."

"Oh, thanks, Mom." Anabel was proud that neither of them had wept or wailed. Her spine was stiff. Her heart was bold. She called the Provost of the university.

Miles Drinkwater, the Provost, had a rich tenor voice well practiced in the art of rolling out phrases of sympathy and reassurance. But when she told him that she had been to the police, Anabel sensed his dismay.

"I am so sorry you felt you had to do that," he said. "I am sure he is all right, Mrs. O'Shea, and you will hear from him soon."

"I can't imagine," said Anabel severely, "what makes you so sure.

I, on the contrary, am quite sure that there must be something that keeps him from coming home, or calling me, and I want to know what it is. The police will do nothing to help me for twenty-four more hours. Will *you* help me?"

"Certainly," he said. "Certainly—whatever I can do, Mrs. O'Shea. Although I think we must keep our heads."

Anabel's head felt in fine shape. "Then will you please ask around, there at the school, whether anyone has any idea where he might be?"

"Why, I . . . er. . . ."

"You won't?" Anabel was sharp.

"My dear lady," said the Provost. "I simply hope that you are needlessly alarmed. Of course, I want to do all I can. . . ."

Anabel said, "I am glad you realize that I am alarmed. Thank you."

She hung up, not violently. Then she put her fingers violently into her hair and held tight to her own skull. But she pulled the phone book to her in a moment, opened it to the yellow pages, and began to call all the hospitals once more.

Miles Drinkwater got up from his desk, smoothing his jacket with both hands. He was most reluctant to "ask around" and thus spread the news that O'Shea hadn't been home all night. Surely it was a private and personal matter between O'Shea and his wife, and the Provost did not like to contemplate scandalous rumors. Mrs. O'Shea would be wiser, he thought, not to risk them. When the young man turned up, no doubt sheepishly, *he* certainly would not appreciate the broadcasting of this escapade among his colleagues and his students.

But, since the matter should be handled with as much discretion as possible, he had better handle it himself. Mrs. O'Shea was in no mood to be discreet. Unfortunately. So, reluctantly, and reflecting upon what multitudes of problems he had seen require no solution at all, given enough time and inattention—nevertheless, he left the Administration Building and walked across campus to the Science Building, nodding benignly in progress.

Joanne Knowles, the girl on the divisional switchboard, was quick to understand the Provost's desire for discretion. She told him what she had already told Anabel, that Mr. O'Shea had left at his usual time last evening and, as far as she knew, in no kind of state, except perhaps a bit of a hurry. She quite agreed that there should be no gossip and the Provost rewarded her with one of his most benign smiles.

He went down the corridor to O'Shea's office, and finding the door wide open, clicked his tongue. But the tiny cubicle was perfectly neat and perfectly empty. It had nothing to say.

He crossed the hall to tap on the closed door opposite, but Adams did not answer. His door was locked, as was proper. The Provost surmised, and even seemed to remember, that Adams had an early laboratory.

The students were now streaming through the building, giving the usual impression of total confusion, although each individual was purposefully going somewhere and would get there. The Provost stood in his little island of unbuffeted space, given as due his rank and authority, and looked benign. One of them had the temerity to approach him. "Mr. Drinkwater?"

"Yes, Mr. Parsons." The Provost was proud that he had the knack of putting names to faces.

"If you are looking for Professor Adams, sir, he wasn't in the lab."

"Thank you very much." Oh, the Provost knew Mike Parsons for what he was. It was the Provost's business to know these things. This boy was eaten with curiosity about the Provost's presence here, but he would learn nothing. By speaking four words, from Olympia, the Provost rendered him helpless.

Then he himself went back to Joanne Knowles to discover the number of the classroom where O'Shea ought to be at ten o'clock. He realized that he had harbored a somewhat irrational hope that O'Shea, whatever had kept him from his home, would have been here, attending to his duties. He lingered now, still half expecting O'Shea to come hurrying along, late but apologetic, and publicly correct enough.

O'Shea did not come. Finally the Provost sighed and turned his steps to the classroom.

It was full of rhythmic noise. The students were doing a countdown. Required by rule to give an instructor ten minutes' grace, they were now, altogether, counting down the last minute.

The Provost's entrance stopped the noise abruptly. He went to the front of the room and faced them, summoning up all his guile. "I am sure that you will all be very sorry to hear," he twinkled at them, "that Mr. O'Shea will not be taking his class this morning."

Some of them accepted his invitation to cheer softly.

"However, I would like to ask those of you who had occasion to speak to Mr. O'Shea and perhaps, also, any of you who saw Mr. O'Shea, let us say, late in the afternoon, yesterday, to remain a few minutes. The rest of you may go."

He nodded benignly.

The class rose and began to shuffle out. Had he not come, he knew, they would have gone whooping forth. As it was, they went slowly, with backward looks.

How he hated them! The Provost clamped down on the familiar surge of this emotion. Damned smart-alecky kids. Oh so shrewd, so bright-eyed, so quick to use their potent energies for troublemaking. But so unteachable, most of them. So full of their own conceit. Hypocrites. Apple-polishers. Always trying to fool their elders, get good grades for no honest work done, work some angle. . . . Smart alecks!

He gazed out of the window, wearing his own mask of benign calm. When the shuffling had died away, he saw that only one student had remained. She was the Adams girl, who stood before him, demure, eyes cast down, feet tight together.

Vee Adams had known, the moment she came downstairs on Tuesday morning, who was expected today. Celia was up, washed, dressed, and she had neatened the house. She had even cut some iris from the neglected garden and was in the kitchen arranging them. She was gay; she said she felt better.

Well, then, Cecil Wahl was coming. Vee knew these signs. Oh, the two of them, with their pale heads and their green eyes! Her father never saw the two of them as Vee had seen them.

Vee poured herself coffee and took her bun, which she ate standing, as usual. She could see, out the window, the open, empty one-car garage. She said, "Dad didn't come home all night? But where is he?"

"I really don't know," said her stepmother, inclining her fair head. "With a friend, I imagine. I wouldn't say anything about it, Vee."

"About what?"

"Why, about your father having his little night on the tiles?" said Celia, looking mischievous, her green eyes crinkling up.

Vee choked on the bun, put it down, and left the house.

When the Provost made his request, Vee saw her plain duty, as Lillian would have seen it. Vee had promised Celia nothing, really. She owed the Provost some obedience. Now the distinction of being the only one who had anything to tell him pleased her.

The Provost was looking at the open classroom door and canceling his impulse to shut it. He knew better than that. He said to her benignly, "Miss Adams, Miss Violet Adams."

Vee lifted her eyes and said, "I happened to see Mr. O'Shea driving away, sir, last night."

"Ah, did you?" He was giving her his full attention.

"I happened to be waiting for my father in the faculty parking lot."

"I see. And Mr. O'Shea left in his car, did he, as usual?"

"He left in his car."

The Provost was a fox. He took in the evasive precision of her answer. He understood a little about this young person. So he said, with a confidential air, "I know that *you* will not spread this rather distressing bit of news, Miss Adams. I am concerned, you see, because Mrs. O'Shea tells me that he was not at home last night, at all. So she begs me to question anyone who may have any notion. . . . You do understand?"

"Yes, sir." But Vee's heart had leaped and she was afraid.

"What is it, my dear?" the Provost purred kindly.

"Nothing."

It was a female "nothing." The Provost ignored it. "I hate to see you look so troubled," he purred on.

"Well, it's my f-father."

"Ah?"

"He drove away so fast he didn't even wait for me. And Mr. O'Shea jumped into his car and drove away too." This man was so kind and discreet. Surely she could tell him this much.

"And it seemed strange to you?" said the Provost in a tone that was careful to muse and explore.

"Because my father wasn't home last night either," the girl blurted.

"Well, then," said the Provost, smoothing his vest. But it wasn't well. It was astonishing. He didn't know what to make of it. "You don't know where either of them may have gone?"

"No, sir. But it wasn't the usual way. They both turned around the Science Building toward the gym. I . . . I had to take the bus home."

"Is your mother worried, my dear?" cooed the Provost, wondering to himself when yet another wife would phone him.

"No," said Vee. Her face turned pink. "*She* isn't worried at all. But *I* am."

"I don't wonder." He touched her shoulder, exuding sympathy and understanding. (The Provost had remembered Celia Adams.) "Of course you are worried, but there'll be some explanation, you'll see." (Privately, he imagined there would be a story invented, for the child.) "Thank you very much for staying to tell me this. But I . . . er . . . wouldn't . . . I think it might be a disservice to your father to . . . er . . . mention this to anyone else—that is, until we know the truth. Don't you agree?"

"Yes, sir, I do agree," said Vee with pathetic gratitude.

"Now then, if anything more occurs to you. . . ."

He saw her swallow.

"Is there anything?"

"No, sir."

"Or, if you are too much worried, please be sure to come to me. You will, won't you?"

"I will. Thank you, Mr. Drinkwater."

Vee moved, making a little ducking motion that suggested an old-fashioned curtsy. Then she went out of the classroom with her head high, her back straight, her feet taking small, dainty, ladylike steps.

Odd girl, the Provost thought. For one thing, she will be quiet.

Then he saw a thin figure pass swiftly by the open door and glance in, with a sharp nose pointed. Parsons. Oh, so smart, oh, so sharp, oh, so bright-eyed—some of them were, when it was none of their business. When it could make trouble.

The Provost left the classroom, walked to the east corridor, and went along it to a window at the end which overlooked the faculty parking lot.

He knew that behind him, at the drinking fountain, there were students and he knew that one of them was Parsons, that he was on the scent somehow and making capital of it with his contemporaries. He knew they lingered there to watch him, to wonder, to buzz, to glean what they could. Oh the little foxes! How he hated the whole pack of them!

Life would get them, of course, he thought with savage pleasure. They'll find out. They, too, would become middle-aged. Their bright promise would also fade. They too, would be stuck, and only if they were very very lucky, stuck in a place where there might be some honor and the salve of some daily respect given. But neither would they—any of them—set the world on fire.

The parking lot had some empty slots. It told him nothing. He walked back, passing the group of innocent children at the drinking fountain and nodding, benignly. He knew how "innocent" they were not. How eagerly they could condemn, without proof or knowledge, an elder to the punishment of their sly and nasty laughter.

On the way out of the building, a student named Rossi stepped aside politely. To him the Provost did not nod. How stupid, the Provost thought, it is to steal!

There had been daylight, now, for some hours; nobody had come.

The old woman had fed him a breakfast consisting of a porridge-like substance and a cup of bitter tea. She had done for him the necessary, helped him to his animal functions in a stolid, matter-of-fact, and unembarrassed fashion, for which he tried to be grateful. But she made him very uneasy.

His head was better this morning, but the flesh above his ankle was swelling painfully against the binding rags, and his hand, he knew, was not what it ought to be. But the head was no longer splitting and his mind worked. Pat considered his situation.

When he had wakened in the dark, he had heard the animal, somewhere beyond a wall, mutter recognition of the fact that he had wakened. He tried to sit up; the dog had growled. Then he had heard the creak of furniture and imagined the old woman's body turning, in that other room. His head had been fuzzy and his notions of place and space confused, his notion of time quite unreliable.

Considering the situation, then, he had thought that Everett Adams would send help soon. So it was not worth the effort to try to put his weight on his right leg, to hobble, hop, or crawl out of this refuge, disturbing the old woman from her rest. Nor could he do it without disturbing her, since he had nothing on but his undershorts and a bandage. He had no idea where his trousers were, and no notion how to make a light in the dark and alien room—much less make his own way, in the night, over unfamiliar terrain, painfully, and toward a telephone.

Considering this, he had let himself drift and, eventually, he had slept.

But soon after first light, he had begun to conclude that Everett Adams was not going to send help. It did not seem possible that help had already come to search that eucalyptus grove and, finding nothing, had gone away without at least asking questions at the door of this house. Would Pat have heard them? Yes, he would. The dog would have heard them and raised a racket. No, help had not come, not all night nor at dawn, either.

Remembering the look in Everett's eye and the stone raised in his hand, Pat knew, now, that he had run into something more serious than a theft. Adams had been beside himself—which was a very fine old phrase, and meant exactly what it said. Now, either he was in collapse somewhere, suffering the pangs of a terrible guilt, gone out of his head entirely—or he was without conscience in the matter and might have even thought it desirable for Pat to have died where he had fallen, injured, exposed to that storm. Ridiculous! Pat wasn't going to *die,* of course. But he really ought to have some medical attention.

Very well; dismissing Everett, there was still Pat's car. Surely, standing there abandoned at the end of the road, it would be noticed by somebody. Anabel would be starting up some kind of search for him by now, in which a description of his car would have to figure. Then questions would be asked at this door and he could call out. . . .

So he had thought, in the dawn. But now he knew that his car was not there. Or so the old woman had told him.

Mrs. Pryde. Ought he to believe her? Had she even understood the question? Could she observe with any accuracy? Or did she answer out of her delusions and her desire?

Four times he had patiently told her his name, his address, his station in life, and four times he had begged her to send for a doctor, send to a phone, notify people. Four times she had ignored his words, quite as if she hadn't heard them at all.

She was not deaf physically, but he suspected that she was psychologically deaf to some words. Any words that would take her son away from her.

He knew, now, that she and the dog had found him lying in the grove unconscious, that she had fetched a blanket and rolled him onto it, and then she and the dog had dragged him to this house. Dragged him up the stoop, into the house, into this room, where she had somehow managed to heave him up and on his bed.

Before the rain.

Remembering the deluge, he realized that no trace of this progress would remain for a search party to find, which was unfortunate. But he would be found, of course.

Still, adding everything up, Pat knew he could put no hope in Everett Adams who possibly—probably, in fact—had gone off in Pat's car. And he feared that it would be some time before the searchers that Anabel—oh, poor Anabel!—would no doubt put to work, could possibly discover this road, this far, dead end of it, and knock on this door. Therefore, Pat had better do something about his situation himself.

Convince the old madwoman that he was not her son Johnny Pryde? Or just get out of here and find sane people?

But now, at midmorning, he had to concede that it wasn't going to be easy to get out of here. His leg was a mess. He was not the strong and agile person he needed to be.

This room had one window at the back, one at the side, both old-fashioned sash windows, both hung with ragged lace curtains behind which cracked green shades were drawn to the sills. Even so, he could tell that there were screens on the windows although he did not think the screens were very strong. He could break out at a window, he guessed, but not without the dog knowing what he was up to. He certainly could not crawl on hands and knees fast enough to get away from the beast, especially when he had no notion in which direction, or for how far, he would need to crawl. There was no hope in speed. There was no hope to cover his tracks from the dog, either, by any kind of stealth.

But the dog was the woman's instrument. If she was not willing to let him go, then the dog would not let him go.

So he must convince her that she had no reason to keep him, that there was no relationship at all. Why should this be so difficult? He moved restlessly. He called out to her. "Mrs. Pryde?"

She came in, through the door to his left. There were two doors to this bedroom. The one directly before his eyes must lead into the front room, the living room, the "parlor" (he imagined), and in that room must be the front door that led to the weather. The door by which she now entered led, at least eventually, to the kitchen. There was a short hall with a door at its end, and a bathroom between.

Pat had hopped that far. Earlier, he had gotten out of bed, at least, and tried out his physical resources. He had rummaged in the bathroom, through the cabinet above the washbasin, and found nothing in it but a large can of talcum powder and a box of corn plasters. He had washed his hands in cold water. He had let the scab on his head alone. His teeth felt slimy. Never mind. His brain worked. His ears worked. He had heard the dog padding, his nails clicking on linoleum, in the kitchen on the other side of that other door.

He now had a sense of the geography of this house. It was a square, or near enough. He lay in the back corner room. The kitchen lay on the other back corner. The living room must run across the front. For all he knew, there was a dining room, another bedroom, a room, on the far front corner, adjoining the kitchen.

What he could not place, could not remember, was this house in relation to any other house on Oleander Street. Or in relation to the inhabited world.

"Oh, Johnny." There she was. She was glad to come to his call. She was glad to hear him, to speak to him. Yet she had not been hanging over him. He had heard her muttering to the dog her litany, her "nevers" and her "no mores." But he could guess that she was unused to another voice, another human presence. And perfectly unfamiliar with any contradictions. Well, perhaps she would get used to him, and his words would begin to wear through. He did not know, now, how to get through to her. Was it any use, now, to say for a fifth time the words she had not yet recognized? Pat decided to try indirection.

"Tell me about Johnny Pryde."

He watched her accept this. He thought, She's in a divided state. One part insisted that he was Johnny Pryde. The other part knew very well that he was not, and this was the part that remained deaf, that would not hear. No, that was wrong. It heard. It knew. It would not let the other part know. The part of her that lived within a stubborn wall, not made of wood and plaster.

"A good boy," she said. "Good boy."

"Your only son?"

"Only son, only one."

The dog barked. She had been careful to close the kitchen door so that the dog was not able to come into this room with her. The dog was jealous, was he?

Pat had given some thought to what he could do, if and when the dog came bounding in on him with hostile intent. Wind his arm in the bedclothes and thrust it into the dog's mouth? Yes. Possibly. If he were quick. But Pat wasn't at all sure that, having done his, he could then deal with so powerful a beast. Swaddle him in the bedclothes? Tie them around the dog, like a straitjacket? That would take a strength that Pat must summon up for his very life, if and when the time came.

Now he said to the old woman, "I can't hear you when the dog barks."

"Quiet, Rex. Quiet. Eh, Rex?"

The dog muttered, saying, "I don't want to obey. I obey."

"Sit down," Pat said, "and tell me. Why didn't Johnny come home a long time ago?"

"He would come when he could," she said. "I knew." Her eyes slipped sideways as the gears slipped in her mind. "You're feeling better, Johnny? Eh, Johnny? You'll see." This was the happy half of her, and in that happiness lay his problem. The poor old soul must have been solitary here for years, and happiness she had not known.

"How long have you lived here by yourself?" he asked her.

"Straight here, I came, when they took you away. Straight here, to wait here. Because you'd know. Eh? Where to come. Where to come home, eh? I knew you would come." Saliva slipped over her lower lip.

"Where is Mr. Pryde?"

She shook her head. It was as if she couldn't remember such a person this morning.

"You have friends, though? Neighbors?"

She cackled. "They're scared of me," she announced proudly. "They don't bother me. No more. No fear."

"Mrs. Pryde, do you get any mail?"

"Never wrote. No mail," she said. "But I knew why, Johnny. I knew. All the time, I knew you'd come as soon as you could. And that was what you'd do."

"But you get some mail?"

"I don't bother. Mail don't bother me. Box is down the road," she said carelessly.

Pat remembered the lines of country mailboxes standing together at intersections, saving the mailman long journeys to solitary houses. No mailman would come to this door, then.

He said, "How do you live?"

"Eh?"

"How do you get food?"

"From the store," she answered. "No fear."

Pat narrowed his eyes. "That's the store at the other end of Oleander Street?"

"Johanneson." She was looking sleepy and contented. She had not sat down. She swayed, supported on two feet and the staff.

"You go to the store, then?"

"Ah, no—no more. No more."

"I don't see how you get your food then."

She cackled. "Why, the boy brings it. He comes on a day, then he don't come, then he comes, then he don't, then he comes and then he don't for two days, and then he comes again."

"Monday, Wednesday, Friday," Pat said aloud. (Today must be Tuesday, he reckoned.)

"What shall we have to eat, Johnny?" she said with sudden excitement. "What shall we have to eat, eh? What do you like? I know what you like. Meat. Meat, eh? I'll write down meat."

She turned. She moved quickly. She went off through the door and returned, almost immediately, with a small pad of paper and a stub of pencil. "I wrote down, already," she told him. "And Rex, he gets his meat—but you don't want that kind. Good meat, eh, Johnny? Eh?"

"That's right," he said slowly. "I see. The boy comes with an order and you give him the next order."

"Certainly, certainly," she said impatiently. "The boy gets my check out of the box, and I sign, and Mr. Johanneson, he takes care. He pays the bill for the water, and all. Nobody bothers me."

"Your check?"

"Pension. Pension," she said. "It's plenty. No fear." She sat down on the one straight wooden chair.

"The boy comes the day after tomorrow?"

"Today," she said. "Today."

Tuesday, Thursday and Saturday, thought Pat, with a spark of excitement.

She was writing something on the paper now, laboriously. Pat watched her. Poor old thing, a hermit here. All her people dead, no doubt, or somehow lost. And her only son in prison. He had figured out that much.

"Why did they put Johnny in prison?" he asked her, hoping to catch her unawares.

"For nothing," she said. "He didn't do what they said. It was them girls, them lying, sneaking girls. Oh, they said he did terrible things. They said he come on them in their cars and he beat their boys and he did terrible things to them girls. But they were just lying. He wouldn't do that. Johnny wouldn't do that. I knew he wouldn't do that. They didn't listen to me. But I knew they'd never keep him. Never. Never."

"Mrs. Pryde," said Pat, "could you please tell the grocery boy, when he comes, that I need a doctor? Or let me talk to him myself? Then I promise you I'll do all I can to find out about your Johnny."

But her ears had closed. "The boy don't bother me," she said. "Good meat, eh, Johnny? Beef, you like, and lamb too. But you never was a one for ham, eh, Johnny?"

He said for the fifth time, "Mrs. Pryde, my name is O'Shea. I am a teacher at the university. I live in town. I have a wife and a little girl."

"No more," she said. "No more. Nobody bothers me. No more. No cops. No doctors. Aplenty. Aplenty." She rocked from side to side absorbed in bliss.

Pat said in a moment, "Is there plenty of bread?"

"Bread," she said. "That's right. Bread." She bore down with her pencil.

"I'll need some medicine," he said. "Write it down, will you?"

She didn't seem to hear.

"Ma?" he said.

Life flashed across her face. She'd hear him now.

"Doesn't the store have medicine?" he whined.

"Oh, yes," she said. "Oh, yes. Certainly. Certainly." All her wrinkles had curved up joyfully.

"Then write it down." Pat's wits were working. "There's one kind," he said plaintively, "would do me a lot of good."

"Rest is the best thing," she said happily.

"Comes in a bottle. You can put it on the order. I'll spell it for you, shall I?"

Her hands were still.

"Ma?"

"Eh, Johnny?"

"Put it down," he said, and began to spell, loudly, evenly. "P-O-S."

She did not move.

"I feel terrible." He rolled his head. "Don't you want me to feel better? Ma?"

"I know better than them doctors."

"That's right," he said. "No doctors. None of them. Write down the name of the medicine. P-O-S—"

Her pencil began to write.

"H-E—"

The pencil continued.

"A," said Pat. "Have you got it? Ma?"

"I got it," she said tenderly. "The boy can bring it, eh? And the good meat and all?"

"And fruit," he said. "Apples?"

The pencil wrote.

Pat thought, Oh, what nonsense! What do I think I am, the prisoner in the tower? Sending a cryptic note to the outside world, with my name hidden in it. Oh, come *on*. He sat up.

"Help me out of bed," he said loudly. "I want to go outdoors."

He let his legs over the edge of the bed. His right foot touched the floor and pain flared. He leaned on his hands and felt from his right hand a long stab go up his arm. He looked at that hand. The lacerations were pus and flame. He didn't like the look of it. "I want to go out in the sun," he said firmly.

She had her old lips pursed and they pushed in and out. He could almost see the gears shifting. "The sun don't shine today," said the part of her that knew he wanted to escape.

"I want some fresh air."

"The air's no good."

"Who's going to see me?" he challenged. "Kids maybe? You afraid?"

She put the pad in her pocket, and holding to the staff with both hands, she rose and swayed, looking down into his face.

"They don't come," she said. "Never. No more. I'm the old witch. That's what they think. They're good and scared of me, the kids are. And Rex, he knows how to keep them away. They don't bother me. Eh, Rex?" Her voice lifted.

Something in her tone communicated with the dog. The beast began to bark and snarl. His heavy body thudded on the door.

Pat let himself slowly back on the pillow.

"Down, Rex. Good dog," shrilled the old woman, with triumph in her voice.

She tucked the staff's end into her shoulder and came to lift Pat's legs. His right leg throbbed. But it was the hand that worried him. He said, "All right, but will you please boil some water and I mean *boil* it. And bring it and a clean rag and I mean *clean*."

He was feeling sickish. The door was so frail and he was in no shape to contend with the animal.

"My head aches," he said to her. "Keep Rex quiet, will you?"

"He's a good dog. Good dog."

"I'm sure."

"He minds me."

"Yes?"

"You mind me, too, Johnny. You mind your ma, and nobody is going to get you. Never. No more."

He said to her boldly, "Old lady, I am not your son and you know it."

"I'll take care," she crooned. "You'll see. You'll see. I don't mind. It don't bother me." She was leaning over, patting his left arm, and the mask of that crazy happiness was too close.

"Boil the water," he said feebly. "Ma?" He closed his eyes.

"Hot. Hot. Hot." She patted him. "You'll see. You'll see." He heard the rustle of her clothing.

Pat lay there when she had left the room and he saw, all right. The old woman was mad and he was her prisoner. Furthermore, unless he played up to her fancy, or whatever it was, this room and this bed were not even safe. She had a deadly weapon, which was the dog.

Pat took a little time to believe all this, including the flaws in the old woman's reasoning, and watching for flaws in his own. But there it was. And no living soul knew where *he* was, unless it was Everett Adams, who must be mad in some way of his own.

But then he thought of Anabel. Pat took no time to worry for Anabel's worry, for her confusion and her hurt and her fear. He had worried about that already. And she was well into that by now. He could not cancel out what she had already endured. And must still endure.

He tried to guess what Anabel would do. Go to the police. He felt sure of that. He relaxed a little. It might take a little more time, but it would not take forever. They would find him.

Furthermore, there was the grocery boy—sometime today.

Anabel's mother stopped her five-year-old Oldsmobile in the driveway at about a quarter to noon. She put her plump little feet to the ground and hauled a suitcase out of the tonneau in a businesslike manner. After embracing Anabel and searching her face, Mrs. King greeted little Sue with all grandmotherly comfort and good cheer. Anabel almost fell down with relief.

But not twenty minutes later, Mrs. King having taken house and child into her sure hands, Anabel was driving her mother's car over Pat's accustomed route to the university, feeling full of energy but a little confused by sudden freedom.

All morning, caged in and waiting, she had been scheming and plotting, pushing against the nothingness of no news at all. But, as the way wound through decent residential streets, she wondered how anyone was to know what dwelt in any one house, what innocence, what evil, and she saw the ordinary world, which only seemed to be buzzing along its ordinary way, to be perfectly opaque and mysterious.

She whipped the car into a familiar gas station and asked the man to fill up.

"You get yourself some transportation, Mrs. O'Shea?"

"It's my mother's. Tell me, did you see Mr. O'Shea going by last night, about dinnertime?"

"Can't say as I did."

"Would you have, I wonder?"

"Well, I was here till seven o'clock. See, I was waiting on the brother-in-law. . . ." The man rambled on.

Anabel caught herself murmuring, "I see," and looking wise, and she thought, This is futile. This is only making talk. It's going through motions. The idea frightened her. She said flatly, "He never did come home."

"Oh-oh. Well, gee, I'm sorry, but I didn't see him." The male face became, in some subtle way, pro-male.

Anabel thanked him, paid him, and drove on. The ordinary world was not only mysterious—a good part of it might not even be on her side. But Anabel stiffened. Just the same, just the same, she must *do* something.

She crossed the highway and entered the campus through the main gate. She drove to the parking lot behind the Science Building, put the car in Pat's slot, went through the glass doors, up the metal stairs, along the east corridor. Joanne Knowles waved at her, looking startled. Anabel turned the corner and went directly to Pat's office. The door was open. The little space was quiet and empty. She went in and sat down behind the gray metal desk. Its surface was neat. She flipped the pages on the calendar. Saw one note, *Saturday, 8* P.M. *Drinkwaters.* Oh, yes, if he never came back, she would have that last silly squabble to remember forever. Anabel beat away the sentimentality. Come on now, she said to herself sternly. What you are going to do is this. You are going to look for Pat. *Look,* then.

But there was nothing here to see. No clues. The desk drawers were locked. Anabel had no key. Nothing on the bookshelves but the usual books. Nothing on the floor, on the other chair, on the clothes tree. Nothing on the clothes tree? Then he had his raincoat with him. And what difference did that make? A head came around the edge of the open door and startled her.

"Mrs. O'Shea?"

"Yes?"

"My name is Mike Parsons." A thin boy came sliding in. "Mr. O'Shea isn't here?"

"No," said Anabel.

"Well, uh, do you know where he is?"

"No, I don't. Do you?" she asked crisply.

"Well, uh, no, I don't, naturally. I just happened to see them take off, last night. First Evvy and then O—I mean, Mr. O'Shea. And it looked kinda funny to me at the time."

Anabel stared at him. "What time?"

The boy put his knuckles on the desk and leaned on straight arms. He fixed her with a stare. "Have you called the FBI?" he said hoarsely.

Anabel shoved Pat's chair backward and put up her hand to beg for respite. "Just a minute. First, who is Evvy?"

"Oh, I'm sorry. That's Professor Everett Adams."

"Adams?" Anabel knew Everett Adams, having met him at faculty parties. She knew the daughter rather better. The new wife she had met once or twice. Anabel didn't much like any of them.

"He's gone too," the boy said, with his air of portent. "Didn't you know? Look, they both took off. One right after the other. And fast. Evvy went tearing out of here. And then O—I mean, Mr. O'Shea— went tearing after, and they took off in their cars and nobody knows where they are. I mean it's kinda obvious." The boy stopped speaking and watched her.

"If there is anything that is obvious to you," said Anabel with dangerous calm, "will you please tell me what that is?"

"Two American scientists?" the boy said breathily.

"Well?"

"Well, shouldn't the FBI get on it?"

"On what?" said Anabel.

"Well, I mean . . . they took off. They're both gone"—the boy lifted one hand to snap his fingers—"like *that*. Something could have tipped them that this was the time. So if they're defecting to the East, probably the FBI could have stopped them from getting out of the country."

Hollows appeared in Anabel's cheeks. "Is this *your* idea?"

Joanne Knowles spoke from the doorway. "Anabel, excuse me, the Provost would like you to come to his office, please."

The boy took a step backward and muttered, "Who can help wondering?"

Anabel said, "If you *wonder*, then you think it is *possible* that my husband has run away out of this country because he is or wants to be a Communist. Or have I misunderstood you?"

"Listen, I only wondered." The boy shuffled his feet doorward, but Joanne Knowles was a big girl and she was in the doorway. He looked back at Anabel. "That would be one thing you wouldn't know, would you?"

Anabel was on her feet.

The boy managed to duck around Joanne and get away. Anabel said to Joanne stormily, "You told the Provost I was here?"

"Well, I knew he'd want to see you. Listen, Anabel, he is only trying to stop a lot of talk and all that—"

"He's been doing just fine, hasn't he?" said Anabel furiously.

Anabel walked over to the Administration building with such an air of angry purpose that people melted out of her path. She clacked into the building, raced up the stairs, and marched through Miles Drinkwater's secretary as if she had been made of smoke. But then Anabel said to herself: What are you *doing? You are looking for Pat.* Keep that in mind.

Miles Drinkwater was gallant with chair, cigarette, ashtray. Anabel endured these ceremonies, but as soon as he had put his rump solidly into his chair she said brightly, "Well? What have you done?"

"I am so glad you came," he said. "I'd been expecting you to telephone. Well, now, as far as I can determine, your husband left his office and the building at about five thirty, which is his usual hour, and he drove away, toward the gymnasium."

"With Everett Adams?"

"Well . . . perhaps coincidentally." The Provost looked wary.

"But Everett Adams is also missing? Is that true?"

"Well, yes. That is to say, he isn't here. But I cannot believe that there is any connection. I spoke to Mrs. Adams on the phone and she is not . . . er . . . too concerned."

"Does she know where he is?"

"Well, perhaps not . . . but she presumes that he was with a friend last night. If he hasn't taken his classes today, then perhaps something to do with this . . . er . . . friend has detained him."

"What kind of friend?" said Anabel stonily.

"I really can't say." But the Provost's tone was answer. "That, of course, is why she has not . . . er . . . spoken to the police. I daresay," the Provost purred on, "that the wisest course—"

"Mr. Drinkwater," said Anabel, "frankly, I don't give a hoot in hell where Everett Adams is." He blinked at her—this slim, charming young woman who had always seemed to him to be the kind of wife a young teacher ought to have. "I want to know where Pat O'Shea is," said his wife. "What else have you done?"

The Provost fingered his pince-nez.

"Have you called the faculty together?"

"Since he . . . er . . . left at his usual time—"

"Or called the students together? Or in any way broadcast for information all over this place?"

"I spoke to his ten-o'clock class," said the Provost stiffly, "and received the information I've just given you, which seemed to me—"

"Mr. Drinkwater," said Anabel, "you, and only you, could question this entire school. Not even the police could do that. But you haven't!"

"I . . . er . . . am inclined to think," said the Provost, working at a modified twinkle as best he could, "that your husband might be rather disconcerted, on his return, if too much of a fuss were to be raised."

"Oh?" said Anabel. "Then you think he, too, spent last night with a 'friend'?"

"No, no, my dear young woman! I simply say that his absence would seem to have nothing to do with the university or his work here. Most plausibly, it is something personal and therefore his personal privacy ought to be respected."

Anabel said, "The police won't act because they think Pat should have time to come privately out of some drunken stupor or get privately out of some floosie's bed. You have done nothing really, because you wish to give him the same respect?"

The Provost was not liking Anabel much at the moment.

"Well," she said hotly, "I don't think anything of the sort. Shall I tell you what seems most plausible to me? Will you remember, kindly, that I know this man, privately, rather better than the police? Or you? Or anyone else? The only thing plausible to me—and I hope to God it isn't true—is this. Pat may have given someone a ride and that someone just hit him on the head, and dumped him out, and stole the car. That is the only thing that explains to me why Pat hasn't called me. It's because he *cannot*. He is not able. He is hurt, somewhere. Or he is dead."

"Oh, my poor child," the Provost said. "Try to believe that he will turn up and explain all this, quite simply. You must not upset yourself—"

"Oh, yes, I must," she cut in sharply. "Tell me how you know that Pat left, as you say he did."

"Why . . . er . . . Miss Knowles saw him leaving the building. And Miss Adams, Miss Violet Adams, saw him leave in his car."

"Vee Adams?"

"You know her?"

"Oh, yes. She's been at the house."

Anabel began to chew her lip. She had been hoping to find some clue that had to do with the school. But if there was none, then there was none.

The Provost said, "I really cannot believe that there's anything to worry too much about. Isn't it the wisest thing. . . ."

But Anabel was not after the kind of "wisdom" that merely soothes. She said icily, "When and if Pat turns up, as you expect, he is going to be rather more than disconcerted to discover that he and Everett Adams are supposed to have defected to the Communists."

"What?" The Provost snatched for his glasses.

"That is what your student body is wondering. Didn't you know? Two American scientists. Both missing. To them it is obvious."

"It's ridiculous!" cried the Provost. "Who told you that?"

"A boy named Parsons."

"Ah, that one." The Provost was furious. "Well, this sort of thing must be stopped immediately." The Provost glared about him. He snatched his phone. "Get me Captain Murch at Police Headquarters." He nodded, sightlessly, at Anabel. "I know the chief of detectives, or at least *he* certainly knows who *I* am. Now, we'll see. . . . Hello . . . no, no, Captain Murch himself. This is Miles Drinkwater speaking and the matter is urgent."

Anabel sat mouse-still.

"Murch? You have a Missing Person Report on one of our people, Elihu O'Shea, which you are holding. . . . Yes. . . . Now I am going to beg of you," the Provost let his voice go sarcastic on the phrase, "that you go about locating this man, and quickly. I'll tell you why. A Professor Everett Adams is also missing—more or less, that is—and we are being riddled by a rumor which must be stopped and stopped once and for all, by an open exposition of the truth here, before the school and my faculty is damaged by talk of *this* kind. . . . Eh? . . . Oh, defected to the East, which is ridiculous!

. . . No, no, impossible! Science teachers, certainly, but of no importance. . . . Now, you know very well, sir, how easy it is to start such a rumor and how difficult it is to stop one. So I insist—" The Provost went on very forcefully but Anabel had stopped listening two sentences ago.

He hung up finally and beamed on her. "Captain Murch is assigning men to the case at once," he said, "and an all-points bulletin will go out on his car. They'll find him."

Anabel stood up. "Mr. Drinkwater."

He scrambled to his feet. "Don't thank me."

"I hadn't intended to thank you," she said bluntly. "I'll tell you this. If it turns out that Pat is very badly hurt or if he is dead—and that, had the police begun their search at nine thirty this morning when I first called you, he would not be in such a desperate state—then I won't forgive you and I won't let you off anything."

"Mrs. O'Shea!"

"If you knew this captain and could have phoned him hours ago but did not—and if *therefore* anything happens to Pat—"

"But please—"

"—who is of no importance—" said Anabel with glittering eyes.

"Mrs. O'Shea. I meant, to the enemy. Please, you are emotionally upset. Naturally. But let me call the infirmary—"

"It is infirm," said Anabel, "to care about what happens to my husband? In whom I believe?"

"No, no, of course not. I only wished to spare him—"

"That much respect?"

"I cannot talk to you while you are so emotional," cooed the Provost, retreating to Olympia. "Won't you go home now? And rest? The police—"

"No. I am going to look for Pat."

"My dear Mrs. O'Shea!"

"I have at least one advantage," she said. "I know some places *not* to look." She swept out.

The Provost polished his glasses. Young. Idealistic. Full of faith. But life would sour her, too. Probably it would. Then he snatched for his phone and demanded the presence of Mike Parsons here, at once. The Provost was going to clobber somebody.

He had been touched. Yes, he had. He was not pleased with him-

self. He was having a glimpse—very upsetting. A classical idea. Death
was better than dishonor? What? In this year of Our Lord?

Anabel knew where not to look, but not where. Kidnapped? Amnesia? She had tried but she hadn't been able to take these alternatives seriously. Dead in a ditch, then? But which ditch? Anabel was
crying, but she held her head high and clattered, by blind luck, in
quick and accurate rhythm down the stairs.

The information counter could not locate Vee Adams.

The library had not seen her; she was not there.

Anabel walked the wide campus paths, wild with energy. But she
mustn't waste it in busywork. Knots of students swerved to let her
by. She stopped none of them to inquire. I should wear a placard, a
sandwich board, she thought, reading, I AM ANABEL O'SHEA, LOOK-
ING FOR MY HUSBAND, WHO IS MISSING. HELP ME, IF YOU CAN. For
how could she tell which student could or would, and how could she
ask them all?

She could ask one. If she could only find her. Anabel raced into
the Science Building and demanded of Joanne Knowles the phone
book. Everett Adams' home address burned into her mind. Then, a
thought struck her. "Joanne, did either Pat or Everett Adams get a
phone call late yesterday?"

"Oh, no, I'm sure not. Anabel, I'm sorry. . . ."

But Anabel turned away. It wasn't that she had believed what that
boy had suggested. But he had given her a vivid picture of two men
moving suddenly. Why? Not because of a phone call, anyhow.

As she hurried down the stairs toward the parking lot, she ca-
romed into a sturdy boy who steadied her.

"Sorry," said Anabel.

"That's OK." The boy, whose name was Dick Green, had to get
going to his part-time job at a gas station. He never had time to hang
around. His days were full.

He wasn't quite sure who Anabel was; he looked after her a brief
moment as she hurried away.

Anabel started the car, remembered something, turned to her left
out of the lot. Toward the gym, the Provost had said. That wasn't
the shortest way. The campus drive wound gracefully to a fork where

she might turn toward the dormitories. But that made no sense. Anabel went on to the South West Gate.

Nothing to see. Just the ordinary street. The usual traffic. The people of the world, coming and going. She blew out her breath, made a left turn across traffic, proceeded to a spot just outside the Main Gate after all, and so back into town.

The house was an undistinguished two-story tan stucco. Anabel had never been here before. She poked the bell.

A man opened the door and Anabel took a backward step, trying to remember where she had seen him. He was not as tall as Pat, yet he was tall. His hair was a very pale color, his face smooth and of a design familiar to her. His eyes were green, and inquiring, and as if irrepressibly, they were also admiring.

"May I see Mrs. Adams, please?"

"I'm sorry," he said pleasantly, "but Mrs. Adams isn't feeling well at all. Could I—"

"Is Professor Adams at home?"

"He isn't here. I'm sorry."

"Is Vee at home, then?"

"No." Now the man smiled to apologize for all his negatives. He had fine teeth. "I am Mrs. Adams' brother. My name is Cecil Wahl."

"I am Anabel O'Shea."

"O'Shea?" He tilted his head.

"Will you please ask Mrs. Adams if she'll see me? I think she might, since both our husbands are missing."

"I see. I see." He threw the door wide, instantly. "Come in, Mrs. O'Shea," he said warmly. "Of course. I'll ask her."

Anabel stepped into the foyer, gratified by this response.

"Come in, and please, be comfortable," the man said in an anxious, and yet irrepressibly gay, manner. His green eyes were not missing any of Anabel's feminine charms as he led her to the living room.

The room was dull and even shabby. It seemed old. It had no clear line or dominant idea. It didn't seem the background for Celia Adams, whom Anabel had met at a few faculty gatherings, to which Celia had come, dressed in a high fashion unsuitable for these occasions. If Celia had a circle in this town, Anabel was not of it, nor did Anabel gossip in her own circle about Professor Adams having married so young a wife. If anything, Anabel supposed she felt a bit sorry for Celia, as a displaced person—but never sorry enough to have been much interested.

She saw that there was an open door at the far end of this room in which the man stood and spoke, very distinctly and quite loud enough for Anabel to hear.

"C? It's Mrs. O'Shea."

"Oh?" The woman's tone was tinted with indifference.

"Do you think that you could talk a little? She says *her* husband is missing, too."

"Oh?" The female voice went higher and was less feeble. "Well, then. . . ."

"Of course," he said. He turned and smiled. As Anabel walked toward him it crossed her mind that this exchange, so very open, so very loud and clear, was in some way unnatural.

But she concentrated on the sight of Celia, struggling to lift her head. She was lying on a couch, her pale hair spread, her face smooth, her eyes green. "Don't move," said Anabel quickly. "I'm sorry you're not feeling well."

"It's this misery in my tummy," Celia said, sounding childish.

Her brother was putting a straight chair behind Anabel, who thanked him and sat down. He moved to the couch and perched, seeming to make himself light, on the narrow edge beside the afghan that covered his sister's lower body. He said to Anabel's wondering gaze, "Twins. That's right."

"I'm sorry if I was staring. . . ."

"We're used to it. Aren't we, C?"

His sister didn't answer. She seemed to be studying Anabel through long, pale lashes.

"I thought I'd better come," said Anabel, rallying to her purpose, "because it is so strange. Pat—that's my husband—left the Science Building last night about five thirty and so did Professor Adams and. . . . You *haven't* heard from him, have you?"

"No," said Celia. "No, we haven't." She seemed faintly hostile now.

"C called me in the middle of the night," said Cecil Wahl. "So I took the bus over from L.A. this morning. Now she has this 'misery.' I wish she'd let me call a doctor."

"It'll go away," said Celia.

"You were worried?" said Anabel. "But you haven't called the police?"

"Have you?" said Cecil pleasantly.

"Oh, yes," said Anabel. "And I suppose they'll be talking to you, now, because. . . ." She told them what the Provost had done. Celia's only reaction was to roll her head restlessly. Anabel thought she must be in pain.

The brother, however, was looking keen. "The Provost called here this morning, didn't he, C? He didn't seem quite so . . . excited about it, then?"

"He wasn't," said Anabel dryly, "until he found out the rumor that's going." She told him what the rumor was.

"Oh, Lord," said Cecil Wahl.

Anabel couldn't help it. She had been talking to him. The woman on the couch didn't seem to have his instinct to chat, to exchange, to make ease between strangers. He was now twisting his handsome mouth to a shape, part mirth, part scorn. "That's pretty damn silly, if you ask me," he said.

"It sure is." Anabel found herself smiling back, almost comfortably. "But where"—she brought herself to her problem—"where *are* they?"

The man responded to her change of mood at once. "That's the question. Well, we've been pretty sure that Everett's off on some . . . oh, toot or other. Do you think they are together?"

"I can't imagine why they would be," said Anabel. "Can you? That's what I came to ask you."

Celia said, "I can't even remember anybody 'O'Shea,' O'Shea," she repeated, rather distastefully.

Cecil said, "Well, *I* don't know what to think. Unless Ev is where we thought and your husband is somewhere else . . . maybe where you've thought."

Anabel told him what she had been thinking, about a vicious hitch-hiker.

"I guess," he said sympathetically, "you can't help wondering these days." He looked a trifle smug—or was it mocking?

"But," continued Anabel, "if there are *two* men in *two* cars, then that doesn't seem possible. Does it?"

"You are right," he answered promptly. "That would be different.

But we don't know it wasn't coincidence. This is a cockeyed world, you realize."

"That's what the Provost . . ." Anabel began. Then she was struck by an idea. "But surely the Provost told you that Pat O'Shea was missing, too?"

"I don't know," said Cecil quickly. He glanced at his sister.

Her green eyes were wide and round. He bent to her. "Don't be scared, C," he said softly. "Probably nobody hit Ev on the head. He's probably quite all right and he'll be coming along soon." His soothing sentences were overdone.

"He might be dead," his sister said, monotonously.

"No, no." He looked around at Anabel; his eye was warning, challenging, and also flattering her.

Anabel said, "I don't mean to frighten you."

Celia said, "Well, I can't help anything, now."

"Of course not," said her brother quickly. "Of course you can't. You lie still. Lie still, C. Don't even think about it. Excuse us?"

Anabel rose and went with him into the living room. He was rubbing his short fair hair. "Oh, boy," he said, looking sideways with irrepressible mischief, as if to say, "Look at me, in such a fix. I am not the type, really." "I think I am going to have to call the doctor. And I suppose I had better call the police, too. I certainly don't think she is in any shape to let *them* in on her."

"You may have to go there," said Anabel helpfully, from her own experience. "You may have to make out a Missing Persons report. That's what I had to do. They'll ask you all kinds of questions."

He was listening, with a cocked eyebrow.

"Is he wanted by the police?" Anabel went on. "That sort of thing. And they'll want to know everything about his car. Then they look for the car, you see. Some marvelous cure-all, called an APB."

He grimaced. His eyes, irrepressibly merry, appreciated her bitterness. "How can I go there, when C's the way she is? Well, I'll see." He didn't say so, but Anabel knew she was being nudged to leave. She started toward the house door.

Still Anabel, however much she had been gratified by this man's quick responses or by his irrepressible admiration for herself, was not forgetting her real mission. Something else perplexed her. "But didn't Vee tell you that she was the one to see them leave in their cars?"

"Vee?"

"She saw them. So I understand."

"Vee's a funny little kid," he said thoughtfully. "I'll talk to her." He had an uncanny way of communicating without words.

Anabel said quickly, "You are going to be busy." She went to the house door.

He reached around her with his left hand to open it. He said, "Listen, about cars. . . ." Anabel, almost in the shelter of his body, looked up. "They look for cars, you know," said Cecil Wahl, "because they can spot a car. But a man, loose on his feet, has no license plate. Or make, model, or a too obvious year." He grinned.

"I see," said Anabel.

"I don't drive a car myself," he said. She was thinking that this was irrelevant, when he added, "Darned if *I* could describe Ev's car. Could you?" The last was whimsy.

"If your sister can't, then probably Vee could," she reminded him.

"I suppose." He smiled.

"Well, thank you."

He was still smiling down. "On the other hand," he said gaily, "in this cockeyed world, your husband could be home, right now, pestering the police to find out where *you* are. Good luck, Mrs. Anabel."

Anabel sighed. She went down the walk to her mother's Oldsmobile, feeling chastened. She seemed to have been in contact with . . . what? Something experienced. Something not as painfully direct as she tended to be. Something that lived in a cockeyed world and did not permit it to surprise him. He didn't even take it seriously. She seemed to understand now why, the situation being what it was, Mrs. Adams had not called the police or raised a fuss. She seemed to understand . . . it seemed to have got into her mind in some underneath manner . . . that Vee Adams was no kind of objective reporter of facts. Perhaps the two men had not left, in any way at all, together. Anabel also seemed to understand that she herself would do best to rely on the police and their methods, because they were sophisticated. She had been naïve.

Beyond all this, as if in a spell, she drove home as fast as she could because Pat might be there.

Pat was not there. The police were.

Cecil Wahl closed the front door, crossed the length of the living room, went into the den, sat down where he had been before. "Cops," he said. "Now we know. So, when they pick up our Ev, what is he going to say?" She hunched one shoulder. "I'd better know, C." His voice held warning. "And right now, before the kid gets home, or something pops."

"How do I know what he'll say, the old fool?" said Celia petulantly.

"I can be good and lost," said Cecil lightly, "in an hour or even less. On my feet, without a license plate. What I want to know: Is this trip necessary?"

She raised her head. "Let's go, C?" she said, eyes bright, lips ready to smile.

"You? With a tummyache?"

She let her neck muscles go limp again and watched him out of green eyes.

"Take ten minutes and run it all the way through," he invited. "You took the gadget from the lab at the college. Right?"

"Right," she said mechanically.

"Told me to sell it and keep the change. Said it was Ev's contribution to my general welfare."

"I thought it was Ev's gadget," she said sullenly.

"Maybe so. You can be pretty dumb at times. And you can't tell me many lies, C."

"He said he couldn't lend you any more money. Then he was showing that silly thing off, C. He said it cost five hundred dollars. Well?"

"Oh, you did it for me." Her brother cocked an eyebrow. "But after a while, you told him what you'd done? And how was that again?"

"Oh, he was carrying on. I don't know. He's such a fool, C."

"That's when he phoned me. And I played stupid, said I'd thought it was his, and his contribution. Said I'd cashed it in. Hadn't the money to buy it back. Then what?"

"You made a mistake, C," she murmured.

"All right. Believe it or not, I didn't have the money. Now, I need to know exactly what Ev said *then*."

"Said the police could recover stolen property. Said the only thing to do was tell the whole story and ask for mercy. Blubbered all over the place. Said I'd taken what I'd thought was his, and they'd have to believe me if he believed me. Said you'd sold stolen property but you'd get off, if you hadn't known that, and if they believed you."

"Ah, we're getting to it. *Now,* exactly what did you tell him?"

"Well—the police, C? I just told him that if the police got into the act at all, they'd pick me up for murder."

"Pick *you* up?"

"I told him they had my fingerprints from that whiskey glass."

"*Your* fingerprints?"

"Because he wouldn't give a damn whether they picked you up or not," she said rather heatedly. "So that's why I lied. To shut him up, C."

"I wish you'd had more imagination," said her brother. "Why did you lie on the edge of the truth? You know damned well that my prints were on that glass."

"I knew," she said, wide-eyed.

He stood up. "Not me," he said. "Not on account of the fat man conking out, five years ago, from one Mickey, which was practically an accident. I've paid," he said. "I've never put my thumbprint on a driver's license in the State of California."

"You don't have to anymore."

"Go on," said Cecil. "What did Ev say to *this* revelation?"

Celia giggled. Then she turned her head, cheek to pillow. "He said it was practically an accident. He said I was only a child five years ago. He said I'd never had a chance. He knows a little bit about Mom. I'd had no moral training." She was mimicking, now. "But I was a human soul and he would save me." She had a perfect mouth, but it went crooked. "Just about what I thought he'd say."

Her brother's mouth twisted, too. "Mom, being dead, isn't going to get picked up for rolling the fat man. Right, C? Nor am *I.*"

"You left me," she said wildly. "And I was so sick. And he took me out to the desert. And he's saved me, already. And I can't stand it much longer. . . ."

"Done is done," her brother said calmly. "Now, Ev sent the money. I got the damn thing back. He had it yesterday. What happened, yesterday?"

"Nothing."

Her brother took two steps. Away.

"He was going to sneak it back into the lab, somehow," said Celia. "That's all I know."

"Did it get back there? I wonder."

"You wouldn't let me ask the Provost." She rolled her head.

Cecil ran his tongue around his fine set of teeth. "I've got something going for me in L.A. that I don't want to run out on if I don't have to. But this ice is pretty thin, C."

"Oh, probably he's dead," she burst. "He must be dead, or he'd be whining around here."

Cecil said nothing.

"If he is dead," she said, watching him, "I get half."

"Half of what?"

"This house." She could cock her eyebrow, too. "Some bonds."

"Be right nice," drawled Cecil in a moment, "if our Ev was dead. Who can be sure? What about this O'Shea? What could *he* know?"

"Nothing. Ran out on his wife. I wouldn't blame him." Her eyes were greener.

Cecil's mouth quirked. "A square, Mrs. Anabel. Pure and simple." He looked thoughtful.

She looked at him. "C?"

"Yeah, C?"

"Don't go." Sweat broke on her brow. "If this damned thing didn't hurt me . . ."

He looked down at her, the green of his eyes cool and cruel. Her eyes met his with the same look, a cool acceptance of the existence of cruelty in a cruel world. "As it is," she said, "if you do go, why should I care where? It might as well be jail."

In a moment he smiled at her, as if he appreciated and even admired her use of threat. He touched her cheek. "Everything might work out," he said lightly. "It depends on where the old fool is."

Her head wagged over and imprisoned his fingers between cheek and cushion.

"I'll call the doctor," he said. "You be sick. And silent."

"All right, C." She was smiling, not looking at him.

"When Vee shows up, be sick. And silent. Or—a little bit worried? That's not a bad idea."

"All right." Her eyes closed.

"She doesn't know anything, does she?"

Celia's lids were tight.

"C?"

"No," said his sister, writhing. "There it goes." Her eyes popped open. "I'm scared, C. Something's wrong with me."

"Keep your mind strictly on your health," her brother said amiably. "That's the idea." He stretched lazily, without haste, for the telephone.

Pat was dozing when the dog gave tongue. He lifted up on an elbow. The old woman spoke; the dog broke rhythm. Pat thought he heard a horn blow. The dog began again.

The old woman began to shout and when the animal at last subsided, Pat could hear her saying, "Guard, Rex. Eh, Rex? Stay, Rex. Guard."

Was she going to the front door? Would she open it? Had someone come? He listened hard, waiting for the exact moment when he could most effectively shout his name and the news of his plight to any sane ear. He heard the door close, sharply. What? Had someone shown his face there, in perfect silence?

Pat got out of the bed. His leg was impossible; he crawled. His head throbbed, his hand hurt, he paid no attention. When his ear was near the bedroom door, he heard the dog growl low, on the other side. Pat could feel the vibration. He did not dare try to open that door.

But what must he do, then? Crawl, now, to the window? Burst through, get out, *now?* Was anybody there? Had he heard an auto horn?

He became aware of a loss of pressure in the house, something was not in it that had been in it. The old woman had gone out! That was it. So Pat yelled. On the instant his throat opened, the dog barked. The dog barked and Pat yelled and the thin wood quivered between.

Stan Simmons looked nervously down from his panel truck at the old woman who stood there, at the broken gate, with her box of groceries in her arms. "He can't get out, can he?"

"He can't get out," she said. "No fear. He's a good boy." She looked merry and sly.

But Stan's spine was crawling and he seemed to hear, at twenty yards, the very thud of the beast's body on the walls. The dog was hysterical or something today. There was an almost human cry in the animal throat.

"Well, OK, Mrs. Pryde," he said. "See you the day after tomorrow." Stan made the truck move and turned it recklessly in his panic to get away from here. "Dog's getting about as nutty as she is," Stan muttered to his dashboard. "And one of these days, it isn't going to be safe."

When the old woman had struggled up on the stoop and in at the door with her load, and had soothed the dog, and had come the roundabout way through the kitchen, Pat was back in the bed, staring at the wall.

She was puffing; she had the big carton in her arms still. "See," she said, putting it on the bed, "I told you. See here, Johnny?"

"Didn't the boy help you with that?" said Pat drearily.

"He don't get out of his truck even. Never. Never." She cackled. "I told you he don't bother me. See here, Johnny? Pretty? Eh?"

He didn't want to turn his head, which was swimming a little. His eyes felt hot and almost ready for childish tears. He felt that he had failed, hadn't been quick enough, brave enough, smart enough. His head rolled and he could see her, taking the packages of food—the few cans, bottles—one by one into her hands and caressing them. He thought she was pitiful as she feasted on these. The gay colors, the clever shapes, the handsome labels of commercial packaging. For how many years had such things been her only news, her only pleasure?

"They are pretty," Pat said gently.

He thought, if I could make friends with the dog—that would be a way.

Stan bumped along Oleander Street, stopping and starting. Mr. Johanneson kept his trade by his delivery service. After all, if people had to get out a car, they might as well go to some big supermarket.

Stan made one special stop at Jamie Montero's observation point.

The little cripple was the whole street's pet. His father had been inspired to build him his perch, which even had a canopy for summertime. Here Jamie was king. No other child was allowed to share his throne, but the children liked to play around it. So Jamie was in the weather and in the world, and by no means shut away. And Jamie knew everything that came or went on Oleander Street.

Stan tossed him today's tidbit, which was a banana. The boy leaned forward. "Did you look?"

"Sure thing," said Stan. "I was all the way to the witch's house and I looked real good, believe me. This killer wasn't there."

"But he didn't come back."

"You ought to forget it, you know that?"

"I didn't see him. The nice man, yes. I saw the Rambler. But not the blue Chevy."

"Listen, you missed him. That's all it is, Jamie."

"I didn't sleep all night, Stan."

"Aw, go on. You dozed off." The little boy was shaking his head. "Then he went by in the rainstorm."

"I don't think so," Jamie said. "Nobody went by in that rain. Tell Mr. Johanneson thanks for the banana, and you, too."

"You bet," Stan said, as he always did, and went on.

One of the policemen was the young man Anabel had met before. Carlson was his name. The other was an older man, a very ugly man, big nose, furrowed cheeks, blue chin, a totally bald head. His name was Maclaren.

Anabel's mother made the introductions; both men nodded and sat down when Anabel did. Mrs. King took up her chatty thread. No, as far as she knew—and wasn't this right, dear—Pat had no relatives nearby. Just the one aunt in—New Hampshire, wasn't it? And a sister, in Maryland. It wasn't at all likely that he had gone to attend to some family crisis without letting anyone know.

Anabel asked whether they knew that a Professor Adams was also missing. But she knew that they must know. She could feel herself faking a question, making talk, wasting, not the time of those present, but Pat's time. Her purpose came flooding back, in all its purity, to stiffen her.

She told them, flatly and briefly, that she had just been to the Adams house, that Celia was ill, her brother there; they didn't seem to know anything. Vee Adams, the daughter, was the one to interview. When she had finished these statements the young man said he didn't suppose she believed there was anything *in* this idea that the two men had gone out of the country. His face was bland, his manner a shade too respectful.

Anabel, feeling as if she'd been slapped in the mouth, said it was ridiculous. Her mother began to amplify, chatting along, saying all the nice things she so often said about Pat and Anabel, and the two of them together.

The man named Maclaren kept quiet. Anabel forgot he was there. She watched this Carlson's young face for the infuriating skepticism that she had seen on it before.

When her mother ran down, Carlson said smoothly to Anabel, "About this—er—quarrel that you mentioned, Mrs. O'Shea. If he's trying to get even, where would you say. . . ."

Anabel felt her top blowing, again. She had not mentioned a quarrel, but she had told him, just the same. And his mind had closed. She remembered. "I'll tell you the gist of this famous quarrel," she said. "He made a date, without consulting me, on a night when I wanted to go somewhere else. I didn't like it. Now, what kind of people do you think we are? Do you seriously imagine that Pat O'Shea could be so stupid, so childish, so small, and so mean, as to run away? Just vanish? Leave me and his baby—and his job, too, by the way— just because I didn't want to go to the Provost's party and I said so? I don't care if the statistics say that ninety-nine percent of the people are complete morons. Pat is *not*. Nor am *I*. And I'd like to ask you what you are doing here anyway?"

Anabel's top had now blown completely.

"You won't find him here, you know," she went on. "That he *isn't* here is the whole point! Or do you think he is hiding in the broom closet, to punish Mama?"

"Not at all," said the young man and his cold control only made Anabel worse.

She said, "What you are doing is busywork! If you don't know that, then I'll tell you. Nothing but busywork! It isn't really doing *anything*. It's taking time. It's going through motions."

Her mother said gently, "Anabel. . . ."

Anabel stood up. She couldn't sit there. "But I keep telling him that Pat's in some terrible trouble," she cried. "That he *must* be. Why don't they *do* something?"

"We have an APB out on the—"

"Oh, well, then of course," she cried bitterly, "everything is just ducky, isn't it?"

The young man was looking grim now but still had the control not to answer.

The older man said, "One more question, Mrs. O'Shea. Might help us."

His very voice startled her out of her fit of temper and despair. It was a deep, warm, beautiful voice. She looked at him.

"Please tell us about his health," said this Maclaren.

"His h-health?"

"Is his heart all right? Or is he a diabetic? Anything like that, at all?" The beautiful voice was like a poultice upon the raw pain of her frantic frustration.

"No," she said with a feeling of clamping her head back to her shoulders with two fierce hands. "No, he had a checkup in the fall and he was fine. He hasn't had his spring checkup yet. He's only thirty-one."

"If there was anything like that, you see," said Maclaren, "it might give us some idea *where* to look. In a pretty big world."

"I know," said Anabel, ready to bawl.

"That's why we try to find his car," said Maclaren, in gentle music. "Because to find it would certainly tell us a lot more than we know now, wouldn't it? The police of four states are watching out for it, Mrs. O'Shea, while we talk here."

"Yes, I . . . Mr. . . ." She couldn't remember his name. "I'm sorry, but I am so scared."

"Surely," he said.

"I know a car is easier. . . ."

"It's a material object," he said, "and a big one. Statistically, we can usually find a car."

Anabel stood up. She had been clinging to the sight of the kind brown eyes in the ugly face and to the sound of that voice. "Will you promise me you'll tell me? The very first thing? Whatever you find?"

"I promise."

"If I *could* help you. . . ." She choked.

"God knows you would." This man believed her.

"Yes. Please, excuse me." She went blindly to her bedroom and fell upon the bed, and began to cry as hard as a woman had ever cried.

Mrs. King, without apologizing for her daughter, led the men to the door. They did not apologize, either. They got into their dark-colored unmarked sedan.

Carlson said, "Well, they do say that the wife is the last to know."

"This one knows," Maclaren said.

Carlson did not look at him. "Where to?"

"Up to you."

"The Adams bunch?"

"Fine."

Carlson made the car move. In a moment, Maclaren said, "You're new."

"As new as they come." Carlson was chipper.

"While I'm as old as they go, just about. And Friday night, I go. I guess you heard."

"Yeah, sure. I appreciate," the young man was cool and polite, "your letting me conduct the—"

"I suppose I've got to say something," Maclaren cut in.

"Benefit of your experience?" said the young man lightly. "Captain probably thought of that."

"He didn't think of a thing. Drinkwater was on his back, so he sent two."

"Listen, what you were going to have to say . . . go ahead. I can take it."

"Maybe that's what I was going to say. Take it. *Some* people know what they're talking about. Otherwise, why be a cop?"

"Well, I'll tell you. It's a living, Dad," said Carlson blithely.

While Anabel bawled her head off, her mother did not come into the room but went about the house, tending to the child, the kitchen, the daily chores.

After a while, Anabel could weep no more. She rolled over on her back and stared at the ceiling through the red ruin of her eyes. Fat lot of good I did, she thought with her blood cold. I was going to find him. What did I accomplish? Got the Provost mad at me. Screamed at the police.

What to think, what to think, besides the awful thought that a car does not decay like flesh or even bone? No more of that. She thought about the Provost, and Mrs. Adams, and the brother. Funny that the Provost hadn't told them about Pat being gone or about Anabel's having been to the police. Why wouldn't he? Oh, he was just cagey. Yet . . . why hadn't Vee told her stepmother anything, either? Or had she? And was that Cecil Wahl the cagey kind?

Now there came back to her the fleeting impression, the first impression, that loud clear open passage between brother and sister that seemed to be proclaiming, "Look, nothing up our sleeves." Why should they think she might think there was something up their sleeves . . . unless there was?

Oh, come now. Maybe that Cecil was one of those people who go sideways, just in case.

But Pat goes straight. If Pat does not go straight, then I am an idiot of the world—which I am not. Pat does go straight. I believe it. I know it, or I know nothing.

This was the basis of her life and the very foundation of her woe.

Her mother put her head in. "Are you hungry at all, Anabel?"

"Some," said Anabel. "What time is it?"

"Early. Only about five thirty."

"That's twenty-four hours," said Anabel. Then, she grinned up at her mother. "Not long."

"Wash your face," said her mother gently.

Anabel got up and washed her swollen face.

When Vee came into the house with her load of books, she found Cecil Wahl in the living room. For once, his mood was sober. No, her dad was not here. Very worrisome. He was worried about his sister, too. The doctor was with her now.

Almost at once, the doctor came out of the den and phoned for an ambulance, saying he would get in touch with a surgeon immediately. So all was crisis and confusion.

When the doctor had gone, Vee didn't know what to do. But this was her home; she had lived here before Celia. She must be gracious, as Lillian would have been. She went to the door of the den and looked in on the two of them. Celia seeming spent and limp, Cecil with his hand upon his sister's brow. "I'm so sorry, Celia," said Vee, in Lillian's cadences. "Is there anything that I can do?"

Celia scarcely stirred her languid eyelids but Cecil took his hand away and said, "You don't have any idea where your dad is, do you, Vee?"

"No."

"You saw him leaving the school yesterday."

"Yes."

"And you saw this Mr. O'Shea leaving, too?"

"Yes." Vee hung on to the doorframe. Two pairs of eyes stared at her now. So shallow-bright. So deeply cold. She would never let *them* know one solitary real thing about her. Such as a dream.

"Well?" said Celia irritably. "Didn't you say this O'Shea 'might know'? What did you mean?"

"Nothing. Just that he could have seen. I mean, which way Dad went. Dad came out," said Vee, desperately stupid, "and got into his car. He drove away. Then Mr. O'Shea came out and got into his car, and he drove away." She stopped.

Sometimes Vee got a funny feeling about these two. They had their own odd ways, such as calling each other by the same first initial. For a long time, Vee had thought they kept saying "See." And they had other ways. They could agree, without saying anything out loud. They were like one, sometimes, instead of two, and uncanny. Then sometimes they were like two—and that was worse.

They were one, just now.

"For pity's sakes," said Celia weakly. "Is that all?"

And Vee was dropped, just dropped. Now she stood, unseen, unregarded, as if she didn't live here, or didn't even live. She didn't know what to do, or where to go. She drifted to and fro in the living room. When the phone rang, she started nervously toward the phone in the foyer.

But she heard Celia saying, "Yes?" Celia was like a cat sometimes. She could go from being limp to being completely energized. Celia said, with friendly calm, "For pity's sakes. How are you?"

Cecil Wahl could move like a cat too. He sprang from his post at the far end of the couch in there and came swiftly to Vee in the living room. He took her arm and turned her, saying in a low voice, "Don't worry her about your dad right now, that's a good kid? She's pretty much in pain. . . ."

Vee pulled away from his touch. "You asked me," she said, ready to cry from the injustice of it.

"Then, I'm sorry. The police are looking for your dad, you know."

"The police!"

In the den, Celia said "Really?" on a long-drawn note. It seemed odd, because Celia didn't have the kind of friends with whom you gossiped on the telephone.

Cecil was rubbing his fair head. His body seemed to be crowding Vee. "They're looking for O'Shea at least, and they know your dad is missing too. So there isn't anything better that we can do. I'm wondering if you . . . Vee, will you help?"

"How?"

But his eyes were a little blind. He wasn't really seeing her. "I wish I'd asked the doctor. Listen, do you have any idea what C ought to take to this hospital? I mean, could you possibly get some of her stuff together?"

Everett was tumbling pent-up anguish into Celia's ear. "I can't tell you why, darling. I don't remember, now. I only know O'Shea is dead and I left him there and it's riding me and I'm sorry. . . ."

She said gravely, "I'm sorry, too." (He could not tell that her green eyes had swiveled toward the open door to watch the two figures in the next room.)

"I know I have to give you up. I only wanted to save you. If I can still save you, then I don't care for anything else. What is it to eat, sleep, without my love? So I'm going to give myself up, my darling. I have to do that. There is my child to think about. In prison I could gather myself . . . gather myself . . . try to make her understand. But darling, remember I am the thief. I'll say so. He caught me. So I . . . well, I went out of my mind . . . I must have . . . and so I killed him."

"Are you sure of that?" she said rather gingerly.

"Of what, darling? But they must have found him!"

"Where?" said Celia, as if she were asking him to repeat.

He began to have a sense that someone was listening at her end. "At the dump," he said. "Where I left him. The old dumping place. I ran. Oh, Celia, I thought I had to think. Well, I have thought. It rides me, Celia. I am not the man to cast it off. You were not guilty, but I am guilty. I knew better." Everett sobbed.

"Why don't I meet you then?" she said brightly.

"What?" He was astonished.

"I'll meet you. I'd like to."

"When?" he said on a tremendous sigh.

"Tomorrow?" (She was craning her neck, watching through the door.) "Let me see. Maybe not tomorrow. But the day after? Is that all right?"

"Would you do that?" Everett said in awe. "Oh, my darling! Oh,

God knows I was out of my mind . . . I never meant. . . ." At his end, Everett was thrilling to a crazy hope.

At her end, in the living room, Vee said, "The simplest thing is to ask her." She took a side step to get away from Cecil, to get around him.

"Don't trouble her."

"If she can talk on the telephone . . ." Vee moved toward the den. She thought he hadn't been seeing her, he hadn't heard a word she'd said, he scarcely knew what he had been saying himself . . . a lot of silly talk about toothpaste, hairbrush. . . .

She could hear Celia saying, "And if I'm late, just wait for me?" *Those* green eyes were seeing her, Vee could tell.

At his end, Everett was seeing a strange and unexpected glory. "Ah, yes. . . . Ah, do. . . . The two of us. Somewhere on this earth, surely. . . ."

"It's a date then," Celia said crisply. "Just tell me—"

Cecil had moved faster than Vee and now he slipped around her and snatched the phone. "Who is this? . . . Oh, *Mary!*" He swung away, turning his back as his fingers cut the connection. "Mary dear, C is out of her ever-lovin' mind. She can't make any dates. She's on her way to the hospital, right now. . . . Well, we don't know how serious . . . I guess, not *too.* . . . An appendectomy, which isn't so much these days, even if it is—well, you know, a little quick. . . . Right, I'll tell her. . . . Certainly."

He put the phone down and said to his sister severely, "Are you delirious or what?"

His sister lay with her eyes shut. "I can't go to the hospital," she said in a sullen monotone. "I don't want to go. I'm not going."

Cecil hushed her, glancing up at Vee, his eyelids signaling a weary patience with a balky baby. "You just pack what you think," he said softly. Now *these* green eyes were really seeing her and searching her somehow. "You'll have better sense about it. And thanks very much, Vee." Somewhere in the neighborhood a siren sounded. "Better hurry."

Vee ran across the living room and up the stairs. She didn't like Cecil Wahl. She never had. It was funny that he should be the first to notice how, in this house, Vee was the long-suffering mother-house-keeper and her stepmother the irresponsible child.

Cecil said, "Quick."

Celia said, "He says he killed O'Shea."

"How? Never mind. Where?"

"He said at some dump. 'Old dumping place,' he said."

"Where is that?"

"I don't know."

"What else? Quickly." The siren was outside.

"Wants to give himself up. Said he'd tell them *he* stole the gadget."

"Oh-oh. Our Ev will never stand up to a police interrogation." Cecil drew away as if in spirit he had gone a hundred miles.

"I know," she said stonily. "That's why I said I'd meet him. He'll wait."

"OK. *I'll* go."

The doorbell was ringing. Two pairs of green eyes met, cool and cruel. "Probably he won't get to say anything," Cecil murmured, "which is best all around. Right, C?"

"Why bother?" she said, green eyes sliding.

"Come on. Where is he?"

"You grabbed the phone," his sister said drearily, "I don't know where he is. He didn't have time to say."

Cecil put his lips into whistle position but made no sound.

She lifted her torso. "And he'll call back, C. Sooner or later." The doorbell insisted.

"That's all right. I'll be here, C. I'll get it."

"Watch her, C. Watch li'l ol' Vee."

"Don't worry." He ran to let in the men from the ambulance, not noticing that, by some hocus-pocus, he had been induced to commit himself to stay around.

When Vee came running down with Celia's overnight bag, Cecil was on the phone in the foyer calling a taxi. The front door was wide open. They were lifting the stretcher into the ambulance. Vee didn't know what to do with the bag.

Cecil held the phone lower and said to her, "Look, you can go along and sign C in, and all that, can't you, Vee?"

"No, I can't," she wailed, everything being too much for her. "I can't *do* it. Nobody ever sees me or hears me. . . ."

"Then we'll both go," he said soothingly. "You certainly mustn't be left here all alone."

She looked up at him. He was smiling. His teeth showed, but she seemed to be seeing them in a skull.

When Carlson and Maclaren pulled to the curb, the stucco house had a blank and empty aspect. The neighbor's twelve-year-old boy, big-eyed with the delight of telling news, said there had been an ambulance—sirens and everything! Naw! nobody was there, now, in the Adams house.

In the hospital corridor, on the fourth floor. Vee shifted from one foot to the other. White-clad people had brushed her outside. Celia didn't care whether Vee was in the room, or out here, or anywhere. Cecil Wahl had not come up to this floor at all. He was in the Admitting Office, or the lobby. Vee didn't know what else to do, finally, but try to find him.

She took the elevator. The hospital frightened her. She didn't belong here. (But where, then?) She stepped out into the lobby and saw a face she knew.

"Violet Adams," the young man said. "Hi, Vi. Remember me?"

"Beau Carlson." She could tell right away that he didn't like that old nickname anymore, but she couldn't remember his real name. "I mean—Mr. Carlson?" She was confused. This was a hospital. Somebody of his must be ill.

"I'm in the Police Department now. This is Lieutenant James Maclaren. Violet Adams. She was a frosh—wasn't it, Vi?—when I was a senior, back in high school."

Vee couldn't get it through her head that Beau Carlson was really stopping to speak to her. He'd been a big wheel, a football player—in fact, *the* football player. The older man, with the clown face, wanted to know how her mother was.

"My stepmother?" Vee wondered how they knew about Celia. "I guess they are going to operate, just about right away. I'm looking for my—well, I guess he's my step-uncle, Mr. Wahl."

She looked around the lobby. Cecil wasn't in sight.

"He's not around," said Beau Carlson. (How did they know about Cecil, too?) "Tell us about your dad, Vi. And this Mr. O'Shea."

(What did he know? Did he know *everything?*) Vee sucked in her breath. "Oh, you are *looking* for my dad," she cried. "Somebody told me."

(These are the police, she told herself, and the police are looking for my father. She didn't know whether to be frightened or not.)

"But you haven't f-found him?" she stammered.

"Not yet," said Carlson, "but we'll find them. Both. Why don't you just tell us what *you* know?"

Vee became rather stiff. She told them how she had seen both men leave, the order of their leaving, the direction in which they had gone. The older one asked her whether her father had seen her waiting there.

"I guess he couldn't have."

"Was it an appointment? Did he expect you to be there, Miss Adams?"

"Well, sometimes I wait for him. Sometimes I go home another way." She wasn't going to say that she took the bus. Let them think she got rides with boys. Beau Carlson really was terribly good-looking. He'd been in the service, she remembered. Now he was back and some kind of policeman. He'd be *good,* too. He was one of the lucky ones.

He began to ask her about her father's car and Vee stumbled through the best description of it that she could give. Imagine Beau Carlson remembering who she was! Talking to her, easily, as if they were friends—of old. She thought, When the time comes, I could tell *him* the secret that I know. He's the police and it's about a crime. She was gathering up material for a dream.

"I guess we can talk to your moth—I mean your stepmother, right now," he was saying.

"There wouldn't be much point," said Vee, more frankly than she had meant to speak. "*She* doesn't know where my dad is."

"They don't get along too well?" He was interested.

The secret was in her mouth. (Celia is a thief. She stole something.) But Vee put her teeth over her lower lip. "I can't talk about that, really," she said primly in a moment, as Lillian would have said.

Cecil's fingers on her bare arm made her jump. "Ah, there you are, Vee. Gentlemen? I believe you were asking for me? I'm Cecil Wahl. I see that you've met Miss Vee Adams."

Beau Carlson began to talk to Cecil. The spotlight swerved and refocused. Vee was in shadow. She had a sense that the two young men were getting along just fine. Overtones went between them, two young bucks exchanging amusement at the antics of an old buck, as if they could understand what Vee could not. As if she hadn't known, for a long time, that her father was possessed, and it wasn't so very funny. They shouldn't think they were so smart.

Then, the one named Maclaren said into her ear, "You've had a rough time." It was just as if he had pushed a button. Vee began to sob. She was furious at herself for this. She hated herself. Cecil's arm came around her shoulders. She hated him and twisted away. She hated Beau Carlson, who took a step backward as if he resigned himself to the nuisance of her tears and would wait. She hated that other man. She was *very* brave. Didn't she go her brave and lonely way—mysteriously sad, perhaps—but a princess, not a cry-baby? Vee hid her face from them all. (Except that there was no such princess. Just in the old baby stories read to her, long long ago, when everything was better. When all you had to do was to be a "good girl" and you would be praised and petted.)

"Poor kid," said Cecil.

Well, *he* just didn't know! None of them knew. Maybe *she* was the key to this whole business. So let them think she was just a "poor kid." Then, someday. . . . A dream, to lean on.

On the way back to headquarters, Carlson said to Maclaren, "Any of that get us anywhere?"

"Not far. Better check on this Cecil Wahl."

"He wasn't even in town."

Maclaren was brooding. Finally, he said, "Call it experience."

"Call what experience?"

"The knack of smelling them."

"Smelling *what?*" Carlson was very much startled.

"No, no," said Maclaren, "I mean the outsiders. The ones who'd just as lief knife their old mothers as anybody else. The bums."

In a moment Carlson produced a rusty laugh. "Excuse me, but he smelled to me like a young fellow just trying to get along."

Maclaren sank a little lower in his seat.

Carlson drove in silence for a moment. Then he said, in a light cool manner, "You've got another knack, I notice. Sure do know how to make the girls cry."

Maclaren said nothing. Carlson bit his lip and then said, rather angrily, "What hit *her?*"

"You used to know her, did you?" Maclaren murmured.

"Listen, I knew who she was. This Violet—in those days, strictly a pig from pigsville."

"That so, Beau?" The powerful voice was frosty.

"You know my name," the young man said stiffly.

"You a young fellow just trying to get along, are you? Or do you want to be a cop?"

"I am a cop."

"Then stop with the pigeonholes."

"What do you mean?"

Maclaren just sighed.

"Uh huh," said the young man in a moment. "But you can smell them. You got a pigeonhole for the bums. Right?" His voice was in control.

"I used my own nose," Maclaren said. "How did you know this Violet Adams was a pig? Was the word around?"

The lad blew air through his pursed lips, making them flutter. Then he turned his head and smiled. "Listen, I didn't mean to get out of line, sir. I appreciate you've had a lot of . . . experience. I'll try and learn. Don't call me Beau. OK?"

"The young lady seems to prefer to be called Vee these days," said Maclaren wearily, looking out of his window. "Don't call me 'sir.'"

"No, sir," said Carlson.

In the cab, Cecil said, "Vee, I wonder if you've got a girlfriend who'd let you stay overnight?"

"Oh?"

"It might not be circumspect—Hey, that's a good word!—for you and me to stay alone in the house. Not that anything. . . . But you know what I mean."

Vee felt like screaming and jumping out of the cab. Certainly she knew what he meant.

"Somebody you could talk 'female' talk to, anyhow," he went on. "I've got things. . . . Oh, phone calls. Want to be on hand, just in case. How about it?"

"I'm trying to think." All Vee could think was that she couldn't go home to her own home. And when he said "female" talk, he meant stupid chatter.

"What about the neighbor lady? What's her name?"

"Mrs. Newcomb? Not there." (No, she *wouldn't*.)

"I've got a lot on my mind," he said, moving restlessly. "Could we drop you now?"

"You can drop me," said Vee regally, "any time."

"Give the man the address, there's a good girl," said Cecil, who bounced up in spirits now that he was going to be rid of her.

But Vee thought, It's *my* father. It's *my* trouble.

She gave an address.

Anabel heard the cab, looked out, saw it stop, and she burst the front door open. Coming up her walk were Vee Adams and Cecil Wahl. She called out, "Yes?" She was scared.

The man's feet broke stride, but the girl hurried ahead of him. "Mrs. O'Shea, I came to ask you, please, may I stay here tonight? Celia's in the hospital, and Dad's not found yet, and I thought. . . . You are all alone too. I could help you with little Susie and be somebody around?"

"I see," said Anabel quietly.

Cecil Wahl had come nearer now. "Mrs. Anabel, I give you my word, I had no idea. . . ." He seemed upset.

"Will you come in, both of you? Have you talked to the police?"

"Oh, yes, they caught up with us," he said. "Not that we had anything to say. Look, I've got a cab waiting. . . . Come along, Vee," he said sternly. "This is not a good idea. The lady mustn't be bothered."

But Vee stood still in the half-dark; the house light fell on her bent head and her clasped hands. She seemed to sway and catch her balance. Anabel distinctly caught her aura of being lost and in great distress. Great need. She had never liked Vee Adams. "Wait," she said.

"Really," said Cecil, "I thought she was directing us to some girl-friend. There is no reason why you should put her up."

"There's no reason why not," said Anabel gravely. "Go on in, Vee, please."

The man moved as if he would physically interfere, but he did not, and the girl walked, with her head still bowed, up the few steps, past Anabel, and in at the open door.

"I'm afraid she'll be trouble," Cecil said. "She's a strange kid. Don't do this. It isn't necessary."

"You are going back to the Adams house?"

"I've got to be there in case there is news or something I ought to do." He was very uneasy.

"Your cab is waiting. She'll be all right."

"Yes." He hunched his shoulders and let them fall. "Well," he said, irrepressibly gay, "call it a star in your crown, Mrs. Anabel. Good night, and good luck to us all." He made her a jaunty salute and loped toward the cab.

Anabel went slowly into the house. Vee and Mrs. King were staring at each other. "Mother, this is Vee Adams. Professor Adams' daughter."

"But I thought. . . ." The girl began to twist her hands. "I thought you were *alone*," she cried, "I honestly did." She had been crying.

"I believe you," said Anabel. "You haven't any night things with you?" Vee shook her head. "That's no problem. But have you had dinner?"

"I don't need any."

"Oh my," said Mrs. King. "But there's plenty left over. You come with me now—Vee, isn't it? I don't know whether you like leftover stew but it wasn't bad. . . ."

Mrs. King swept the girl away with her on the tide of kind and hospitable chatter.

Anabel stood still, chewing her lip. The phone began to ring.

It was so silent, so silent, in the night. Sometimes a plane went over and noise bored through the high air. Sometimes a coyote barked, distantly. Otherwise, silence. No voices, traffic, footsteps, music . . . only the night, breathing around the old bungalow.

No moon? Those shades drawn, how could he tell? What night was this, anyhow? Pat's attention span was not what it ought to be. He kept starting a train of thought and drifting away from it and then finding himself unable to remember what it had been. Now, now. . . . He rolled his head.

What had he been thinking? No guts, eh, O'Shea? That's right. Pursue that. So it would hurt him to walk on a broken leg? So what? He had a broken leg, a wounded hand, and a half-broken head. But that leaves half of me, he thought and grimaced in the dark. Half or more, and don't they say that half a brain is better than no brain?

How come I lie here and let a crazy old woman keep me here?

He lifted his head. Ah-ha, the dog hadn't heard *that*. How could he make friends with the dog when he never saw the dog? Only heard him. If he had any poison, he could poison the dog. He had never thought of himself as the kind of man who would ever poison a dog. . . .

Back. Back. He had been trying to think. . . . What about?

About getting out of here. Sure. That was the only thing there was to think about. "And I had better think fast," he muttered, "because I don't feel so good, and that is a fact."

He heard the dog's toenails scrape on something. Bare floor?

"Got your ears up, boy?" muttered Pat.

Well, he said to himself, I'll tell you what. I'll just get out of this smelly bed and I'll get me over to that back window, and I'll put up that shade and I'll see what's to be seen, and if there's any light out there—or maybe even if there isn't—I'll bust the screen, I'll heave myself out of here . . . and what happens then is what is going to happen.

This seemed very simple, very clear.

He sat up and his head swam. The dog growled.

"Wake her up, then," said Pat. "What can she do? I'm Johnny Pryde, her Pryde and joy. So why will she set the dog on her own darling Johnny? Who is Johnny Pryde, anyhow? Where is he now? Where are the snows of. . . ."

He caught himself swaying on the edge of the bed, thinking about something else instead of the project at hand.

At foot. All right. Pat got out of the bed. The leg didn't hurt so much at that. Or else it hurt so much his brain wouldn't believe it.

She never left any matches around, damn it. He could have lighted the lamp. In fact, he would have lighted the world. Throw the lamp out the window. Takes a lot less than that to start the State of California burning. Pretty soon, fire engines.

"Fried alive," Pat said, quite loudly. "Fried alive, in my own grease? I don't care for it."

He guessed he wouldn't try to light any matches. Anyhow, he didn't have any matches. He didn't have any trousers, either. For my manly modesty, must I rot in this room? There comes a time . . . comes a time . . . when first things have got to come first and that's right and a man has got to sort out his values . . . and you can take the collision course because maybe you were wrong and you don't collide there wasn't anything there where was I?

He was standing, in a rubbery sort of way. The dog was giving out short yelps now. He couldn't hear the old witch moving or speaking yet.

He tottered to the back window and with his left hand grasped the shade at the bottom and tried the little teasing tugging that would release the spring and send it up. But the spring no longer functioned. The shade tore from the roller, a quarter of the way across, and sagged crookedly.

Now the dog was making a lot of noise.

Pat brushed the shade aside and got it behind him. It was dark out there, but not perfectly black. There was light arched above—some kind of skylight? But clumps of blackness, knots and lumps of blackness. Trees? He couldn't see the ground. Dirty glass? He put his left hand (his right hand wasn't much use to him, since he couldn't open the fingers nor could he close them, all the way) . . . left hand on the lower sash, groping for a handle. Got it. The sash moved upward.

The dog was throwing himself at the door. *Thump.*

Pat put his shoulder against the ancient rusted screen and, as it tore, he pitched forward. The screen cut at his cheek. Now, wait a minute. He'd better not go out of here headfirst, because his head was in no condition to be landed on. His half-head.

Like a swift dawn, light came up behind him.

"Now listen," he said, staggering on bent knees, half turning, "I'm getting out. I mean, that's all there is to it. So don't argue."

She was in the doorway and the dog was at her side. She had one hand on the dog's collar. The dog was muttering low. In her other hand, she held a lamp. She was wearing a shapeless gray garment. It was her nightgown. He could see her gnarled bare feet. He could see, for the first time, something of that outer room. A patterned rug. A bit of carved mahogany.

He said, "Well, maybe the front door would be more convenient." His bent right knee would not straighten. All his weight was on the good left one.

The old woman put the lamp down on the chest of drawers. The dog crouched.

"Now listen," said Pat, reeling, "I'm sick, old lady. I am as sick as a dog! Hah!" He raised his left hand and began to shake his fore-finger at her. Once begun, the motion would not stop. "You want me to die? That's what you want? Eh, Rex?" He mimicked her. "Eh, Rex?"

The dog's feet scrabbled for a better hold. But the old woman made the dog stay and she came silently to Pat. Her strong hands went under his armpits.

Pat yelled. It hurt. The dog began to bark furiously.

"Quiet, quiet, *quiet!*" shouted the old woman. Then she said gently, "Johnny, you ain't well enough to go anyplace."

"Yeah, well, I know *that*." Pat sagged.

"Tomorrow," she said. "Tomorrow."

"Yeah, well—all right. Tomorrow."

She was helping him toward the bed and he was going there. She lifted his shaking legs. She pulled up the blankets.

"I'm burning," he said, throwing them off violently.

"No, no. No, no. *They'll* never burn Johnny Pryde."

"Never?" he said feebly.

"Never. Never."

His mind was drifting. "My mother died. . . ."

"No, no," she crooned. "No, no."

"Tomorrow? Eh, Rex?" (That dog doesn't like me, Pat thought. I never did anything to him. Did I?)

"Tomorrow," the old woman said. "You'll see."

In a little while she left him, picked up the lamp and, in silence, ordered the dog to precede her out of the room. She shut the door.

"A touch of the influenza," she muttered to the dog. "That's what it is. Tomorrow the medicine will come, eh, Rex?" She padded on the dirty carpet to her nest on the couch. "Sleep's the best thing," she said. "Quiet now, Rex. Quiet. Mind." She blew out the lamp. "And the good meat, too. *I* know what's good for him. You'll see. You'll see."

The old house was dark and silent. Outside, the night breathed.

She said in the dark, suddenly, "The day *after* tomorrow, I mean. That's right. That's right."

Wednesday

ANABEL WOKE from heavy sleep and sat up in her bed. It was morning. It was nine thirty in the morning. "Oh, no!" she cried aloud. The sound produced her mother, who said, "You were so exhausted, dear. I've talked to the police."

"Nothing?"

"Nothing yet. I'll fix your eggs."

Anabel squeezed her eyes shut and dropped back to her pillow. That made two nights. Two nights and one day. Here was another day. Wednesday. And he wasn't here. And she didn't know where he was.

She made herself think about all the phone calls last evening. Friends, Pat's colleagues, acquaintances, even students—full of concern. And curiosity. But Anabel had developed a technique of turning the questioning the other way. Not one of them had been able to tell her anything. At last she had become panicky and begun to say, as rudely as was necessary, that her phone must be left open for important calls.

There had been no important call.

When, at last, the phone had subsided, Mrs. King had decreed bed for them all. They had made up the living-room couch for Vee. Mrs. King was in the guest room-den. So Anabel had come, again, to the big cold double bed, alone. Too exhausted to weep, too numb to pray, she had slept. Too long.

Although no matter, if there was no news yet.

She lay wondering where to get any purchase on the mystery. What about Everett Adams? Had he anything to do with Pat's disappearance? Was there anything odd about his wife and her twin brother? Why had Anabel taken Vee in last night? Why had Vee come?

Anabel knew that the girl was in the throes of a student crush on an attractive young instructor. Vee had turned up at his house several times, asking for special help, and Pat had given it, in his amiable way, at the same time warning Anabel that she must not, under any circumstances, leave the room where he and Vee Adams were. So Anabel had finished the best part of a sweater during those sessions. She didn't much like the poor silly kid—an adolescent poseur.

She knew that she hadn't taken the girl in last night for sweet charity alone, being under no illusion that Anabel O'Shea was pushing for sainthood. Nor had she done it with some superstitious notion that to turn any distressed person from her door would rebound upon Pat somehow. Anabel now judged that she had done it partly because Cecil Wahl had not wanted her to do it, and partly because Anabel had hoped she might find out something. And partly for charity, after all.

But Vee had been very prim, forlorn, polite. Yes (she said), she had seen the two men drive away, first the one and then the other. She had said no more, *asked* no more, which was peculiar.

It had been Mrs. King who, after some friendly prying into Vee's affairs, had called the hospital to inquire for Mrs. Adams and had been told that Mrs. Adams had come through the operation very well and was resting.

Anabel threw off her coverings and jumped out of bed. But her mother's very charity and kindly wish to make the poor girl more comfortable had stood between, last night, and had prevented any detailed inquisition by Anabel of this girl who was, although a pitiable human being, yet also a puzzling one.

Meek as milk, but with the crust to come here and beg lodging.

Anabel bathed and dressed quickly and sallied forth. Vee was in the kitchen, wearing the same small-flowered pink print dress. Mrs. King was trying to let herself be "helped."

"Vee couldn't go to her classes today," said Mrs. King. "For one thing, she'll want to go to the hospital. For another, the poor child has no clothing. Anabel, I wonder if you can't drive to her house and pick up her things? It would be all right, surely, if you were along."

Anabel said, "Mother, go deal with Sue, would you? I want to talk to Vee alone."

Mrs. King read her daughter's expression and left them without protest or comment.

"Sit down," said Anabel, putting herself before her breakfast. Vee sat down the other side of the table. "You came here," began Anabel, "first, because you thought I might be all alone?"

"I did. I really did, Mrs. O'Shea."

"I know," said Anabel, "and I know you have a crush on Pat, besides."

"I—like him very much. He is a wonderful teacher."

"This is not," said Anabel, "the day to be mealymouthed."

Vee swallowed and turned her eyes.

"All right," continued Anabel with good humor, "I can't say that I understand it entirely, but here you are. So since you were *there,* in that parking lot, I wish you'd tell me whether you think that the two of them went off together."

"They drove off in their cars." The girl's voice was low and it evaded. She was nervous. She was pitiable.

But Anabel snapped, "Don't be literal. I heard you say that before and I believed you. What I want to know, now, is this: Did it seem to you that there was any connection between the two of them?"

"I don't know." Vee began to sniffle.

Anabel said, "I'm not going to stop asking questions if you cry. Not when my husband is missing."

"My dad is missing, too," Vee mumbled defensively.

"All right. We are both worried, both scared, and we'd both like to know what's happened. So please tell me. Did they go together, in any sense at all? What did you think at the time?" she prodded.

The girl was using her handkerchief. "Don't pay any attention to what I thought," she murmured.

"Why not?" said Anabel flatly.

"Nobody does."

"That's too bad," said Anabel. "But you're not worth much attention, the way you are behaving."

The girl looked up, startled and hurt.

"I am only asking for your opinion. Why can't I get it?"

"Because . . . because I'm probably stupid."

"You had a 'stupid' opinion, then?" said Anabel, undaunted.

Vee said, "Yes, I did."

"Well?"

"I thought maybe my dad didn't like it that I had a 'crush.' That's what *you* call it. . . ." The voice was muffled.

"Why do you say that? That he didn't like it."

"Because. . . ."

"You won't get out of answering now," said Anabel cheerfully but firmly. "Go on."

Vee looked hostile suddenly. "I thought they were fighting," she said, "if you want to know."

"Fighting? Pat and Everett Adams? All right. You must have had some reason to think so."

"I did," said Vee. "Dad came out of the Science Building, almost running, and Mr. O'Shea came out and shouted his name. But Dad just ran to his car and took off as fast as he could go, and the wrong way, too, and then Mr. O'Shea ran to his car and took off right after him, and he was *mad*."

Anabel straightened very high in her chair. "Mad? Angry, you mean? You thought they were 'fighting'? About what?"

"I don't know."

"But you thought," insisted Anabel. "You had a 'stupid' opinion. What was it?"

Vee put her arms on the table and her head down on her arms. "Maybe my dad said something to Mr. O'Shea—about us. And honestly, Mrs. O'Shea, I knew you always watched us, but we weren't doing anything wrong. If I'm in love with him, I still . . . I *know* . . . I didn't expect. . . . Well, I just think Mr. O'Shea probably got mad at my dad. . . ." Her voice droned, dreamily.

"Over you?"

Vee sobbed.

"I see. Well, let me put it this way," said Anabel. "You are an idiot."

Vee's face came up pink and startled.

"And you'd better get this romantic little opera right smack out of your romantic little head," said Anabel with fairly good humor. "You kids with your crushes can be quite a menace. Pat always does insist that I stick around. He knows some of you get some pretty whacky notions and he'd better always have an honest witness."

Vee sat up straight, very red. "I didn't realize. . . ."

"I'll tell you another thing you do not realize. If your father was silly enough to query Pat on the subject, then Pat would have told him, very kindly, how careful he knows he has to be. Not to guard you from harm, but to guard against the harm that you could do by what you call being-in-love."

Anabel choked off her rising temper. "Now, in the name of something more *like* love," she said, "tell me the truth. Did Pat shout after your father? Or did you just imagine how thrilling it would have been if he had?"

"But he did," said Vee furiously. "'Adams,' he yelled. And he was very mad, I mean angry."

"And they were running, you say? Hurrying?"

"Yes, they were and I can't *help* it."

Vee was trembling.

Anabel said, "All right. Calm down. I believe you." Then she snapped her fingers. "Wait a minute. That boy. Do you know a Mike Parsons?"

"He's a snoop," said Vee sullenly. "He listened outside the door."

"What door?"

"The classroom door when I was talking to the Provost."

"No, no," said Anabel. "That wasn't it. *He* told me that he saw the two of them—first your father, then Pat—hurrying out of the building. Now, wait a minute. It goes together."

"You said you believed me," Vee muttered.

Anabel shot her a withering glance. "You know, if you could leave yourself out of this, for two minutes. . . . Did you think that Pat was *following* your dad? That your dad was trying to get away from Pat?"

"Maybe," said Vee.

"They were 'fighting'? That's what you thought?"

"Probably I was wrong." Vee was sullen.

"In your best judgment, they were fighting about *something*?"

Vee sniffled.

"You say they were running? You say Pat shouted? You say they drove off and went the wrong way?"

"They did," sniffled Vee.

"I wonder why," said Anabel. "I wonder why."

"I don't know why."

"Neither do I. Let's think about it." Then Anabel said suddenly, "Thank you."

Vee got up and stumbled away.

She didn't belong here, Vee knew that. She'd just made a fool of herself. As usual. She huddled miserably in a big chair. Mrs. King was very nice and very kind to a stranger, but Vee was beyond that somehow. She needed more than kindness from a stranger. More than charity. Or maybe less. Something. Vee didn't know what.

Mrs. O'Shea wasn't very kind, really. Not like Mrs. King. She wasn't like Lillian, either. She was different. Vee shivered and summoned up resentment. Anabel. Well, Anabel was one of *those*. A lucky one. Always "in." Anabel's got a husband, and a baby, and her own house, and her own mother to come and help her. *She* doesn't know what it is to be all alone, with nowhere to go. So she doesn't care what she says to hurt somebody's feelings. She'll be sorry. . . . Vee tried to dream, but the mechanism had struck a snag. The dreaming process would not start. It had jammed.

About an hour later, Anabel took one more turn down the carpet on her long legs and said suddenly, "Come on, Vee. I'll take you over to get your things. Mother?"

Mrs. King said, "I'll take care of things here."

Vee had the sense of message between them.

Anabel looked at the weather (which was dull again), dashed for the keys, her purse, and then into the hall closet for her coat. Then she stood and looked around her house with a kind of blank look. "I don't know what I might do."

"All right," Mrs. King said.

"Hurry up, Vee," said Anabel.

So Vee got out of the chair, feeling strangely bare in her rumpled dress.

When they were in the car, Anabel said, "Vee, if your father was trying to get away and he didn't come home, where would he go?"

"I don't know."

"Maybe you do. At least, you'd know better than I."

"I don't know what you mean."

"Then listen," said Anabel. "If Pat was following your father, then Pat would go where your father went. Your father would be leading. Don't you see that?"

"I guess so."

"Will you help me?"

"I can't imagine. . . ."

"That's not what I'm asking you to do," said Anabel. "Or maybe I am. Let's try to trace them."

"I don't see. . . ."

"You know your father. You know this town. You must have been places with him. You'd know *something*."

Vee drew in her breath, ready to sniffle again.

"Listen," said Anabel, "what I want to go on is what you told me. Maybe you were right. They were fighting. I'm taking that for the truth. And I'm asking you to help me. Help your father, then. Help Pat. Won't you? At least you could try."

Vee felt queer. "I don't see how—"

"Never mind how," said Anabel. "You can't always see how. If you just try, then sometimes you can see how, as you go."

"All right," said Vee. "All right. I will."

"OK," said Anabel. "You didn't want to go to the hospital anyway." Anabel's sideways glance was challenging.

"No," said Vee, "I didn't." (It was true!)

"We'll get your stuff," said Anabel, in high spirits. "You need a coat. And then we'll try."

Cecil Wahl must have seen them park because he opened the door and looked out at them. Anabel said, "Hurry, Vee. I'll wait here. I doubt if you'll be raped."

"I'll hurry." Vee ran up the walk and in the door, past him, and up the stairs. Of course she wouldn't be raped. What nonsense!

Cecil put a foot out on the porch, changed his mind, drew back into the foyer. He slipped the phone there from its cradle.

When Vee came pelting down again, with lipstick on crooked, wearing a clean dress, a light coat, and dragging her suitcase, he advanced to the bottom of the stairs and blocked her way.

"What's all this?" he said.

"Let me by."

"What's the hurry? Where are you going?"

"To find them." She looked him right in his green eyes. The eyes narrowed.

"What makes you think you can do that?"

"Never mind."

"Wait a minute. What have you heard?"

"Nothing. Nothing. But Mr. O'Shea was following Dad, and we think. . . ." Vee's head was up.

"Oh, he was, was he? How do you know that?"

"I *saw* that."

"And you told her that?"

Vee said to him boldly, "I don't always tell everybody everything I know. You'd just better let me by."

Cecil was looking up at her with shining eyes. "Well, well."

"And I could tell a little more, too," said Vee, "if you don't get out of my way."

Then he laughed. He slipped one arm around her waist and lifted her down the few remaining steps. Still embracing her, he swung her out the house door, firmed the door behind them, and hurried her down the walk, as gaily as if they were dancing.

Anabel, in the driver's seat, was leaning to hold the car door open. "Hop in," said Cecil. "You in the middle, Vee." Vee got in. She was panting. Cecil snatched her clumsy suitcase, tossed it over the seat into the back, got into the front himself and slammed the door. "What's the plan, girls?"

"We're going to try to trace them," Anabel said. "We don't need you."

"Maybe you do," said Cecil. "What do you mean? Tire tracks? Spoor, do you think? The bloodhound bit?"

"It'll take time. I'd rather not waste any." Anabel made the car move. "We can let you out at the first red light."

"Listen," said Cecil, "I want to find them just as much as you do. How are you going to proceed?"

"We'll see, as we go."

"But what if they call?"

"They won't call any sooner, for us agonizing by the telephone," said Anabel tartly.

He sank back upon the seat. His mouth seemed pursed to whistle but he made no sound.

"We can drop *you* any time," said Vee tightly.

"That's true," said Cecil softly. "That's very true."

Something made Anabel put her right hand on Vee's knee. She said, "We can try. You never know."

At this moment, for the first time since the storm, the sun came out.

In Vee's mind there was breaking, like Fourth of July spangles in the sky, a new vision.

Pat was sitting high against the headboard, shouting with all the force he had in his lungs. "You go to the nearest house. You hear me, old lady? You tell somebody there's a sick man, needs a doctor. You go. Do that. And take your dog along." The dog raged in the other room. "Hear me? Am I getting through to you? Go on. Get going. Tell somebody. Otherwise, you'll have a corpse in this stinking bed and, sooner or later, the corpse will stink and what will you do then, old lady? Somebody's going to come and say 'It's O'Shea. O'Shea. O'Shea.' *Listen* to me. And get going."

She was standing by the door to the front room; all her wrinkles were turned downward.

"I'll help you," shouted Pat. "I told you that I would. But you've got to help me. Take your dog and your stick and walk to the nearest house. What is it? Half a mile? It won't kill you. But if you don't, it'll kill *me*. So go on. Hurry. *Get out of here.*"

His good left hand caught at a pillow and ripped it from behind and threw it. The old woman put up one claw. The pillow did her no harm.

Pat yelled, "All right. Then *I'll* go. Set the dog on. Let *him* kill me. I see no difference, old lady. Not anymore."

Her other claw turned the doorknob. She put her body into the yawn of the door, keeping the dog away. "Quiet, Rex. Down, Rex." She looked at Pat. "No fear," she said.

Then the door closed and he was alone.

He listened. The dog's noises died away. Pat saw himself in the dusty glass over the old chest of drawers. Black clot on the side of his head, beard starting—he looked insane. He lay back and felt his entire frame quivering from his effort. Had she gone? Everything was still. He let his head loll. Damn it, he wasn't insane, but he was sick. He put his right hand to his chest, and chest, hand, leg, all of him throbbed in one beating measure.

Not much longer, though. He closed his eyes. Wondered what time it was. Why he had been lying here so passively, with the old woman sitting on the chair, talking and talking? He had not listened. He seemed to know all about Johnny Pryde, even so. His mother's joy. A beamish boy. A paragon. Who wound up beating the boys, raping the girls, and worse. With the stubborn old woman, doting and blind. . . . Pat could still hear her muttering voice, always with that latent cackle, that shrill strain, and that pounding repetition. It ran in his head like a tune, he'd be hearing it in his dreams.

"'Wants his way. Wants his way.' That's what your pa says. 'Johnny wants his way.' I says, 'You never had your way,' I says to your pa. 'But Johnny shall have his way. He's a good boy, my boy. No fear.' 'Twelve years old,' your pa says, 'too young to run with them big kids.' But I says, 'No,' I says, 'Johnny Pryde, he's got no fear,' *I* told them kids. I says, 'You stay away from Johnny Pryde.' And they don't bother you. Eh, Johnny?" She cackled.

Pat opened his eyes. He wasn't dreaming. She was sitting there, in the chair. She hadn't gone anywhere. In her cracked mind, Johnny Pryde was just getting younger. Twelve years old and wants his way. *But doesn't get it,* thought Pat with a burst of light.

"Never," she said. "Never. No more."

He stirred. Then he saw that the dog was there, sitting beside her, mute, ready.

Her voice went on but Pat closed his eyes. Some other way, then. Outwit her. Use his brain. His brain went darting, this way and that. His body felt heavy and immovable. "Anabel?" he said.

Anabel drove into the parking lot behind the Science Building, turned solemnly all the way around, and headed out again. Now, to the left. They would soon come to that fork, where one could turn off toward the dormitories. "Would Professor Adams go to the dormitories?" Anabel asked the question aloud, but in her mind she snatched at an incomplete memory. There was some student about whom Pat was very much concerned. What was the name? Anyhow, there had been a theft and Pat felt that this boy was being damaged by unjust suspicions. Could Everett Adams have gone to accuse and Pat, angry, to defend this boy? But what was his name? And did he room in the dorm?

Before she could recollect anything about the name or ask another question, Vee said, with finality, "They didn't go that way. I would have seen them from where I was."

So Anabel drove on toward the gym. After all, two men, two cars could scarcely be hidden anywhere near the anthill that was the dormitory area. She brought herself sharply to the problem of the next step and stopped beside the tennis courts. There was only one court in use.

"Is it too dark for tennis by five thirty? Maybe not to be finishing a match. Better ask."

"I'll ask," said Vee with unusual vigor.

Cecil opened the door and got out to let her out.

"Why don't you get in the back seat?" Anabel said to him. He bowed. He got into the back seat.

The boy and girl on the tennis court had not been here Monday and knew no one who had been. They stood still, staring after the car as it went on to the South West Gate.

There Anabel stopped again. "If we go left, we only get back to the Main Gate and that makes no sense at all. So I say turn right here. Agreed?"

"OK," said Vee.

"And you, Mr. Wahl, please watch to our left."

"What am I watching for?" He was irrepressibly amused.

"For a place where a car might have been wrecked and not easily seen. For a place where somebody is stationed who would naturally be watching the street."

"Such as?"

"Such as," said Anabel severely, "an old character in a rocking chair. An invalid in a window. A newsstand. Anything. And Vee, you watch to our right."

"I will, Mrs. O'Shea."

"Please call me Anabel."

They turned into traffic and went along. Just a street. A few scattering houses. Some vacant lots. Nothing to see. No one to ask. At the first intersection Anabel stopped the car once more.

"Right, left, or straight ahead? Vee, do you know of any friend's house, any place at all—any reason for your father to turn here? One way or another?"

"To the right is a dead end. It bumps into the campus. To the left . . . I don't know. I've never been." The girl was trying.

"We'll get into some fancy mathematics," said Anabel, "with so many alternatives. We can't explore every one."

"Not without," said Cecil, "our deerstalking caps."

Anabel turned around. "I am looking for my husband, Mr. Wahl. Vee is looking for her father. What are you looking for? Fun?"

"Please call me Cecil," he said sweetly, "and why are you so mad at me today?"

"No reason," said Anabel, conquering irritation. "I'm not." She looked straight ahead.

"Are *you* mad at me, Vee?" Cecil was being charming.

"Don't be so silly," said Vee. "What shall we do, Anabel?"

"We can't explore every way there is to turn," said Anabel, dismissing Cecil from her thoughts. "The only thing we have to go on is a tiny bit of probability. What do you think, Vee? Which way might your father go?"

The sun was shining. But Anabel had a gray feeling now. Which of them was silly?

Within the four walls of your own place, or inside the cave of your skull, you could scheme, dream. But when you got out into the world and the weather, it didn't work as you had dreamed it would.

But in a moment, Vee said, "Listen, sometimes if Dad wants to go to some store at the west end, he does take the next big street—you know?—and go back to town that way."

"Does he?" said Anabel. "All right, Vee."

She sent the car straight ahead. But she thought, Not back into town. How could two men, two cars have vanished from the middle of town? She plodded along, looking to right and left herself—at a stand of tall grass where a man's body might lie, at a hedge, at a clump of shrubbery. Couldn't examine every one.

The most one could say for this expedition, it might beat sitting by the telephone. It might beat listening to the Provost's tenor coo, or people asking curious questions, or a police voice saying, "No, ma'am. Not yet."

She said, "I'd better call my mother every once in a while, in case anything has been found. Vee, what about *this* street?"

"I can't think of anything, Anabel."

Cecil kept quiet in the back seat. He was thinking that this expedition was typically square.

The car plodded on. At last they came to a traffic light, where a major street crossed their path. Again, three choices. But there was a gas station here, and Anabel drove in deep on the pavement. They could ask. They could try.

A voice called, "Hi."

Vee answered, "Oh, hi, Dick."

The boy who walked over to them looked vaguely familiar to Anabel.

"Dick, you know my father, Professor Adams?" Vee was saying. "Did you happen to see him go by this corner around five thirty or six o'clock, Monday night?"

"No, I didn't," the boy said, with proper solemnity. "What's up, Vee?" But he was looking past her at Anabel. "Excuse me, but aren't you Mrs. O'Shea?"

"Yes, I am."

"I saw Mr. O'Shea," the boy said, "about that time."

Anabel's blood leaped. "Tell us," she cried. "They are missing. We are trying to trace them. So tell us every bit about it."

"Well, see, he was honking," the boy explained. "I was washing a car, way back there. He honked real fast, you know? Like he wanted to say 'hello.' But he didn't see me. Looked more like he was trying to honk to some car ahead."

"A Chevy?" said Cecil quickly, from the back seat.

"I wouldn't know," said Dick Green. "Whatever car it was, it must have been pouring it on because Mr. O'Shea, *he* took the turn on about two wheels."

"Which way?" cried Anabel.

The boy pointed.

They left him with a babbling of thanks. Anabel's heart was singing. "Now we know they came this far," she cried. "They turned this way." She took her hand off the wheel and Vee's hand came up to touch it.

"So far, so good," said Cecil thoughtfully. "What's out this way?"

They didn't answer him.

Up in the pass, Maclaren and Carlson were standing at the side of the road, watching a slim uniformed man in high leather leggings who was walking up the steep mountainside toward them, hauling himself hand over hand against a long rope that was snubbed around a rock and held at the brink by two of his colleagues.

"No lights," said a big sheriff's deputy who was in charge here. "Somebody saw the sun bouncing off the chrome. Fellow had some field glasses. So we get this report. You were looking for a Rambler. It's registered to Elihu O'Shea, 3407 Pine. That's your man, eh?"

"Nobody, you say?" said Carlson.

"Not in the car. But he could have crawled clear. Could have been thrown, too. Both doors open. So maybe he's someplace in the chaparral. Oh boy!"

Maclaren said, "Did I mention the windshield wipers?"

"He'll check. He'll check."

"Want me to go down?" said Carlson eagerly.

"You're not equipped." The big man looked at Carlson's trousered legs.

"Snakes?" said Carlson.

"Snakes? Oh, man, there's a million of 'em. Poor S.O.B. Say he was hurt and crawled out. Before he gets a yard he coulda been bit and he coulda rolled on down."

"Service Detail coming?" asked Maclaren.

"Sure. Sure. Fingerprints. Bloodstains. What they can get out of it. Me, I got to organize this search, and what have I got here? A whole damn mountain, that's all. Just a whole damn mountain, crawling with rattlesnakes. It's going to take time."

Carlson crouched and peered over. The Rambler was almost invisible from the road. "Didn't turn, eh?"

"It musta flew," said the deputy. "What we kinda figure is, the fellow flew off the road in that big storm. That should be the size of it."

"So much for O'Shea, eh?" said Carlson.

"What was he doing up here in the pass?" murmured Maclaren.

"Not going to make much difference. He's just as dead," said Carlson. His gray eyes searched below. Maclaren stood still, looking up at the hills.

Finally, the man on the rope reached the brink and was helped over it. He dusted himself, panting. His colleagues in uniform and the two plainclothesmen waited respectfully until he had more breath.

"Keys are in it, ignition's on. Headlights off. Brake released. Windshield wipers are on."

"Good for you," said Maclaren heartily.

The man grinned at him. "And here's a funny one. Lever's in reverse."

"So what do you think?" The big deputy frowned. "Reverse?"

Carlson said, "Could the lever jolt into reverse when she rolled or hit?"

"Hard to say. I'd doubt it. If not, what was he doing? Trying to turn around?"

Maclaren said, "I'm wondering if he was in it at all."

"Listen," exploded the man, "if you can figure out some proof there was nobody *in* that thing when she went over, you'll be doing me one great big favor. A whole damn mountain, crawling with rattlesnakes."

"I wish I could do that."

The deputy grunted.

"Well," Maclaren said, "we'll go on up the road. See you, Harry."

"Right. Right. We'll *be* here, don't worry."

Carlson drove on up the mountain. His young face was frowning with thought.

"In case O'Shea went on up the road," said his partner, "there's a hamburger joint up here a little bit."

"Yeah, I remember it. O'Shea got missing Monday night. The big storm was Monday. About seven, seven thirty?"

"We can check on that." Maclaren was respectful.

"So when he sent the car over, he forgot his wipers were on. Giving the time."

"*If* he did that."

"Who's going to be trying to turn around, in the dark and the rain, without lights?" said Carlson. "Looks pretty much as if he sent it over. Got rid of it. Took off."

Maclaren sighed.

"What's the matter now, Dad?" drawled Carlson, in a minute.

"You're jumping. First, he's dead, you're pretty sure. Now, you're pretty sure he's voluntarily disappeared. *But you don't know*. You don't know the man, for one thing. That's something to keep in mind."

"I'll remember," said Carlson blithely. "But if he did ditch the car and get lost, voluntarily, I was thinking about Mrs. O'Shea's ever-lovin' hero. A wife"—Carlson stopped and licked his upper lip— "could be wrong, I suppose."

"Anybody can be wrong," said Maclaren, shifting restlessly. "I'll have to call Mrs. O'Shea."

"Why? She's just going to get all upset and we don't *know* anything." The young man glanced sideways.

Maclaren said nothing.

"Yeah, I guess you promised," Carlson said. He frowned.

The first stroke of luck was the last stroke of luck they'd had.

Now they were getting into the country, going north slowly, slowly, corner by corner, stopping at every one. Anabel insisted. Anabel had gone to ring doorbells. It was people who cost them so much time, by not understanding what was wanted. Or by wanting to know the whole story before they would answer questions at all.

Anabel was thinking that it might have been smarter to put a notice in the newspapers, broadcast their questions by such public means, and let the information seek them out. It was plain that this expedition was bogging down. Vee was tiring, drooping. Couldn't stand up to repeated failures. Cecil was restless. Anabel had braced herself, long ago, to hear him begin to argue the futility of going any farther.

But Anabel dogged it and slogged it and went slowly, slowly, asking, watching, seeking—and failing. They might have, long ago, missed a turn, for all she knew. In fact, it was probable that they had.

One more, she thought. And then, One more.

She stopped the car again, and both her passengers sighed.

"How about here?" she said to Vee.

"Where is this?"

"Oleander Street," Anabel read the sign.

"Oh, yes," said Vee wearily. "We used to come out here. A long time ago. When I was just a little kid."

"Why was that?" Anabel made herself spark up.

"Oh, there used to be a place where you could dump stuff."

Cecil in the back seat said, "Dump?" There was something odd, drawling in the word. Skepticism, Anabel supposed. She was inclined to agree. How could this possibly be significant?

"Way out at the end there's a place," said Vee. "I used to ride out with Dad, and sometimes Mama, too." Vee's voice broke with fatigue and discouragement.

"Way out at the end? Maybe we'd better—"

Cecil said, "Listen, this poor child is starving. And so are we all. Why don't we go home now?"

"We better at least ask here." Anabel was hungry herself. "In the store. We could buy something to nibble on."

Cecil said, "They've got a phone, I see. Maybe you'd better call your mother?" He seemed to have livened up. He was full of ideas.

"All right," said Anabel. She pulled around the corner into Oleander Street and parked. There was a delivery truck and a boy was putting boxes into it.

Anabel would have spoken to the boy, from nothing but inertia, but Cecil cried, "Come on." He was out of the car and helping Vee out. "You don't know what you're doing anymore. You're punchy. Come *on*, Anabel."

So Anabel got out of the car. The three of them went into the little store. The boy looked after them.

It was crowded and dim, inside, with narrow aisles. Near the check counter, an elderly man was putting up orders, holding a sheaf of them in one hand. He said, "What can I do for you?"

They were blinking in the changed light. Cecil said, "Phone?"

"Right over there."

"You go ahead, Anabel. How about a box of cookies, Vee? You have a carton of milk, sir?"

"In the case," said the grocer, gesturing. He went back to his work.

Anabel walked to the phone on the wall and began to hunt for a dime. She thought, Maybe I am getting so numb that I'm stupid. She knew that Cecil was picking a box from a shelf and using his thumbnail on the dotted line to open it. She knew that Vee had stumbled to the refrigerated case and was opening it to get a wax carton of milk. She knew that the boy had come inside and was talking to the grocer. She felt her fingers tremble with fatigue as they pursued a coin. She did not listen to their voices.

"That's all for today, I guess, Mr. Johanneson?" Stan said. "I finished Martinez."

"Yep. That's it. I'm trying to get a head start on tomorrow. Say, Stan, can you make any sense out of this?"

Stan's young eyes had been noting, out of their corners, young Vee, sagging against the case, drinking her milk, looking kind of sad and kind of . . . well . . . mysterious. He brought his gaze to the paper in Mr. Johanneson's hand. "What's this?" he said.

"I'm asking *you*," the grocer said testily. "Posh something. Posh —what? What's she *want*? Polish? What am I supposed to send? Shoe polish? Furniture polish? Silver polish? Nail polish?" The grocer sputtered.

"Mrs. Pryde, eh?" said Stan. "Say, listen, has she got a license for that dog?"

"Why?"

"That dog is dangerous."

"Oh, go on."

"I'm telling you . . ." Stan said. He was stalling and he knew it. These strangers intrigued him.

Mr. Johanneson put the orders down. "Ask her when you see her —what she *wants*," he said irritably. "It's not going to make a lot of difference if she don't get to polish up something or other tomorrow. And you can tell her, she's got too much. . . . Yes, sir?"

Cecil said, "How much?" He was selecting a cookie from the open package. "These, and the milk the young lady has."

The grocer peered at Vee and began to ring up the sale.

Anabel had found a dime and was dialing. There was no sound-proof booth. The pay phone hung on the wall. Over the space fell the silence that is embarrassing.

"Mother?" she said. All of them could hear.

Mr. Johanneson, wishing not to eavesdrop, snapped at Stan, "I said, that's it. You got a job to do. Do it."

Cecil turned to offer the cookies to Vee.

Then Anabel cried out. "Oh, no!—Where? Where?"

Cecil dropped the cookie box on the counter and went racing toward her. Vee straightened and milk from the tipping carton in her limp hand dribbled on the floor. Stan was riveted where he was. Anabel, phone to ear, turned a wild and anguished face to the others. Cecil put the flat of his hand upon her back as if to hold her up. He bent his head to listen with her. Vee was paralyzed.

Mr. Johanneson did not like a disturbance. He needed his days to go evenly, as he had planned them. He had as much as he could do to manage that. He said to Stan, "Get along, will you?" So Stan tore his feet from the floor and went outside.

Anabel hung up. She wondered whether her heart was literally breaking. She put both hands up to hold it in.

Cecil said in a caressing tone, "We'll go home. I'll drive. Try to take it easy, Anabel. They said there was nobody in it. I heard that. Come on, please. You're so exhausted. You've done everything you could. . . ."

"But I don't think they know, for sure," said Anabel, resisting him as if he were the devil. "So we'll go up *there*," she cried.

"Oh, no. Should you? Really,"

"Where else would I go except where Pat might be?" Anabel pulled away from him and ran toward the door.

Stan was still sitting in his truck as the three of them came running out. He craned his neck. He stretched his ears. The woman was white, but blazing with purpose. The man was frowning. The girl was sobbing. They piled into the car, Anabel seizing the wheel in hands that were convulsively strong.

Stan yelled, "Hey, something wrong?"

Nobody answered him.

Anabel roared the Olds around in a U and turned into the highway going north. Could not wait to answer. The police had found the car. Need not wait to question. Their desperate and amateurish busy work, time-wasting, useless expedition was over.

Mr. Johanneson had come out of the store to look after them.

"Hey, what was all that?" Stan called to him.

"Damned if I know," said Mr. Johanneson. "Fellow didn't pay for the stuff, even. Well, I guess they got trouble." Johanneson sighed. His heart was too soft, his brain knew it. Sometimes he sputtered or spoke too sharply, trying to protect himself from himself. He said, "Listen, Stan, maybe the dog is sick."

"Huh?"

"You didn't notice the meat order Mrs. Pryde's put in? That dog's going to live it up, looks like. Well, her budget won't stand for it, not more than this once. You'll tell her, tomorrow."

The strangers were far away now. Stan would never know what it was all about. He looked down at the grocer. "Hey, Mr. Johanneson, why doesn't somebody put the old witch in a home or something?"

"She's not doing any harm." The grocer was turning to go in.

"She's not all there, I'm telling you," Stan said.

"Listen, she hasn't been all there since Johnny Pryde went to the gas chamber. Let her be, poor soul." Johanneson's heart was soft; his conscience was quick. He said to Stan, "I don't mean you should take any chances with the dog, see? So . . . I mean take care of yourself?"

"Oh, believe *me*," said Stan enthusiastically, "I won't bother *him*, Mr. Johanneson."

Anabel kept her mind on the driving, to go as fast as she safely could, to get through two towns and on, over the foothill slopes, into the pass and up the mountain. She wouldn't think about it. She would get there. She was grateful to Cecil for telling Vee the news, very briefly, and to Vee for sitting still and keeping quiet. She was grateful to them both for a companionable tension.

Having shaken out of town traffic, they raced up into the pass and Cecil said, "How will you know where?"

"I'll know."

It was easy to know. There were police cars, some kind of truck, many men. Anabel pulled up at the side of the road and set her brakes. As she opened the door, two men, whose faces were familiar, came quickly toward her. Maclaren said, "Just the car."

Anabel got out then, shakily. "It really is our car?"

"It didn't burn, Mrs. O'Shea. The registration."

"Where is it? Let me see."

"Down there." Maclaren began to guide her around the hood of the Oldsmobile to where she could look over. There was a car, far down, very far away, very small, and pitiful. It was a dead car; one knew that. Ours? thought Anabel. With my sunglasses in the glove compartment? And the maps from our trip? The hole where my high heel gouges the mat? It was the death of a friend, in a way.

But Maclaren was looking over her head and he shouted, "Watch her, Jimmy. The young lady."

Vee had slipped out at the other side and was peering over the brink. Carlson scampered around the back of the Olds on his lively young legs and caught her by the arm. "You better get back in, Vi," he coaxed. "You don't want to go sliding down there. Too many rattlesnakes. Come on, Violet. Vee, I mean." He almost lifted the girl into the front seat and stood between her and the brink.

Cecil, who had gotten out of the Olds and followed them around the hood, said demandingly, "What's the official version? What happened here?"

"One version," said Maclaren gently, "could be that the Rambler stalled in the heavy storm and had to be abandoned. Somebody comes along, blind in the rain, hits it—it goes over."

"With nobody in it?" Cecil asked.

"Nobody's in it now?" said Anabel. "You're sure?" She leaned and Maclaren took her weight.

"Now, you know that we are sure," he chided.

"Yes, I . . . I believe you." Anabel was feeling confused.

"Come away." Motioning Cecil out of the path, he led her to the other side of her mother's Olds, between the traffic, which was the world going about its business, and the vast, sad mountainside.

Cecil was leaning and peering. "Pretty far to crawl back up to the road," he said crisply. "Could he have gotten out at all?"

"Seems so," Carlson answered.

"He wouldn't get far."

Carlson said, "Hard to see what's in the brush."

"Watch it," said Maclaren. "Get her head down."

Carlson's strong hands began to bend Vee over, forcing her head toward her knees. But Vee said, "I'm all right. I'm all right. Don't do that."

"You're sure?"

"It doesn't *matter*."

She was struggling to sit up and he let her sit up, murmuring, "Take it easy." But she looked at him with a naked expression, devoid of any consciousness that she was a young female and he was a young male and that they had once encountered each other (or might have) in the high school jungle where the hunt is on. Every kind of defense or offense was peeled away. Carlson felt shocked. He said, "Shove over." He got in beside her and shut the car door. "She's just got the shakes a little bit," he said to the others in explanation. "She'll be OK." He put his left arm around behind her. Pig or no, whatever . . . this poor kid!

But Vee wasn't even noticing. (Death was not romantic! It was terrible! It was awful! She didn't want *anybody* to be dead. Not Dad. Oh, no, not poor Daddy. Not Mr. O'Shea. Please. Not even a stranger. Out here on the terrible mountain, alone. Alone. But what she wanted, or didn't want, would not matter. No dream of hers could change anything that was or had been. She had the shakes, yes.)

Maclaren said, "Are you all right, Mrs. O'Shea?"

"Yes." Anabel was numb, which was "all right" enough.

Cecil had come back to where they stood. "What makes you think the Rambler might have been abandoned?" he demanded.

Maclaren answered, a little lamely, "That's only an idea. We don't know what really happened. But there's something else I think you'd better—"

"Go on," said Anabel forcefully.

"Sit down, Mrs. O'Shea?"

"No, just go on." Anabel had sensed, already, that there was more to be told.

"All right. If you don't mind," said Maclaren, and she received a strong impression that he was fond of her, that he was both respectful and affectionate, that he was on her side. "I'm going to tell you a little story." In his voice there was a promise. She was absolutely sure that he wasn't going to tell a story for nothing, that it would be important. They were all quiet, and Maclaren went on.

"Up the road," he said, "there's a small café. I called your mother from there, Mrs. O'Shea. My—er—partner was taking a cup of coffee. The man behind the counter told us this story. A funny thing, too.

"It seems, the night of the big storm—and that was Monday—lots of people took refuge in his place. There was a bus, for instance. Thirty or forty passengers crowded in. There were several cars that couldn't go on. The driving was terrible.

"Well, in the midst of the worst of the rain, a man came in alone. But he seemed to think he had a companion. When Mr. Mueller—that's the man we talked with—told him he'd seen nobody else come in, this fellow went to the door and looked out, as if he couldn't believe it.

"Well, he saw nobody. So he came and had coffee. And when the rain stopped, everyone else went on his way except this one.

"He asked Mueller whether he'd ever watched certain TV programs," Maclaren continued. "The kind that . . . well, I guess you could say they flirt with the supernatural? He was pretty much shaken up by something, Mueller tells us. Finally, he said there had just been a miracle. He had to believe that his life had just been saved—by a ghost."

Strange, on the side of the mountain road, in the late daylight, with the traffic swishing by, and that knot of men so busy with their ropes, and their shouts to each other . . . strange, in this place, at this time, to be held and suspended, listening to the ghost story.

"It was the ghost," said Maclaren, "of a man in a shiny brown raincoat."

And Anabel's breath rushed into her.

"And a tannish rain hat."

Anabel smiled at him.

"It seems," said Maclaren, not missing her reactions but starting a flashback chapter, "this chap had been caught, on this road, going up in that downpour. He was driving alone. He was pretty scared. He didn't dare stop, for fear he'd be run into from the rear. But he hardly dared go on, either. He couldn't see. He said he prayed."

"Yes?" Anabel hung on the story.

"Then, suddenly, there was this figure on the road. Right about here, as far as we can judge. It was a man, in the shiny brown coat and the tannish hat. The motorist stopped and yelled to the man to get in and he asked if the man would please put his head out the right window and watch for the edge, while he himself with his head out the left window could just make out the white line.

"So the man in the raincoat did as he was asked. They crept along and they made it, to the café. It's only another mile. So the driver pulled up there, pretty glad and thankful. He said he'd buy his friend a cup of coffee, dashed through the rain. . . .

"But, you see, the man in the brown raincoat—just vanished."

Maclaren stopped and smiled, a little wistfully, at Anabel.

"Pat's raincoat is shiny brown," she said, "and he had it with him, and one of those limp plastic sou'westers in the pocket of it. A tannish color." She was feeling well and strong. The air was wonderful.

In the car Vee whimpered, "But how could he vanish? What does he *mean?* Was it . . . Was it a real. . . ."

"Ghost?" said Carlson. "Oh, no, wait a minute."

Cecil snapped, "She asked a good question. How could he vanish?" Cecil was tense. He didn't seem to think that anything was amusing at the moment.

"There was a bus," said Maclaren. "I mentioned that. We think it was a real man, but that instead of following into the café, he spotted the bus standing there and boarded it and waited. And when the rain was over, the bus carried him away."

"Where?" barked Cecil. "Where was this bus headed?"

"Victorville, Barstow, Vegas, on to Salt Lake."

"So you're looking for. . . . Wait a minute." Cecil seemed to grind his teeth. "I suppose you can turn up that bus driver?"

"Surely," said Maclaren. "I've already talked to him, in fact, on the phone." He paused. He seemed to be waiting for the next question. When no question came, he went on. "He can't, unfortunately, confirm this guess. He says it is possible. He was in no mood to be counting heads. Felt he should be making up lost time and on wet roads. Then, when he got to his first rest stop, he had to contend with his superiors. He might, or might not, remember a raincoat of that type or color getting off . . . somewhere."

Cecil Wahl was looking at Maclaren with narrowed green eyes. "I suppose you've found the haunted motorist, too?"

"No way to do that," said Maclaren. "No name given. Mueller didn't even see what he was driving."

And Cecil said, sunny with amusement now, "Be a shame, anyhow. Let him have his miracle. Change his whole life."

Anabel spoke from the new and deep sense of trouble. "But Pat— would have called me."

"Oh, look, honey," said Cecil, "he's *all right,* at least." He said to Maclaren, "I suppose you've got the word out for O'Shea in Victorville, Barstow, and Las Vegas?"

"Surely."

"I don't understand this," said Anabel, standing straighter. "Did the . . . the ghost tell the motorist that his car had stalled? Or why he was on foot in the rain?"

"Not that Mueller was told, ma'am," said Maclaren, in soft sadness.

Carlson piped up, "Going to be tough to tell whether the car backed up a little too much or whether somebody just—"

Anabel whirled around and caught his young face with his mouth open and his foot figuratively in it.

"Somebody just what?"

Vee Adams chimed in, "Somebody just what?"

Carlson's face smoothed out. "Sent it over," he answered quietly. "Supposing somebody wanted to get rid of the car and just disappear."

"Why?" cried Anabel. "Why would he? Why?"

Nobody said anything until Vee spoke, in a shaky voice. "Where is . . . where is my father?"

And Carlson said quickly, as if he wanted to comfort her, "If he's down there, they'll find him."

She was right under his arm. He could feel the stab going into her. "But look," he tried to back water, "that's only. . . . Nobody knows. Look, don't. . . ."

Vee was not yielding to the sheltering pressure of his arm.

Anabel faced the other man. "Then they *are* looking for a body down there?"

"They have to do that," Maclaren said.

The air was cold. Anabel was freezing. "How soon will they be sure?"

"That will take some time, Mrs. O'Shea. Reasonably sure? In the morning. To be absolutely sure might take days."

"Days?" It made her stagger.

"They've been trying to figure how to rig some lights," said Carlson, as if to be helpful with chatter. "But it doesn't look as if they can do too much without the daylight. Shadows can be pretty tricky." His voice died.

Anabel was bracing herself against the fact of a long uncertainty. "There is nothing we can do here," she said.

"No, Mrs. O'Shea."

"I'm sure you will tell me, as soon as they find anything. Whatever they find."

"I will, Mrs. O'Shea," Maclaren said, in his warm beautiful voice.

"That's right," said Carlson, rather humbly. "We promise."

Anabel said, "I don't understand this. I still say that Pat would have called me, no matter what, if he was able. But maybe I should remind you"—she was holding her head proudly; the cold wind was cutting at her nape—"that Vee did think the two of them were fighting."

"Ah, did she?" said Maclaren. The music was deep and sad.

In the car Vee lifted both hands as if to clutch the air and began to turn her head from side to side. Carlson's left hand came up to press her head against his jacket and stop that frantic motion.

Cecil, coming out of a stunned moment, cried, "Oh, Anabel. Look, Anabel, if something happened and your husband had to run away . . . it's none of *your* fault." (As if this might comfort her.)

"Fault!" she said, high and clear. "What an idiot you are! It would be my sorrow. It would cancel me."

She ducked her head and got into the car.

Cecil, quick as a cat to change his position, said, "I'm sorry. I'm sorry. I know. I know. Let me drive home, Anabel. Please."

She slid over to the middle as Carlson got out at the other side, seeming to prop Vee up against the seat as if she were a doll. There was some polite murmuring on Cecil's part.

Maclaren said nothing. His ugly face was sad.

The young man said nothing but seemed to listen and watch and almost inhale every tiny impression.

Vee said nothing.

Anabel said nothing. She would trust to the truth and trust that she knew some of it. And if she were mistaken, then she would be canceled. If Pat had done some terrible deed and run away, then she would have to start all over again, and from the bottom. But not yet. Not yet. Not yet.

They drove all the way back to Riverside without a word spoken.

When they were well into that town, Cecil said apologetically, "Do you think you could get home all right, if I stop to see my sister?"

Anabel said, "Of course."

So they went on to the hospital and stopped. Cecil sat a moment, sliding his hands up and down, up and down on the steering wheel, as if he were trying to frame something to say. At last he sighed and got out. "Coming, Vee?"

Vee began to fumble at the latch of the door. Then she twisted to reach over into the tonneau for her suitcase.

"Let it ride with me," said Anabel. "I won't wait. But we'll wait supper."

"Am I supposed," gasped Vee, "to stay with you, *now?*"

"Don't be silly." Anabel's lips felt numb.

Vee said quickly, "Then I'm going home with Anabel. I don't need to see Celia."

Cecil was on some kind of tiptoe, as if he were held to earth by the merest thread, as if he could fly. Yet he was tethered. He didn't seem to know what to do, what to say, whether to argue with this decision or not.

Anabel said, "Thank you for. . . ." She didn't go on. She'd lost her phrase. Wasn't in the mood for polite murmuring.

Cecil lifted one hand, as if to reject any thanks, but then irrepressibly, the gesture became a gay flip that said "So long." He loped away toward the entrance.

Up on the mountain, it was beginning to get dark. Carlson said, "If you want a theory, *why* he would send the car over, you can say maybe he did have a body in it. Say they did fight. O'Shea doesn't know his own strength or something. He panics, afterward." The young man glanced at his partner. "This is just a theory. There may be a couple of things we don't know yet. Right?"

"In that case, where's the other car?" Maclaren brooded.

"Oh. Yeah. The Adams car." Carlson walked restlessly away to look over the brink where the work was ceasing with the falling darkness. It was as if he thought there might be two cars down there and meant to check. Rooted on his two tall, muscular legs, he stood. Maclaren tilted his ugly head, as if fondly.

Cecil came swiftly into the hospital room, cast one glance at the other bed, which was rumpled but empty of its occupant, and bent over his sister. "What does Vee know? I better have it. And fast." He was on tiptoe, to be gone.

Celia was looking better. Very beautiful, with her pale hair drawn cleanly back and tied up in a ribbon. Her color was better. She lay on the high bed with the white covering pulled tightly and smoothly around her as if she had not moved since she had been tucked in. She did not move now.

He straightened. "Just checking," he said distantly.

"No, no," she said. "Nothing."

"She doesn't know, for instance, about the night the fat man. . . ."

"Impossible."

"Tell me how it's impossible."

His sister lifted her head, looking strained and uncomfortable. "Because Ev told me, about a hundred times, not to let her know. Because he kept saying she was too young to 'understand.' What do you want, C? What's the matter?"

"So the kid's got ears. She overheard."

"She did not. She wasn't even in the house. Not one word was said in the house while she was there."

"Then what's she hinting about?"

"Who knows? She's just a moony little kid, C. Who's going to pay any attention to her, for pity's sakes?"

He sagged a little and his mouth pursed to whistle. "It was a long day I had for nothing, then."

"What?"

"Where's your. . . ." He jerked his head, indicating the other bed.

"Walking around. She's going home tomorrow. Not soon enough for me," said Celia viciously. "Did Ev call?"

He eyed her and his lids winced. "I wasn't around. But it was just as well I went with them, I guess." He told her quickly what had been found on the mountain.

Celia lay, still as a mummy.

"Listen, C," her brother rushed on. "The man in the raincoat must have been our Ev. *We* know it couldn't have been O'Shea. Although what the devil Ev was doing in O'Shea's car. . . . Never mind. Right now, the cops are looking for O'Shea along that bus route. So far, so good. But the minute they pick up Ev. . . ."

"They'd better not pick up Ev, then," she said sullenly.

He blew out breath. "You still think I can fix it?"

"*I* can't. I would if I could."

Green eyes spoke to green eyes. Her mouth quirked. "Oh, sure. When I'm sick. When you can't take *me*. . . ."

He shifted his weight.

"Too bad," she said listlessly. "I'd get half. If you could fix it. And I'll get well. We could. . . ."

"I'd get better than that," said her brother. "Off the hook. OK. Let's say I would, if I could, too. O'Shea's no problem. The problem is, where's Ev?" He rubbed his head.

She began to walk her fingers on the smooth band where the sheet was turned over the spread. She was smiling faintly.

He said, "Listen, Vee did this sort of thing all day. You try it, C. Where would Ev go? You know him. Try and think. Must have been chance that he got on that particular bus for Victorville, Barstow, Vegas, Salt Lake. Wait, you took that crazy honeymoon up that way."

"The cure, you mean?" she said bitterly. "Good old Bedelia's? Two and a half months. In a motel. A mo-tel."

"He wouldn't go where he'd be known. Or would he?" Cecil was jittery.

"Why worry?" she said. "You'll find out when he telephones."

He didn't speak but she read his mind. "You know why he didn't, don't you?" she cried. "He's waiting for me. Probably hasn't got the faintest notion that I don't know where he *is*, the old fool. So. He'll wait until tomorrow, late, when I don't show."

Cecil said softly, "That may be, but you *don't* know where he is. And neither do I."

"There's time."

"Time for what, C?"

"You should have a car, ready to go. The minute he calls—"

"Where will I get a car?"

"Rent?"

"No license."

"Borrow?"

"From whom? Anabel? Not a chance."

"Mrs. Newcomb? Next door?"

"Old curiosity shop?"

"You could, C."

"And I'm a sitting duck," he said, "until some time late tomorrow?"

"They're looking for O'Shea, you said."

"And suppose they find O'Shea? That body will turn up. Right then, the cops are looking for Ev. And I'm not crossing their path."

"But the cops are wrong."

"Looking for the wrong man? That's what I said."

"They're looking in the wrong *place,*" she said fiercely. "Don't be stupid, C."

He cocked an eyebrow.

"They're looking for a body on the mountain, you said. But Ev left the body at some dump or other. He told me. I told you. Why will they find it tomorrow if they haven't found it yet? Maybe Ev buried it."

Cecil said nothing but she heard the inaudible click in his mind. "What?" she demanded. "What?"

He rubbed his head. "I've got a hunch that I know where this dump *is.* That's a funny thing."

Her head lifted. Her eyes shone.

"I don't mind taking a bit of a chance," he said, "but this is ridiculous." His eyes were merry.

"There's time," she insisted.

"For what, C?"

"For *you* to bury O'Shea."

"For what reason?" he drawled.

"For *time.* Time to keep the cops looking for *him.* Until Ev calls."

"So I bury one body and what do I do with the other one?"

"What one?"

"Ev's."

She shrugged. She closed her eyes. "What will you do with *your-self?*" she inquired listlessly. "Otherwise?"

"Be a little bit careful," he said and her eyes popped open. "Don't pressure me. I can start in two minutes." He shrugged. "From now."

She said drearily, "When I'm sick. . . ."

His eyes were cold. "You are sick, C."

She said, "Then, they'll be asking *me,* won't they? Where would your brother go? You know him. Try and think."

The telepathy between them was very strong. He winced and chewed his lip.

Then Celia's roommate came walking in, wearing a long maroon robe of surpassing ugliness. "Well, hi!" she boomed. "Company, I see. Say, are you two *twins?*"

"Yes, ma'am," said Cecil. Then he touched his sister's cheek lightly. "I'd better. . . ."

"Get on with it?" she murmured.

"I'll see, C."

"Shall I wait, then?"

On his face broke the irrepressible mischief. "Why don't you take a bit of a chance?" he said teasingly. The cobweb that tethered him broke and he was gone.

The roommate was letting her chunkiness down upon the other bed. "Must be real strange to be a twin," she said. "Real strange, you know?"

"I know," said Celia. Her mouth twisted. She turned her cheek to the mattress and folded her pillow over her upper ear.

"OK, little sunshine," grumbled the roommate.

The Provost was an unhappy man. He had forbidden his wife to discuss the matter at the dinner table, but afterward he had retreated into his study, pleading work to do because he simply could not discuss anything else, and her obedient chatter seemed fantastically irrelevant.

At about nine o'clock he had called his friend—by now the Provost and Captain Murch were old buddies—only to be told once more that there had been no developments and probably would not be until morning.

But the Provost knew that he had a responsibility. He must say what he could to poor Mrs. O'Shea. He had put off calling her. He had told himself that he had been hoping for better news.

But now, at about nine thirty—when it would soon be too late for an evening phone call—he found her number and braced himself.

A woman answered. She said she was Mrs. O'Shea's mother.

The Provost exerted himself to be very very happy that Mrs. O'Shea was not alone during this trying time. Then Anabel came to the phone.

He stated his concern, he spoke of not giving up hope, he spoke of her courage. She seemed calm, he thought, and he was glad of that. He went on to something else that was bothering him.

"You must realize, Mrs. O'Shea, that the newspapers are going to report the—er—accident in tomorrow's editions and I think perhaps you should be prepared to—"

"They've been here," she told him.

"Oh, indeed? Already? I . . . rather hope that you did not—er—say very much about Professor Adams having also chosen this moment—"

"They know about that."

"Oh, me," said the Provost. "I *am* sorry."

"I'm not," said Mrs. O'Shea. "Somebody may read about it who knows something and can tell us."

"Oh, me. I had hoped. . . . I spoke to Mike Parsons, you see, and I did hope that I had done something to squelch. . . . You did not discuss that reckless speculation?" He was worried and he was a little sharp.

She said, "No, but I can't worry about it, Mr. Drinkwater."

"I understand," he said (which was the truth). "Please believe that I couldn't be sorrier for this tragic accident."

"Accident?"

"Why, that your husband's car went off the road in that cloudburst. A terrible thing! A very terrible—"

"Mr. Drinkwater, don't you know about the man who was picked up? In the brown raincoat?"

"Oh, yes, of course. But I am very much afraid that it was just some hitchhiker. . . ."

The Provost checked himself. He was not really a brutal man. He had human compassion. He was truly sorry for this poor young wife. He was inclined to believe, with her, that only tragedy explained the events. Still, he ought not to argue, to her, that her husband was dead, by accident, on that mountain. Even though this was, in his view, not the best, not the happiest, not the most desirable solution, but the simplest, certainly. A simple accident in an automobile. Tragic loss of a bright young man. And a "nine days' wonder."

The Provost was fond of declaring, at dinner parties his unchecked theory about the origin of that phrase. He would say, twinkling, that a "nine days' wonder" was actually the observation of a truth, made by generations of the folk. Empirical knowledge. Nine days was the exact time it took for news to become stale.

He thought, now, that a tragic accident was of course tragic, but after nine days it would be forgotten by everyone—except Mrs. O'Shea, naturally.

"I can be wrong," he said compassionately.

Anabel said, "You still think that Professor Adams has nothing to do with this?"

"I do tend to think so. By the way, I—er—"

"And you also tend to think," she said—now he heard her voice pick up vehemence and sparkle—"that although a man was on the road, just about where the car went off, wearing a raincoat the color of Pat's raincoat and a rain hat the color of Pat's rain hat, *he* has nothing to do with it, either?"

The Provost said, "I would say, probably—"

"As a mathematician's wife," said Anabel tartly, "I know about probability."

"Ah," said the Provost, piqued, "and isn't it very probable that, in the rain, most men wear raincoats?" He was ashamed of himself immediately. "Please forgive me," he cried. "I certainly don't mean to quibble in the face of this very tragic— You must continue to be as courageous as you—"

"Courageous enough," she said, "to have thought of the hitchhiker."

"Now, my dear. . . ."

"My hypothetical hitchhiker," said Anabel, "who, if he stole the car, stole the raincoat right along with it. Which, I have to admit, would explain to me why the man in the raincoat did not go into the café, where there was a telephone, and call me."

The Provost felt shocked. When he'd spoken of courage he had not meant anything like this. He had had in mind a certain womanly patience and restraint. "You must not think—" he began.

"Oh, yes, I must," snapped Anabel.

"We must wait," he said piously but rather rapidly, "and hope. I have not been able to get in touch with Mrs. Adams. I am wondering. . . ." He was anxious to change the subject. He felt he needed no additional taste of Anabel O'Shea's temper. Although she astonished him, and also touched, somehow, a buried nerve that was not quite dead yet.

"Mrs. Adams is in the hospital," she told him. "An appendectomy. Last evening. She is all right."

"Indeed? Thank you, very much. But the daughter. . . ."

"She is here, with me."

"Oh, indeed. Well, I am very happy to hear that." The Provost didn't know whether he was happy or not. He was surprised. "I wonder if I could speak to her, please?"

"Of course."

"And we will all hope and pray. . . ." The Provost did not go on with this sentiment, because he seemed to know that Anabel was no longer holding the other phone to her ear.

Vee's voice said, "Mr. Drinkwater?"

"My dear Violet." He warmed up his voice. "I am so glad to have discovered where you are. I have been worried about you. Are you all right?"

"I'm all right, I guess."

"No news yet about your father. Too bad. Too bad. I didn't know that your mother was ill, my dear. I have called your number several times during the day, but there was always the busy signal. Well! It's good to hear your voice. Please try not to worry too much, and if there is anything *I* can do, remember."

"Thank you."

"I am very glad that you are not alone."

"So am I." Her voice was fading.

"Then, good night," he said caressingly. "You are a very brave girl." He hung up. He felt he had done passably well with her, at least. But he was not a happy man.

Mrs. King was mending a rag doll for little Sue, who was sound asleep abed at this hour. She looked up from the work and exclaimed, "What is it?" Her hands put the work aside. "Why, child, you look as if you've seen a ghost!" Mrs. King began to wiggle out of her chair.

Anabel whirled and saw Vee, hanging on to the back of the sofa.

They had not said much to each other during this strange evening. Anabel had not discussed with the girl the proposition that Anabel's husband might have sent this girl's father over the mountain to his death. Anabel would have been glad to proclaim her own conviction that this had not happened, but even to deny it would have raised the question. Furthermore, it would have raised the question of Anabel's hypothetical and vicious hitchhiker, to which horror she had not wanted to give any more substance than it already had in her mind. So the miserable girl had simply been here, in the house, and Anabel's mother had created what ease she could.

But now Anabel, having just been forthright with the Provost and found it a relief, too, sent herself swiftly across the carpet.

"Anabel?" said Vee pitifully.

"All right. Whatever it is. I'm listening."

"My father must be home."

"What do you mean?"

"Because"—Vee swallowed—"the Provost said—" She looked scared. So Anabel touched her. "Just tell."

"The Provost said he called our house several times and always got a busy signal."

"Yes?"

"But there wasn't anybody home." Vee stuck her hands together. "So how *could* there be a busy signal?"

Anabel had been expecting a blow, somehow. Now she felt her brain snatch up the point. "That's right," she said. "Your stepmother's in the hospital. Cecil was with us, almost all day. I see. I see."

Color flooded into Vee's face.

But Mrs. King said, "Oh, my dears, that doesn't necessarily. . . . Think how this phone has been ringing. I do believe that if two calls are trying to come in at once, one of them gets a busy signal."

"Ye-es," said Anabel. "I think so. But. . . . He did say several times?"

"Yes, he did."

Anabel said, "I don't know. You might as well figure that the Provost laid it on a little thick. Maybe he called *once*. People will do that."

"I know it," said Vee. Then she burst out, as if she had found new courage to speak up. "But the thing is—Anabel, you keep saying that Mr. O'Shea would call you. Well, my father. . . . It's the same thing. He's so crazy about her. He would call Celia, if he could. Not *me*. I know that. But he just wouldn't keep away from *her*, if he's alive. So maybe he has been calling. Or else, come home."

Anabel said gravely, "You know, I think you are right." She went to the phone. "What is your number?"

Vee gave it to her. Vee's cheeks seemed to have lost some of the childish plumpness. Vee's eyes were not now sliding or evading. She was not being demure. She was gazing at Anabel and Anabel knew that Vee was in the process, and had been for some time, of making herself a new crush, a new idol.

Anabel did not especially want to be anybody's idol. She turned her attention to her dialing. No answer at the Adams house. But no busy signal, either. "Hm." Anabel wiggled one foot on the ankle. "Cecil may still be at the hospital, I suppose. But it's late."

"Maybe when he got home, Dad was *there,* and they both went to see Celia?" Vee was breathless.

"Hm." Anabel wiggled her eyebrows. "That could be, too." She found the number of the hospital.

"Mrs. Adams, please? What's her room number, Vee?"

"I don't know, but the fourth floor. . . ."

"On the fourth floor," said Anabel.

"We have no way of connecting you with a patient after nine P.M.," the voice said pleasantly enough.

"How can I find out. . . ."

"I'll connect you with the floor nurse."

The new voice was annoyed. "We *cannot* permit a *patient* to take a *phone call,* after nine P.M."

"Yes, but—"

"Mrs. Adams is doing very well. You may call her in the morning."

"Just a minute," said Anabel. "Is Professor Adams there?"

"No visitors now. Too late."

"Has he *been* there?"

"I really couldn't say."

"Had he *phoned* there, then?"

"It's too late," the voice snapped. "We cannot have the patients upset. Or disturbed."

Then Anabel sat with a dead phone in her hand.

She got up and took a few turns up and down the room. "I wonder. . . . They could be on their way back to your house."

"Or else," said Vee, "the neighbors might have seen Dad. If he did come. . . . If he is home. . . ." Then Vee Adams smiled, with a peculiar sweetness. "It might not have anything to do with you, Anabel."

"I could bear to know," said Anabel. "Shall we go?"

Vee gasped and went running to the coat closet.

The Adams house was dark. Anabel parked at the curb and peered out at it, leaning across Vee, who said, "They're not there now, I guess. Shall we get out, Anabel?"

"Well, we're not going quietly. What's the best place to ask?"

"Mrs. Newcomb," said Vee promptly.

Mrs. Newcomb put on her porch light before she opened her front door. "Why, Violet!" she cried. "You poor dear child! Come in. Come in!"

Vee said, "We just came to ask you. . . ."

But Mrs. Newcomb went right on talking. "Your—er—I mean Mr. Wahl, only just *told* me that you were with a friend. I've been wondering where you'd got to. How *is* your mother? I called this morning and they said she had come through just splendidly. Won't you come in?" This woman had a long nose and little eyes, set close. "Both of you?" she simpered. She made the question, Who is this?

"This is Mrs. O'Shea," said Vee, rather helplessly.

"Mrs. Newcomb," said Anabel briskly, "have you seen Professor Adams?"

"No, but I've talked to him," the woman said. "Come in, do."

"Wait a minute. You say you've *talked* to him? When was that?"

"Why, just a little while ago. Poor man. Imagine, not even knowing that his own wife had been taken to the hospital in an ambulance. Imagine, *my* having to be the one to tell him." Her lively little eyes reproached the daughter. "So strange. Of course, I was glad to do it."

"This is important," said Anabel. "Has he gone there?"

"To the hospital? Well, I couldn't say, of course. But I think he had intended to phone there. As a matter of fact, he asked me to find the number for him. Won't you come in? No one's at your house, Violet. I let Mr. Wahl take my car, you know. He had some important errand and taxis are so inconvenient. I was glad to do it. I'm sure he is perfectly reliable."

Anabel said, "You didn't see Everett Adams, then? You talked to him on the phone?"

"Why, yes, I thought I had said—"

"Your phone?"

"Well, no. You see. . . . Poor Mr. Wahl. All this trouble on his shoulders. His poor sister. And then the Professor being out of town and nobody able to get in touch with him. Or so I assume." Mrs. Newcomb tossed her head. "After he had left, it occurred to me. . . . I thought it would be only neighborly. And I have always been a good neighbor—"

"You went to my house?" Vee burst.

"You know," said Mrs. Newcomb accusingly, "that your back door can be opened. I did think I might just look around. Perhaps I could lend a woman's hand, to straighten up the place a bit." Her nostrils pinched.

There was no speeding her up. Anabel nerved herself to wait.

"Well, I went over. And do you know, I noticed that someone had carelessly left the phone off the hook? Naturally, I replaced it. And the professor must have been trying to get the number all along, because I hadn't been in the house ten minutes before he called!" She nodded, as if pleased about this.

"Well, when he asked for Celia, you know I was quite shocked. Fortunately, I was able to tell him that she had come through the operation just splendidly." The woman beamed and nodded as if she congratulated herself.

"This was how long ago?" Anabel asked.

"Why, I can't say—exactly." The woman peered at her suspiciously. "Oh, half an hour, something like that."

"From where was he calling?"

"Why, I don't believe. . . . As a matter of fact, he didn't *say*. He was very much upset, you know. Naturally. Do come in."

"Thank you. No," said Anabel, with decision. She took Vee's arm and hurried her away. Mrs. Newcomb, taking obvious offense, stood on her lighted porch and openly, and rather hostilely, watched them scurry to the Adams door.

Vee had her key. They went in and turned up the light. Anabel was looking at the phone in the foyer. It was as if she spit on her hands.

"This is Anabel O'Shea again."

"Yes?"

"Did Mrs. Adams get a phone call from her husband this evening?"

"There are no phones in the patients' rooms after nine P.M." The starched voice indicated dutiful patience.

"All right. Did he *try* to call? Who would speak to him? Would you?"

"All I can tell you is that we do *not* permit calls to *any* patient after nine P.M., and that is an inflexible rule. I *cannot* and *will not* break it. Not *tonight* or *any* night." The patience was exhausted.

"Don't you hang up!" Anabel was sharp. "This is a police matter."

"Are *you* the police, madam?"

"No, I am not."

"Then why don't you call the police?" Starched voice was skeptical.

"I intend to. What is your name, please?"

"More. *Miss* More." Starched voice was proud of it.

Anabel hung up. "I think he did call. I think he did. She's just too ornery to say so." Anabel snatched up the phone again and in a little while was talking to Captain Murch himself on a special line.

When she hung up this time, Anabel sat still, wondering what more there was that she could do. Nothing—about Everett Adams. The police would check on him now. He had either called the hospital or he had not. The police would either find out where he was or they would not. The chance that he would know where Pat was seemed remote. But surely Everett Adams wasn't on the mountain. It was Pat's car, Pat's coat, Pat's hat. . . . And in Anabel's imagination a ghost, in a brown raincoat, hitched rides. She let the pang go through her.

Then she sighed and looked around. This house was drab and chilly and foreign. What was she doing here?

"I'm sorry, Vee," said Anabel. "I guess I'm just the bossy type. I shouldn't have taken over like that. But at least you know that your father's alive and evidently well." Anabel tried to smile.

But the girl was looking white and strained and she was watching Anabel intently.

Anabel rose. "Do you want to stay here, in case he tries to call you?"

"He won't," said Vee, in a low intense voice. "He doesn't even remember me."

Oh, no, sighed Anabel in herself, as if I haven't got my own troubles. She said, "Well, that's up to you. I guess there's no point in our going to the hospital. Unless *you* want to go there. If so, I'll take you."

"No," said Vee in the same manner. "Celia doesn't want to see me. She doesn't care."

"All right," said Anabel mildly. "We'll go home, then, I suppose."

"I don't know what to do," Vee wailed.

"And I can't tell you," said Anabel, rather severely, "but I'd suggest you come with me. I wouldn't think there was anything more that either of us can do tonight. Tomorrow. . . ." She started for the door. (Tomorrow they would search the mountain.) She turned to hurry up the girl.

Vee stood with her head hanging, in that attitude of distress.

Anabel said, "Oh, come on. This just isn't the time to worry about who cares for you and who doesn't. In fact, you could cheer up a little. You were pretty sharp about the telephone."

Vee lifted her head and gave her a strange look, a shaky smile. Then Vee stumbled out the door. It was Anabel who turned the light out. She was frightened and very weary from having been frightened for so long. It did cross her mind to wonder who had left that telephone off the hook. But it didn't seem to matter.

Going home, she was grateful for Vee's silence.

"So I guess you better get on over there," said Captain Murch to Carlson on the phone, "and get hold of this Miss More and get it out of her, whether Adams already phoned there. If he shows up, you grab him. Don't worry about a thing. I want to know where he's been and what he knows."

"Yes, sir."

"And if he hasn't phoned there yet, you may have to stick around until he does. You can let his wife do the talking, but be sure you find out where the hell he is."

"Yes, sir."

Wednesday Night

PAT SAID, "For better or for worse. Stand up and you say it. Why? Because she's such a sweetheart, you can't stand it. You gotta get married. *Ev*-vrybody has to say that. Don't know what you're in for."

The lamp gave a flickering light.

The old woman said, "A real strong constitution. Your pa was the weevily one. Not my side. Healthy, all the Mayhews. Your Grandma Mayhew, she was ninety-nine when she passed on. She used to say, she says to me. . . ."

The air was very dry.

Pat said, "Then there's a day and the next day and a week and the next week, a year and the next year. This Anabel turns out to be quite a dame. You didn't know the half of it. Tell *me* it's just the old rat race, the job, the bills, the baby. I don't know. . . ."

The bed was hot.

The old woman said, " 'Estrella,' she says to me, 'you're a Mayhew and Johnny's a Mayhew, too. I can tell,' she says. She's ninety-six or ninety-seven, that time, and you was only four years old, Johnny. She was blind by then, too. Well, she was old. But she put her fingers on your little face. 'He's a Mayhew,' she says. 'No fear.' "

Pat said, ". . . what they think life's made of. Sugar and spice and all things nice, like the job and the bills and the baby . . . and Anabel. That ain't no rat race. That's my life. My wife. She's not going to sit in the corner and cry for me. No sir. No ma'am. In sickness or in health. . . ."

The dog barked.

The old woman said, "A little touch of the influenza. That don't bother me. Ninety-nine, she was, when she passed on and I'll be, too. And so will you, Johnny Pryde."

She cackled.

Pat said, "Because this kid's not what you'd call the passive type. I ought to know. And I pity the world. I really do. Be turning it upside down. So long as we both shall live."

He rolled his head. The air was dry and still. The lamp was spluttering. The dog was barking.

"Eh, Rex?" he shouted.

The old woman said. "Eh? Eh, Rex?" She got up, using her staff, and went to the bedroom door. She looked back over her shoulder. Pat lay hunched up, his eyes squirrel-bright, shrewd, and a little mad, with fever.

Grumbling to herself, the old woman came back and picked up the lamp. She took it with her. Long shadows wavered up the walls. She left him.

Cecil was holding Mrs. Newcomb's flashlight close to his body, directing the light almost straight down. He was well within the grove now, following some ruts, along which he had not dared drive Mrs. Newcomb's Ford. He had left it at the end of Oleander Street, but well away from where, muffled in neglected shrubbery, there was a house with a dim light in it.

Surely no one could hear his feet on this still-soaked, mushy ground, and no one would notice his light if he were very careful. He dared send the beam a little farther ahead and it seemed to leap, as if suddenly nothing obstructed its range.

He turned it downward and went on, very gingerly, until he came to the end of the ground. There was a cut in the earth. A drop. Cecil shuffled sideways and found a tree trunk to which he clung with his left arm. Then he sent the beam of light down over the edge. A dump, all right. There was the old shoe, the inevitable one old shoe. There was a rusty gallon tin, from some nursery. There were heaps of ancient weeds and cuttings. There was a tire. The tire was on a wheel. The wheel was on a car. The car was upside down. It was Everett Adams' car.

The flashlight's beam trembled over its somehow indecently exposed underparts. No way to see from here, at night, whether there was anybody in the car. But that was where he was, all right. O'Shea.

Cecil, seized by the notion that he had no idea what might be watching him from the other side of this gulch, slid the button and the dark became seamless. It was so silent here. All sound was distant. Close by, one seemed to be able to hear the rotting process. The sweet smell of decay came up to his nostrils. He let go of the tree and turned around. He could glimpse that faint light in the house. It must guide him. Cecil began to hurry, shuffling in order not to stumble, anxious to get away from here, especially since, somewhere, a dog was barking.

He had his left arm stiff before him, to guard against bumping into anything. He began to fumble with his right thumb to slide the flash-light button and give his feet some light and hurry on.

But light became greater over there, around the house. And the dog was louder. But Cecil could see the grayish look of the open road, beyond the grove. He began to run, fearing that the dog was out of the house. He slipped and threw up his right arm for balance. The flashlight fell out of his hand. The dog was out. Cecil did not fall. He kept his feet, his feet raced, he made it.

Then he was panting, inside the glass and metal fortress of the car. He turned the key, pulled the lever and, without lights, he backed the car and turned it around.

The dog raced on the road behind him, swift and silent. But not as swift as he, as he drove away from Oleander Street.

Pat heard the racket of a car starting up in the night, the motor racing. Then he heard the sound diminish as it went away. He had not heard it come. He was leaning on his left elbow. His right arm was beginning to swell up. He heard the old woman shrieking for the dog and he heard the dog's return.

And he thought, as he heard the house door closing, She'll bury me. She'll put up a stone. The stone will say *Johnny Pryde*.

The whole bed seemed to tilt. He started to count. Count something. Anything. The hours. He didn't know this hour. The days, then. Monday, Tuesday, Wednesday. . . . This must be Wednesday night. . . .

Wednesday night.

Jamie Montero was lying the wrong way on his bed, with his head where his feet ought to be. This way, he could look out the window at the pool of light under the high streetlamp. He'd lain this way for two nights in a row already. This night, he saw the Ford go by, very fast. He had seen it before. Now he saw it coming back. He checked it off. It wasn't a two-toned Chevy. The driver probably just hadn't known this was a dead-end street.

But that was the trouble. Oleander Street went nowhere. So where was that Chevy? Jamie was sure he hadn't missed it Monday night. Nor Tuesday night either. By day, he had taken little naps in his chair, but he'd had the little kids watch the street for him by day. And the Chevy had *not* come back. Where was it then? Stan hadn't helped very much. Stan, the grocery boy, was nice and all that, but maybe he wasn't serious. He was too old to be serious, really. But the little kids, who knew how to be serious, wouldn't go out to the end to look around, not even for Jamie. They were too scared of the old witch and her dog. Jamie sighed. He wasn't scared, but he couldn't go.

Wednesday night.

The Newcomb house was dark. Cecil Wahl ran the Ford into the Adams driveway, rubbed his fingerprints off the wheel by habit, and got out. He let himself into the house, frowned at the telephone. He got a beer and a sandwich and went into the den, where he sat down to keep vigil. A bit of a risk? Maybe. Maybe not. At least O'Shea was well hidden.

Wednesday night.

The O'Shea house was dark. The little girl slept sweetly with her nose snubbed into the plush hide of a toy animal. Mrs. King slept. Vee, on the couch in the living room, curled up, uncurled, turned over.

Anabel wasn't beautiful. She wasn't *anything* like Celia, thank goodness. Anabel listened. She even went and did things, on the basis of what Vee told her. It was a little frightening. It made Vee feel real. So she was trying not to dream, not to comfort herself with a dream about Beau Carlson, for instance, who had been very nice to her. But it did not mean anything and she must not pretend that it did. Must not pretend at all? That was very hard.

But Anabel wasn't like Lillian, either. Not "sweet." Not thinking about how "sweet" her manners ought to be or whether she was acting like a lady. The thing about Anabel, she was real. And Vee had seen the vision, but she wasn't sure that she herself could bear it. Vee didn't know what she really was. She had always been trying so hard to be, or to dream that she was, something else.

Anabel was loyal. But she said what she thought, too. Vee did not know whether to be loyal still, or what? Or what? There were some things Anabel didn't understand. Some things she had not believed. Vee couldn't blame her, but she wished. . . . But if Anabel ever did understand those things . . . !

Vee curled, uncurled. . . .

Anabel was trying to lie quietly in the big bed, all alone, and not give the terrible shadow of the hitchhiker any more substance than it deserved. But logic ran. If the man in the raincoat had been Pat, Pat would have called her. He had not. Therefore, he wasn't Pat. If he wasn't Pat, then he had taken Pat's raincoat. If he had taken Pat's raincoat, how had he done that?

No, no, wait. The premises were only probable. All right, she knew about probability. She knew that, however great, it still remained only probability.

Could she dream up any other premises? What if Pat had been hurt, say, going off the road in the car? Had been thrown out, or had jumped out and got up to the road? Had been dazed? Hadn't been able to think who he was, who she was? Had been the man in the raincoat after all?

It's possible, she whispered in the dark.

Wednesday night.

Carlson sat on a hard chair in the hospital corridor, outside Mrs. Adams' door. There was a certain fluttering around the nurses' station. Women in white tripped past him rather more often than was absolutely necessary. Miss More was haughtily quiet, trying to forget how she had fallen apart under those cool young eyes. Well, the man on the phone had sounded *hysterical!* How could she have let his call go through to a patient? She *had* told him that his wife was doing very well, nothing to worry about. She *had* done her duty. Her full duty. She was forty years old and she'd been doing her duty a long,

long time and that young man needn't have been so insolent. Not that he had said anything. He had been insolent, just the same.

Miss More "humphed" to herself, remembering how they had moved Celia Adams' roommate, how Celia had played possum. Oh, she hadn't been asleep! Oh no—lying there, so pretty! Mrs. Adams had seen the young man peering in at her. And the green eyes opening, and that long cold stare between them. The insolence of young good-looking people who recognize their kind. Miss More settled her starched feathers. None of *her* business.

Carlson shifted his rump on the hard chair. Nobody had showed. He'd had a bit of a shock. If it hadn't been for the uncanny resemblance to Cecil Wahl, he would have picked the old biddy in the maroon thing to have been the Adams woman.

Thursday

ANABEL MUST HAVE been asleep; something had wakened her. The sound of weeping. Someone was weeping in her house. In the night? In the first faint dawn. It wasn't the child.

It isn't I, is it? wondered Anabel.

After a minute she put her feet out of the bed, felt for her slippers, and groped for her robe. She turned on no lamp; she knew where the furniture was. It was Vee Adams, of course, weeping on the couch in the living room, and Anabel felt impatient with her, for the sound of her distress that was so distressing. She went into the living room, made her way to the couch, and sat down on the edge of it, saying nothing.

"I'm sorry. I'm sorry, I'm sorry." The girl lashed herself.

Still Anabel did not speak, but silently, now, she gave the girl permission to weep. Very well, then, weep. In a world that is too much for you. Poor kid, you cannot cope, and so you weep. So do we all.

Vee said, "I think about myself too much. I know I do. But my mother is dead. And my father isn't my father anymore. Or anything like my father used to be. Celia doesn't see me. There's nobody to think about me, except me. I know. I know. Probably I am jealous. But even when I leave myself out of it, there is still something wrong with her.

"You don't know, Anabel. It was wrong, a long time ago, and it gets wronger and wronger. It isn't only that she steals. She doesn't do *anything* like other people. And you can't love her. I mean, if you do, she doesn't give anything back. I know because I did love her, at first. And my father still doesn't care for anything else on earth but Celia. She doesn't care for him one bit. She only. . . . But I don't hate her, either. You can't even hate her. You can't do *anything* with her. There's something wrong."

"*Ssh.* . . ."

"I'm sorry. I'm sorry. I don't know what's right to do. For me to do, I mean."

"It wouldn't be right," said Anabel softly, "to wake my mother."

"I know. I know. Were you asleep?"

Anabel put her hand on the girl's shoulder where she could feel the vibrations of distress. She was wide awake now, and she began to think that she had made a hasty judgment, fitting this individual into a familiar pattern, the stepchild, the beautiful young stepmother, and . . . oh sure . . . the "inevitable" reaction of jealousy.

So Anabel said, very softly, "But I'm listening, now."

Vee turned over. "Sometimes I think she wasn't all-the-way born. I know that sounds crazy. But she's not alive, except when her brother comes and then. . . ." The girl's whole body shuddered. "Sometimes I think they didn't get split evenly. She hasn't got her whole half."

Anabel's brain said "fraternal twins," but she did not voice a correction. She listened.

"She's been killing my father for a long time," Vee said quite soberly.

"Oh, Vee. . . ."

"Yes. Listen. She went to the college and stole a very expensive thing out of the lab. And when my father found out, he covered up for her. If it had been me. . . . Oh, Anabel, my father and mother would have marched me right up. . . . But my mother died."

"Celia? Stole?" said Anabel. "But now wait . . . Pat told me about that. About some boy."

"Yes. Jim Rossi."

"But, Vee, if you knew. . . ."

"Yes, that's it," said Vee. "So now, you see? It makes me think that I could have stopped it. If my father is doing terrible things, it's because she's made him. If I had told somebody *then,* maybe . . . I mean, if anybody had known what she was like and what he was getting to be like. I was either being loyal or else . . . just chicken. But I never was one of the lucky ones. Anabel, I don't know how to do things like that. Nobody ever listens to me. Except *you.*"

"*Ssh.* . . ."

Anabel was bewildered. She was getting the sense of the girl's conviction that her father had been progressively corrupted. A jealous delusion? Very probably. Yet, *stealing!*

"How could your father cover up stealing?" she demanded.

"He took it back," said Vee. "Or one just like it. It came in the mail, on Monday morning. I . . . knew."

"Took it back? To the Provost, maybe?"

"He was going to sneak it back."

"Sneak? And just let that boy—?"

"He was so upset, Dad was. It was just about killing him. Just killing him, Anabel. But he was going to do it, just the same. For her. I mean, do you see?"

Anabel said, "Pat must have found that out."

The girl sighed herself deep into the couch cushions. "Yes," she said.

"He would have been furious."

"Yes."

Anabel gnawed her lips in the dark. All right. This explained what Vee had seen in the parking lot. Pat, angry, pursuing Everett Adams to thrash it out, and Everett fleeing. But it explained only that and no more.

"But what could have happened, then?" murmured Anabel.

"If I had only gone and told. . . . If I had only gone and told. . . . Then my father couldn't have tried to save her. And nothing would have happened to Mr. O'Shea." Vee turned over again, face down.

Now, in Anabel's mind, the pattern turned over, end-for-end, and she understood what Vee was thinking. It was true, since Everett Adams' phone call to Mrs. Newcomb, no one could any longer imagine that Pat had sent him over the brink in the Rambler to his death, or to hide it. He was not dead. But Vee had been thinking of it the other way around. His own daughter seemed to be able to imagine that Everett Adams could have killed and run, and he could have become so lost a soul. In a brown raincoat.

"No, no," said Anabel aloud. She was thinking, Because of a theft? What was that? Kleptomania? Why on earth should Celia Adams steal anything unless she had an illness? But that could be understood. That could be treated. Everett Adams would be upset, yes. But not as upset as this, surely.

"What would you do?" Vee whispered. "Would you go to the police and tell them now?"

"Would I? Yes, I probably would. I'd certainly tell the Provost. That doesn't mean I'm telling you. . . ." Anabel lost track of what she was saying. She was tired, very tired, and sick at heart.

"It's too late now," burst Vee. "*I* can't do anything about it. I'm sorry. I'm sorry. But *I* don't mean anything. I never will."

"Try not to feel so. . . ." Then Anabel O'Shea pulled herself up. All right. Here is this girl. I didn't like her. I didn't want her. I didn't ask for her to be around. But here she is. So Anabel said quietly, "Try not to be so stupid. Your mother died. Your father's left you, in a way—or so you say. But you didn't die. If your heart goes on beating, you had better mean something."

The girl was very still. Anabel could feel how Vee's heart was beating. She could feel her own. "Look at what you are saying," she went on. "Your father fell in love with Celia, who has got something wrong with her. He's let that make him do, you say, terrible things. But we don't know whether there's been a terrible crime. And if there has been, we don't know who has done it. And I'll tell you this. If Pat has done it . . . and somebody proves that to me . . . I'll still love him. But it's not going to make me be a criminal. Other people can make you very unhappy. But *they* can't make you meaningless."

She touched the girl's hair. "Think about what to do, in the morning. There's not much left of this night anyhow. All right?"

Vee said, very calmly and thinly, in the dimness, "I could never come and live with you."

Anabel said, "No."

"All right," said Vee. "Then I won't dream of it."

Anabel got up and made her way back to her bed in her quiet

house. She got in, shivering, and pulling up the blankets. Not much left of this night . . . so cold upon the mountain.

At a few minutes before eight in the morning on Thursday, Cecil Wahl parked Mrs. Newcomb's car three blocks away from the hospital, where he had found a spot just behind a driveway so that he could get the car out fast, if need be. He supposed that wherever he went from here, it would be quickly. If Celia, and only Celia, knew (by now) where Ev was, then that was one thing. Otherwise, then otherwise. Cecil fancied himself the little pig who got up an hour earlier than the wolf.

But as he swung into the lobby, he almost collided with one of the wolves. "Morning, Mr. Wahl. I guess you've heard," said Maclaren.

"I hear from the neighbor that Ev phoned last night," said Cecil brightly. "Does anyone know where he is?" Cecil was tethered to the floor by the merest thread. If Ev had turned himself in somewhere, then Cecil was turning around and getting out, right now. But he read on the other face that this was not so. "Has he phoned my sister?" Cecil inquired.

"He hasn't talked to her. They told him last night that he could speak to her by nine A.M. Carlson's upstairs, been waiting on him. After you?"

Cecil preceded him into the elevator. He didn't like the sound of things. He might have one hour's margin left.

Maclaren pushed the button for the fourth floor. "What business you in, Mr. Wahl?"

"What? Oh, excuse me. Sales." Cecil looked vague.

"I see. This development changes the picture a little bit. At least, we know that Adams is alive somewhere."

"May have nothing to do with O'Shea," said Cecil, nodding wisely.

"That's right. But the Service Detail got a fingerprint off the Rambler. Did you know?"

Cecil's head went high, his ears seemed to cock.

"Back of the mirror, as usual," Maclaren went on. "Somebody readjusted it. Well, sir, they lifted the prints and one thing . . . they aren't O'Shea's."

"Is that so?" drawled Cecil.

"We haven't gotten hold of Adams' prints yet. We don't have everybody's . . . handy." Maclaren smiled at his own pun.

Cecil did not smile. He looked as if he might whistle. The elevator stopped. Cecil had his hands in his pockets, his mouth pursed to whistle, his eyes staring at nothing. Maclaren reached out and opened the door.

Cecil went springily down the corridor. Maclaren seemed to amble after him. Carlson got off his chair to greet them. Cecil gave Carlson one quick nervous nod and hurried into the room where Celia was. A nurse came fluttering to protest, but Maclaren stopped her. Then the two policemen stepped silently into the room.

The two faces, so alike. The two very blond heads, almost white. The two pairs of green eyes. It was like watching somebody look at himself in a mirror.

Cecil murmured, "Poor C. I won't stay now. Only be in the way. Good luck to us all, eh?"

Celia said, "Poor Ev. He's such a fool, C. Maybe he won't call."

Cecil said, "Maybe not. Even so. Another hour—? Shall I call you, C?"

She closed her eyes. One source of green flame went out. Cecil looked around, saluted with a lift of his hand and a nod of his head, and sprang away.

But the words between them hadn't told the half of it; not the half of what had been said. Maclaren muttered something, raced down the corridor, and got into the elevator with Cecil again. Cecil eyed him sideways and said nothing.

Maclaren said, "She's right. Maybe he won't call. The thing is, if he sent O'Shea's Rambler off the road, then we can be pretty sure he knows where O'Shea may be. Will you be at the Adams house later on? If we can get Adams' prints there for comparison, that would be helpful."

Cecil said sweetly, "Naturally, I want to be as helpful as possible."

"Then could you let me have a key to the house?"

"No key. Sorry. But the back door won't lock. Be my guest." Cecil had his hands in his pockets. His head was bent. He seemed ready to sprint off his mark. Maclaren was the one who opened the elevator door.

Maclaren watched him go. He watched him through the revolving door. Then Maclaren went over to the switchboard, to wait there.

Upstairs, Carlson sat down in the comfortable chair beside Celia's bed. There was no phone in the room yet. When a call came for her, the nurse, following the normal procedure, would bring one and plug it in. Nothing to do but wait. Carlson said so, out loud.

The beauty on the bed rolled her fair head and said, "Who are you, pray tell?"

But she didn't care.

The old woman had actually bathed him. She seemed to realize now that he was seriously ill. She seemed to have been hearing echoes of his cries for cleanliness. So she had bathed him and dusted him lavishly with talcum powder as if he were an infant, muttering all the while her private affirmations and incantations. No fear. No fear. He'd see. He'd see.

Pat saw, well enough, that he was in a bad way. He did not know what was happening to his leg, except that it was nothing good. The head he didn't worry about. But the arm, his right arm, had swollen all the way to the shoulder. His heart, he thought, was fighting the good fight. He seemed to be able to detach and observe the civil war within, the poison attacking, and his body's defenses.

Time would tell. Time would tell. But he didn't think it would take much longer for time to tell.

The old woman was wringing out her rag over the bowl on the table. Pat put his left forefinger into the thick coating of white talcum that lay upon the sheet. Almost whimsically, he lifted it and began to write upon the back of her black dress.

She felt his touch and turned.

"Ma?" he murmured. It was the magic word. He knew he was almost smiling, a sickly smile.

"I'll take care," she said. "No fear. You'll see." She turned back to her task and Pat wrote upon her back the big letters S O S. She seemed pleased that he had touched her. She turned again and beamed upon him. As she carried the bowl away toward the kitchen, Pat saw with squinted eyes that he had got the *S*'s backwards, like a child's printing. Oh well. . . .

In a little while, he would get up and walk away from here.

In another little while. . . .

He lay and breathed in the perfume from the talcum. It was a small, keen pleasure.

Celia said, "Why should you eat three meals a day? Why not six? Five? Four? One? Why should you sleep eight hours? Suppose you don't feel like it? Why should you wear a skirt? A shoe? Why should you wash your teeth or pay money? Or work at some stupid job? Why should you do what everybody else does? Get married? Say 'please' and 'thank you?' Why is that?"

Carlson felt his Adam's apple moving. He had no answer. Her face was pale and her green eyes expressed an inner state to which he had no clue at all.

"Stupid," she said. "When nobody lives forever, why won't they let you live while you're at it? Why do you always have to do what they say? Who says?" Her head rolled.

"Shall I call a nurse?" He was reduced to conventional concern.

"Even when you're sick they still tell you what to do. Who gave them the right to tell you what to do? What *not* to do? Why is it?" cried Celia out of some anguish he couldn't understand. "Why is it they won't let you be with the only one—? Who are they to say? Who *are* they?" She raised herself up. "Who makes all these rules, any-way? For this game? I'd just as soon not play anymore." Her green eyes met his eyes. "And you," she said, "can. . . ." She told him, in language that raised his eyebrows, what he could do. But she didn't care what he did.

A nurse stood in the door. "Telephone for Mrs. Adams. It's early, but the man downstairs said to let it through."

"Let it through," said Carlson.

As soon as the phone had been plugged in, Carlson was right up beside her on the bed. He knew now that she was some kind of kook, and he wasn't going to trust her for one minute. His hand was on the shank of the phone with hers, forcing the instrument to stay an inch away from her ear. His cheek was on her pale hair. She didn't care. She said, wearily, indifferently, "Hello?"

"Oh, my darling, are you all right?"

"Everett?" Her voice was flat.

"Mrs. Newcomb said you were fine. I tried to call. . . . Are you all right, really? Truly?"

"I'm fine," she said languidly. "How are—?"

"I understood, then, that you wouldn't be coming. Darling, I only wanted to tell you to bring some money. But that's no matter. You would have come to me if you could. That made me happy. But now we've had our answer. You are to live. I am to die. Because I am the guilty one. I killed O'Shea. Killed him."

Carlson's hand jerked in shock. He let the phone go, grabbed wildly at a lipstick that was lying on the table, snatched up a magazine, wrote on a gray inside page WHERE IS HE? There was a killer at the other end—a shy bird, then.

"But you are not guilty, my darling," continued Everett's ranting voice. "I want you to live and be happy. Oh, Celia, let me have something from this ruin? Celia, promise."

"I promise," she said passively, even stupidly. "Are you coming home now?" Carlson began to shake the magazine before her eyes.

"Going to my long home, darling. Long home. You must understand. Tell my poor Violet to try to grow up and be happy and forgive and forget me. Tell Mrs. O'Shea there is nothing . . . nothing to say."

Celia stared at the big red words that Carlson had written and read them, numbly, aloud: "Where is he?"

"O'Shea? Why, at the dump. Didn't I tell you? I left him . . . left him. And not found yet? Well. . . . Well. . . ." His voice was falling, note by note, on the scale. "I can't talk. This was only to say 'good-bye.' My darling. My lovely girl."

Carlson, with his teeth clenched, was scribbling on another page, WHERE ARE YOU?

"I'm at the desk," said Everett, as if he could see the words. "The woman's gone, for a minute. I knew they kept a gun ready—in case of trouble. I'll be sorry to trouble them. I was happy here."

Carlson was holding his new message and glaring fiercely, but Celia's green eyes looked into his eyes, not at the writing. He had a strange idea that there wasn't anybody there, behind the green.

"I shall look up at the mountain I named for you one night—remember?" Everett was raving. "Then, to die. It's nothing. I don't mind. I truly do not mind."

Carlson's fingers were bruising her shoulder. Celia winced and said at last, "Where are you?"

"Why, at Bedelia's, darling. Where I loved you. Where I do love you. I called to say. But I must go. I can't even pay for this, darling. Will you? I have no time. She'll be back. So the rest is—"

Carlson wrenched the phone to himself and shouted, "Adams? Where are you? Adams?"

"Cecil?" The voice was shocked.

"This is the police."

"Ah . . . Celia. . . ." It was a long wail for the great sorrow of a final betrayal. Then Everett said, with quaint dignity, "I owe a cock to Asclepius. . . ." The phone went dead.

Carlson was looking grim. "They were tracing it," he said to the woman, "so you may as well tell me. Where is he? Where's this Bedelia's?"

"It's just a motel," she said lazily, "outside of Las Vegas."

While Carlson was getting the telephone ear of Captain Murch himself, Celia walked her fingers on the spread where it lay across her body.

"Adams is talking suicide in a motel called Bedelia's, outside of Vegas," said Carlson, putting the emergency first. "He's got a gun."

Murch spoke aside. "OK. We're on that," he said in a second. "Go ahead."

"He says he killed O'Shea and left the body at the dump."

"That's for the Uniformed Branch. They'll get on it."

"That's about it, sir."

"Paid off, eh?" said Murch, relaxing. "Why did he kill O'Shea?"

Carlson's crispness abandoned him. "He didn't say, sir."

Afterward, he said to the woman on the bed, "Don't give up yet, Mrs. Adams. Las Vegas police officers will get there and they may be in time to stop him."

She said sulkily, "Why should they? If he doesn't want to play anymore?"

"He's wanted for murder, for one thing," snapped Carlson, who was a cop.

She paid no attention. "Won't meet *him* again." She shuddered. "I don't believe that. This is all there is; there isn't any more. And who needs it? It's not so—great."

The young man stared. He stirred himself and went away.

Carlson got down to the lobby and looked around for Maclaren. He was standing by the switchboard with his ugly head bent as if he were praying. Carlson shook off a feeling of irritation. "You on the line?" he asked cheerfully.

Maclaren lifted his head. "Yes."

"Well, now we know, eh? I got it out of her where this motel is."

"I was on the line to Murch, too."

"They may get to Adams."

"They may. A gun's quick, though."

"Poor slob," said Carlson. "Well, maybe they won't. But even so, at least we know."

Maclaren said nothing but began to walk toward the exit.

"Headquarters?" chirped Carlson, keeping pace with him.

"We'll have to go tell Mrs. O'Shea. And the little Adams girl."

"Yeah, that's right." Carlson's spirits were suddenly sent down. "Why the hell *would* Adams kill O'Shea?" he demanded almost indignantly.

"We don't know that," said Maclaren sadly.

"Cheese," said Carlson to his private section of the revolving door. "Does a cop have to know everything?"

When they got to the car, Maclaren took the driver's seat. Carlson sat beside him, pulling at his own fingers. They were almost to Pine Street when Carlson spoke at last. "Oh, boy," he said, "that Adams dame—she's a bird. I'm telling you. She couldn't care less."

Maclaren shot a glance at him.

"What did you think," said the young man, "of her and her brother? Kind of weird. Right?"

"Brother has taken off."

"What do you mean?"

"Oh, he's gone. And she knows it."

"What's the matter with *him?*" (Carlson felt this to be true. Maclaren was right.)

"Something."

Carlson sucked air through his teeth. "Yeah," he said, "something. Maybe I see what you mean. Those two. I guess there's a lot of strange things. She gave me the shakes, practically."

"How was that?"

"Oh—Why should you do like everybody else? Why should you join the human race? That's what she was saying. She wants to know who makes the rules. She doesn't want to play anymore, she says. And I'll tell you another thing." Carlson cleared his throat. "She's got no religion. 'I won't meet him again,' she says, 'and who needs it? Life's not so great.' "

Maclaren was braking the car. He waited for an opening and made a U-turn.

"What's up, Dad?" said Carlson, a little too brightly because he could guess.

"We've got rules," said Maclaren grimly. "Being cops, we're not supposed to let it happen."

They raced back to the hospital, where they came too late.

Anabel was talking to the Provost on the telephone. She'd reached him at home; it was not quite twenty minutes after eight in the morning. "Vee Adams and I agree that you ought to know. Celia Adams stole that objective (wasn't it?) from the lab. Everett Adams knew it, covered up, and was going to sneak it back. So at least you can put that student, whatever-his-name-is, out of his misery."

"My dear Mrs. O'Shea!" Anabel's style was too fast for Mr. Drinkwater. He was almost panting. "I do wish that Adams had come to me. I would have done everything in my power, I assure you. . . ."

Anabel had no time for his regrets or his assurances. She excused herself. She wanted the line open for news. From the hospital, she said. (From the mountainside.)

She nodded at Vee, who smiled and went down on the carpet to join Sue and the doll family. Vee wasn't going to her classes. She had announced that she intended to go to see Celia later today. She looked very tired, yet better somehow.

Anabel could see her mother out on the porch rummaging in the mailbox. She fingered the morning paper where, over a short article on the front page, the headline said PROF'S CAR WRECK IN PASS.

"The whereabouts of popular young instructor, Elihu (Pat) O'Shea. . . ."

The whereabouts. Whereabouts. The word fell out of all its associations, a freakish collection of sounds. Anabel shook herself and wondered whether to call anybody and ask for news or whether to wait. And whether she could wait. It was the waiting, the waiting, the not knowing yet, the waiting, that ground one down. Her mother came in with a package in her hands which she was turning over and over. "Anabel, what's this?"

Anabel took it, a manila envelope fat with some content not its size. It was addressed to Pat, but Anabel tore off one end without hesitating. The thing inside was Pat's wallet. There was no money in it, but all his credit cards, his pictures. One of herself simpered up at her. Anabel couldn't believe her eyes. She peered again at the envelope and the postmark.

Then her heart went heavy because there was only one explanation that she could think of, and it was very probably the right one. She went back to the telephone and dialed the police. Neither Maclaren nor Carlson was there, so Anabel demanded, and got, Captain Murch. "Mr. O'Shea's wallet just came in the mail," she told him, speaking low. (The game on the carpet was going well.) "I've heard that when a thief strips a wallet and throws it away, anyone who finds it can put it in a mailbox and the post office will return it to the owner. Is that true?"

"I believe, in some communities. . . ."

"It was mailed in Barstow." (There *was* a thief. And if a thief, was there a hitchhiker?)

"I see. Thank you, Mrs. O'Shea." His voice changed. He was gathering himself. "I'm sorry to have to tell you some news that is not very happy for you. You are not alone, are you?"

Now everything fell down about her, her heart, her tensions. She felt all heavy and flabby, a lump, with arms and legs.

"No. Go on."

"Adams phoned the hospital at 8:06. Carlson was on the line. Adams says. . . ."

"Go on." The lump could speak. It was alone, of course. In the universe, it was all alone.

". . . that he left your husband's body at the dump. He says he killed him. Adams now—"

She kept on listening, politely, because this was confusing. It was probably true, but impossible, of course.

"—says he is going to do away with himself." The captain cleared his throat. "In a fit of remorse. We have alerted the police in Las Vegas. They may get to him, but frankly, it is not likely. Adams has a gun."

Both of them dead, then? thought Anabel. *"Where* did you say?" (Pat's child was not twenty feet away, playing with the dolls. And the other man's child.)

"At a place called Bedelia's, a motel—" the captain began.

"No, no. Where he left—"

"Oh—the dump. We have men on their way to the city dump, Mrs.

O'Shea. I am very sorry. We don't know how or why it happened. This is really all we know, so far."

"Yes."

It's enough, she thought. She put the phone down. The whole world was colorless. Her little golden daughter, on the sea-green rug, played in black and gray. "Anabel?" said Mrs. King.

Anabel got up and walked very fast into her own bedroom. Her mother followed her.

"Mother," said Anabel, having told her, "there is only one thing you can do for me. Be with Sue. Take that off me. I've got to get out of here until I can bear it. Until the time comes to tell her, or bear to wait and not tell her. Mother, you are the only one in the world who can do that for me. A little while? A little minute?"

"Of course I will, Anabel. But shouldn't you lie down? Take something?"

"No, no. I'll walk," said Anabel. "Just walk. It has to sink in. What's the use of making that take longer? One thing, though, before I can go. I'll have to tell Vee. Oh, what shall we do with her, Mother? How can I leave her on you too?"

Mrs. King said, "You do what you must do, Anabel. So will I. And so will she. And so will Susie too—when the time comes. I'll send Vee in here."

Anabel looked at herself in the glass. You are going to be a widow, she said to herself. A very young widow. Very soon. Just as soon as your whole soul can stop screaming that it can't happen to you. It can happen.

When Vee came in, Anabel said quietly, "I can't do anything for you, Vee. So, I'll just tell you what was said to me." She repeated the words of Captain Murch exactly as they were burned, forever, into her brain. "Adams has a gun," she finished.

Vee had put her palms to her temples and pulled back the flesh of her face. She looked like a cat. "I was afraid. I was afraid."

"Hang on now," said Anabel sharply.

"I'm sorry."

"We're all sorry."

"My father . . . must have been sorry—?"

"Yes, he was sorry. Vee, I've got to go. Stay in here if you want to."

Vee said, "But oh, Anabel, we were so close. So close."

"What?" Anabel was, of all things on earth, powdering her nose. She would get out of here in a minute. She was only waiting for the girl to collapse. Or not, as the case would be. Or maybe Anabel wouldn't get out of here. She might have to just . . . rock with it right now.

"Yesterday," Vee said, "we were so close. We were even *on* Oleander Street."

"What are you talking about?"

"But that's . . . where, isn't it? I told you, there's a dumping place. Didn't you say a dump?"

"Yes."

"But that's where, then. It was on their way."

Anabel was astonished that her brain could receive and function. "We never did say anything to the police about the gas station, the boy . . . the way Pat went. The *city* dump's the other side of town!"

"I know. That's what I mean. This place is way out at the very end, where Dad used to. . . ."

Anabel knew what she was going to do. She didn't ask it to be wise or sensible. She didn't query it at all.

She said to Vee fiercely, "You've got to take a thing like this right in your teeth. *You've* got to live. I told you. Will you do something for me?"

Vee staggered and said, "Yes, I will, Anabel." She took her hands from her head. They trembled.

"Call the police. Get Captain Murch. You can do it," Anabel insisted, as Vee quailed. "You're the one who *can* do it. Tell him about this dump, at the end of Oleander. They are going to the wrong place. Tell him. Just that. That's all."

"I. . . ."

"It's something for you to do."

"All right. Where are you going?"

"I am going where Pat is," said Anabel, without taking any thought at all, "because if I don't, I will never, to the end of my life, forget that I didn't."

Carlson gazed upon the smashed thing on the sidewalk as coolly as became a man and a cop. Then he swallowed the sour spittle in his mouth and looked around for what needed doing. Maclaren was talking to an intern. Celia had jumped almost as soon as they had driven off. There had already been photography, questions and answers. The ambulance stood ready. Celia was for the morgue.

Carlson spotted a wretched lad almost prostrate on the curb, still being sick enough to constitute a public nuisance, so he strode over to pick him up. He put the sufferer up on a low stone wall and asked whether a doctor was needed. "What's your name?" Carlson would not have been surprised to see the boy lose consciousness.

"Name's Parsons. Mike Parsons. I never saw anything like that. I never want. . . ."

"All right. All right." Carlson waved away a gathering audience.

"I was actually trying to get in and find out . . . about her. Then I saw her jump. Why did she do it?" The green face turned up. (Parsons could not imagine. Parsons had snooped once too often.) "Terrible," he whimpered.

"Take it easy," said Carlson. "You wanted to find out *what* about Mrs. Adams?"

"Well, see, it's so kinda funny. They say . . . around school, I mean . . . maybe she didn't really have an operation. Maybe there was something going on. . . . Her and O'Shea."

Carlson fixed him with a cold glare. "I'll tell you something, sonny," he said. "You're never going to find out anything, the way you're going."

"Hey, look! She better not. . . ."

Carlson looked. A car had stopped across the street on the rim of the gathered people. Vee Adams was getting out of it. So Carlson went pushing through, as fast as he could go, and put himself in front of her. "No," he said. "I won't let you."

"I had to come." She was already shuddering, in great waves.

"Well, you're going back again."

"It is Celia?"

Maclaren was there suddenly. "There's no question of identity," he said in his sad way. "This isn't necessary, Miss Adams. Who called you?"

"The Provost. He'd been called. He knew I was at Anabel's. I tried to reach Celia's brother, but he doesn't answer. So I. . . . My Dad would have wanted her to have somebody of her own. Maybe that's silly. . . . But *I* have to live. . . ."

Carlson almost knew what she was talking about. Maclaren

seemed to understand perfectly. "Stand aside, Jimmy. It's not too bad. She can take it."

So Vee looked between the standing people, then over their heads as the stretcher went up into the waiting vehicle. Just a red-and-white sheet over something flat.

Carlson grabbed her. "All right. Now you had better go home. Will that man take you?"

"Mr. Dickenson? I don't know. He lives next door to Anabel's house. He was very nice. . . ."

"*We* have to see Mrs. O'Shea," said Carlson. "Listen, we can take you." He signaled to the frightened-looking face in the car and the car moved away. Carlson led her to their car and put her into it. He told her what would be done now with what was left of Celia.

She was shivering. He didn't know how to tell her any more. Then he realized that he need not. Vee said, "It seems as if everybody's dead. Mr. O'Shea. My dad. And Celia. It's . . . awfully strange."

Carlson got in at her right and put his arm behind her. "Oh, look, Violet—I mean Vee—I'm sorry."

"We are all sorry."

"But I mean because I goofed this one. I don't know what to say to you. I should have figured what she had in mind. I just goofed, that's all. If I had only. . . . If I'd had any sense," he said bitterly. "I just didn't take it in. It didn't get to me. I didn't know her really, but that's the more reason I should have listened."

Vee said, "I guess you can't be sure you could have made any difference."

He looked at her intently. Listening.

Maclaren was standing at the other side of the car now. "Mrs. O'Shea is at home, is she?"

"Oh no, Anabel's gone to the end of Oleander Street. Because that's where Mr. O'Shea must be. And she. . . . Well, she *would* go. I mean, if you knew her. . . ."

"Where?" said Maclaren. They both had their heads turned to her now and seemed to be listening, very intently. So Vee managed to tell them about the old dumping place, the gas station boy, the reasons to believe.

Maclaren had heard of the place. "Out by Mrs. Pryde's," he said. "Old Mrs. Pryde lives way out there—that's if she's still alive. I guess you wouldn't know about her and her son Johnny Pryde. That was before your time."

Carlson said impatiently, "Does anybody else know about this? Does the department?"

"I told them," said Vee. "I said I would." And then she lifted both her hands, "Did I? Oh yes, I did! A long time before the Provost called. I *think* I did. I *promised.*"

"Don't worry," said Carlson, watching her. "We can check." He opened the glove compartment and took out the phone that was hidden there. He spoke into it. Finally, he said, "We'll get out there, right away. *I'd* say Miss Adams knows what she's talking about."

He put the phone away and said, "Yes, you told them. But they've got men out taking a good look at the city dump and they're being thorough. We better. . . ." Then Carlson, ignoring his partner's claim to be familiar with the end of Oleander, let his left arm come down around Vee's shoulders. "You can show us how to get there, Violet? I mean, Vee?"

"Violet's all right," she said dully. "Yes, I'd be glad if I could do something."

Carlson looked over her head at Maclaren, rather defiantly. Maclaren nodded and started the car.

Stan Simmons, who lived on Oleander Street, took the truck home with him nights. This was permitted because Mr. Johanneson and Stan's father were old friends and there was an unwritten covenant that Stan was not only apprentice but also heir to the grocery store. Stan's future was clear before him and he was content with it. He had the temperament for neighborhood business. So, of course, Stan would not skylark in the truck on his own time. And it was convenient.

As he came along Oleander Street on Thursday morning, Jamie Montero was already on his perch by the gate, waving at him to stop. Mary Montero was out there too.

"Stan! Stan!"

"Hi, ma'am. Jamie? I got something for you." Stan tossed the gift. Jamie caught it. "Take me out to the witch's, Stan?"

"Well, gee, I suppose so." Stan, once in a while, had taken the little cripple on his rounds, although never without permission from his mother and from Mr. Johanneson. "I'll be going out there this afternoon. OK?"

"No, now. Right now!"

"Gee, listen. I'm supposed to—"

"Something's funny. There's a Ford."

"Yeah? Thought it was a Chevy." Stan winked at Mrs. Montero.

"No, no. This Ford came by last night, real late, and it went away but now it's back. He's looking for the bad man."

But Mrs. Montero said, in a nervous way, "If you could take five minutes. . . . Honest, Stan, I don't see how else he's going to get any sleep at night. Maybe if he got out there once he'd stop all this. *I* can't get it out of his head. His father wants to whip him, but that's not going to get him to sleep either."

Stan looked at the wan little face. "Listen, Jamie, you don't want to make yourself sick, do you? You ought to forget it. I mean it."

"I wish I could walk," said Jamie passionately.

That did it, of course. Stan winced and looked at the mother's face and he said, "Hey, come to think of it, I do have a question to ask the old witch at that. Make a good enough excuse, I guess. So. . . . OK, Mrs. Montero?"

"Yes. I wish you would, Stan. But take care of him."

"Oh, don't you worry." Stan got out and lifted the boy into the truck. "You keep your window rolled up, mind. In case the dog is out. What's the matter with you anyway? Didn't I tell you there's nobody out there?"

"There's somebody out there now," said Jamie confidently.

Cecil Wahl was out there.

With a wary eye on the house where the dog lived, he was hunting for the flashlight. It belonged to Mrs. Newcomb. She would know it, say it traveled with her car, say who had had her car. Cecil had no intention of being quite that helpful to the police.

He was a slow and conservative driver (with his peculiar handicap) and it had taken him forty-five minutes from the hospital to the end of Oleander. But it wasn't quite nine o'clock yet. He could afford to hunt until he found the flashlight with his fingerprints on it.

Then he'd be gone. Once he got out of the cul-de-sac of Oleander Street, it would be simple.

Even when they picked up Ev—the man was such a fool, he'd stall around battling his "conscience," whatever that was—it would take them awhile to get the whole story. Even after that, since Ev thought he was protecting Celia, they'd have to check *her* out. Dig up that old incident? Take time.

Celia could tell them all about it, of course. But he knew his sister. She wasn't really vindictive. She hadn't the energy for that. She might very well just give up, just not bother, just stare at the wall. (Until somebody like Everett Adams came along and knocked himself out to "save" her.)

All of this would give Cecil, who was interested in saving himself, plenty of time. The only question in his mind right now was whether to steal the Newcomb car. For all his bravado about a man on foot, it might be smart to take the car as far as L.A., say. Or South?

The whole silly affair was a nuisance to him. He didn't have much cash. He hated work, the kind of labor he'd have to do to eat. For a while. It was too bad that Ev, having got himself into this jam, was alive to tell the tale and start the police along the way that Cecil couldn't afford to have them go. Cecil would have found it rather relaxing to move into Everett's comfortable house, fake up a skin disease, perhaps, on his right hand. (He had done that before.) Just hang around, comfortably, until the estate was settled. That would have been quite an improvement over running.

But Cecil did not doubt that he could run successfully, that he would eat. He had a superabundance of self-confidence, a kind of extra portion. It made him merry and quick and willing to take chances. But the only chance he saw now was that Everett might not break down under police inquiry and tell about that old affair. Cecil could lie low, and if this miracle were to come to pass, he could always reappear.

So he'd find the flashlight . . . except that he couldn't seem to find it. Well, if some kid had already picked it up, it was safe enough. At least the police would not be the ones to find it. And a kid would cherish such a treasure and soon blur off the signs of Cecil's handling. This place was like the end of the world, though. No kid-signs. He had better keep on looking around. There was still time.

When he saw the panel truck come around the last curve, he did not startle or run or hide. He stood there, a little way in among the trees.

Stan parked the truck ahead of the Ford. "Hi!" He recognized this man as the one who had been in the store yesterday.

"Hi, there." Cecil was casual.

"Anything I can do?" Stan was full of goodwill and curiosity.

Cecil strolled nearer. "Just wondering about this land. A playground, is it?"

"No, no. Kids don't play out here. They're too scared of the old lady lives in that house. They think she's a witch." Stan grinned. "She might be, at that. You looking for a playground?"

"No, no. Who owns this grove, do you happen to know?" Cecil was improvising.

"Can't say I do. Maybe Mrs. Pryde owns it. Wait a minute and I'll ask her." Stan hit his horn.

He debated whether to ask the man for the price of the milk and the cookies. But he dismissed this as being too small. The cookies, opened, had been unsalable. But they had disposed of the cookies, they could hardly. . . .

Jamie said, "Mister? Are you looking for a blue Chevy Bel Air?"

"Am I what?" Cecil cocked an eyebrow.

Stan started to explain, but the dog was barking, the door of the bungalow had opened. The old woman came out on the stoop, closing the door behind her against some opposition. She began to hobble down toward the broken gate and she was screeching, "You bring the medicine? You, boy?"

She was thin, with wild white hair. She wore a black dress that looked as if it had been on her frame for years. She had a staff in her hands. Her eyes were wild. "Witch" was the only word for her.

Jamie quivered a little. Stan said, in an easy friendly tone (to reassure the boy), "Hi, Mrs. Pryde. What's this? Did you say medicine?"

Cecil had taken two steps backward, as if to put himself in a spectator's position, but the old woman had seen him. "Who's that?" she glared.

"Just a man wants to know if you own the eucalyptus grove."

"Not me. Not me. It don't bother me. Where's my stuff, you, boy?"

"Oh, I don't bring it yet," Stan said. "But listen, we couldn't read one of the items. Hey, I'll bet that was the medicine."

She glared at him.

"Listen, if we can't figure out what you want, Mrs. Pryde, we can't put it in your order. Let's see, now. P O S H E A. That's what it looked like. What kind of medicine is it?" She didn't answer. "You're not feeling so well, Mrs. Pryde?"

She *was* looking wilder than usual, as a matter of fact.

Jamie piped up, "Did you see a blue Chevy Bel Air—?"

He might as well have been speaking Greek. Mrs. Pryde lifted her staff and pointed it at the child. "You don't come around here!" she shrieked. "Johnny Pryde don't want to play with you!"

"Listen, listen," said Stan placatingly, "if you're sick, Mrs. Pryde, do you want me to get you a doctor?"

"None of them. None of them." Her roving eyes caught Cecil's fascinated stare and she suddenly looked sly. "A touch of the influenza," she muttered. "No fear."

"Gee, that's too bad." Stan was doing his best. Mr. Johanneson carried some drugs and Stan knew what they were. "How about aspirin, maybe. You want me to bring you some aspirin, Mrs. Pryde?"

"You bring my stuff. You bring the good meat and all."

"Sure. Sure. This afternoon. My regular time." She had become calmer. Stan went on with his duty. "But Mr. Johanneson wants me to tell you—Listen, he's going to send that big meat order *this* time. But it's pretty expensive, he says."

The old woman suddenly lifted her staff again and pointed it over the hood of the truck to where Cecil was rooted. "I know you! I know you! You're a liar! Don't you say Johnny Pryde done it."

The dog, in the house, was frantic to get out.

Stan, despairing of the conversation ever making sense, put the truck in reverse and began to back it around the Ford, watching his rear. Jamie was trying to pierce through the trees with long eye-beams, looking for the Chevy. It was Cecil who saw the old woman turn her back. There were some whitish marks on the rusty black of her dress. A crooked squiggle, a drunken O, a blur. She beetled back to the stoop.

So Cecil knew, with one thing and another, where Pat O'Shea was now.

Then Stan was calling to him. "Hey, better watch out for the dog, mister. He's pretty vicious and the old lady's nuts. You can see that. So if you don't want to get bit, better watch it. Boy, she's *really* nutty today."

"I'll watch it," said Cecil.

"See, she had this son, this Johnny Pryde." Stan was feeling chatty. "Well, he got into all kinds of bad trouble and actually, they ran him through the gas chamber, a long time ago. But you just heard her, talking as if he was still alive? Oh boy . . . I wouldn't tangle with her if I was you."

"Thanks a lot." Cecil looked tiptoe, ready to fly. But he did not move.

Stan, perceiving that he wasn't interesting his audience, began to back the truck farther. He said to Jamie, "I got to go, OK?"

The little boy's face was pale, his eyes were bright. He said nothing.

Cecil, left standing at the end of the road, was thinking hard. O'Shea was alive. The crazy old woman had him in there. He must have been injured.

So Cecil's time was up. By now Ev must be blubbering and blabbing somewhere, and the cops would be out here, very soon. When they got here, they'd find O'Shea, who could tell and would tell, and right away, whatever it was that *he* knew. So time was up. Cecil must get lost, fast. Never mind the flashlight. He turned his head and looked into the grove and saw a brightness twinkling on the ground.

Maybe Cecil was a little bit obsessed about fingerprints. Sometimes he suspected that this was so. But this was the one thing, the one chance he never took, if he could help it. Something to do with Mom? Maybe. But if that was Mrs. Newcomb's flashlight shining in there, he could not leave it.

"Hey, Stan," said Jamie in the truck, "there *is* another road, in the trees."

"Naw, there isn't. It doesn't go anywhere." Stan wasn't thinking about Jamie. He was wondering about that tow-headed fellow. He had to get Jamie back and get to work; he'd lost enough time.

"Hey, Stan, Johnny Pryde really is dead, isn't he?"

"Oh, sure. Long ago. Listen," Stan said. "You get your sleep, now, and stop worrying your folks. OK? You don't want to get sick, do you?"

"Sick people die," said Jamie intensely.

"That's right," said Stan. "They sure do. I mean, sometimes."

"Johnny Pryde was a bad man. It was OK if he died."

Stan was not following; he was watching the road. He said, "Well, for Pete's sakes!" An Oldsmobile was coming toward him along Oleander Street. And the woman in it was the same one—Stan hit his brakes.

Anabel had been driving skillfully, alertly, and quite fast. She had thought, at first, that she ought not to be on the roads at all, but this was not so. Everything seemed clear and sharp to all her senses.

The thing was, she could not wait anymore. She must go, now, to the end of the waiting. Get there. She had waited and waited too long already. A terrible sorrow kept coming up in a wave, ready to catch her by the throat. But it always subsided, it sank away. And she could see the road, the roadside, the cars, the world going about its business; then what she was doing would seem absurd. Incredible.

But she was moving. She was going right into it, toward it, *for* it. To an end. And a sad beginning.

She turned into Oleander Street and wondered whether the police had somehow passed her by. Maybe they were there . . . out there at the end, where the end was. It didn't matter. She had to get there. Then she saw the panel truck and she saw that it was stopping, and that the boy in it was staring at her.

Oleander Street was narrow. Anabel slowed. She braked. She stopped because, in some way, the boy in the truck knew her and it was a meeting.

She said, "Can you tell me? Is there a dump of some kind, out at the end of this street?"

The boy's long, thin freckled nose seemed to twitch. He said, "No, ma'am. Well, not exactly. Well, yeah . . . I guess some folks do throw stuff over into the arroyo. Can I"—he seemed to know her and be curious about her—"do anything?"

"I'm Anabel O'Shea," she began, mechanically. (She had done this all day yesterday.) "I am looking. . . ." She stopped, because this was stalling, busywork, bitterly unnecessary, now.

"You looking for the bad man?" It was a boy's voice. It rang out from the spot beside the driver of the panel truck. There was a little boy in there.

The driver said, "Aw, come on, Jamie."

"I am looking for my husband," Anabel said.

"Oh," said the truck driver. "Yeah. Well, *he's* out there. I just been talking to him."

She was stabbed by the shock. Her breath came in. Her rib cage came up high. The heart jumped. The blood raced.

"With Pat?" she cried out. "With Pat?"

"Well, I mean," said Stan, "with the fellow in the store yesterday."

"The . . . what?"

"The grocery store? You made a phone call? I mean, there was this man with you. And *he's* out there."

The uproar in Anabel's body began to sicken and turn sour. "Out there?" she said.

"Oh, well listen. I mean out at the end of Oleander. I mean, he's out there. I was just out there. Talked to him."

"To Cecil Wahl?" Anabel's head was spinning. "Has he found Pat?"

"I don't know what you mean, ma'am."

"Pat. Pat O'Shea." The boy looked stupid. Didn't understand. Anabel's head felt thick itself. They stared at each other.

Then the little boy said, "I guess I got to tell. The old witch has got him. The bad man." He sounded ready to cry.

The driver turned his head and said severely, "For Pete's sake, Jamie, skip it about the bad man, will you?" He turned and said to Anabel. "Don't pay any attention. He's got something in his head and it isn't so. He doesn't know what he's talking about."

Anabel did not know what either of them was talking about. The truck driver had given her a terrible shock. Her whole body still throbbed and quivered with it. She said, "Well, thank you." She started the car moving.

Stan started up the truck and stopped, abruptly, at Jamie's gate, hurried to pluck him from the seat and put him back on his perch. He brushed off Mrs. Montero's gratitude. He was going to be late. He hurried along the rest of Oleander Street. That woman had looked awful wild or sick or something. Stan was feeling uneasy. He should have warned her about the dog. Well, but that tow-headed fellow was out there still. And Stan guessed he wasn't her husband after all, but at least they knew each other. Stan had warned *him*. So he guessed it was going to be all right. But it was certainly funny.

What was this all about, anyhow? And where was that third person, he wondered, the girl who had been with these two in the store yesterday?

She was snug between Maclaren and Carlson. She was trying not to think about Celia, because she knew she would be thinking about Celia for a long time. She didn't think about her father. She had let him go, a long long time ago. And he was gone. She didn't think about Mr. O'Shea. She tried to think about Anabel.

Although Maclaren drove fast, they seemed to be rushing through veils and cobwebs and many impediments. It was taking time. They were past the gas station where Dick Green worked, and getting out into the country, but there was a long way to go yet.

Vee said, "I'm afraid she's there already, all alone."

"We'll get there," Carlson said. He wasn't driving but his foot was on the floorboard, hard.

She breathed in deeply and sighed breath out. "It's all so. . . ."

"Take it easy."

Vee looked at the rushing scenery. It wasn't easy. But it wasn't too hard, either. It was odd. To have them both dead and find herself all alone was not as lonely as it had been before. She said quietly in a moment, "Do you know, for sure, that my father is dead?"

Maclaren said, "Maybe we can check."

Carlson said, "Right." He got out the telephone. "Carlson. Any word from Vegas on Everett Adams?"

"Oh, there's word, all right," the voice said. "There's no such place."

"No such—?"

"No such motel. Captain Murch has had them trying Barstow. No soap there either. And it's getting mighty late for this Adams. Somebody blew it."

Carlson choked. "Yeah. Thanks."

His smooth young face was blooming slowly red and redder. "Um, boy," he burst. "Dumb cop! That's me. Oh, listen, Violet. I'm sorry—I goofed that too. Your father. . . . She lied to me, that's all. So there wasn't any chance for him."

"I don't understand, Beau, I mean, Mr. Carlson."

"Celia. *She* told me this motel—this Bedelia's—was around Vegas.

But she didn't want him stopped. She didn't give a— She lied, and I fell for it, and God knows where he is."

"Take it easy," said Maclaren.

"Oh, sure," the lad said bitterly. He stared out his window. Maclaren drove steadily on.

"It isn't *named* Bedelia's," said Vee thoughtfully, in a minute. "I think the name of it is Sunset something-or-other."

"What?"

"Well, they had a long honeymoon. I was a camp counselor that summer. They always called it Bedelia's, but I used to send postal cards and it was to Sunset-something. Courts, maybe."

"Do you know the address of this place?" asked Carlson quietly.

"I don't know the number. It's only up in Apple Valley."

Carlson's strong young hand trembled as he reached for the telephone.

After Carlson had sent the message, Maclaren said, "I ought to have asked you, Miss Violet. Didn't think to. Should have thought. There wasn't *much* chance for him, but there could have been more."

Vee said, "Celia killed him a long time ago, Mr. Maclaren. I mean, it isn't as if he was himself anymore. *My* father couldn't have done that terrible thing—to Mr. O'Shea, I mean—if he was himself, the way he used to be. I don't want to sound—hateful. I don't hate her. I didn't ever hate her, as far as I know. But there was something wrong with her."

"With Celia?" said Carlson. "I guess *so*."

"It's awful hard to explain, Beau. I mean, Mr. Carlson."

"Beau's all right," he said, "if it's easier."

When Anabel came to the end of Oleander Street, there, sure enough, was Cecil Wahl, standing beside a car. When he saw her he took a kind of quick step, almost a dance step. Or, he was something like a cat, twisting to land on its feet.

Anabel parked the Olds crookedly and tumbled out. She went pell-mell toward him. Toward the end.

"Where is he?" she cried.

Cecil grasped both her hands. "What's up? What's happened? What are you doing—?"

"He's dead. Everett Adams says so."

"Where is Ev?"

"He's dead too," wailed Anabel. "Did you find Pat? Please?"

"Now wait," said Cecil. His hands were so tight they hurt. "What is this about Ev? He is *dead,* you say?"

"He was going to shoot himself." Anabel fought to remember that other people had other concerns. "He called. He killed Pat. He left Pat . . . at a dump. But the police have gone to the wrong dump."

Cecil said, "Anabel, please. Ev is dead? Shot himself? What did you say?"

"They've told the Las Vegas police, but they don't think there's much chance—"

"Las Vegas?"

"Some *silly* name. Bedelia's. . . . He had a gun."

"I see," drawled Cecil (who knew where Bedelia's was). "And the cops have gone to the wrong—dump, you say?"

"The wrong place," said Anabel. "There's a dump here somewhere. And Pat. . . ."

She could feel that his hands had turned cold somehow. They began to release her. Cecil said, "There is a dump, Anabel. It's beyond those trees. Along that track."

"Have you . . . been?" Now she was not held and not leaning on him in any way at all. She was leaning on no one and nothing. Anabel was on her own feet. She said sharply, "Will you tell me, please?"

"Look," he said, "why don't you sit in the car? I'll go . . . I'll get. . . ."

"Is he there?" she demanded.

One of the man's eyebrows drew up. He cocked his pale head. His green eyes watched her. "Yes," he said, "he's down there."

He didn't look like a man who was telling bad news reluctantly because he felt sorry. He looked like a man who was trying out a little jab and watching to see the result.

Anabel felt a revulsion. She took two steps backward. She turned away from him. She started into the grove, along some ruts. She walked, then she began to skip along faster, in a half-stumble, half-run. Because this was the end of the road, the end of one world. She was almost there.

Cecil watched her go.

He'd seen a glimmer on his horizon. Ev was dead? The cops had gone to the wrong place? Twice over? They would not find Ev in time. They would not find O'Shea. Yet.

If Ev was dead, that left *only* O'Shea.

But Cecil knew where O'Shea was. And he was officially, you might say, already murdered. He was needing medicine, in the witch's house. Suppose he were to die in there? It would be the same murder. For which the cops already had the murderer's confession and his suicide.

Safe as houses.

Cecil thought he could manage his sister.

Risky? But the stakes were so high. Why not? He thought. When he had just been presented with what you might call a free murder. Right here. If there was time for it. If he could manage.

He had meant to divert Anabel and run. Well, she was diverted. He could see her. She had sat down upon the ground. Probably she was going to sit there and cry.

He could always say he'd been looking for a phone in the witch's house. What about the dog, though?

Ah, now. When there is a gift—of time, of chance—while the cops look in the wrong places, and Cecil was in the right place and smart enough to see his chance, he must be bold enough to take it!

Maybe around at the back of the house. There might be a way that he could get at O'Shea. Because if he could . . . if he could . . . and then phone Celia . . . Cecil was home free!

He slipped between the two cars and put a tree between him and the witch's house.

Anabel had come to the end. She was sitting on the brink of the arroyo, gazing down at a rubbish heap upon which had been thrown her husband's body. In a moment her sick and frightened, straining eyes would see it. Cast off. A piece of rubbish, like the rest. Then she would know, at last, that Pat himself, that gay and loving man, was not here at all. And not anywhere in this world.

At the back of the bungalow there was a window with a busted screen. Cecil, hugging the wall, could hear the dog carrying on somewhere inside, and the old woman talking. Mad? She must be. Well, the point was, could he do it?

He crept to the window, which was rather high off the ground. His eyes came a foot above the sill, but he couldn't see in. There was a blind hanging crookedly.

Cecil said, "O'Shea?"

Within a man's voice answered clearly, calmly, "That's more like it."

When Stan came into the store, Mr. Johanneson was leaning over the morning paper. "That was Mrs. O'Shea," he announced.

"I know," said Stan, astonished.

Johanneson glanced up at him. "I mean the woman who was in here yesterday."

"I know," said Stan again.

"You saw it in the paper? You figured it out too?"

"Huh?"

"Look here. Look here." The grocer rapped the paper with his knuckles. " 'PROF'S CAR WRECK IN PASS. The whereabouts of popular young instructor Elihu (Pat) O'Shea. . . .' You didn't even hear her say she was going 'where Pat was.' How did you—?"

"Yeah, but she said 'Pat'—just now."

"Huh?" It was Johanneson's turn to be bewildered.

Stan leaned on the paper. "A Rambler? But how could he—?"

"How could he what? That was some rain last Monday night."

But Stan said, "Wait a minute. Wait a minute. You see how they spell O'Shea, Mr. Johanneson? You see the initial?" Stan was hearing Jamie say, "The old witch has got him."

The grocer looked at the paper. He looked up.

Stan said, "Gee, Mr. Johanneson, maybe we better call the police, or something. Because Mrs. Pryde, she's *really* nutty today."

"O'Shea?"

There was no sound in the landscape. The house held sound, but not the land. The wild land baked, beyond the back of the house.

"Present. Future. What? Who's that?" said the voice in the house, closer than the dog's racket.

Cecil said, "I want to help you. But what about that dog?"

"Eh, Rex?" The voice was jubilant. "Anabel sent you," it proclaimed.

"Yeah. Right. Do you think you could get over here? To the back window?"

"Why, I might as well be over there as where I am," Pat said. "Maybe better." His head was light. "I'll give it the old try. If the good half of me can make it, stands to reason the other half will go along. Wouldn't you say? Friend? That's logical."

Pat slid his good left leg out of the bed. He struggled to lift himself and turn, so as to get his right leg over and out, but his right arm was such a big fat mess, he had no leverage.

". . . big fat mess," Pat muttered. "Now, I can't walk, you understand. I absolutely cannot walk. On *two* legs, I mean. That's out of the question. What is the question? *That* is the question."

Cecil waited.

Time passed.

Then Cecil's hands were through the window, batting the brittle, rustling blind aside. "Just close enough," he coaxed, "so that I can help you out. I've got a car. I'll get you to the car." (He would prefer to get this over with, right here. And then go virtuously around to the front door.) "I'm scared of the dog," he said.

"You're so right, friend," came the voice. "No you're not, either. Ought to be scared of the old woman."

"I am. I am," snapped Cecil. "Can you make it, O'Shea?"

"Why, I certainly can. Very happy to meet you. Halfway. Half. . . ."

Then there was a long silence within the room. The dog was barking. But the dog was not in that room. Was the dog out of the house? Cecil's toes began to feel for a hold on the wall. He got himself higher and thrust his head and shoulders in.

The man was collapsed, arched backwards over the edge of the bed. Strange sounds were coming from his arched and naked throat.

Cecil thought, Sixty seconds would do it!

He couldn't afford *not* to take the risk. Could he?

Must be inside the car, she thought. Inside the car, then. Or in the trunk of the car.

It was so silent here. The sun was shining. She could see right through the car, the way it was tilted, to the other side of it. There was a shoe down there but there wasn't any foot in the shoe.

It struck her that this was a beautiful place. What a mad thought! She lifted her eyes and saw the wild hills. She turned her head and saw the colonnades of the pale, barkless tree trunks. She could see, down a kind of *allée,* that there was a house, way off and a sound. The sound had made her turn her head. On the stoop of the old house there was the figure of a woman dressed in black, and beside her there was a big black dog. The woman looked like a witch.

Anabel got to her feet. She knew that in the back of her mind a lot of things were adding up, like a column of figures in plain arithmetic. But she didn't know what any of the items were.

Yes, *one.* Cecil Wahl had lied to her. He said he had seen. But he couldn't have seen. Because Anabel could not see. But how cruel!

Then there was the remnant of the uproar of the adrenalin or whatever . . . the aftermath of her shock, when the grocery boy had made her think for a moment that Pat was alive. And there was something. . . . And there was something. . . . Idea in somebody's head that wasn't *so.*

Suddenly her temper flared. Anabel began to take strides toward that house. Cecil Wahl wasn't visible. The two cars stood at the end of the road. She could see them.

Something was wrong with the picture.

Something was wrong with the whole setup. There was an idea in somebody's head that was not *so.*

Then she saw the woman duck back into her house, taking the dog with her. She saw it. The furtiveness of it. People lying to Anabel, hiding from her. . . .

Anabel was getting good and mad.

She began to run. She ran through the grove and through the gap in the fence where the gate hung crooked. She ran up on the stoop and she knocked, imperiously, at the door. The dog was barking furiously inside. Anabel was not afraid of dogs.

She saw a mad old face, bobbing at the window. Anabel didn't care that it was mad. "Let me in," she cried. "I want to *know.* Is Mr. Wahl in there?"

Mr. Wahl was climbing in at the bedroom window.

The old woman was muttering, undertone to the dog's noise. Anabel didn't care what she was muttering. She kept on knocking, hard and loud. She kept on calling, "Let me in." She pushed. She couldn't *wait!*

The door opened. There was the old woman and the big black

fierce dog, held at his collar not as much by her old hand as by her old authority.

"I am Anabel—"

"You are not," cut in the old woman ferociously. "He don't mean anything by that. He don't mean a thing in the world. So you git! You hear? You, girl? None of *you*. You don't bother me."

The dog was turning and twisting as if he, too, were mad. Or of two minds. As if there was more than one alien thing against which he must defend his mistress.

Where? Beyond that closed door, directly across this room? (The old witch has got him.)

Anabel said, "The police are coming."

"None of them," screeched the old woman. The dog's frenzy now turned her body. Anabel saw the back of her dress.

"You had better tell me," cried Anabel. *"Who* doesn't mean anything? By *what? Where is he?"*

"I'll set the dog on you!" the old woman shrieked. "Or anybody else. *Nobody* bothers me."

But Anabel said, "Me, either."

Her long legs scissored across the room, past the old woman and the struggling straining snarling beast, straight to the door that was closed.

Anabel opened it. The inner room was dimmer. But there were people. Anabel stepped out of the way of what light she had let in, through the door, and she saw a pair of hands. A pair of hands. In the air. Held out—fingers tensed—in the air.

Behind her the old woman screamed, "Get 'em, Rex. Eh, Rex? Get 'em! Get 'em!"

And the black dog came like a bullet, hit the door. The door whanged all the way open, to slam upon the wall.

Maclaren steered around the corner into Oleander Street. He had slowed, to take the turn. Suddenly there was a figure, semaphoring at the side of the road, beside a panel truck.

"Hey! Hey!" Stan yelled. (The police had told him that the police were coming. He recognized the *girl!*)

Maclaren braked and Carlson leaned.

"He's in the witch's house," Stan yelled. "O'Shea. O'Shea. And she's crazy and watch the dog!"

Maclaren tramped on the accelerator. His body was very solid, as Vee could sense. Carlson calmly loosened his jacket. He had a gun under there. His body was solid. Their calm was very solid. So was their competence. Maclaren was driving very fast, but carefully, too. He hit the horn. The car bounded on the twisting road.

Vee's heart was up. It was thrilling! But this was the way they *did*. They did what was to be done. Solidly, calmly, fast and sure.

She wanted to cry. She wanted to laugh.

They spun to a stop where the Olds was, and Mrs. Newcomb's car. "Cecil?" gasped Vee.

Carlson said to her, "Stay," as if she were a dog.

The two of them then, policemen, shoulder to shoulder, their guns ready, ran for the trouble, ran up on the stoop of the bungalow, because from inside there was the noise of screaming, the sound of violence.

Vee stayed in the car and said out loud, "Oh yes! Oh yes!" and couldn't have told what she meant.

Carlson hit the door. The first room was empty. The old woman was standing square in the bedroom door. She was screaming. She had a staff in her hand and it was raised high. She was going to whack something or somebody. Somebody on the bed.

Maclaren got the staff in his left hand and took it and the old woman to one side.

Carlson could see a man and a dog threshing on the dusty rug in there. The shade had been torn from the window, giving light to see by. Something had been broken. They threshed over broken glass. There was blood and the man was screaming. The dog was going to kill him, if once the dog could shift his jaws from the forearm, just at the shoulder, to the throat.

Carlson was quick and smart. He fell prone upon the floor, gun in hand, got the gun under the dog, and fired upward.

The dog died without making too much fuss about it.

The man screamed, "Get him off me! Get him off!" Carlson went on his knees to try to loosen the dead jaws. "Take it easy," he said to the white face and the green eyes of Cecil Wahl.

Carlson jumped about six inches when there was a *thunk* behind him. He looked and the dog was not twitching. The old woman had plunked her bones down on the floor beside the dog's carcass.

Maclaren was lifting, with gentle hands, the bare legs of a man up on the mattress. Anabel O'Shea was lying across the bed, holding the man with one arm over his chest and one over his thighs, holding him up and away from the late violence as best she could, leaving her back vulnerable to the old woman's staff. The blow had not fallen. Anabel forgot about it.

She sat up and took the man's head against her breast. "He is burning," she said clearly and calmly in the sudden silence. "Get the doctor. Call. Find the phone."

The man was unshaven; he was a very sick man; he looked as if he were dying. But he opened his eyes and croaked reproachfully, "I would have called you."

"Don't you think I know that?" said Anabel, and her voice was so . . . so . . . something, Carlson's young eyes stung.

She said, "Will you get some help please? Will you hurry?"

Carlson looked down at the man on the floor, who was lying in the posture of the Dying Gladiator, heaving at the chest.

Maclaren said, "I'll watch it."

So Carlson stepped over the dead dog and around the old woman, who was stroking the dog's fur and muttering.

"Good dog. Eh, Rex? Be fine. You'll see." Or something like that.

Carlson tore out to the car and grabbed the telephone. "O'Shea's alive in there," he told Vee. "Cecil Wahl's been bit."

Stan Simmons was standing at the other side, looking in. "Oh, my gosh," he was saying. "Oh, my gosh, why didn't you ask me? I saw him. Jamie, he saw both of them."

"Went out on that already," the voice said on the phone. "Ambulance to the end of Oleander. Ought to be there in half a second."

So Carlson asked for more men, more help.

"Hey Carlson"—the voice held him—"what do you know? Adams chickened out on the suicide deal. They found him—where you said."

Carlson put up the phone.

Stan said, "Listen. I *told* them there was a sick man out here in the witch's house. O'Shea, I told them."

Vee hissed at him. "*Sssh.*" She said to Carlson, "I heard. You *go*." Because she understood.

Carlson went racing back into the bungalow.

Cecil Wahl was sitting on the straight chair now, his jacket and shirt pulled away from his wounds. He was saying to Maclaren, "I thought I could get him out of the house, away from the dog. I might have done it if *she* hadn't come flying in like that, letting the damn dog in."

He glanced nervously and resentfully at Anabel.

She wasn't listening. She was touching her husband's face in certain small caresses, sending as best she could her life to him.

Cecil got up. "I can drive. My sister's in the hospital. I think—"

"Your sister is dead," said Carlson. "She jumped from the fourth floor."

Maclaren looked quickly at Carlson, who was having no pity, to whom this Cecil was beginning to smell.

Cecil's green eyes winced, briefly. "Oh, no! Poor C." But the cold eyes slanted to glance at the unshaven dirty haggard unconscious face of Pat O'Shea, a pitiful sight on Anabel's breast. "Will he live?" asked Cecil.

Nobody answered. Cecil glanced at Carlson. He held out his hand. "I guess you saved my life, pal," he said heartily, "corny though it sounds." (One young buck to another.)

But Carlson did not take the offered hand. He said, "Don't you care why?"

"Why?" Eyebrow went up.

"Why your sister jumped?"

"Oh, well. . . ." Cecil swayed. "Her husband. . . ."

"You think so?" said Carlson.

"Best I get out from underfoot," said Cecil. "You've got your hands full here." He staggered; he was trying to be charming.

"Better wait on a doctor," said Maclaren mildly. "And there'll be a few questions."

Cecil took a step. Carlson snapped, "You heard the lieutenant. And by the way, your sister's husband isn't dead. They've got *him*."

Cecil's face went very still. He was hunched protectively over his own wounds. Now he swayed and went down. Suddenly he was sitting on the floor. His right hand began to grope. It found the thin shards from the lamp chimney. It took Carlson a moment or two to realize that the man was busily and deliberately mutilating his own fingertips.

When he saw it, he stopped it; there was noise outside. Ambulance. Then a police car. Then another. People.

They took O'Shea. They took the old woman. They took the dog's body.

Carlson stood beside Cecil Wahl. Maclaren said, "How did you know O'Shea was in there? Why did you have your hands on his throat? What was the idea?"

"Not I," said Cecil. "Not I."

"I saw," said Maclaren quietly, "the red marks of your ten fingers. Nobody else was in this room."

"He's got fingers," snapped Cecil. "O'Shea has."

"Only five," said Maclaren.

After that, Cecil would not speak. They took him away. They took Vee Adams back to town; a uniformed man drove her in Mrs. King's Oldsmobile.

Because nobody—not all the converging agents of law, order, and mercy, separately or together—had been able to take Mr. O'Shea anywhere without also taking Mrs. O'Shea.

Friday Evening

VEE ADAMS WAS SITTING with Carlson in his car. Mrs. King was awfully nice, but they wanted to talk. About Carlson, who had always had a desire to get into police work, although he'd never said too much about the way he felt to anyone before. People don't always understand.

About Vee, who was moving into the dormitory tomorrow. The Provost had fixed it, for the rest of the term. After that, it depended, some, on where and how her father was.

"I guess you saw your father, did you, Violet?"

"This afternoon. He doesn't seem to know what's happened. It was awfully hard to talk to him at all."

"I'll bet."

"You know, Beau, I don't feel as if I ever really, in my whole life, knew him. Not himself. My own mother, well . . . she always wanted things to be nice. Maybe it wasn't fair. I could have been nicer *to* him."

"Kids," said Carlson, "get impressions. I guess they have to be too—well, you know—too simple? I had a stepfather."

"Did you?" She turned to him in sympathy and wonder.

"We got along fine. He died last year. See, my Mom divorced my real father when I was six years old. She's been dead three years."

"We're both kind of orphans then," Vee said. "My father's alive, of course."

"So is mine," said Carlson. "It's not generally known."

He fell silent but she knew there was something else he wanted to tell her.

"Beau? Oh, I'm sorry. I keep using that old nickname because . . . I just don't even know your real name."

"My real name is James Maclaren," said Beau Carlson, tasting it.

The Provost couldn't do a thing with Mr. and Mrs. O'Shea. He wanted to discuss the whole affair with maturity, compassion, mercy, and understanding. They wouldn't even be serious.

As far as the theft was concerned, he had told them, the university would no doubt recover the cost, and, after all, the poor woman was dead. The poor man—pitiable.

"Pity me?" said Pat. He was clean-shaven and there was a neat piece of tape over the healing cut on his scalp. His right leg was strung up in one of the intricate contraptions that a hospital provides. His right arm lay quiet, but Anabel was tucked under his good left arm. Up on the hospital bed, she was—committed not to jiggle, but with her ankles crossed insouciantly, and looking very pleased to be there, not caring who knew it.

"He clobbered you good," she said.

"Well actually, what he did, he hit me in the head."

"Stole the car."

"Stole the money. You always forget the money, Anabel."

"How much?" she asked shrewdly.

"Oh, just the two or three hundred I usually carry—for tips, you know."

"Then he goes and casts our perfectly good car off the mountain."

"Had that dent in the right fender. Needed a lube, too. Still. . . ."

"Stole your raincoat. Only six years old."

"And my hat, don't forget. A dollar eighty-nine."

"A dollar ninety-eight," cried Anabel.

The Provost sighed. He knew all the anguish they were leaving out. They were good kids.

"She argues, all the time," Pat told the Provost happily, "but she sure smells good. So do I. *I* feel like a blooming rose. I tell you, there's nothing like a hospital."

"For fainting?" said Anabel.

"Well, it ain't hay."

The Provost was absolutely lost, not being an "Alice" fan.

Maclaren put his head in. "Dropped by to see how you are doing, Mrs. O'Shea. Mr. O'Shea. Mr. Drinkwater."

The Provost said he was just leaving. He thought he might as well. O'Shea was, no doubt, still a little feverish, and his wife giddy with relief. He could forgive them. As he went out, he heard Pat say loudly, "Hey, Lieutenant, how can we railroad Adams into some cushy hospital? Do we do a deal? Who do we have to bribe?"

"Whom," said Anabel.

The Provost was halfway down in the elevator before he realized that there already had been compassion, mercy, and understanding. It would be only a nine days' wonder, then.

He braced himself. The Press was downstairs. Well. His school was a good school, a great school. Those young people, up there, were good young people. The Adams girl was a good kid. There were thousands of good kids on his campus. Many fine teachers. None of them were going to be hurt if he could help it. *He'd* deal with the Press. He had his skills.

"Hey," said Pat joyously. "We have here none other than the Answer Man. Where's our list, Anabel?"

Maclaren said he had just retired, as of one hour.

"Never mind. Sit down. There are a few little points. I'm not going to ask you why Celia Adams did the Dutch and Everett didn't."

"I spent some time with him today. He doesn't know." Maclaren's beautiful voice was kind.

"*Was* Celia Adams mixed up in an old murder?"

"We don't know."

"*Yet,* you mean. OK. Why did my car go off the mountain?"

"We don't—"

"Yeah. Yeah. But what does Adams say?"

"As near as I can figure, he skidded. Rear wheels were on the edge. He got scared, for a guess—afraid that somebody *would* stop to help him. Don't know, really."

"This is proceeding famously," said Pat. "Eh, what? Why was my wallet mailed in Barstow?"

"We don't know," said Maclaren flatly.

"Somebody put it in a mailbox," said Anabel, mischievously. "I'll *bet* that's it."

"It's a theory." Maclaren grinned at her fondly. "Maybe Adams dropped it on the bus. Somebody kicked it off in Barstow."

"And we'll never know," said Pat. "OK. Why the dickens was Cecil Wahl out at the end of Oleander on Thursday morning?"

"Or in the night before?" chimed Anabel. "Jamie saw him. That's the 'chicken' boy. I drove Mother and Sue out there today and talked to him. Had to make it clear that *I* was married to the 'nice man.'"

"Anabel," said Pat, "Kindly stop yakking?"

But Maclaren was shaking his head. "We don't know why Cecil was out there. He's not talking."

"He was mixed up in the murder with his sister, wasn't he?" demanded Anabel.

"We don't know," said Maclaren. "But we will probably find that out. We're hanging on to him. How is your throat?"

"Fine. Fine. He didn't have time to get set, really, before Anabel let the dog in."

"Nobody needs to kid me," said Anabel cheerfully. "I let Cecil in. Well, didn't I? Something I said. Then I went off and gave him his chance." She didn't sound too upset.

"You never know, sweetheart," said Pat soothingly. Then to Maclaren. "He messed up his fingerprints. A guilty conscience?"

"Well, they're not the only kind of evidence in the world," said Maclaren comfortably.

"Anyhow, you've got them now," said Anabel.

Maclaren said, "Wait a minute. We have?"

"Don't *you know?*" Anabel laughed with delight. "Well, let me tell you. Cecil bought a box of chocolate-covered cookies. He left them in the store. Stan gave them to Jamie. Jamie conked out all day yesterday; he was pooped. So nobody ate them. Well, Cecil had touched one and there it was. Now of course," she continued, looking wise, "that may not stand up as evidence in court, but it *is* a clue."

"Who told you this, Mrs. O'Shea?"

"Why your . . . I don't know his first name. Carlson."

"James," said Maclaren, his kind ugly face suffused with a foolish tenderness.

"He was out on Oleander Street, being a regular beaver," Anabel told him.

Pat said suddenly, "How is the old lady?"

"She can't live alone."

"No more?" said Pat sadly.

"She won't be kicked around. She's still saying he isn't dead."

"Johnny Pryde?"

"Yes—but I meant the dog."

"Pour soul," said Pat. "One rotten son."

"And that was the end of her," said Anabel. (She would feel pity some other day.) "Wow, but I'm lucky. Or else, smart."

"Lucky is what *you* are," said Pat severely. "A fifty percent chance that dog would have jumped you."

"A thirty-three and a third percent chance," said Anabel indulgently, and then to Maclaren. "He teaches math, you know."

Maclaren was laughing, when Miss More put her starched head in. "Visiting hours are over," she caroled. Then shocked, "Mrs. O'Shea! Not on the *bed!*"

Anabel reversed the position of her ankles delicately. "How kind of you to come and tell us," she caroled dangerously.

Maclaren was a man who knew when a rule needed breaking and a lie needed telling. "I'm from the police. I wonder. . . ." He took the starched one firmly away.

Mischief

Chapter One

A Mr. Peter O. Jones, the editor and publisher of the Brennerton *Star-Gazette,* was standing in a bathroom in a hotel in New York City, scrubbing his nails. Through the open door, his wife, Ruth, saw his naked neck stiffen, saw him fix his image with his eye, heard him declaim over the rush of running water, "Ladies and gentlemen. . . ." She winked at Bunny.

Ruth in her long petticoat was sitting at the dressing table, having resolved to be as perfectly, as exquisitely groomed as ever a woman was in the world, this night. She was very gently powdering her thin bare shoulders. Every fair hair on her head was already in shining order. Her carefully reddened lips kept smiling because she knew this long-drawn-out ritual, this polishing of every tooth and every toenail, was only to heighten the wonderful fun.

It was The Night. Ruth sighed, from a complexity of emotions.

What a formula, she thought, is a hotel room. Everything one needs. And every detail pursued with such heavy-handed comfort, such gloomy good taste, it becomes a formula for luxury. The twin beds, severely clean, austerely spread. The lamp and the telephone between. Dresser, dressing table. Desk and desk chair (if the human unit needs to take his pen in hand). Bank of windows, on a court, with the big steam radiator across below them, metal topped. Curtains in hotel-ecru. Draperies in hotel-brocade. Easy chair in hotel-maroon. The standing lamp. The standing ashtray, that hideous useful thing. The vast empty closet. And the bath. The tiles. The big towels. The small soap. The very hot water.

Over this basic formula they had spread the froth of their preparations, in that jolly disorder that a hotel room permits. Her rose-colored evening dress swung with the hook of its hanger over the closet door. Peter's rummaged suitcase stood open on the luggage bench and his things were strewn on his bed. The dresser top was piled with stuff that at home would have been hidden in the drawers. Powder and ashes had spilled gloriously on the carpet. All the lights were blazing.

All the lights were blazing in Bunny's room, too, the adjoining room that was exactly like this one, except that left was right and maroon was blue.

Peter turned the water off, reached for a towel, stood in the bathroom door in singlet and his dress trousers with his suspenders hanging down over his rump. Turning out his patent-leather toes, he bowed, "Ladies and gentlemen. . . ." He began to pantomime, clowning for Bunny. Ruth thought, fondly, How clever he is! She turned to watch what she loved to see, the smooth skin of Bunny's face ripple and twinkle as it always did before the giggle came out.

Bunny was nine. Her dark brows went up at the outside just like Peter's. In her blue woolly robe, Bunny hunched on the foot of Ruth's bed, her arms around her ankles, and one bunny-slipper stepping on the toe of the other. Her dark hair went smoothly back into the fat braids, so often living and warm in Ruth's hands. Ruth's heart felt as if something squeezed it, quickly, and as quickly let it go.

Peter, with a fine-flung gesture, called down fire from heaven to be witness to his wordless passion, and bowed to make-believe applause. Bunny took her cue, let go her ankles, clapped once, lost her balance, and toppled over, giggling. "You see!" said Peter, poking the blue bundle on the bed in a ticklish spot. "Going to mow 'em down!"

"Peter," said Ruth in fright and curiosity, "do you know what you're going to say?"

"Well, I know what I'm going to *do*. I'm going to rise up and take a good grip on the rug with my toes and open my mouth. Oh, sure, I know what I'm going to say, in a way. I don't know how I'm going to put it, if that's what you mean."

"Oh, Peter!" She sucked in breath. She didn't understand how anyone could do such a thing as make a speech. Something made her heart jump at the mere thought of it.

"Don't get me wrong," said Peter. "I'm terrified." She knew he was. She knew he'd make the speech, nevertheless, and do it well.

She knew, too, that her own tense partisanship was helpful to him, and even her fright was a channel that drew off some of his.

". . . time is it, honey?"

"Quarter after six." Their eyes met briefly. Hers with a flick of worry. His with that quick dark reassurance.

He picked his dress shirt with the studs all in place off his bed. "Which one of you two dames wants to button me up?"

"Me!" squealed Bunny. So Peter sat on the hard rim of the footboard. "Daddy, why does your shirt pretend it buttons in the front when it buttons in the back?"

"Civilization. Tradition in the front. Business in the back. How you doing?"

"OK," said Bunny with a puff of effort. She never questioned Peter's polysyllables.

Business, thought Ruth darkly. "Peter," she said, "I hope you know what I think of your sister, Betty!"

"I couldn't print it," he answered promptly.

"Business," said Ruth as darkly as she felt. "Her and her business appointment! On a Saturday night! *I* think she's got a heavy date."

"Can't tell," said Peter lightly, cautiously.

"I don't see *how* she could break her date with us! Do you? Really?"

Ruth heard again Betty's high and somewhat affected voice on the phone. ". . . Terribly sorry, darling. Of course, if you simply can't get anyone, I'll cut this thing and I *will* come. . . . But I thought perhaps, if you *could* . . . ?" and Ruth stiffened once more with that shock and the anger.

Important! What kind of business appointment could be so important for Betty Jones—the silly little chit! Here in New York six months, with her job that paid what? fifty dollars a week? What on earth could Betty Jones do on a Saturday night that could be Important Business?

For years, now, Ruth had resented but been unable to combat her sister-in-law's manner that assumed, so ignorantly and unjustly, that Ruth was done for. Ruth's goose was cooked. Oh, Ruth was buried with the rank and file, and the drab stones all said Housewife, that drab and piteous label. There was no use. One could only wait and someday. . . .

"We'll try, Betty," Ruth had said, very coldly, and hung up and turned an anguished face to Peter. What if she had to plead and beg? Or not go to the ball?

But Peter had fixed it. By some hocus-pocus, he had fared forth into the halls and passages of the hotel, and he had fixed it. And Ruth had called Betty back and said, coolly, "Don't bother. . . ."

"But how could she welsh like that," murmured Ruth, "when she knows. . . ."

"Hold still, Daddy."

"Excuse it, pet. Look, Ruthie. Sis takes herself awful hard as the career girl. You know that. Someday . . ." Their eyes met and the gleam in Peter's was satisfactory. "Besides," he went on, "I don't suppose she thinks this convention amounts to much. Corn-fed gathering of country editors. Provincial, hm?"

"There you are!" said Ruth indignantly. "There *you* sit, seeing *her* point of view. But can she see ours? Night of the banquet, and your speech, and it was all arranged weeks ago. What if we couldn't have gotten anybody?"

"She did say she'd come if she must. No use to be bitter."

Ruth bit her lip.

"Don't fret, Cinderella," grinned Peter. "You shall go to the ball."

Ruth blinked, because he was right . . . no use to be bitter. She kicked off her mules and bent to reach for her evening shoes, feeling the soft brush of her own hair on her bare shoulders. "Oh, dem golden slippers . . ." whistled Peter, and Ruth saw Bunny's solemn eyes peek around his shoulder. For the audience, Ruth fell back into the rhythm. She arched her pretty feet and put them slowly, ceremoniously into her golden slippers.

"Someday," said Peter, with his dark eyes glowing, "do you know, girls, who's going to be putting on her golden slippers to go to the ball?"

"Bunny O. Jones," said Ruth at once.

"And who's going to be sitting with her bedroom slippers on, watching her?"

"You and me," Ruth said. Their eyes met, smiled. We'll grow old. It won't matter.

Bunny said, in a practical voice, "Is my sitter coming pretty soon?"

Peter pinched the toes in the furry slippers. "Pretty soon. And you're going to go to sleep in your room with two beds, one for each pigtail. And what are you going to do in the morning?"

"Telephone," said Bunny.

"And say?"

"Room service."

"And then?"

"This is Miss Bunny O. Jones. I want my breakfast, please."

"In room?"

"Room 809." Bunny flushed and started over again. " 'This is Miss Bunny O. Jones in room 809. I want my breakfast, please.' And if they don't know what I'm talking about, I'll say, 'My Daddy, Mr. Peter O. Jones, ordered it last night.' "

"And when the man knocks on the door?"

"I'll unlock the door and run quick back in my bed."

"That's right. The key's in your door. And then they'll bring in the wagon."

"Daddy, it isn't a real wagon."

"No horses, I'll admit. A mere pushing type of wagon. And on it's going to be a whole bunch of silver dishes and your orange juice sitting in the biggest mess of cracked ice you ever saw, enough to make about four snowballs. And you'll eat your breakfast, putting on as much sugar and cream as you want, and after a while Daddy will groan and wake up."

"And tomorrow's the day," Ruth said, "you're going to the magic eating store."

"I don't believe it!" said Bunny, but her face was rippling.

"Oh, you don't, Miss Bunny O. Jones? Well, you'll see!"

They all three had the middle initial O. Ruth's name had been Olsen, and Peter was delighted with the coincidence. People named Jones, claimed he, had to do something. Peter O. Jones, he always was. And Bunny ran it together so that, more than once, school records had used the apostrophe.

"Quite a lot like a zoo," Peter was explaining. "A whole bunch of little glass cages and in one there's a hot meat pie, and in the other there's a big fat salad, and all you do is put in your nickels and presto chango."

"But you have to have nickels," said Bunny shrewdly.

"Well, yes," said her daddy. "In the olden days, a magic wand was the thing. Now, of course, it's nickels." He grinned. He had begun the struggle with his collar.

"Peter," said Ruth suddenly, "do you believe in the elevator boy? Do you believe in his niece? Is she coming?"

"Certainly," said Peter, with his brows winging. "Why would he say so?"

"I don't know—" For Ruth, the room was rocking. The bright box it was had become dreamlike. And the city over which it hung was fabulous and all its denizens were phantoms.

"Said she'd be glad to," Peter was saying. "First, I spoke to that colored woman, that awfully nice-looking woman, the one who was so friendly? But she's—uh—dated up. So this Eddie overheard us and he offered. Glad to earn the money, he said."

"It takes nickels . . . ?" murmured Ruth.

"Papa's wand. Imagine, hon. This Eddie's been running the same elevator for fourteen years. You know which one he is, don't you?"

"I guess. . . ."

"Lives up in the Bronx. No children, he told me. He'll tell you, at the drop of a hat. Speaks fondly of his wife. Must be a nice woman. This girl, now . . . they seem to have taken her in out of the goodness of their hearts since his brother died." Peter sucked his cheek. "Fourteen years, up and down. And he still runs that elevator as if his heart was in it to do it perfectly. I've seen 'em so blasé—make your hair curl. Wonder what he gets a week?"

Ruth sighed. Her momentary feeling that it was all myth was blown away. The little man who ran the elevator was real, of course . . . a human being, with a life, a wife, a budget . . . with brothers and sisters like everybody else and a niece to oblige. It was just like home, after all. You needed somebody. You asked around. It was just like asking the Johnstones who might say all their sitters were busy but they knew someone who knew somebody. You set up a kind of chain of inquiry and after a while it dredged up what you wanted. People were people and they passed the word and obliged each other and that was the way it went all over the world, truly.

"The niece comes from the Middle West someplace," Peter was saying. "Experienced, he says. I suppose a little extra means something in a setup like that."

Ruth thought, all at once, that it was better to be paying someone, hiring someone, having the leverage of that power, than taking such a one as Betty's time for free. She smiled and reached out her hand.

"Oh boy," said her husband, "comes the twelve-dollar smell!"

"Twelve dollars and fifty cents, don't forget!" Ruth took the tiny stopper out, touched her shoulders with the precious stuff.

Peter bent over and sniffed violently. He said in her ear, "Would a couple of symmetrical toothmarks look good?" She saw herself laughing, in the glass, and Peter's dark keen face against her yellow hair.

". . . me smell," demanded Bunny.

So Ruth crossed with her pretty petticoat swirling, turned the plump little paw, touched the back of it with the perfume. "Deelicious!" said Bunny, sniffing violently as her daddy had done.

Ruth looked down at the white clean part in the dark hair. All of a sudden, she saw their two connecting rooms, the two bright boxes on the inner rim of the doughnut of this eighth floor, suspended above the boiling city. And the rising noise surrounded them like smoke . . . the honks, clangs, shouts and murmurs, the sound and fury . . . and her heart was squeezed again. And she thought, We couldn't have left her two thousand miles away . . . but we shouldn't have brought her . . . but we couldn't have left her. . . .

The Hotel Majestic was neither large nor small, neither cheap nor costly. Not the last word, it wasn't dowdy, either. It was conservative. It tried to be smart about it, in a modest way. It took the middle road. Even the elevators, although they ran smoothly, did so with a modest speed.

Eddie Munro stopped for a light at the eighth floor. A young man got on, turned at once to face the door. They sank downward in silence.

Out of the corners of their eyes, they typed each other, quickly. Eddie saw the easy grace of a tall body, the arrogant carriage of the high head, the crew cut that was somehow arrogant, too. The sharp cut of the good-looking face, the long nose with the faint flare at the nostrils, the cool gray eyes, long lashed, and almost beautiful in that hard-boned young face, but very cool and asking for nothing. A type. One of those young men who had come out of the late war with that drive, that cutting quality, as if they had shucked off human uncertainties and were aimed and hurtling toward something in the future about which they seemed very sure.

His name was Jed Towers. It was his last night in New York. He had a dinner date.

If he saw the little man out of the corner of his cool eye, it was just a little man, with his shoulders pulled back from his narrow chest in a frozen strut. With a gray face. With pale hair that never had any color to lose, lying long and lank over the bald part. Pale eyes that blinked often, as if Eddie Munro were never quite sure of anything.

The car stopped smoothly at the main floor. Jed put his key on the desk without interrupting the long fluid strides that were taking him to the outside, to the city, to the evening.

Eddie ran a nervous glance around the quiet lobby. He said to the next boy, "Gotta make a phone call. Watch it, will you?" He scuttled around a bend of wall with his nickel in his hand already.

"Marie?"

"Yeah, Eddie?" said his wife's placid voice.

"She leave?"

"She went, yeah, sure."

"How long ago?"

"In plenty of time," his wife said. Everything she said carried the overtone, Don't worry, Eddie.

"Take the subway?"

"Of course."

"Listen, Marie, I think maybe I oughta stay around after I'm off. Folks might be late. Some kind of big shindig, the man said. OK?"

"OK."

"I think I oughta stay and bring her home, don't you?"

"Good idea, Eddie."

"You do think the whole idea's a good idea, Marie? She can earn a little money? You know? Get started?"

"Sure it is, Eddie."

"She—uh—liked the idea, didn't she?"

"Sure she did."

"Well . . . uh . . ." He didn't want to let go of the wire leading to Marie and her voice saying, Sure.

"Say, Eddie. . . ."

"Yeah?"

"I think maybe I'll go to the show. Miz Martin said she'd go with me." Eddie squirmed in the booth, blinking rapidly. His wife's voice went on. "That picture we didn't think we'd better take *her?* You know?"

"Yeah."

"So I thought I'd go—got the chance."

"Oh. Well. Yeah. Sure."

"Don't worry, Eddie," Marie soothed. "I'll be home long before you and Nell, probably."

"Sure. Sure," he said. He heard his wife's tiny sigh whispering on the wire. "Go ahead," he said, vigorously. "Have a good time."

"It'll be OK," she told him. (Don't worry, Eddie.)

He went around the wall to his car. His eyes searched toward the revolving door, across the depth of the lobby. He threw back his shoulders, trying to stand erect, to look as if he were perfectly sure.

In 807, Ruth slipped the rose-colored frivolity off its hanger and expertly lowered it past her shining hair. Peter's strong fingers zipped her up the back. She made her curtsy to the audience.

"Something like a princess," said Peter judiciously, "don't you think?"

"Zactly," said the audience solemnly.

Ruth kissed the back of the audience's neck. "And now!" she cried. Oh, they were clowning for the audience, and if the audience was having fun, so were they!

"Ah *ha!*" Peter made fending, clear-the-decks motions with both hands. He took up his ridiculous garment. Ruth skipped to hold it for him. Peter wiggled in and patted the flying front sections.

"You said it was *tails!*" said the audience in high sweet scorn.

"You don't think so?" said Peter. He put both hands under the coat at the back and suddenly he was marching up and down with a Groucho Marx kind of crouch in his knees and his tails were flapping.

The audience was convulsed. It rolled over in a helpless giggling heap. Bunny wasn't (zactly), thought Ruth, a pretty little girl, but how beautiful she was, laughing! How irresistible!

And she herself gasped, "Peter, oh stop!"

"O. Jones."

"Oh, stop! I'll ruin my mascara. Oh *my!*"

The whole long, sweet, slow, mock-solemn ceremony of dressing for The Night crescendoed in hilarity.

Somebody knocked gently on the door.

Something squeezed Ruth's heart quickly, and as quickly let it go, so that it staggered.

Chapter Two

"MR. JONES, here we are, sir." Eddie's bright blinking eye, the thrust of his neck, were as of a mouse at the door.

"Oh, yes, Eddie. Right on time. How de do. Come in."

"This here's my niece, Nell Munro. Nell?" Eddie came in, too.

"How de do, Nell." Peter's tails were a graceful appendage to the Speaker of the Evening. Ruth, herself, moved toward them, the gracious young matron. All the fizz had gone out of the room.

"Good evening, Nell," she said. "It was nice of you to come on such short notice. Had you very far?"

"Don't take long on the subway," Eddie said. His Adam's apple jumped. He stood with his skinny shoulders thrust well back. "Really don't take long at all. She came right straight down." He seemed proud of this.

The girl, Nell, said nothing. She looked to be nineteen or twenty. She stood demurely with her ankles tight together. Her shoes were shabby black pumps with medium heels. Her head was bent, her lashes lowered. Her hair was the color of a lion's hide, cut short, not very curly. She wore no hat, a navy blue coat of a conservative cut and a little too big for her. Her hands were folded on a black handbag and Ruth was pleased to see that the nails were bare. Then she hooted at herself for so quaint a connecting of character with nail polish, for, after all, her own nails were a glossy rose, the shade of her frock. Still. . . .

"Won't you take your coat off, Nell?"

Eddie said, "Take your coat off, Nell. Go ahead." The girl wore a neat dark-silk dress. She held the coat on her arm as if she didn't know what to do with it.

"Just put it here, won't you?" purred Ruth. "And your bag, too? I suppose you've sat with children before, Nell?"

"She did, back in Indiana," said Eddie. "Did it a lot. Not around here, so much. She only came East about six months ago."

"Is that so?"

"She's living with me and my wife, now. My brother's girl. . . ."

"And do you like it here, Nell?"

"She likes it fine," said Eddie. "We've got room in the apartment, plenty of room for her. My wife's real glad to have her."

Is the girl mute? Ruth wondered. Eddie's interposing chatter was nervous, as if it covered something lumpish and obstinate in the girl, who was not helping. As one ought to chatter, and push time past this kind of stoppage in its current.

Eddie said, "What I wannida say, I'll *be* here in the hotel. I mean, I'm going to be around, see? So if you folks are going to be late, you don't need to worry."

"We may not be so very late," said Peter smoothly. The effect was as if he said, What are you talking about? He had a towel in one hand and was swiping it recklessly across the shining toes of his evening shoes.

"What I mean," Eddie blinked, "I can take Nell home, see?"

Peter looked up, drawled, "That's nice of you." Ruth heard his surprised pleasure. The job of taking the sitter home is one of the meanest chores that falls to the lot of the married male. "But I'd have seen her home, of course," said Peter virtuously.

Ruth was, at the moment, turning. She thought the pupils moved under the lowered lashes in that bent face. She said, pushing brightly at the sluggishness of things, "Bunny, dear. Nell, this is Bunny and Bunny, this is Nell."

"Hello," said Bunny.

"Hello," the girl said. Her voice was low and colorless, but at least it worked. She spoke.

"My wife, see," Eddie was saying, "took a notion to go to the show so I might's well wait around." Swallowing made a commotion in his skinny neck. "We was thinking it might be a real nice idea for Nell. There's a lot of guests bring their children. And me being right here, why, it ought to work out good."

He showed no sign of going back to his elevator. An anxious little man, the kind who keeps explaining himself, although nobody cares. Terribly concerned to do the right thing. The conscientious kind.

"Suppose we show Nell your room, Bun?" Ruth led them. "You see, this door can be left a little bit ajar because Bunny does like to go to sleep in the dark. I thought *you* could sit in here, Nell, in our room, where you can be more comfortable."

Bunny had marched ahead of them into 809. Now she threw one leg possessively over the edge of one of the beds, the one on which her stuffed dog from home was already established.

"Perhaps she ought to turn in quite soon now," Ruth said gently. "She's had a pretty exciting day, and tomorrow we have all sorts of plans. Perhaps you'd read her a story? If you don't mind?"

"No, ma'am," said Nell passively.

"That'll be nice, won't it, Bun?" It *was* like pushing, pushing something heavy. Ruth said with a bright smile, "Suppose you see if Nell would like some candy."

Bunny got the box, offered it, as Ruth had taught her, with a gracious little bend of her small body. Nell said, "Thanks a lot." And snatched. Ruth felt her heart lighten. Surely that was nice of her. That held some understanding. No grown person could care that much for candy. That greedy quickness must have been exaggerated for the child's sake.

"You're welcome." Bunny dipped in herself, companionably.

Ruth felt easier. "Bunny's such a big girl," she went on, "there really won't be anything to *do*." She realized that Eddie's voice and Peter's monosyllables were still going on behind her. "Bunny's bathroom is over there, of course." Ruth stepped to dim down the lights, leaving the lamp between the beds. "And this door," she waved at the exit from 809 to the corridor, "is locked, of course. Now, Bunny's to have one more piece of candy and then she's to brush her teeth and have her story and by that time I expect she'll be pretty sleepy." She touched the little girl's munching cheek. She looked back through the connecting door.

Eddie's high voice said clearly, "Well—uh—probably I'll look in on Nell, once in a while, if that's all right with you folks."

"Surely." Peter picked up his wallet. Ruth could tell from his back that he was both annoyed and resigned. "Well—uh—thanks very much."

"No, sir." Eddie backed away from the dollar bill. "No, I'm glad to do it, sir. It's such a good idea for Nell. You just pay her what she earns. Fifty cents an hour. And that'll be fine. That's the arrangement. Nell's mighty glad to have a chance to earn a little something. It's going to work out real nice for her. So—uh—" he looked rather defiantly past Peter. "You folks go on out and have a good evening, now."

Ruth guessed he was speaking to her. "Thanks very much, Mr. Munro. Good night."

"Good night. Uh—good night. Have a good time now, Mr. and Mrs. Jones." His hand hovered in a kind of admonishing gesture. It fell. At last, he was gone.

"OK, Ruth?" said Peter with a touch of impatience.

"In a minute. Nell?" Summoned, the girl moved. Ruth could hear Bunny making a great splutter, brushing her teeth. "Peter, do you mind looking up the number where we are going to be? Where we can be reached? We'll just leave it by the phone in here, Nell, and if there is anything at all, why, you *can* call us. You must remember to ask for Peter O. Jones. Don't forget the O. It takes so long to comb out the Joneses otherwise." She laughed.

Nell said without humor. "Yes, ma'am."

Ruth began to turn off lights in 807, leaving only the standing lamp over the big maroon chair and the little lamp between the beds. "That's enough, Nell?" The girl nodded. "And if you'd like something to read, there are all these magazines. And please help yourself to the candy. And if you get drowsy, you must lie down in here. I'm sure that will be all right. And," she lowered her voice discreetly, "perhaps you had better use this bathroom. Now, is there anything I've forgotten?"

She stood in all her finery, her brow creased just a little, feeling unsatisfied. The girl had said so little. Yet, what was there for her to say? Something, thought Ruth impatiently, some little thing volunteered . . . *anything* to show she's taking hold! "Can *you* think of anything else?" she prodded.

The girl's head was not so bent anymore. Her face was wide at the eyes with high cheek bones, and the eyes were large and a trifle aslant. Her chin was small and pointed and her mouth was tiny. The face was not made up, and the skin had a creamy yellow-or-peach undertone.

She wasn't bad-looking, Ruth thought with surprise. In fact, she might have been stunning, in an odd, provocative way. Even her figure was good under that ill-fitting dress, now that she was standing more erect, not so meekly bent. The eyes were blue. There was too much blue in them, as if the seeing center were too small, the band of color wider than it needed to be. The tawny hair straggled over her ears, but Ruth noticed that they were tiny and tight to the head.

"I guess you've thought of everything," Nell said. The tiny mouth seemed to let itself go into a reluctant, a grudging smile. Her teeth were fine.

Ruth watched her. For just a flash, she wondered if, in that perfectly flat sentence, there had been some mischief lying low, a trace of teasing, a breath of sarcasm.

"Better get going." Peter moved, full of energy. "There's the number, Nell, on this paper. Ask them to page us. Doubt if you'll need it. *We* may call up, so if the phone rings. . . ." He tapped the slip of paper on the phone table. He started briskly for the closet. The whole world, for Ruth, seemed to take up where it had left off.

Bunny was curled around the jamb of the connecting door, toothpaste lingering on her lips. "Pop into bed, baby," Ruth said. "And Nell will read to you awhile."

Herself in shadow, she watched them obey . . . Bunny peel out of her robe, climb in and pull the covers up, toss her pigtails behind . . . watched the girl move nearer and seat herself tentatively, rather uncertainly, on the edge of the bed, where the light haloed her hair.

Suddenly Bunny took charge. "Read me about Jenny and the Twins." She pitched her book at the girl.

"OK," said Nell, meekly.

Ruth turned away. She bustled, putting things into her evening bag, her wristwatch, her compact, handkerchief, hairpins, lipstick. Her heart was beating a little fast.

Peter was standing silently, with his overcoat on, with her velvet wrap over his arm. She went over and he held it. She looked up at him, wordlessly asked, Is it all right? Wordlessly, he answered, Sure. What can happen? The wrap was soft and cool on her bare arms.

"Eddie's got his eye on," said Peter in her ear. And she saw at once that this was true. Eddie was responsible. Eddie had worked here fourteen years. He couldn't risk losing that record. No. And Eddie was conscientious to a fault. He'd be fussy and watchful. It was Eddie they were hiring, really. He'd have his anxious eye on.

"Take us awhile to get across town," said Peter aloud. Together they went into the other room. The girl was reading. Her voice was low and monotonous. One word followed another without phrasing. She read like a child.

"All cozy?" said Ruth lightly. "Night, Bunny." Her light kiss skid-ded on the warm little brow.

Peter said, "Don't forget about your breakfast. So long, honey bun."

"So long, Daddy. Make a good speech."

Oh, bless her heart! thought her mother. Oh bless her!

"I'll see what I can do about that, sweetheart," said Peter tenderly, as touched as she.

The girl sat on the edge of the bed with her finger on her place in the storybook. She watched them go. As they crossed room 807, Ruth heard her voice begin again, ploddingly.

Not all of Ruth went through the door to the corridor. Part re-mained and tasted the flat, the dim, the silent place from which she had gone. After all the lights and the love and the laughter, how was it for Bunny? Hadn't all the fun too abruptly departed? A part of Ruth lay, in advance of time, in the strange dark. Heard the strange city snarling below. Knew only a stranger's hired meekness was near when something in the night should cry. . . .

Peter put his finger on her velvet shoulder. An elevator was com-ing. (Not Eddie's, and Ruth was glad. Not again did she wish to hear, "Have a good time, you folks. Have a good time.")

She shook at her thoughts. She knew what Peter wanted. By her will, she pulled herself together. (Bunny was nine. Bunny would sleep.) She drew the tardy part of herself in toward her body until she was all there, standing by the elevators, dressed to the eyes. She looked up at Peter and showed him she was whole.

It was The Night. At last, it was!

Chapter Three

JED TOWERS picked up his date at her family's apartment on East Thirty-sixth Street. Her name was Lyn Lesley and she was more than just a date. She had achieved a certain ascendancy on Jed's list.

In fact, she was right up there on top. Lyn was slim, dark, with a cute nose and a way of looking out of the corners of her eyes that was neither sly nor flirtatious but simply merry.

He'd known her a year or more, but not until these two weeks, all free time, between jobs, had he seen her so constantly. This had happened easily. A kind of rollicking slide to it. Very smooth and easy to slide from "see you tomorrow, question mark" to "see you tomorrow, period" to "what shall we do tomorrow?" They had fun. Why not? But this next morrow, Jed was off for the West, all the way to the coast, in fact, where he'd be pinned down awhile, in the new job. Tonight, their last night, had accumulated without any deliberation on Jed's part the feel of being decisive.

Maybe it wasn't their last night together—but their last night apart. He didn't know. He wasn't stalling. He just didn't know.

They were not in evening clothes. Lyn wore a fuzzy blue coat with big pockets and big buttons and a little blue cap on the back of her head. They decided to walk. They didn't know where they were going, anyway. The mood was tentative and merry . . . no tinge of farewell in it yet. Lyn hopped and skipped until Jed shortened his stride. They drifted toward the deepest glow in the sky. They might go to a show, might not. It depended.

On Thirty-ninth Street, the block west of Fifth, a beggar accosted them, whining to the girl, "Help an old man, missus?"

"Oh . . . Jed?" She stood still, impelled to compassion, her face turned up confidently.

Jed's fingers bit her arm. "Sorry. . . ." He dragged her along. "Just a racket," he said in her ear. The man's muttering faded in her wake, audible in the shadowy quiet, for the city's noise was, like fog, thicker afar, never very thick near around you.

She was really dragging her feet. "How do you know?" she said.

"Know what?" He was surprised. "Oh, for Lord's sake, Lyn, grow up! That old beetle probably's got more in the bank than we'll ever see."

"You can't know that," she said, stubbornly.

He stopped walking, astonished. Vaguely, he realized that his brusque decision back there may have broken something in her mood, some enchantment maybe. He had no patience with it. He said, "Now, look. Of course I can't know it, but the chances are I'm right. You know that. And I don't like being taken for a sucker, Lyn. Now, skip it, shall we?"

She walked along only somewhat more willingly. He said teasingly, "But you'd have fallen for it, eh? Softie!"

"On the chance he really needed help," she said in a low voice, "I'd have risked a quarter."

"Don't be like that." Jed laughed at her. "Sentimental Sue!" He wheeled her into a restaurant. "This all right?" Jed had been there before. The food was good. He wasn't guessing. He was sorry the mood had been broken. It was his instinct to change the setting, and use the difference and food and drink to bring back whatever it was between them.

They took their table and Jed ordered dinner. Lyn had her lower lip in her teeth, kept her eyes down. When their cocktails came and he lifted his glass to her, she smiled. She said, "I'm not sentimental, Jed. It isn't that."

"No?" He wished she'd skip it. He, himself, was finished with that trivial moment. "Drink your drink, honey." He smiled at her. When the cool beauty of his face broke, in his smile, to affectionate attention, it pulled on the heart of the beholder. Jed did not know that, in such terms. But he knew, of course, statistically, that what he offered was not often rejected.

But Lyn said wanly, "You have an awfully quick way of mistrusting people." Her voice was gentle but he thought there were stormy signs in her eyes and anger stirred in Jed's own.

He said evenly, gently, "I didn't think you were that childish, Lyn. I really didn't."

"I can't see," she said, holding scorn out of the voice carefully, "how it would have hurt. Two bits. Or even a dime."

"Spare a dime," he mocked. "For Lord's sake, Lyn, let's not fight about it."

"No." She pushed her glass to and fro on the cloth and she smiled. "But you do expect the worst of people, don't you, Jed? I've . . . noticed."

"Certainly," he grinned. "You damn well better, as far as I can see." He offered her his certainty with careless cheer.

She took a deep swallow of her drink, set down the glass, and looked across the room. "I don't think I care for cheap cynicism," she said.

"Cheap." he exploded. Women were the limit! What a thing to come out with, just like that! He realized he must have hurt her, somehow. But he also knew he hadn't meant to. "For Lord's sake!" he said, "that's about the most expensive piece of education I ever got myself. I'd hate to tell you what I had to pay for it." He was still genuinely astonished.

"You don't believe . . ." she began and her lips were trembling.

"Don't believe!" he scoffed. "Listen—aw, you baby! What I believe or what you believe makes no particular difference to the way things are. Lyn, honey, sooner or later you get to know that. All the difference it makes is whether you're comfortable or not. Well, it just happens I don't like to be fooled and I've got to the point where I don't even enjoy fooling myself." She flicked her lashes. "This," he said soberly, "is a pretty stinking lousy world."

"Is it?" said Lyn.

He was annoyed. "If you haven't noticed that you're unintelligent," he said crisply.

"And what do you do about it?"

"Mind your own business. Take care of yourself, because you can be damn sure nobody else will. Lyn, for the love of Mike, let it go, will you? Anybody thinks *he* can save the world isn't weaned yet. You're old enough to know that much."

"If everybody figured the way to do . . ." she began, looking unhappy.

"You like the boy-scout type?" he challenged. "The sunshine kids?"

"No."

"The dreamy boys? The old stars in the eyes?"

"Stop it!"

"OK," he said. "So I'm not going to water myself down and play pat-a-cake with you." He canceled his anger. He offered, again, his smile and himself.

"I don't want you to," she said. "I'm interested in what you think about things." Her voice was low again.

"But you don't think much of my way of thinking?" he said, more challenging than he had intended to be. "Is that it?"

She turned her hand.

"Well . . ." he shrugged. "I'm sorry, honey, but one thing that stinks high in this lousy world is the lip service to sweetness and light.

Everybody's for it. But does their left hand know what their lip is saying?" At least, I'm honest, his eyes were saying. I'm telling you. "Look, I didn't expect an inquiry into my philosophy of life. I thought this was a date . . . you know, for fun?"

Her lips parted. He read in her look that they both knew it wasn't just a date . . . for fun. But she didn't speak.

"Show?" he said lightly. If they went to a show, it would deny, somehow, their ability to be together. He felt that, suddenly.

She said, "In such a stinking lousy world, what do you expect?"

"Oh, say, the love of a good woman," he answered lightly, because he *didn't* want to discuss this kind of thing seriously anymore. And then he was sorry. He saw her lips whiten. He'd hurt her, again, when all he wanted was to get lightly off the subject. "Aw, Lyn, please. . . . What are we yapping about? How'd we get off?"

"Coffee now?" inquired the waiter.

"Coffee, honey?" Jed put his hand on hers.

"Please," she said, not smiling. But it seemed to him that her hand was on his and he thought if he could kiss her, hard, right now, it would be a fine thing.

Bunny listened politely to the story. When Mommy read, the story seemed more interesting. When Daddy read to her, it was interesting, too, although Daddy never did finish a story. He always got off to explaining something, and the explaining turned out to be *another* story. She sat quietly against her pillow, her stuffed dog under her arm, until the voice stopped. Nell looked at her then. "I better go to sleep, now," said Bunny, "I guess."

"OK." The mattress moved, the spring changed shape, as Nell stood up.

"I can turn off my light," said Bunny kindly.

"OK then," Nell said. She put the book down on the other bed. She walked away. She picked up the candy box, looked once over her shoulder, and went through the door.

Bunny snapped off the light, watched the pattern of shadows establish itself. She wondered if the window was open. Nell hadn't looked to see. The room felt stuffy and dusty hot. Bunny wasn't quite sure she knew how to work the Venetian blind. She lay still quite a long time, but it didn't feel right to go to sleep, not knowing whether the window was open. She sneaked her feet out and felt the bristles of the carpet. She fumbled with the thin ropes and after a while there was a soft rattle and the slats changed. Now, she could see. The window *was* open. It was all right, then. Bunny crept back under the blankets. The air smelled dusty, just the same, and the pillow didn't smell like her pillow at home, either. Bunny pushed her nose into it and lay still.

Nell set the communicating door at an angle that almost closed it. Then she stood absolutely still, tipping her head as if to listen. Room 809 was quiet, behind her. Room 807 was a pool of silence. Her eyes shifted. The big lamp flooded the spot near the windows where the big chair stood. The small lamp touched the upper ends of the twin beds. Elsewhere, there were shadows.

Nell put the candy box down on a bed and walked back with a silent gliding step to the windows and tripped the blind. The court was too narrow to see very far up or down. Across, there was only one lighted window. The blind there was up a third of the way, and she could see the middle section of a woman, seated at the desk. A black-and-white belt marked a thick waist on a black dress. There was nothing else to see. Not many spent their evenings in at the Hotel Majestic.

Nell pivoted, glided in that same step to the middle of room 807, and stood still. She did not stand still long. Although her feet remained in the same flower of the carpet pattern, they began to dance. The heels lifted and fell fractions of an inch, only, as her weight shifted. Her hips rolled softly, and her shoulders and her forearms. Her fingers were the most active part of her body in this dance. They made noiseless snaps and quick restless writhings of their own. Her chin was high and her head, swaying with the tiny movements of her body, wove the pattern of a wreath in the silent air.

Meantime, Nell's eyes, wide open, darted as she danced. Very alive and alert, they were. Her whole face was vivid, more sly than shy, not in the least demure.

In a little while, the feet danced daintily, in the tiniest of steps, off the one flower. Nell swooped over Peter's suitcase. Her hand, impiously, not tentatively at all, scooped through its contents. Handkerchiefs and ties flew like sand from a beach castle. There were some letters and a manila folder flat on the bottom. The girl snatched them out, opened the folder awkwardly, and all the paper slid out in a limp curve. She stood with the empty folder in her hands and looked down at the spilled papers in the suitcase. Then she yanked the letters from the clip that held them to the folder. They didn't interest her for long. She dropped all the paper out of her hands, as if it were merely paper, with no other meaning. She flipped the lid of the suitcase with one finger and it fell.

She made three long steps and pivoted with one leg out like a dancer's, pulling it slowly around. She sat down, with an effect of landing there by sheer accident, on the bench in front of the dressing table. Ruth had turned the two little lamps out. It did not seem to occur to Nell to switch them on. She rummaged in Ruth's box of jewelry. There were three bracelets and Nell clasped them all on her left arm. There were two brooches and she pinned one above the other on the left lapel of her dress. There were a string of coral-colored beads, and Ruth's three-strand pearls, and a silver locket on a silver chain. All these Nell took up and fastened around her neck. A pair of tiny turquoise and silver earrings that matched one of the pins she put at her ears. She looked at herself in the shadowy glass, solemnly, lumpishly. She smiled. Slowly, she began to take everything off again. As she removed each piece she did not return it to its place in the box. When the table top was scattered with most of the things, Nell seemed to lose interest. She still wore the earrings.

She turned, very slowly, sliding around, moving her legs as if they were in one piece. She kicked off her black pumps. Ruth's aquamarine mules with the maribou cuffs were standing neatly under the dressing table. Nell put her feet into them. She rose and walked up and down in them, watching her feet, acquiring more and more skill and arrogance in the ankles and the arches. At last, she seemed almost strutting. Then she seemed to forget and moved about as easily as if the mules had long been her own.

She ate three pieces of candy, slowly.

Then she sat down on the bench again and picked up Ruth's perfume. The tiny glass stick attached to the stopper she discarded. She tipped the bottle on her forefinger and dabbed the forefinger behind her ears. She held the forefinger under her nostrils and inhaled dreamily, swaying to and fro as if she tantalized her own senses in a dreamy rhythm. The little bottle dropped out of her left hand, cracked on the table top, lay on its side. The liquid began to seep out among the jewelry. (The twelve dollars that had been Peter's, the fifty cents that had been Bunny's, last Mother's Day.)

Nell noticed it, finally. Her face did not change. She picked up Ruth's hairbrush, dipped it, making a smearing motion, in the spilled perfume, and began to brush her tawny hair. She brushed it sharply back from her ears. Now her face took on another look. Now the shape of it, the sharp taper to the chin, the subtle slant of the eye sockets, became older, more sleek, reptilian.

She drew the hairbrush once around her throat.

She rose and walked between the beds, turned, and let herself fall supine on the one to the left of the telephone. After a little while she lifted her right arm, languidly, letting her hand dangle from the wrist, looking up at her fingers that hung limp off the palm.

Then she sat up, propped her back with pillows, and opened the fat phone book. She opened it almost at the center and looked at the pages with unfocused eyes. She lifted her left hand and dropped it on the fine print. Where her left forefinger nail fell she gouged a nick in the paper.

She picked up the phone with her right hand, asked sweetly for the number.

"Yes?" A man's voice came out of the city, somewhere, hooked and caught at the end of the wire.

"Guess who?" Nell said in a soft high soprano.

"Margaret, where are—"

"Oh-ho no! Not Margaret!"

"Who is this?" said the voice irritably. "I'm not in the mood—"

"By the way, who *is* Margaret? Hmmmmmmmmm?"

"Margaret is my wife," said the voice stiffly. "What's the idea?"

"Ha!"

"Who is this?"

"Virginia," crooned Nell. "Don't you remember me?"

"I think you have the wrong number," the voice said, sounding very old and tired, and he hung up.

Nell sucked her cheeks in, turned pages, gave another number.

"Hello?" A woman this time.

"Hello. Oh, hello. Is Mr. Bennet there?"

"No, he's not. I'm sorry." Brightly, "This is *Mrs.* Bennet."

"Oh," said Nell without alarm. With nothing. Flatly. Her head tilted, listening.

"Can I take a message?" the woman said, somewhat less cordially.

"Oh, dear," simpered Nell. "You see, this is Mr. Bennet's secretary. . . ."

"Mr. Bennet has no secretary that I know of."

"Oh," said Nell. "Oh dear me! Are you sure?"

"Who is this?" The voice began to sound as if the face were red.

"Just a friend. You know?"

"Will you give me your name, please?"

"Why, no," said Nell flatly and then she giggled.

The phone slammed shut at the other end. On Nell's face danced a look of delighted malice.

She stretched. She called the girl downstairs again. "Long distance."

"One moment, please."

Rochelle Parker, at the switchboard, was efficient and indifferent. She dealt with the barrage of calls from 807 for a long time without much comment, even to herself. She got in on part of a wrangle between the long-distance operator and whoever was calling, up there, over the existence of an exchange in Chicago. The person upstairs used language, softly. It was as bad as Rochelle had ever heard over the wires and she'd heard some. And this was worse, sounding so hushedlike.

"Jeepers," said Rochelle to herself. The eyebrows that Rochelle, herself, had remodeled from nature's first idea went up to her bangs. It crossed her mind that she might say a word to Pat Perrin, the house detective. Probably, she thought, they were drinking up there. People had a few and went on telephone jags sometimes.

She decided it was none of her business. What went over the wire wasn't disturbing the sacred peace of the Hotel Majestic. If 807 began to do that, somebody else would catch on.

And the telephone bill would be part of the hangover. "Oh, boy," she thought and grinned. Then 807 suddenly quit calling.

The phone book had fallen off the bed. Nell rolled over on her stomach and looked at it, lying on the carpet.

She sat up, curling her legs under her. She yawned. She listened. Her rambling glance passed the half-open closet door and returned. . . .

Chapter Four

A TALL MAN looks best in tails, they say. Ruth thought that although Peter O. Jones was not too terribly tall, he looked wonderful. She saw no man there who looked more distinguished than he. Erect, compact, controlled, he walked beside her. And if the bold lines of his face were not handsome, they were better than that. People remembered Peter.

She saw herself, too, in the mirror walls of the passage to the ballroom and she began to walk as if she were beautiful. For the frock was becoming, and in the soft light she even liked her nose. Maybe it did turn up, as Peter insisted, against all evidence, that it did. At least it had, as he said, the air of being *about* to turn up any minute.

Her hand with the rosy nails pressed the black cloth of his left sleeve and Peter crossed his arm over and touched her hand. Here they stood, at the portal. Black-and-white men, multicolored ladies, flowers, table-and-chairs like polka dots over the floor, but the long white bar of the speakers' table dominated.

"Peter O. Jones," said her husband very quietly to somebody. A black back bent. They followed toward the speakers' table and Ruth could see their path, opening, and the turning faces marked it as if flowers were being thrown under their feet.

Somebody stepped into their way, holding out his hand. "Peter O. Jones?" he said joyfully. "Want you to meet. . . ." "Beg pardon, sir, but this is. . . ." "How do you do?" "*Mrs.* Jones, ah. . . ." They were in a cluster. Yet they were moving slowly, surely, toward the speakers' table. Peter had the nicest *way* about him. So many people knew who he *was*. Ruth struggled to remain balanced, to lock names to faces. It was confusing! It was glorious!

Jed and Lyn were still sitting in the restaurant. Coffee, brandy, more coffee, and many cigarettes had gone by. They'd had no ambition to stir themselves, to go to a show. They were caught in the need to settle something. Maybe it was never to be settled. This was what they needed to know. Jed shared, now, Lyn's feeling that it was important. They were hanging onto their tempers, both of them.

They'd about finished, speaking awkwardly, obliquely for the most part, with God.

"What I know," he said, "the Lord ain't Santa Claus. You got them mixed, honey. Santa Claus, sure, *he'll* open his pack if you been a good girl. I don't think it's the same." His brows made angles.

"You don't believe in it at all," she said wearily.

"I don't nag myself about it." He shrugged.

"All I'm trying to say, Jed," she was making an effort to be sweet, "is just this. I'd like . . . all right, call it soft . . . call it anything you want . . . I'd have *liked* it, if you had given that old man a coin. What would it matter if he really needed it or not? It would have been good for *us*."

"Aw, that's junk, Lyn. Pure junk."

"It isn't junk!"

His voice slipped. Dammed-up irritation slipped out. "It's ridiculous!"

Her eyes flashed. They had worked to smile, too long. "I'm glad to know you think I'm ridiculous."

"Maybe it's a good idea to know these things," he agreed coldly. "You called me a cheap cynic, remember?"

"And perhaps you are," she said shortly, "just that."

"It's no chore of mine, Lyn," he fought to sound reasonable, "to contribute to the income of a perfect stranger who's done nothing for me."

"It's not a question of your responsibility. It's your charity."

"Nuts to that kind of charity. I intend to earn what I get. . . ."

"People can't, always. There's such a thing as being helpless . . . through no fault. . . ."

"The rule is, you get what you pay for, pay for what you get. You grow up, you know that."

"Suppose *you* needed food . . . or a place to. . . ."

"Then I go beg from organized charities who recognize that so-called helplessness and, incidentally, check up on it to see if it is real. *I'll* never expect a stranger on the street to shell out for me. Why should he? Why should he believe me? It works both ways. You look out for yourself in this world, that's all I—"

"It's not true! People have to believe. . . ."

"Why?"

"Why, anything, then?" she blazed. "What are you living for?"

"How do I know? I didn't put me here. Of all the idiotic—"

"I think you'd better take me home."

Their voices came to a dead stop.

"Why?" he said finally, his eyes glittering.

"Because this isn't fun."

"Why should I take you home?" he said, smoldering. "Ask some kind stranger."

She stared. She said, "You're quite right. I do nothing for you. Or your ego. Do I? I'll be leaving now."

"Lyn. . . ."

"Yes?" she said icily, half up, her coat on her shoulders.

"If you go. . . ."

"Why should I not? You're not entertaining me. Nothing's for free, you say."

"If you go. . . ."

"I know. We'll never meet again. Is that it?"

"That's it, I'm afraid."

"Jed, I don't want to. . . ." She was more limp, more yielding.

"Then for Lord's sake," he said irritably, assuming it was all over, "sit down and quit talking like a little jackass."

Her sidewise glance was not merry at all. "Good night," she said quietly.

He settled in the chair, took a cigarette out of the package. "Got your mad money? Here." He threw a five-dollar bill on the tablecloth.

Lyn's lips drew back from her teeth. He could feel, like a strong sudden gust, her impulse to hit him. Then he thought she'd cry.

But she walked away.

He sat, staring at the messy table. Of all the stinking lousy dates he ever had in his life! Protectively, he thought of it as just a date. He was furious. He advanced to being outraged. His last night in this town! Last night in the East! Last date! And she walked out on him.

For what? He oversimplified. Because he didn't give that mangy old deadbeat a quarter. Of all the . . . ! He sat there and let anger become a solid lump. After a while, he paid the check and put his coat on. Outside, he looked east, then west. Lyn was nowhere about.

He began to walk, fast, hands dug in his coat pockets. He supposed gloomily it was a good thing he'd found out what kind of stuff passed for thought in her head. (Lyn, with the dark head, his shoulder high.) So . . . cross *her* off the list. Yeah. Couldn't she see he hadn't tried to hurt her? Couldn't she concede he'd learned a few things, formed some opinions, had to have a core of conviction that was, at least, honestly come by? No, she couldn't. So, she walked away.

But Towers would have a date tonight, just the same. His little book (with the list) was at the hotel, damn it. He swung north. Hadn't thought he'd need it. But he *had* it. He could put his hand on it. His pride, his proof, his very honor began to get involved here. Towers would have a date his last night. Wouldn't be stood up, not he!

Jed slammed through the revolving door. It stuttered, not moving as fast as he. He stood, towering, teetering, smoldering, at the desk, crisply after his key. He went up to the eighth floor, unlocked his door, put on his light, flung off his coat in one swift surge of entering.

He visited the bathroom.

He came out with the bathroom glass in his hand and stared around him. He dipped into his bag for that bottle of rye. He could think of nobody on his list who'd do him good. And the preliminaries. He was in no mood for them. Call any girl, this time of night, and you could hear her little brain buzzing. Oh, will I look unpopular if I admit I'm not busy? They all wondered, the nitwits. So she'd say she had a date. And he'd say, "Break it for me?" Knowing damn well she probably was just about to wash her hair or something. So, she'd "break it." Phony. Everything was pretty phony.

(Not Lyn. She was just too naïve to live.)

He looked at the telephone. Call her and apologize? But what was there, honestly, to apologize for? He'd only said things he believed. He couldn't change his spots. They'd only start over again. They didn't think the same. And nobody walked out on Towers twice! This she'd find out.

Aw, quit stewing.

The blind across his bank of windows was not drawn. He realized that he stood as one on a lighted stage. It felt, too, as if eyes were on him. Somebody was watching him.

He moved toward the windows that looked out on a court.

He was looking directly across the narrow dark deep well into another lighted bank of windows. The other room hung there in the night like a lighted stage. The scene had no depth. It was lit by a lamp near the windows. The light fell on a female figure. There was a girl or a woman over there. She was dressed in some kind of flowing bluish or greenish thing. She seemed to be sitting *in* the window, probably on the flat top of the long radiator cover. Her neck was arched. She had short yellowish hair. She seemed to be looking down at a point on her right leg just above the knee. A garter or something? Her right foot rested on the radiator top. The nicely shaped leg was bent there, framed and exhibited, with the bluish-green fabric flowing away from it.

She was not looking out, not looking at him. He was absolutely certain that she had been. He knew he must be silhouetted in the frame of his own windows. He stood still, watching her, making no further move to pull his blind down. He was absolutely certain that she knew he was there.

She moved her right palm slowly down the curve of her calf. Her head turned. She looked across at him. He did not move.

Neither did she.

Her hand rested on her ankle. Her garment remained as it was, flowing away from the pretty knee. Her head was flung up from the neck. She looked at him.

There was something so perfectly blunt about the two of them, posed as they were, each in his bright box, suspended, aware. . . . It was as if a shouted *Well?* crossed the court between them.

Jed felt himself grin. The anger that hummed in his veins changed pitch, went a fraction higher. What was this? and why not? he thought, pricked and interested.

Chapter Five

THE GIRL took her hand from her ankle, put both hands on the radiator top behind her, bent her body to lean back on the stiff support of both her arms, kept looking out at him. There was something direct about it that fitted with his mood.

Jed was reading the floor plan of the hotel that lay in his head. He was counting off numbers, calculating. He had the kind of mind that carried maps and floor plans with him always. He felt pretty sure he knew what the number of that room must be. He put his bottle of rye down and raised both hands where the shape of them would be silhouetted for her to see. He signaled with eight fingers, with both hands bent in an O, and then with seven fingers.

She sat up suddenly, wrapped both arms around her middle, and turned so that the knee slid down. She was facing him, her head tilted as if to say, What do you mean?

He took up the bottle in his left hand, pointed at it, at her, at himself.

Her chin went high, as if her head fell back in laughter.

He put down the bottle, pantomimed himself at a telephone. She understood because her head turned and she looked behind her toward where the phone in that room must be.

She made the sign of seven.

Jed backed away from the window. He knew he was still perfectly visible, perhaps even plainer to her sight now, in the glare of the overhead light. He picked up his phone. He said to the girl, "807, please."

Downstairs, as Rochelle made the connection, a thought no clearer than the word "huh?" crossed her mind fleetingly. Pursuing it, she remembered. Oh yeah, 807 was the whispering foul-mouth. What now? Probably, she surmised, 821 was going to complain. She was tempted. She heard a man's voice say, "Well?" It was blunt and a trifle mocking. It wasn't going to complain. Rochelle's interest, faint in the first place, faded. The muscles of her mouth made a quick cynical comment, soon forgotten.

Jed could still see the girl, in the little puddle of light by the beds in there, answering her phone. He waved. "Hi," he said over the wire.

She made a soft sound, like a chuckle. "Hello."

"*Would* you like a drink?"

"I might," she said.

"Alone?"

She knew what he was asking. "You can see, can't you?" she said and the hint of laughter came again.

"If I walk around, will you open the door?"

"I might."

"It's a long walk," he said.

He had the impression that she would have teased him, but something happened. He saw her head turn. Some sound . . . that she could hear but he could not. She said, in a different mood and a different tempo, "Wait a few minutes?"

"This is an impulse," Jed said frankly. "It might not last."

"Five minutes," she said, sounding eager and conspiratorial, now. "There's somebody at the door." Then she said, "Oh, please," very softly and very softly hung up.

Jed sat on the bed in his room and automatically put the phone down. He saw her at the window, lowering the blind, but she tripped it so that he could still see into the room. He knew when she went into the shadowy part, when she opened the door. The visitor came in the direction that, to Jed, was downstage, came in far enough so that he could identify the hotel livery.

Bellhop, or something. Oh, well. . . . He went into his bathroom with a vague sense of stepping into the wings for a moment, out of the footlights. He looked at himself in the glass. His anger was no longer so solid. It had broken into a rhythmic beat. It came and went, ebbed and flowed. When it pulsed high he felt reckless and in a mood to smash. When it ebbed low he felt a little bit blank and tired. But the pulse was strong, the beat was urgent. It seemed necessary to do something.

Eddie said, "Little girl went to sleep all right, did she? You all right. Nell?"

"Umhum," Nell murmured. She'd fallen into the maroon chair and looked relaxed there. Her lids fell as if they were heavy over her eyes. Her face was smooth and seemed sleepy.

"What you got on? Nell!" Eddie's voice was thin and careful.

"I'm not hurting anything."

Eddie's flitting eye caught the top of the dressing table and the condition it was in. His gold-flecked teeth bit over his pale lip. He moved closer to the dressing table. After a while he said, in a low voice, "You shouldn't monkey with other people's stuff, Nell. Really, you shouldn't."

"I'm not hurting anything," she repeated and her voice was more truculent than before.

Eddie gnawed his lip. He rescued the perfume bottle and replaced the stopper. Almost furtively, his fingers began to neaten the tumble of jewelry. He began to talk softly, coaxingly.

"It's kind of an easy job, though, isn't it, Nell? Don't you think so? Just to sit for a few hours in a nice room like this. And just think, you get paid for it. Fifty cents an hour isn't bad, for nothing but being here. If you was home, you'd be sitting around with Aunt Marie, waiting for bedtime, just the same. You like it, don't you, Nell?"

"Oh, sure," she said drowsily.

"Nell, you . . . better take off that negligee . . . and the slippers. Honest. I don't think Mrs. Jones would like that."

"She won't know the difference," said Nell shortly.

"Well," said Eddie, "I hope you. . . . Will you take them off, like a good girl?"

"Umhum," she murmured. "Sure I will, Uncle Eddie." She lifted her eyes and smiled at him.

He was enormously encouraged and pleased. "That's right," he cried. "That's good. Take them off, Nell, and put them where they were, so she won't know. Because you want to get paid. You want to get more jobs like this. Don't you see, Nell? It'll be a real nice kind of little work for you. So easy. And you can do what you want with the money after. You can buy some fancy slippers like those for *yourself,* Nell. Or a pair of earrings. Wouldn't that be nice?"

She turned her cheek to the chair.

Eddie wished he knew how it was Marie talked to her, what it was she did. Because Nell was good when Marie was around, real quiet and good.

"Tell you what I'll do," he said heartily. "When I get off duty, I'll bring you up a coke. OK? Have a little refreshment, you and me. It won't seem so long. You'll be surprised how the time will go by."

"Sleepy," she murmured.

"Well," he said, bracing his shoulders, "nap a little bit. That's a good idea." He looked at the perfume bottle that was now nearly empty. He cleared his throat. He said in a nervous rush, "And you ought to apologize for spilling the perfume . . . right away when she comes back."

Nell's lids went up slowly until her eyes were very wide. "It was an accident," she said an octave higher than before. Her whole body had tightened.

"I know. I know," said Eddie quickly. He stepped near her and put a gentle hand on her shoulder. She twisted away from it. "Of course it was an accident. I believe you, Nell. Sure it was. The only thing I mean is, it's a good idea to say so, real soon, before she notices. Anybody can have an accident like that. She won't blame you."

Nell said nothing.

"It'll be all right," said Eddie comfortingly. "You couldn't help it. Now, you just—just take it easy a little bit. I'll be back." He looked nervously behind him. The open elevator, standing too long on the eighth floor, was present in his consciousness. "I gotta go. But you're all right, aren't you?" He swallowed. "Please, Nell," he said in a thin pleading voice, "don't get into no more mischief with their things?"

"I'm not doing anything," she said sullenly.

But, when he sighed and paused in his progress toward the door as if he would plead some more, she said quickly, "I'm sorry, Uncle Eddie. I'll put everything back. You know I get . . . restless." Her hands moved to the earrings. "I'll take them off."

Immediately, he was pleased. "Sure, I know you get restless. I know you don't mean anything. I want you to . . . kinda get used to this idea. The thing is, to *think*, Nell. We could work up a kind of a little business, here. If you'd just . . . if you like it."

"I do like it," she said, sounding thoughtful and serious. An earring lay in her hand.

The little man's face reddened with his delight. "Good girl! That's swell! And it's a date, now. Don't forget. I'll bring the cokes." And so he withdrew, pointed little face going last, like a mouse drawing back into its hole.

Nell waited for the door to close. With no expression on her face she put the earring back on her earlobe. She got slowly to her feet. Then they began to move on the carpet in that tiny dance. She listened. She went to the blind and it rattled up under her hands.

Jed was standing in the middle of his room, his weight even on both feet, looking rather belligerently across at her.

She flung up both hands in a beckoning gesture, let them go on, until her arms were in a dancer's high curve, and she whirled backward from the window. Jed stood still. And the girl stood still, posed with her arms high, looking over her shoulder.

In a second, Jed put the bottle in his pocket and his finger on his light switch. His light went out.

Nell pawed, disturbing the order Eddie had created, and she snatched at Ruth's spare coral lipstick.

Chapter Six

JED'S IMPULSE had been flickering like a candle in a draft. He put the bottle in his pocket for the necessary little drink that you take while you look the situation over, put his key in his pocket, too, heard the elevator gate closing. So he waited for the faint hum of its departure before he went around the corner to his right and passed the elevators and turned right again.

His mood was cautious when he tapped on the door marked 807.

She was not very tall, not very old, not bad-looking, either. But he couldn't type her. No curly blonde. Not a sleek blonde. Her face, tilted to look at him, was a triangle and the eyes were set harlequin-wise. Jed's nostrils moved. She reeked . . . the whole room reeked . . . of perfume. She opened the door wider, quickly. He took a step and the door closed behind him as if she had fanned him into this perfumed place. His glance went rapidly around. He looked, and knew it, as if he were ready to take the step back again, and out.

"What's in the bottle?" she asked.

He took it out of his pocket and showed her the label. He said, mechanically, "Too nice a night to drink alone." His cool gray stare examined her.

Her blue eyes examined his. For a minute he thought there wasn't going to be any act . . . and he was fascinated by that same sense of blunt encounter that he had felt before.

This wasn't a type he knew.

She turned, tripping a little on the aquamarine hem of the negligee, so long it puddled on the floor around her. She said, "Won't you sit down?" Her voice was flat and matter-of-fact. Yet he wasn't sure whether she used a cliché or mocked one.

He set the bottle on the desk and walked past it, going warily to the big maroon chair. "Nice of you to let me come over," he said, perfunctorily. His eye caught certain signs and he was not pleased. He thought he had better get out of here as gracefully as was quick. Obviously, this room was half a man's.

She walked over a bed on her knees and then was standing between the two of them with complete dignity. It was an odd effect, almost as if she didn't notice how she had got there, as if she assumed that of course she must have walked around the bed like a lady. She put her hands on the phone. "We must have some ice," she said grandly.

"Fine."

"Ginger ale?"

The name on that envelope caught in the hasp of the suitcase was Jones. "Whatever you like, Mrs. Jones," Jed said.

She was startled. Her body stiffened as she held herself high in surprise. Then her reddish lashes swept down. Into the phone she said grandly, "Please send ice and ginger ale to Mrs. Jones in 807."

Jed guessed she was being some movie star or other. But they'd cut a line out of the picture. She forgot to ask for room service. The operator obliged. Looking over Jed's head, posed like a model for a photograph of glamor, the girl repeated her order with exactly the same inflections. It was mimicry, all right.

But when she hung up her whole face changed. "I'm not Mrs. Jones," she told him with sly delight. "Mrs. Jones went out." This wasn't mimicry. It was . . . odd.

Jed looked mildly interrogative.

"This isn't my room," she chuckled.

He thought to himself that this was no worse a dodge than any. "That's funny. The room over there isn't *my* room, either. Coincidence?" He leaned back, grinning.

"Mr. and Mrs. Jones went out," she said frowning.

"The fellow whose room I was in went out, too," said Jed, still grinning. "He's got a date." He felt anger pulse in his neck and jaw. "Lucky guy. Or is he? Or am I?"

She sat down on the bed and stuffed a pillow behind her. "I'm going to South America tomorrow," she remarked lightly.

"Oh? What part?" She didn't answer. "I'm off to Europe, myself," he lied cheerfully. He didn't believe a word she'd said so far.

"Mr. Jones is my brother," said the girl. "I hate him. I hate all my relatives. They won't let me do anything. They don't want me to have dates." She looked both dreamy and sullen. Jed began to believe some of this. Something was real about it.

"Shall we make it a date?" he suggested. "Would you like to go dancing?"

Her head jerked. He saw her quick desire to go and her recollection of some reason why not . . . the jump of a flame and its quick quenching. "I haven't any evening clothes," she said, and he gawped at such an excuse. If excuse it was. "Mrs. Jones had a beautiful evening dress."

"Your . . . sister-in-law?"

"And a velvet wrap the color of this." She touched the negligee. "You can't buy that for fifty cents an hour."

Jed made no sense of what she was saying. A rap on the door cut into his puzzling. Boy with the ice. Jed got up and turned his back, looking out through the blind as if there was something to see. There was nothing to see but some old biddy writing letters there. Jed hardly noticed even that. He was annoyed by the notion that he ought not let himself be seen in there.

Still, a hotel, he guessed, in its official consciousness, usually knew by some nervous sympathy what went on within its walls. It pounced or it did not pounce. But it knew. Probably he wasn't fooling anybody.

"Sign, miss?" The boy was mumbling.

The girl was at a complete loss. She had never seen this in the movies. Her grand air was punctured. She didn't know anything about signing a check.

Jed turned around. "Better let me get it, honey." He fumbled for money. "What time did your brother go out?" he asked her over his shoulder.

She said nothing.

"Do *you* know?" Jed watched the boy's worldly young eyes. "Notice a couple in evening clothes? She wore a wrap, that color."

"Mr. and Mrs. Jones?" said the boy smoothly. "Yeah, they left quite a long while ago."

"How long will they be?" Jed asked the girl.

She shrugged. "Some shindig. . . ."

"Yeah? Well. . . ." Jed watched the boy whose eyes were first satisfied, then veiled. The boy took his tip and departed.

The boy, whose name was Jimmy Reese, went down the corridor jauntily, his lips pursed to whistle, shaping a tune without the breath to make it audible. Eddie's elevator picked him up. They eyed each other with a kind of professional contempt. Jimmy's whistle went right on.

The guy in 807 belonged in 821. This Jimmy knew. Who that girl was, Jimmy did not know. So she was Jones' sister. For all he knew. He didn't know she had anything to do with Eddie. He looked up at the grillwork, coming to the chorus. He didn't think 821 was looking for Jones in there, though. Jimmy kept a lot of amusing things to himself.

Eddie didn't know that Jimmy had just been to 807. He'd listened hard at the eighth floor. He'd eyed the boy. All seemed quiet.

So they sank down, professionally aloof, exchanging no comments, no gossip, no information.

Jed, fixing drinks, thought it over. He hadn't been trying to set up a picture of himself, the dropper-in who had missed his host. He guessed he wasn't fooling anybody. On the other hand, he had established something. Mr. and Mrs. Jones *had* gone out. Who was this, then?

"You got a name?" he asked gently.

"Nell." She told him so absentmindedly he believed it was true. Nevertheless, he lied, saying, "I'm John." He handed her a glass.

She took a deep swallow, looked up, and laughed at him. "You don't know what to think about me. You're nervous. You're funny."

He let it ride. He went over and fixed the blind. Then he sat down on the bed next to her. "Where you from, Nell?"

"California."

"What part?"

"All of it."

"You can't do that. California's too big."

"It's not so big."

"San Francisco?"

"Sometimes."

"Tulsa?" he said.

"There, too," she answered serenely. She was rolling this stuff off the top of her head, not even bothering to make sense.

"Where is Tulsa?" he asked, in sudden suspicion.

"In California." She looked surprised.

"Nell," he said amiably, "you're a liar."

"Oh, well," she said, suddenly soft as a kitten, leaning against his arm, "you're lying to me, too."

"I haven't said anything."

"You're lying, just the same."

He took her chin in his left hand, turned her face and searched it and his pulse jumped, recognizing the cockeyed honesty there. You're a liar. I'm a liar. Well? No, it wasn't a look, given cynically, after long practice. There was something perfectly fresh about it.

She was not a type he knew.

"Well?" he said, aloud. He bent his mouth to kiss her.

The taste of her lips was very close when a ripple went down his spine. He turned Nell's quietly waiting face with his hand, pressing it to his shoulder. His neck worked stiffly, slowly. He looked behind.

There was a little girl with dark pigtails, barefooted, in pink pajamas. She was watching them silently.

A wild animal could have startled him no more.

Chapter Seven

THE SHOCK SEEMED to lift him into the air. He croaked, controlling his voice better than his reflexes, "Seems to be an audience." He had pushed Nell to her balance. He had pivoted without straightening his knees. He was suddenly sitting on the other bed, facing the child . . . reaching for his glass. . . .

Jed, going about his business, brushed by the children in the world without making any contact. They didn't interest him. Like philatelists or monks or surrealist painters, they were out of his orbit. Events that had artificially aged him had also knocked awry the continuity of his own memories. It seemed a long time ago, if not in another planet, that he himself had been a child. Fathering none, and, in fact, acquainted with few young parents, Jed didn't know any children as friends. He would have mentioned "a bunch of kids" as he would comment on a "flock of chickens" or a "hill of ants." He didn't individualize them. He simply had no truck with them.

This little girl, with her dark eyes in an angular face, wasn't a pretty little girl. Too thin. Too solemn.

Nell was in a crouch, leaning on her arms. "Get back in there," she said viciously.

"I want. . . ."

Nell went across the bed on her knees. "Go on. Get back in there and go to sleep." Her fingers clawed the little shoulders.

Nobody spoke to Bunny O. Jones in such a fashion. Nobody came crawling at her like a big angry crab. Nobody handled her so cruelly. Bunny was severely startled. She began to cry.

"And shut up!" said Nell.

"Yours?" said Jed coolly.

"She's not mine," said Nell angrily. "She belongs to the Joneses."

"Oh . . . your niece?"

Nell laughed.

"You've got my mommy's things on," wailed Bunny.

"Shut—"

"Just a minute." Jed rose. Glass in hand, he came toward them. He was very tall next to Bunny O. Jones. He had no instinct to bend down. "What's your name?" He felt awkward, speaking to this mite, and was impelled to speak loudly, as one does to a foreigner or someone who may not readily understand the language.

"I'm Bunny O. Jones." She twisted in Nell's harsh hands.

"Let go of her, Nell. Bunny *Jones,* eh? This isn't your aunt, is it?"

"What are you asking *her* for? She's not supposed to be in *here.* . . ."

"Suppose you shut up a minute," Jed said.

"She's my sitter," sobbed Bunny.

"Oh, for Lord's sake." Jed put his glass down and settled his jacket around him with angry shoulder movements. Now he knew what he had got into.

Nell's hands were off the child but not far off. "I don't like you," sobbed Bunny.

"I don't like you either, you damn little snoop," Nell said.

One did *not* speak to these strange little creatures in such terms. Jed felt this much out for himself. It came slowly to him with a sense of how big he was, how big and how powerful even Nell was, and how helpless was the child.

He said, "Nobody's going to hurt you, Bunny. Don't cry."

But she kept on crying. Perhaps she didn't believe him. He couldn't blame her for that. She was shrinking away from Nell. And Nell contrived to loom closer and closer, so that the child was menaced and pursued and sought to escape, although the chase was neither swift nor far, but done in tiny pulses of the foot on the carpet.

"Why don't you ask her what she wanted?" Jed said.

"She wanted to snoop," said Nell.

But it was clear to Jed that the little girl hadn't snooped for snooping's sake. It was clear to him that she had done nothing in malice. He put his arm like a bar across Nell's path and her throat came against it. "No," he insisted. "There was something. What was it, hm? Bunny? What did you want?"

"It's too hot," wept Bunny. "I want my radiator off."

"You might have asked," Jed said scornfully to Nell. "It's simple enough. I'll take care of it."

He strode through the communicating door, which for all his caution he had not noticed to be open. The other room was stuffy. He found a valve. He thought, Towers, fold your tent. He noticed the exit to the corridor from here, from 809, and the key in the lock.

But the crying child, the girl again pursuing her in that gliding stepless way, was in the room with him.

"It's OK now," Jed said. "Cool off in a minute. Better get back to bed."

"*She'll* get back to bed."

Bunny broke and ran. She rolled into the bedclothes. She burrowed as if to hide. She was still crying.

Jed stalked into 807, making directly for the bottle. He had a notion to leave without breaking his stride, snatch the glass, drain it, pick up the bottle, cross the room, and fade away. But he was angry. What a stinking evening! First one thing and then another! Cutting phrases came to his mind. *Now* he understood that crack about fifty cents an hour . . . this late! . . . when it should have informed him, before, if he'd had the wits. He was furious for having been stupid. He was embarrassed and humiliated. He was even half angry with the little girl for having walked in and stared at Towers making a jackass of himself. A baby-sitter!

He wanted this Nell to know he was angry. So he freshened from the bottle the drink in the glass.

As Nell, on his heels, entered 807 and closed the door firmly behind her, he snarled, "Were you going to pay me my two bits an hour? Or wasn't this a fifty-fifty proposition?"

"What?" She spoke as if she'd been preoccupied, as if she hadn't quite heard. Her face was serene. She drifted toward the mirror. She touched her hair. It was as if, now that the door was closed, it might as well never have opened.

But Bunny was crying bitterly beyond the wall.

Jed said furiously, "Why didn't you tell me there was a kid in there?"

"I didn't know she was going to come in here," Nell said.

Jed looked at her. For the first time something nudged him, something said the word inside his head. But he didn't believe it. The word is easy to say. It falls off the tongue. But it is not so easy to believe, soberly, in all reality.

She walked to where he stood, by the desk that had become the bar.

He'd had cats press themselves around his shoes and ankles.

Nell fitted herself into the hollow of his shoulder and turned up her blind face. She was back where she'd been when so rudely interrupted. She was waiting for them to take up where they had left off. Jed stood still, angry enough to throw her brutally away from him, but bitter enough to stand still in unresponsive contempt.

The little kid was crying in there, a tearing, breaking—a terrible sound.

Nell's tawny head rested against him. He grabbed her shoulder. "Don't you hear that? You got something the matter with your ears?" He shook her.

"Hmmmmmmmm?" She was smiling. She enjoyed being shaken. So he let her go. Her eyes opened. "I heard you. I know what you said. You're mad at me. I don't see why you're mad at me, John. Johnee! I haven't done anything."

"You haven't done anything?"

"No."

"Well," Jed said. He put the stopper in the bottle of liquor and kept it in his hand. He was ready to go. He could make no sense here, no use arguing, no point to that.

"Don't go," Nell said rather shrilly. "I haven't done anything. It's all right now, isn't it? She's gone."

"Gone!" The sound of the child, crying in the next room, was preying on Jed's nerve ends. As bad, he thought, as if a cat had been yowling under his window and he trying to sleep. It was too irregular even to be a background noise. It pierced. It carried you with it into its anguish. "Can't you hear that!"

"That? She'll go to sleep."

"She will?"

Nell shrugged. Using one hand, she lapped the long silk robe so that it didn't drag. She whirled, seeming quite gay. "Can't I have another drink?"

The sounds the kid was making were not, Jed discovered, quite like a cat crying. Either a cat shut up, or it went elsewhere, or you went elsewhere. You got away. And if the cat cried where you couldn't hear it, why, let it cry. He didn't know anything about kids. But you didn't need to know anything. Just listening told you. *This* sound of *this* crying had to stop.

"Does it bother you?" the girl said rather casually, holding out her glass.

"It bothers the hell out of me," Jed said roughly. "She's scared. And you did that. Why did you have to jump at her like a wildcat? This the way you always treat your customers?" He poured whiskey into her glass, hardly aware he was doing so.

She looked sullen. "I didn't mean to scare her."

"She startled *me*. OK. But you knew she was in there. You're supposed to be taking care of her, aren't you? Listen. . . ."

He was listening, himself, all the time. The sound was intolerable. "You better get her to stop that."

"When she gets tired. . . ."

"You want the whole hotel up here?" he snapped.

"No." She looked alarmed.

"Then do something. I'm telling you."

He stalked toward an ashtray, walking between the beds. "If I go in there, you'll sneak out," Nell said flatly. The thought was crossing Jed's mind as she spoke. He put the whiskey down beside the phone. He took his hand off the bottle as if it were hot.

"I don't have to sneak out, you know," he said cuttingly. "I can walk out, just about any time. I won't stay here and listen to that, I'll tell you."

"If she stops crying, will you stay?"

"I doubt it."

She put her glass in her left hand and worked her right as if it were stiff and cold. Her blue eyes had too much blue.

"This is no business of mine, remember," Jed said, slashing the air with a flat hand. "Nothing to do with me. But I'm telling you. . . . Why don't you try being a little bit nice?"

"Nice?"

"Don't smirk at *me*. Nice to the kid in there. Are you stupid? What am I wasting my—"

"This is a date, isn't it?" she began. "You asked me—"

But Jed was thinking how that little throat must ache. His own throat felt raw. He growled, "Get her quiet. Get her happy. Go on."

"If I do?"

"If you do," he said rather desperately, "well . . . maybe we can have a quiet little drink before I go."

The girl turned, put down her glass, went to the door, and opened it quietly. She moved obediently. She vanished in the darkness.

"I'm afraid," Lyn said, "Mr. Towers must have gone out again. His room doesn't answer."

"I can only say I didn't see him, Miss." The man behind the desk at the Majestic wasn't terribly interested.

"But you did see him come in a little while ago?"

"Yes, I did." He threw her a mildly irritated glance.

"Well. . . ." She turned uncertainly.

"A message?" he suggested politely. She was a cute girl, trim and cuddly in the bright-blue coat with the big brass buttons. And she seemed distressed.

"Yes, I could leave a note."

He used a pencil to point the way to a writing desk in the lobby, aiming it between a pillar and a palm.

"Yes, I see. Thank you." Lyn sat down at the desk, put her purse down under her left forearm. She shifted the chair slightly so that she could keep an eye on a spot anyone entering the Hotel Majestic from the street must pass.

She thought he must have gone out again, perhaps through the bar. She hoped he wasn't, even now, upsetting her family. She herself didn't dare call home to ask. If they didn't know she was alone, so much the better. They'd have a fit, she thought. A fit. But . . . never mind. If they were anxious, too bad, but she was actually safe enough and they'd forgive and perhaps they'd even have confidence enough in her not to worry too much.

This was something she had to work out for herself. The family tended to side too blindly with her. Any man, they would assume, so benighted as to quarrel with their darling would never be worth her efforts to patch it up.

But I can be wrong, she thought, not far from tears.

No, she couldn't go home quite yet. She'd stay free for a while, even as long as a date might have lasted. Because this was important. She knew. It would be hard to explain how and why . . . embarrassing . . . maybe impossible. She had to work it out alone.

Anyhow, she didn't think Jed would go to her apartment. It would be capitulation. He wasn't that type. He was pretty proud.

Was she the type, then, to hang around? All right, she thought stubbornly, I *won't* be the huffy female type who, right or wrong, sits and waits for the male to come with his hat in his hand, like the dopey heroines of old romances who huffed and waited their lives away.

Ah, nobody was a type! This was Jed and Lyn, and this had to be worked out on the basis that they were unique and alive, and it had to be worked out *now*. Tomorrow, the plane. . . .

Wherever he was, he'd come back here. He hadn't checked out. It was all so childish. . . . She could at least say that much.

"Dear Jed," she wrote. "It was all so childish. . . ." She watched a man and a woman cross the lobby. "And I don't want you to go West thinking that I. . . ."

Am I doing this, she wondered, because I'm vain? "Thinking that I . . ." what? How could such bitter words have been spoken between them? Because she'd been riding a high romantic crest of expectation and been dragged rudely off it? Maybe for him there'd never been such a crest. No, no. That was a huffy-type thought, a fear to *seem* vain. She *had* known that Jed was fond of her. She'd had *reason* to expect him to say so or say more. Never mind that inside-out kind of vanity.

She tore up the sheet and wrote again, "Dear Jed: I've been trying to find you because—" A tear fell and the ink blurred and she thought, Oh no . . . not this! Wouldn't he be amused!

Would he? Lyn sat a long time with her hands quiet on the desk. She worked it out. It was true. She was in love with Jed Towers . . . in love enough to lash out at him, to get as mad as that, to have it matter.

It was true. She had thought he might ask her to marry him tonight. They'd been together, together . . . until that old man touched this off.

And it was true. She'd have said yes. Gladly, yes. Yes, right or wrong. Yes, just because of his mouth, maybe.

And they had quarreled.

But it was *not* true that she thought him a cheap cynic. He was . . . wary. Yes, he was. And he talked cynically. Part of it was simple reporting—what he saw around him. Part of it was defensive . . . or something like that. But it was talk. People don't always know what they are. They talk *at* themselves a lot. She thought, But I can really be tough. If I believe, then I must do . . . or all *I* said was only talk.

So Lyn worked it out, painfully. It was also true, whoever began it, whatever it amounted to, she had been the one to walk away and cut off communication, and she didn't (she'd always *said*) believe in that.

Very well. She clasped her hands. It was important. Here was a crest from which she would coast away all her life long. And a huff wouldn't do.

But what could she put on a piece of paper? If only he'd come. People crossed the lobby, none of them he. Tomorrow, that plane. . . . Maybe he'd call her. No, it went so early. She could ask in the note. All her thoughts were splintering. Dawn was such a chilly time.

She took up the pen. "Dear Jed: I can't let you go—" But you can't keep him, Lyn. He isn't that type. Maybe he was only something charming and exciting flashing through your life, and what you seemed in his, for a little while, you'll never know. Might have discovered whether there was any meaning but not now—too late. "Misunderstanding," she wrote desperately. It was too late. She ought to go home.

What can I say? she wondered. What can I do? How can I go home?

Get out of here, Towers. Get out, quick. And forget it. Skip it. Jed paid his inner talk to himself no heed. He sat down on a bed. Under the verbalized thought ran uneasy pictures. What if the child were to cry a long time, and he, in his own room, could hear? How was he in a position to be the indignant guest, to protest, to do anything about it? *He'd* been stupid. Nell, the baby-sitter, had already made a complete jackass out of Towers. This rose to word level. He looked into his glass and contemplated this state of affairs.

When Nell came back carrying the child, he knew her reason. She didn't trust him not to sneak away. He remained quietly where he was. He was not entirely displeased. He wanted to watch her quiet the child.

"If you're scared, that's silly. Nothing to be scared about," Nell said impatiently. "Now don't start to cry anymore. Shall I read another story?"

"No," said Bunny. She wasn't quite crying at the moment, but she was shaken by an aftermath of shuddering. It was a reaction not subject to her control.

Nell set her down on her bare feet. Three strangely assorted people looked rather helplessly at each other.

"You know, *you* nearly scared the life out of me," Jed said to the child in a friendly tone. "And Nell, too. That's why Nell was cross."

"She was . . . too . . . cross," said Bunny as well as she could.

"That she was," he agreed grimly.

Nell looked as if she would flare up defensively, but she did not. "You OK now?" Her voice was edgy. "You're not going to cry anymore?"

Bunny wasn't sure enough to say. Her eyes turned from one to the other.

"I'm a friend of Nell's, stopped by to see her a minute," Jed said, feeling his face flush. Why he should be trying to explain himself to this half-pint creature he didn't quite know. "You ought to be asleep, I guess," he went on awkwardly. "How old are you?"

"Nine."

Nine. What was it to be nine? Jed couldn't remember. The drinks were beginning to blur his concern a little. He began to feel these events less shattering, as if his ego went somewhere and lay down.

"I'm too hot," said Bunny. "I'm all sticky."

"Come over here, then." Nell went to the windows. "We'll let some cool air blow on you. Then you'll be cooler. Then you can go back to sleep." She nodded wisely. She pulled up the blind. She pushed up the sash.

Jed jumped quickly out of the line of vision through those windows. His back felt for the headboard. He poured another drink. The ice was all the way over there. So, no ice. Because he wouldn't cross in front of the windows. Place like a goldfish bowl. He knew. And that was where you made your mistake, Towers.

"See the lady, Bunny?"

Sob and shudder answered.

"I see a man down there. He's playing cards."

Jed's warm drink was nauseating.

"I think," Nell went on, "there's a kitten under the table."

"What"—sob—"table?"

"Down there. The card table."

"I don't see. . . ."

"Maybe it isn't a kitten. But it looks like a kitten."

"I've got a cat," Bunny said. "Is the kitten stripe-ed?"

"No."

"Is it gray?"

"Maybe."

Miss Eva Ballew wrote, on the Hotel Majestic stationery, in her flowing script ". . . seems to be a child crying in this hotel and I am so distracted, I hope you can understand what I am writing, since I seem to have two predicates and no subject in my previous sentence! My dear, this trip has really—"

Her pen paused. The child had stopped crying. Thank goodness, thought Miss Ballew. But now the night seemed hollow. She ducked her head enough to glance briefly out under her blind.

The pen resumed, "—been a treat for all us teachers to have visited so many historical sites here in the East. . . ." It was not a sentence.

She put down her pen suddenly and ducked again to look out, across the dark well of the inner court.

"I don't see any kitten," Bunny said, "at all." Her pigtails hung down in front, swinging.

"Well, you're not looking . . ." Nell said softly. "But you won't cry anymore, will you?"

Jed glanced across at the bowl of ice. He rose. Why did she have to put the damn blind up? Dare he cross over? *Was* there anybody taking all this in? He'd just as soon get out of here without some guest having seen. . . .

When he turned his head over his shoulder, the question dropped out of his mind. He stood quite still, puzzling about what was wrong. It seemed to him, definitely, that something was wrong. Bunny was kneeling on that radiator top. And Nell sat there, beside her. Nell's hand was flat on the little rump in the pink sprigged muslin—

Her hand was flat!

And there was some wild throbbing in this room.

Miss Eva Ballew, peering out, exclaimed. Nobody heard her, for she was alone. "No!" she said. Then, whimpering, "Oh, no! Please!"

The back of Jed's neck prickled. Must be his own pulse, doing that throbbing. Just the same, it was intolerable. He began to move silently, with the speed and grace of the young and strong.

"Way down under the table?" Bunny asked.

"Way down . . ." crooned Nell. "Way, way down. Are you going to be quiet, I wonder?"

Bunny screamed.

Jed, with his fingers tight around the little brown ankle, caught her forward pitch with one arm and said, on a rush of breath, "Excuse me. Shouldn't lean out like that, for Lord's sakes. I *had* to grab."

Nell's face turned, tipped back and up. She looked drowsy and unstartled. "What?" she murmured. "What's the matter?"

Jed had the child. "Better come away," he said to her. "You'll catch cold, anyhow." He could feel little twitches the whole length of the arm that held Bunny. He squeezed her as gently as he could manage. "I'm sorry, honey, if I scared you. Trouble is, you scared *me* again. Sure did. Awful long ways down—kind of tough landing."

Bunny, having screamed once in her surprise, did not begin to cry. Her face was pale. Her big dark eyes seemed to turn and keep some wisdom of her own.

Jed said, "You're chilly. You're shivering. Aren't you sleepy now?"

Bunny nodded. She wiggled out of his arm. Her feet hit the carpet. She looked at him gravely. "I can go to bed myself," said Bunny O. Jones.

Miss Ballew straightened her cramped body. Her heart still lurched with that old devil of hers, that hair-trigger onset of the physical sickness of fear. She felt her throbbing throat. But what was going *on* over there? Her pale lips tightened. She'd heard the man say, "Put that blind down!"

So, it was to be secret, and it was male, and it was, perhaps, evil? She focused on her letter. "And even in this wicked city," her pen wrote at last, too shakily.

"Put that blind down!"

Nell was still sitting by the window, still looking dreamy. She stretched to obey and Jed thought there was something snakelike in the smooth uncoiling of her arching back and her reaching arm.

He stood at the door of 809, through which Bunny had marched herself. 809 was quiet . . . dim and quiet in there. So he closed the door, gently.

Bunny's rigid neck muscles let go a little. The head began to dent the pillow. The eyes were wide open. The hand reached for the little stuffed dog and tucked it under the stiff chin. The throat moved against the fluffy toy in a great and difficult swallow.

Jed swung around. You're nuts, Towers, he said to himself angrily, using the words, in his mind, to knock out the pictures. You must be nuts. Where'd you get such a nutty idea? Nobody shoves kids out of eighth-story windows so they won't cry anymore! Made his hair curl, the mere idea, even now. Where had he got it?

He began to fish ice out of the bowl.

It crossed the level of his mind where slang was not the language that there is something wild about total immersion in the present tense. What if the restraint of the future didn't exist? What if you never said to yourself, "I'd better not. I'll be in trouble if I do"? You'd be wild, all right. Capricious, unpredictable . . . absolutely wild.

He looked at the girl. She was leaning beside him, watching the ice chunk into her glass, with a look of placid pleasure. She glanced up. "You've had more than me," she stated.

"That's right," Jed said. He felt perfectly sober. The slight buzz was gone. He didn't bother to put ice into his own glass, after all. He wasn't going to have any more liquor, not for a while.

He gave her the drink. He sat down, nursing his warm glass.

He couldn't get rid of the shimmer on his nerves of narrowly missed horror. Nuts, Towers. Forget it. She was careless. Nobody's going to have an idea like that one. She just wasn't thinking what she was doing.

"I guess I wasn't thinking," Nell said, with a delicate shrug.

"Are you a mind reader?" He sagged back on his elbow. "That's a couple of times you've said what I had in my mouth, practically."

She didn't answer.

"But you sure should have put a good hitch on the seat of her pants or something. Don't you know that's dangerous?" If the future didn't operate in your thinking, you wouldn't even know that word, he thought. Danger wouldn't have a meaning. Would it? He shivered. His mind veered.

If there *was* such a thing as telepathy, why, it would work both ways. If she could catch an idea out of his mind, then he might catch one of hers. Couldn't he? *Hadn't he?* Listen, Towers, don't be any nuttier than you have to be! Mind reading, yet! Fold your tent . . . fade away.

But he was hunting for comfort. He remembered something. He said, "So you couldn't go dancing with me on account of the kid?" (So you did feel responsible?)

"Uncle Eddie's on the elevator."

"Huh?"

"He'd have caught me going out," she said placidly. "He never lets me."

"Your Uncle? Uncle Eddie runs an elevator? In this hotel?"

"Yes."

"Oh." Jed turned this information over. "Maybe he got you the job, eh?"

"Yeah," she said with weary scorn, "my wonderful job."

"You don't like it?"

"What's there to like?" she said. And he saw the answer come into her head. He saw it! He *read* it! There's you, though, Nell was thinking.

He closed his eyes and shook his own head. None of that. But he considered, and on the whole he thought he felt relieved. The future tense had operated. Hadn't it? If she thought ahead of her to Eddie on the elevator?

His mind skipped to his own future. Tomorrow morning on the airplane. By tomorrow night, a continent away, looking back on a weird evening, which was about over, he judged. Time to go.

His anger was gone. *He* was operating in the future tense, looking back, saying to somebody, "And *what* a sitter! What a dame she turned out to be! Nutty as a fruitcake!" he would say. If he ever said anything.

"Well," he spoke. "Nell, I'll tell you. It might have been fun. We'll never know. So here's to the evening. Bottoms up and then good-bye. See you in South America, sometime?"

He grinned. Her eyes were too blue, not in the quality of the blue, but in the quantity. Strange eyes. . . .

"You're not going," she said, with no rising inflection at all. It wasn't even a protest. She just said this, as if it were so.

Chapter Eight

THE UNWRITTEN LAW that links green peas to roast chicken had not been flouted tonight. Peter pointed with his fork and winked. He wasn't really eating.

Ruth could eat no more than he. They picked and pretended. But nobody, she thought, was there for the sake of nourishment. The food marched by, as it were, in a sedate order, perfectly conventional, with no surprises, so that nothing about it should interrupt the real business of the banquet. Be seen, buzz, bow. . . . Preen yourself, flatter your neighbor. Oh, it *was* fun!

But now they were nearly past the ice cream. They were at the coffee . . . the end of the line. Peter's conversation with his neighbors had been slowly lessening. Fewer and fewer words came out of him.

Ruth's nerves tightened right along with his. She let a little ice cream melt in her dry mouth. Peter was taking tiny sips of water, oftener now.

Every once in a while, the buzzing and the bending to chat got a little unreal for Ruth—whenever Bunny came into her mind. It was a little distressing that her vision of Bunny in her bed was shaky and unreal, too. Bunny, she told herself, making words, as if the words had power, was sound asleep. As sound asleep as if she were in her bed at home. Oh, Bunny was real! Warm and beloved, Bunny was there. But those hotel rooms, those formulas, did not wrap her around with the safe sense of being home.

But *of course not!* Ruth said to herself.

Still, it was a great city, vast and unknown, and the West Side seemed divorced from the East Side, where they were . . . seemed far.

"I'd like to call back to the hotel pretty soon," she murmured to Peter. "Where are the phones?"

"Saw them as we came through," Peter said. "Around the corner, past those mirrors. . . ." He dabbled in his ice cream. The toast-master was still chatting peacefully.

"Have I time, do you think?" breathed Ruth. They, at the speakers' table, were as far as it was possible to be away from the double doors to the mirrored place beyond which were the telephones. Parade, in my pink, thought Ruth. Conspicuous. Peter could not go *now.*

The toastmaster shifted in his chair. He sipped his coffee. Ruth felt all Peter's muscles wince. For the toastmaster glanced their way and made a tiny nod. His eyes nodded deeper than his head did.

Imperceptibly, Peter responded. The toastmaster shoved with his hips and his chair began to move backward.

Not now! No time now! Ruth would call afterward. After the man had said whatever he was going to say. Later than that, for without intermission it would then be Peter's turn!

It would be good to call later, with this tension gone. And all clear. Oh, yes, it would be much better.

There was no doubt that Bunny was sound asleep, anyway. Ruth must now lift her chin and turn her head and listen sweetly to the Speaker of the Evening. (Oh, what was he going to say. Oh, *Peter!*)

Bunny was nine and surely had fallen sound asleep by this time.

The toastmaster rose like Fate. Ruth released her glass and patted her cold hands together in tune with the crowd. "I am happy," the man said, "to be here. . . ." Who cares how happy they are? Always so *happy!* She could hear every tiny wheeze of the toastmaster's breathing. Peter had turned slightly in his chair, as if this were fascinating, but no concern of his, of course. . . .

"And I am particularly glad," the man said, "to have this opportunity. . . ." They were always so glad.

Ruth smiled faintly and let her fingers play with her water glass. She must display the perfect confidence she felt, that under her pounding heart lay so truly sure. . . .

Jed fended her off and it was balm to do so. It was sweet revenge on the whole female race who had loused up his evening. He laughed at her. He had her by the elbows, at arm's length. "It's not that automatic, toots," he said. "I know. There's a school of thought that says it is. But make a note, why don't you? There is such a thing as being choosy."

Her rage made him laugh and he let himself go back against the headboard. "The time, the place, and the girl," he mocked. *"I'll* choose them all, and this ain't *any* of them, sweetheart."

She looked ready to screech. But then her face closed down, took on that sleepy look. She leaned heavily on his grasp, limply, now, with nothing but her weight.

"So I'll say so long, Nell," he snapped, watching her suspiciously. "Understand?"

The wild thing about her which, he knew now, had attracted him in the first place, and then made him uneasy, was getting entangled with her will. She wasn't sleepy. Oh, no! Now, he knew that the dreamy look was on her a dangerous sign. Maybe a part of her did go to sleep. Maybe it was the part that took into account the future.

He sat up, thrusting her with stiff forearms. He was a little bit sorry for having indulged himself in that laughter. He wondered just how he was going to get out of here without a row, without, say, too much racket. He said quietly, "I'm really sorry, but I've got to go. Some other time, Nell."

She didn't seem to hear. Then she did seem to hear, not his voice, but something less loud and less near. Her pupils traveled to the right corners of her eyes.

He heard it, too. There came a discreet tapping on the door of room 807.

Oh-oh! Exit Towers! Jed muttered under his breath, "I'll get out the other way, through the kid's room."

"No." She spoke no louder than he, not a whisper, only a movement of the lips that was nearly mute. "You won't." The words were clear and stubborn on her small mouth.

". . . find me," he said in the same fashion, "you'll lose your job."

The tapping was gently repeated. It would persist, insist. It was patient.

Nell's face lit in malice and delight. "No, no. I'll say . . . you pushed in here. Say you're . . . after me."

Jed's eyes flickered. She would, too. She damn well would! He was quite sure she would. For the hell of it! For the sheer wild mischief of it! And, if she did, the benefit of the doubt rests with the female.

"You wait," she said. "I know who it is."

Their almost soundless conversation was taking place in a depth of silence that was uncanny. The room pressed silence around them. The city bayed at the feet of the building, but here, high, they spoke without voices in a soundless place. Although someone kept tapping in gentle hope upon the door.

"Who?" Jed was rigid in alarm. How in hell was he going to get off this spot? What to do?

"It's Uncle Eddie. I can get rid of him."

"I can get out," Jed gestured. His eyes were somber.

"No." She knew her wild will held him.

"What then?" He ground his teeth.

"In there. Be quiet." She intended him to hide in the bathroom.

He rose slowly, letting her go. He could knock her aside. He could get swiftly into the kid's room.

And she was opening her mouth.

Jed stalled by picking up the bottle and hiding it in his pocket. Quickly she put his glass into his hand. And then she had him by the elbow. She was pushing, guiding.

The tapping faltered. "Nell?" someone said softly and a trifle anxiously. "Nell?"

Nell said, "Who's there?" Her very voice seemed to stretch and yawn. But her eye was watching Jed and her face rippled. She would just as leave cause trouble . . . just as leave as not!

"It's Uncle Ed. You all right?"

Nell's brows spoke to Jed. Twitted him with it. *Well?* they asked. *Am I?*

He growled, voice muted in the bottom of his throat. "OK. Make it snappy." He went into the bathroom and pushed the door back behind him, not quite tight.

"Gee, I'm sorry, Uncle Eddie. I guess I must have been asleep," he heard her saying . . . heard her yawning it.

Towers stood in the bathroom and cursed Towers in his mind. What'd she have, a hex on him? Of all the damned lousy situations. He looked at his watch. He said to himself, Let Uncle Eddie get away and I am gone. Brother, will I be gone. I'll really fade. Without a word, he'd go. Without a wasted motion.

You picked up dames, sure. Every once in a while. On a train. Maybe in a bar. Sometimes a thing like that turned out not bad. If it was sour, you blew. In cold blood. You got out fast.

How come Towers was hiding behind a door?

He sat on the edge of the tub, to wait, reciting curses, rehearsing in his mind his swift passage out and away.

Lyn turned away from the phones. No answer.

I will smoke another cigarette, one more. I will wait until ten more people come in from the street, ten more. I can write a better letter. I know I can. I can try.

Chapter Nine

EDDIE LOOKED at his niece in negligee and his eyes were disappointed. He said, "I brought the cokes." Disappointment made his voice bleak. He had the bottles in his hands and he went toward the desk and stood there looking down at the tray, the bowl of melting ice, and Nell's glass. "What's this?" An inch and a half of rye and ginger ale remained in the glass.

Nell said, "You were a long time, Uncle Eddie. I got thirsty. Let me wash that out." She took the glass out of his meek hand. "I ordered ginger ale," she said defiantly to his troubled eyes. "Mrs. Jones said I could."

"That was nice of her," said Eddie.

"Want a piece of candy?" Nell said brightly over her shoulder. "She said I could help myself."

"I don't believe I care for any," Eddie said. "Thanks." His bleak stare went around the room.

Nell pushed in the bathroom door. She went to the wash basin and rinsed the glass.

Not even in the mirror did her eye meet Jed's. There was not a gesture, not a wink, not a sign that she even knew he was there. Jed felt his blood rage. It was an abuse of power. A little grin, a tiny glance, a hint that they conspired to fool this Eddie would have eased the thing somehow. But, oh, no! She'd forced him into this ignominy and now she let him stew in it. He could have beaten her. He ground his teeth. Some baby-sitter!

Eddie said, "Little girl sleeping? I see you closed her door."

Nell left the bathroom, pulling its door behind her. She would have closed that, but Jed threw his strength on the inner knob and they tugged secretly, silently, and she lost.

"Could you hear if she cried or anything?" Eddie was saying in worried tones.

"The light bothered her," Nell lied calmly.

"Now she's sleeping, though, it won't bother her." Eddie, gentle on the knob, released the catch. "I think Mrs. Jones would rather it was a little bit open, Nell."

"OK," she said indifferently. She waited for the coke.

"And it's getting later. It would be better if you took Mrs. Jones' clothes off, Nell. Honest, I thought. . . ." Eddie's Adam's apple betrayed his hurt, although his voice was careful.

"Gee, I meant to." Nell's fine teeth bit her lip. "I was so kinda comfortable . . . I just didn't hurry. . . ."

At once Eddie brightened. "Sure you meant to, Nell. I know that. Uh—" he fiddled with an opener. "Why don't you do it now, though?"

"All right, Uncle Eddie." She sat docilely down on the little bench and slipped her feet out of the mules. Eddie scrambled for her own black pumps and she put them on. Then she took the earrings off, slowly. She put them into the jewel box. Her fingers began to pick up other things, tidying them, putting them away.

Eddie brightened with his lightening heart. "That's right! Good girl!"

She turned her bent head, smiled at him. She rose and her hands worked at the sash of Ruth's gown. Eddie's eyes turned primly down. Nell said, sounding modest and shy, "I'll just step into the closet."

Her Uncle Eddie took a long relieved pull on his coke bottle.

She came out of the closet in her own rumpled dark dress. It had been a heap on the closet floor for some time. But now Nell made elaborate motions of finicky care as she hung the negligee on a hanger and arranged its folds. "There," she said, "that's just the way it was. Is that OK, Uncle Eddie?"

He beamed on her. "That's fine, Nell. Now!" He sighed. "Mightn't be so very long before they get back, you know. But you're all set."

"We'd better drink our cokes," she said mildly. "It might look better if I was alone in here. Do you think?"

"You're right," he said. "Yes, you're right. I told them I was going to drop in, but it *would* be better if they find everything quiet and you on the job, eh? Well, here you are. You know," he blurted, "I want to do everything *for* you, don't you, Nell? You know why I want you to take a nice little job like this. I want you to get started."

"I know, Uncle Eddie." She was all meekness. Her lashes were lowered. She showed no sign of impatience at all.

He took a swig. "Well, it's because I believe in you, Nell. And Aunt Marie does, too." His blink was contradicting the courage in his voice. "I think you'd rather be here with us than back in Indiana."

"Oh, I would," she murmured.

"If the insurance company would have paid on the house and furniture—but as it is, there's nothing left. You know that. So you'd be on some kind of charity, till you got a job, and I wouldn't like that for Denny's girl."

"No," she said.

"You know I haven't got much money," he went on. "I got a steady job. But you can see why it's a good thing if you can . . . kinda get over this trouble pretty soon."

"I'm OK," she said without force.

"You're *better*. That's sure. You certainly are a lot better."

She was looking at him with that blind blue abstraction she sometimes had. "But they ought to pay," she said. "Why can't we make them pay?"

"I don't know how we can," said Eddie uneasily. "I don't know if we can ever *make* them. You see, they claim, because the fire was *set*. . . ."

"It was an accident." Her voice went higher. And he cleared his throat nervously. *"Wasn't* it?"

"It was. It was. That's what they said in the court, yes. It was an accident."

Suddenly her face was calm, her glance cold. "So why don't they pay?"

"Well, the insurance company, they figure—I tell you, Nell. I think it's best to kinda forget about that. Might take a lawyer and quite a lot of money and you wouldn't be sure you could win, you see? I think the best thing is, forget about that and try and get started. . . . There wasn't so much insurance. How's the coke?"

"It's good," she said meekly. "Is yours?"

"Fine." He took another swig. It might have been wine, for he seemed to mellow. "You just needed somebody to stand back of you," he said. "Me and Marie knew that, Nell, at the time. And we do stand back of you. We really do. *I* can understand just why it is you get kinda restless streaks. *I* don't blame you."

"You've been good, Uncle Eddie." Her lips barely moved.

But he looked very happy. "It's just that I can see how it is," he said eagerly. "After such a terrible experience, a lot of little things seem pretty *little*. Don't matter much, eh? That's the way it is, isn't it, Nell?" The little man seemed to hold his breath. Every fiber of his worried little being was yearning to make contact, to understand and be understood.

The girl didn't look up, but she nodded.

He swallowed and leaned closer. He said softly, "You want to remember, Nell, your father and mother don't blame you. You mustn't ever think that they would. They know you wouldn't ever have done anything bad, Nell . . . not to them. You see, wherever they are, *they* must know that even better than we do. And if they could talk to you. . . ."

"I don't want to think about them," she said in a perfect monotone. "I don't want to think about them."

"No, no," said Eddie quickly. "Nobody wants to make you think . . . about that. But I been trying to tell you one thing, Nell. The doctor said it would be good if you'd know . . . and here we're so quiet and all, maybe I can say it. Me and your Aunt Marie, we stand back of you. We believe in you. We don't doubt, for one minute, you set the fire walking in your sleep that night. . . ."

He watched her face. Her lashes flickered. "That's what the court said," she remarked lightly.

"But—but—don't cry," he whispered to the tearless blue of her eyes.

"I'm not going to cry, Uncle Eddie." She turned her empty glass in her fingers. She put it down.

Eddie blinked the tears out of his own eyes. He swallowed the sick flutter of his heart. That Julia his brother married, something about her he never had liked. But surely she'd never been mean to Nell. Denny wouldn't have stood for it. Denny wouldn't be mean to anybody. No, no. There could be *no reason.* She was still shocked, poor Nell. She *couldn't* cry. She *loved* them. She'd meant no harm. She'd cry, someday. *Sure,* she'd cry.

"Tasted pretty good, didn't it?" he said cheerily.

Jed controlled his rage almost immediately. He'd got into this jam by getting senselessly angry and it was about time, he told himself, that Towers used the brains he was born with. He settled coldly to wait this out. He could hear their voices and a part of his brain recorded the words.

But, in part and at the same time, he was reviewing the way he had come. It had come back to him, the year he was nine. Not the events of that year, so much, as the feel of it. By then, he mused, the boy was all adjusted to the family. He had been trained. He knew what the rules of conduct were in so far as his mother and father had taught them. All that was smooth, so smooth he couldn't remember much about it.

But he was also stepping out, newly bold, into the world his parents did not know. He was beginning to test himself more daringly with his contemporaries. School, the gang, society and his personal meeting with it had been the part of life that was filled with interest. Warm security at home and one toe in the cold waters of the outer world, testing to take his weight.

Pretty soon, he remembered, the boy began to pick up the stuff that isn't down in the home rules. The ways and the means, the maneuverings, the politics, the exchanges of influences, the worming one's way, the self-interest of everybody and how to use *this* for himself. Through high school and a part of college, and then the war, and the final bitter tutoring of the peace. Sharper lessons, all the time. Trial and error. What worked and what didn't. Lessons in the possible. Knocking home what's possible and what is not, and what is only a fool's goal.

So now here's Towers. A young man, out to "make his fortune" as they used to say in the old stories when he was nine. Out to make his fortune without a dream in his eye. Wangled himself a damn good job on the Coast. Pulled strings to get it. Young man on the way up, and gangway for him! Old enough to begin to think, if only obliquely, that he might take a wife.

So Lyn was on his mind, eh? A dream, there? He pushed her image away.

So, here was Towers, skipping the whole middle of the country, tomorrow, letting it flow under his plane, not planning to stop and see the family. Why? Oh, business, he'd said. They understood. Not wishing to stop and hear the blind love speaking, pretending he was nine?

Well, he thought, people probably settled on a pattern that worked for them, and there they stayed. And if his pattern was shaping up a little differently, why, no use arguing. Dad talked service. Lived it, too, as far as anyone could see. And it worked for him. Or anyhow, it worked pretty well. It made a kind of guide, a touchstone . . . Jed could see. And Mother talked love—*was* love, dammit. He wished, a little wistfully, that the world really was what they seemed, incomprehensibly, able to assume it was. How come they could hang onto that kind of peace, whatever it was, and make it a shell around them?

Or did they? Were they besieged by disappointments? Were they only huddled in their shell, like people in a fort? He didn't see much of them, these days. It was the family tradition to exchange only cheerful news, as far as one could. Did their hearts despair?

He didn't want to think so. He supposed you battled through, sooner or later, and came out on the other side of struggle, when you accepted something or other and put the blinders on and just kept them on and didn't look anymore.

But when you're young and scrambling in the market place, you have to watch out. Yeah, out. Not in. That is, take a hard look at the way the world operates. You didn't want to be pushed around.

Oh, Towers was a wise one, all right, sitting on the bathtub, behind the door. He knew the score.

His jaw was tight. Definitely a detour, this little expedition. Get on your way, Towers!

Still talking, this Uncle Eddie? Still yammering in there?

"And so, I thought," Eddie was saying, "the best idea is for you to start out easy. Take a little job once in a while. The thing is, Nell," he was expounding his creed, "you do something for somebody else and you do a good job. So they're glad to pay you for it. Then you're earning. You're being useful. You got to get into the idea. After a while, you'll get so you can do a bigger job or a better job. You'll get into the idea. You'll get over being so restless."

"You told me all this," she said. Her ankle was swinging.

Eddie saw it and silenced himself.

"Going?" she murmured. Her head fell against the chair. She turned her cheek. Her eyes closed.

"I'll take the coke bottles. I don't think the Joneses are going to be so long, now. Couple of hours, maybe. Tired?"

She didn't answer. Eddie rose and the bottles clinked together as he gathered them. She was breathing slowly. "I'll be in the building," he murmured. His eye checked over the room. Everything was in pretty good order. Looked all right. He took up the glass from which Nell had sipped her coke.

Absorbed in his own thoughts, his anxieties, his endeavors, his gains and his losses, Eddie went mechanically toward the running water, which was in the bathroom.

Chapter Ten

EVEN BEFORE he met the little man's shocked and unbelieving eyes in the mirror, an appraisal of this new situation flooded clearly through Jed's thoughts. The jig was up, all right. OK. He rose smoothly. The frightened eyes followed him up, still by way of the glass. But Jed was smiling.

This could be handled.

The mind has an odd ability to play back like a tape recorder things heard and yet not quite attended to at the time. Jed knew, immediately, that Eddie could be handled. And that it was a way out for Towers, too.

He knew from what he had overheard that Eddie was by no means sure of his little niece, Nell. Eddie had stuck his neck out, getting her this job. Eddie knew she was unreliable, to put it mildly, although he tried, he struggled, to make himself believe everything was going to be all right. All that pitch about his belief and understanding, all that stuff, was a hope and a prayer, not only conviction. Oh, yes. Eddie had taken an awful chance here and Eddie was liable.

All Jed needed to do was use Eddie's self-interest. Very simple. Jed would apologize. Nothing happened, really. Had a couple of drinks, very sorry, sir, he'd say. I'll be leaving now. No harm done and enough said. Nobody need say anything more about it?

Jed would make it easy for the other fellow. He'd ask silence as a favor to himself. Eddie could escape by magnanimity the consequences of his own folly. Eddie would be glad to say "good-bye" and only good-bye.

So long, Nell, Jed would say, quietly. And he'd be out of it.

So Jed rose, smiling, knowing he had the power of charm and attractive friendliness when he chose to use it. In the time it took him to rise and open his mouth, the little man had jerked with a mouse squeak and backed toward the door, keeping a frightened face toward Jed's tall figure in the tile-lined gloom. Jed, not to alarm him, stood quietly where he was.

But Nell, like a cat, was lithe lightning across room 807. She had the standing ashtray, the heavy thing, in her wild hands. She swung it up. Jed's lunge and Jed's upraised arm missed the downswing. The thing cracked on Eddie's skull. The detachable portion of heavy glass clanged and boomed and echoed on the tile. And Jed said something hoarse and furious and snatched the thing out of her hands cruelly, and Nell jabbered some shrill syllables.

All at once the noise was frightful.

Only Eddie made no noise. He sank down, very quietly.

There was an instant when everything was suspended. Then the phone began to ring in 807, and at the same time Bunny's voice screamed terror in 809. And the glass part of the ashtray, rolling off a brief balance, rumbled and at last stopped rolling, unbroken.

"Now!" said Jed thickly. "Now, you . . ." He squatted beside the crumpled little body.

Nell turned and walked over to the telephone, which in some freak of time had rung four times already.

"Hello?" Her voice was fuzzy and foggy.

Jed touched Eddie's temple and then his throat.

"Oh yes, Mrs. Jones," Nell said. "I guess I must have been dozing."

There was a pulse under Jed's fingers and he stopped holding his breath.

"She's fast asleep," Nell said blithely. (And Bunny kept screaming.) "Oh, no, no trouble at all. Everything's just fine."

Jed, crouching, found himself listening to that voice. It was pretty cool. Just the faintest undertone of excitement. It could pass for enthusiasm. He could feel the child's cries pierce him, and he shuddered. He looked down at Eddie, feeling a blank dismay.

"Yes, she did. Went right to sleep after her story, Mrs. Jones. I hope you are having a nice time."

Phone to ear, Nell pivoted to see what Jed was doing and one stare was as blank as another. Her hand rose to hover over the mouthpiece.

The kid was frantic in there! Frantic!

"Please don't feel you need to hurry, Mrs. Jones," purred Nell, "because I don't mind— What?"

Her eyes widened as her voice acted surprise. "Noise? Oh, I guess you can hear the sirens down in the street." Her hand clamped on the mouthpiece. She said, through careful fingers, "They're just going by. There isn't any fire near here." She laughed. "Oh, no. You just have a real good time," she advised gaily. She hung up the phone.

Her face set.

"It's a wonder he's not dead," Jed growled. "You little fool!"

"Isn't he?" said Nell absentmindedly.

She walked into 809.

Jed's hand, going about the business with no conscious command from his numb brain, felt Eddie's head carefully. The dry hair crisped on his fingertips. He left the dismayed welter of his thoughts to pay attention, here. Couldn't tell what the damage was, but there was, at least, no bleeding. Gently, he straightened the body. He lifted it, shifting it all the way over the threshold within the bathroom and, reaching for the thick bath mat, he slid it gently between the hard tile floor and the head. He took a towel and wet it. He washed the forehead gently, the eyes, and the cheeks.

Eddie's breathing seemed all right . . . a little difficult, not very.

Jed thought the pulse was fairly steady. Knocked out, of course, but perhaps. . . .

He lifted his own head suddenly.

Bunny was not screaming. The empty air pulsed in the sudden absence of that terrible sound.

Jed sat motionless on his heels. A trickle of sweat cut a cold thread of sensation down his neck and blurred in the fabric of his collar.

Ruth stepped with slow grace out of the phone booth. "Have a real good time." The phrase rang in her ears. Not the *mot juste* for a night as this! This Night of Triumph! A time to keep in the mind for reference forever. Even now, so soon afterward, it was an hour to live over again, and feel the heart stop when Peter got up from his chair, and lurch when he began, so nervously. And pound proudly, because she soon knew that all these politely listening people were warming to the man, who began a little bit nervously and shyly, as if to say, "Gosh, who am I?"

And then, Peter getting interested, himself, in what he was saying. Everybody feeling that. First, the words, coming out grammatically, properly placed, in full sentences. Then, the thought transcending, and driving the grammar into vivid astonishing phrases that rang just right. And finally Peter in the full power of his gift, taking directly from his mind and heart the things he knew and believed. The heads turning because they could not help it. They must hear this.

He was still excited (oh, bless Peter!) and he was reaping his reward. Now that his speech was over, now that they were pushing the tables out of the middle of the floor, and music was playing, and people stood in little groups, and he in the middle of the largest group of all.

Peter was reaping an evening's worth of praise and glory. But maybe even more. Maybe even the real thing! Was it possible, the Joneses wondered, that some might remember, might retain and refer to some small part, at least, of what he had told them?

A victory! But the rehashing, the reaping, the wonderful fun of this might go on for hours.

Ruth turned her bright nails into her palms. Bunny was fast asleep. The girl had told her so. Everything was fine. The girl had said so.

But Ruth stood trembling in the hall of mirrors, and she knew in her bones that everything was *not* fine.

"Don't be silly!" she gasped to her own image. "Don't be such a *mother!* Don't spoil it now!"

Peter's head craned toward her out of the group, and she gave him a gay little signal of the hand that meant "all's well."

For it must be so.

But that hadn't sounded like the same girl. Oh, it was the same voice. But it was not the same manner. The girl on the phone, just now, was neither dull nor passive. *She wasn't stupid enough!* No, she'd been too decisive. Too . . . too darned *gay!* Too patronizing. . . . "Run along, little Mrs. Jones, and have your real good time. Don't bother me."

"Don't you be so *silly!*" Ruth told herself once more. "Are you going to be mean and spoil Peter's wonderful night, being such a hick and such a female? What's *wrong* with you?"

She shook herself and walked forward.

"What's wrong, oh, what's wrong where Bunny is?" her bones kept asking.

Peter was in full flight, amplifying something he hadn't touched on quite enough in the speech. Men, standing around him, were smoking with very deliberate and judicious gestures, and nodding, and breaking in to quote themselves. "As I said at lunch the other day. . . ." "I was saying to Joe. . . ." It seemed as if only last week or the other day they'd been thinking the same things Peter thought. They'd been telling somebody, in some fumbling fashion, that which Peter had just told them so well. (Ah, sweet praise!)

"OK, hon?" Peter was tuned in on the wavelength of Ruth's bones. Often and often he'd heard what they were muttering. But now, when she answered, smiling, "All quiet. Everything fine, Nell says." Peter didn't hear her bones proclaim, "But I don't believe it."

"Good." He squeezed her, swung her. "Ruth, this is Mr. Evans, and Mr. Childs, and Mr. Cunningham."

"How de do . . . how de do. . . ."

"Husband of yours has a head on his shoulders and a tongue in his head, Mrs. O.–uh–Mrs. Jones. Fine talk. Fine."

"I thought so, too," said Ruth in sweet accord.

"Isabel, come here. Turn around, want you to meet. . . ." The women murmured.

Peter said, "So, a man says to you, 'Honesty is the best policy.' You don't need to look up his antecedents, and if you find his great uncle stole fifty cents thirty years ago, figure what he *says* must therefore be suspect. What he *says* you can agree to or *not* agree to. However, if he claims he is prohonesty, but expects you to rob a bank with him, you can see the difference, I hope. In fact, you had better learn the difference."

"Right," said a cigar.

"I claim the truth can come out of a rascal's mouth, but how can a rascal fool us, if we learn to sort out words from deeds and keep our heads clear?"

"Just what I said to Isabel. I said. . . ."

"And how old is your little girl, Mrs. O.—uh—Mrs. Jones?" Isabel was cooing.

"Bunny is nine."

"Ah, I remember Sue when she was nine," said the woman sentimentally. "A sweet age. A darling year."

Ruth smiled, bright-eyed. She had no voice for an answer.

Chapter Eleven

MRS. PARTHENIA WILLIAMS said, "I can't help it."

"Aw, Ma," her son said, keeping his voice down in the evening hush of the place where they stood. "Listen to me—"

"I can't help it, Joseph, hear?"

For old Mr. and Mrs. O'Hara in the front suite, the Hotel Majestic had somehow, in the inertia of the years, acquired the attributes of home. Now Mrs. O'Hara wasn't very well. She wasn't ill enough to warrant a nurse, yet they were unwilling to risk her being alone. So Mrs. Parthenia Williams came by day and sometimes, when Mr. O'Hara had to be away, she remained late into the evening. Whenever she did so, her son, Joseph, came to see her home.

As they stood in the hush of the eighth-floor corridor, Joseph said, "You better keep out of it, Ma. You know that. Don't you?" He was a thin nervous Negro with an aquiline face.

"I know what I know," his mother said.

Mrs. Williams' chocolate-colored face was designed for smiling, in the very architecture of her full cheeks, the curl of her generous mouth, the light of her wide-set eyes. Nothing repressed her. Nothing could stop her from saying "Good morning" in the elevators in her beautiful soft voice. She seemed to acquire through her pores bits and scraps of knowledge about all these strangers, so that she would say, in the corridor, "Did you enjoy the boat trip, ma'am? Oh, that's good!" with the temerity of an unquenchable kindness. Mrs. O'Hara, who was sixty-two and so often annoyingly dizzy, felt at rest on Parthenia's bosom. She told Mr. O'Hara it was as if, after thirty orphaned years, and in her old age, she were mothered once more. (Mr. O'Hara crossed his fingers and knocked on wood.)

Joseph knew his mother's ways and adored her, but some of her ways. . . . He tried to protest this time. "Some things you can't— Ma!"

"Something's scaring that baby in there nearly to death," Parthenia said. "She's just a bitty girl. She's in 809 and her folks next door. I spoke to them today. A real nice child. And I can't help it, Joseph, so don't you talk to me."

Her big feet carried her buxom body down the corridor. "If her folks ain't there, somebody ought to be comforting her. It's not good for her to be so scared."

"Ma, listen. . . ."

"All right, Joseph. Her papa, he was asking about a sitter and I *know* they were planning to go out. Now, if her mama's there, that's one thing. But I got to ask. I can't help it. I don't care."

Jed got to his feet. His eyes rolled toward the frosted bathroom window. He unlocked it and pushed it up. Cold air hit him in the face.

The deep court seemed quiet. He thrust his head through to look down into the checkered hollow. He couldn't, of course, see all the way to the bottom. He couldn't see Bunny's window, either, for it came on a line with this one.

He could see that old biddy across the way and she was walking. She walked to a chair and held to the back of it with both hands and let go with a push and walked away. And back again. He could see only the middle section of her body, and those agitated hands.

The fear that hadn't been verbalized, even in his mind, seeped away, and he wondered why he was looking out of the window. He wondered if the dame over there was upset because she had been hearing things. He wondered, and in the act of wondering, he *knew* that someone must have heard all that commotion.

Get out of here, Towers, he warned himself, while you got the chance, you damn fool! Before all hell's going to break loose. This guy's not going to die. He'll be OK. He's resting peacefully. Look out for Towers!

Jed realized that he had a perfect chance, right now. While the wildcat was in 809, Towers could fade out of 807. And Towers would run like crazy away from here.

What he heard himself growling aloud as he stepped over Eddie's body was, "What in hell is she *doing* in there?"

The knock made him jump. Too late? He groaned. He eyed the distance from where he stood to 809. Through there, where the key, he remembered, dangled its fiber tag on the inside of Bunny's door . . . that would have to be the way out, now that someone, and he didn't doubt it was trouble, knocked on 807. He waved. How would he get by whoever it was, once in the corridor. He would, he thought, get by and he'd better.

Then he saw Nell standing in the way. She looked at him and moved her left hand. It said, "Be still." Jed shook his head and tightened his muscles for the dash. But Nell was too swiftly across 807 . . . so swiftly that Jed caught himself and ducked backward into concealment again, only just as she opened the door to trouble.

"Yes?" Jed could see her and he cursed, silently, her dark-clad back (she'd changed her clothes!) and the fantastically cool lift of her chin.

He expected a man's voice, an official voice, cold and final. But the voice was deep music, and not a man's. "I heard the little child crying so bad," it said. "Is there anything I can do?"

"Why, no," said Nell in chill surprise.

"You taking care of the little girl for Miz Jones, ma'am?"

"Yes."

"That's good. You know, I spoke to the little girl and her mama . . . she might know me. I wonder could I comfort her?"

"She's all right now," Nell moved the door. But Parthenia's big foot was within the sill.

"I had so much experience with childern. I get along with childern pretty well, it always seems. She was scared, poor child? I hear that."

"Just a nightmare," said Nell indifferently.

"Come on, Ma," Joseph said. "You asked. Now, come *on*."

"Who are you?" said Nell sharply, peering at him.

"This is my middle boy," Parthenia said with pride. "I've got three boys and two girls. Yes, ma'am, a big family but they raised. Hurts me to hear a baby cry so bad. Just hurts my heart like a pain. Poor little child . . . and all so strange. . . ." It was like a song, a lullaby.

"It's none of your business that I can see," said Nell coldly.

"Maybe not," said Parthenia. But her big foot stayed where it was. A big foot, worn with carrying a big body, bunioned and raked over at the heel . . . a big strong stubborn foot. "Maybe not," the lovely voice said sadly, "but I got to try to stop my pain. Can't help trying, ma'am, whatever child is crying."

"She's not crying now," said Nell irritably. "And it's too bad you've got a pain. Please let me close this door, will you?"

"Ma—"

"You got a charm for the nightmare?" Parthenia asked with unde-feated goodwill.

"If you don't get out of here, I'll call somebody."

"Ma . . . Excuse us, miss . . . Ma, come *away*."

"I can't feel happy about it," said Parthenia softly mournful. "That's the truth. It's just," her soft voice begged, "could I be sure she ain't scared anymore? Little children, being scared sometimes in the night, you got to be sure. Because it hurts their growing if they're not comforted."

"She's comforted," spat Nell. Then she changed. "But thank you for asking," she said in a sweet whine that had a threat to it, some-how. "I guess you mean well. But I really can't ask you in here. I don't know who you are or this man—"

Joseph plucked his mother from the doorway roughly.

"Good night, then," Parthenia said forlornly and, as Nell closed them out, "If I was white I wouldn't—"

"Shush!" said her son. "Hurry up. Get the elevator. Get home. She's trouble."

"Trouble," his mother murmured.

"You ought to know better, Ma. I told you. We can't fool around that white girl. Believe me, not *that* one!"

"I wasn't fooling. Something's bad wrong, Joseph. Baby's mother's not there. I can't feel happy about it."

"Listen, Ma, you better feel happy because you can't win. You know that, don't you? You can't stick your nose in that white girl's affairs, if you're right a million times over." He rang for the elevator, jittering.

"No child," said Parthenia gravely, as they waited, "no child gets off the nightmare as quick as that. No child, Joseph. Nobody's child."

"You can't do anything, Ma. Forget it, can't you?"

The elevator stopped. The door slid. Parthenia's enormous foot hesitated. But she stepped in at last, and Joseph sighed as they sank down.

He heard her mutter, "No, I wouldn't go."

"Shall we stop for a bite?" said he in nervous animation. "You hungry, Ma?" She didn't answer. "Ma?"

"I don't believe I'll stop tonight, boy," Parthenia said.

"Not hungry?" He grasped her arm and pushed her off the elevator, around the bend, to the back way out.

Parthenia said, looking at the stars, "No, I'd make a fuss. I wouldn't go."

Chapter Twelve

". . . NIGGERS!" said Nell.

All of a sudden all Jed's cool purpose to depart was burned up in the flame of his raging need to tell her off.

"You damn wildcat! Dope! Fool! What's the idea of doing what you did? What's the idea of swatting him down like that? What in hell did you think you were doing? What kind of cockeyed dream was in your stupid brain? Answer me!"

He shook her. The dark dress was too short. Also, it was cut to fit a more matronly body. So she looked younger and less sophisticated, but also older and dowdier. Her head went back on her neck, as a snake's head poises to strike, and her tiny mouth over the sharp tiny chin looked venomous. Her face with the yellowish glow to the unlined skin was no age one could guess or imagine.

"Answer me!"

She was angry. "What's the matter with you?" she cried. "You didn't want to be seen, did you? Did you?"

He could see her pupils, pin points in the fields of blue.

"You're the one who's a dope!" cried Nell. "You didn't want him to see you? Well? He was walking right in there."

"So you'd just as leave murder the man, eh? Just for walking? So you don't care whether he lives or dies? Do you?"

"He's not going to die," she said scornfully. "I didn't hit him so hard."

"The hell you didn't! You hit him as hard as you damn well could. Just luck that you didn't. . . ."

"Did you want to be seen?" she hissed.

"So you did *me* a favor? Don't do me no more." He flung her to one side of him, holding both her wrists in one hand. It crossed his mind that time was sifting by. It began to look as if no one had sounded any alarm to authority. Nothing was happening. He yanked her along as he went to peer through the window blinds.

The dame across the court was just standing there. He could see her hands on the back of that chair.

He swung Nell back into the center of the room. She stumbled, unresisting, although she looked a little sullen. She said, "I thought you didn't want to be seen in here. You acted like it."

He looked at her. "Just a point," he said dryly. "The little man had a perfect right to walk in there if he wanted to. He wasn't doing a thing he shouldn't do." Nothing happened to her face, no change of expression. He might as well have said it in Choctaw, or something. "Didn't think of that, eh? I suppose," he mocked. "You 'just weren't thinking'?"

"I thought you didn't want him to see you."

"So you shut his eyes. That's logical. That's great!" Jed wanted to slap her, hit her, worse than he had ever wanted to hit anything smaller than he was. He took his hands off her as if she would soil them. "OK. Where did it get you? What did it do for you?"

She didn't seem to follow.

"I was going. Remember? I'm still going. I'm going faster and farther, if that's possible. And don't think you can frame me with any lying yarn," he stormed. "I'll be gone," he snapped his fingers, "like smoke! You don't know who I am, my name, where I came from, or where I'm going to be. And you'll never see me again in this world, Nelly girl. The point I'm trying to make. You might as well . . . might a hell of a lot better . . . have let your Uncle Eddie show me out! Do you get that? Can you?"

She said nothing. But she moved a little bit, working around, he thought, to put herself between him and the door. He laughed. "Single track, your mind. One-idea-Nell. One at a time is all you can handle? Listen, you never had a chance to keep me here since I found out you were a baby-sitter. Never. Not a chance. All your monkey-shines. . . ."

"Why not?" she said.

"Say I'm allergic," said Jed shortly, "and skip it. I've got nothing against kids." His hand chopped the air nervously. "That's got nothing to do with it. They let me alone, I let them alone. Nothing to me." He didn't like this line. He shifted, quickly. "Start thinking about yourself, and think fast, Nell. How *you're* going to get out of the jam you got yourself into, I couldn't say."

"I'll get out of it," she murmured carelessly.

He didn't hear. He was listening for something else. "It's quiet in there," he muttered.

"She's all right," said Nell carelessly. Her lids seemed to swell at the outsides of her eyes, puffing drowsily.

"What did you tell her?"

"I told her nothing to be scared of. Somebody just fell down." Suddenly Nell laughed, showing her teeth. "Somebody *did*," she giggled.

"How true," said Jed thoughtfully. His anger churned inside of him still, but he had the upper hand of it. He had an uneasy feeling that he had better not indulge in so simple a response. He stepped around one of the beds and looked into the bathroom. "Eddie's going to be missed, you know. Naturally, you didn't think of that."

"He won't be missed," she said indifferently. "He's off duty." She sat down and put her ankles together and looked at her feet. Her toes made a miniature sashay.

Eddie was about the same, still out, breathing better. Jed turned around.

Nell fell back on her elbows, smiling up. "Take me dancing?" she said coquettishly. "Johnee?"

"Dancing!" he exploded.

"Uncle Eddie's not on the elevator now." She seemed to think she was explaining something!

He wanted to say, I'd just as soon take a cobra dancing. But he said, "And? Who sits with the baby in the meantime?"

"It's a dumb job," she said. "I don't like it."

His lips parted, closed, parted. He sat down, facing her. It seemed important to make plain what it was she left out of her calculations. It seemed important to try reason out against unreason. It seemed necessary to try to cut through a wall of fog, to clear things up. "You're in a mess," he said rather patiently. "Don't you know that?"

"What mess?" She was sulky.

"You bop this guy, this Uncle Eddie. OK. Now what's going to happen? Look ahead a little bit. The Joneses come home from the party. There's a body in the bathroom. What are you going to say?"

"It's only Uncle Eddie," she murmured.

Jed took his head in his hands. He meant to make a semihumorous exaggeration of the gesture, but it fooled him. He was holding his head for real.

"Now listen carefully," he said. "What's *going* to happen? Future tense. Consequences. You ever heard of them?"

She used a word that rocked him with the unexpectedness of its vulgarity. "——, Uncle Eddie isn't going to say it was *me* who hit him."

He had to admit that he himself had reasoned along this line. For a moment he was stopped. "OK," he resumed patiently. "So Eddie won't tell on you. Then what *is* the story? Did he knock himself out? What did knock him out? Who? Don't you see, you've got to have an answer?"

"I can say you did it," she answered placidly.

"*After I'm gone,* you'll say it!" He was furious.

"Unless we're out dancing."

He stood up. This time he spit it out of his mouth. "I'd just as soon take a cobra dancing as you."

"You asked me when you first—"

"*Then,*" he snapped. "That was before I knew what I was getting into. Now I see you do the way you do, I retract, believe me." He paced. "Why don't you *think,* first! That's what I can't understand. You swat him down without a brain in your head working. Can't you imagine what's *going* to happen? Doesn't that mean anything to you? Ever plan? Ever figure ahead? What's wrong with you, anyhow? How come you do the way you do?" He looked coldly down. "I think you're insane."

It's easy to say. The word falls off the tongue. This was the first time Jed had ever said it, in perfect sincerity. He did think she was insane.

She lifted her head on the neck, slowly. It was the neck that lifted, as if it uncoiled. She said a few ugly words. Then she was screeching and clawing at him and biting his self-defending hands with savage teeth and her shrill refrain was, "No, I'm not! No, I'm not! Take it back. You take it back!"

He handled her, but it wasn't easy. He got her in a locking hold and he shut her mouth with his hand. "Cut it out! Cut it! You'll scare the kid. You'll have the cops in here."

She was still screeching, as well as she could, "Take it back!"

"OK. OK. I take it back. If that does you any good. So you're a model of foresight and wisdom. So anything! So cut it out!"

She cut it out. She seemed satisfied. It was necessary to her that the word not be used. The word "insane." But it was a matter of words. The words "I take it back" were just as potent. Which, thought Jed grimly, is insane.

He felt chilled. He did not want this to be true. She was a crazy kid, a wild kid, in the slang sense. Only in the vernacular. She was all mixed up and she didn't know how to stop and think. He told himself that was it. But he felt sad and chilly. He didn't know what to do. She was limp in his hold. Then he knew she was not so limp, but too happy to be held so tightly.

He loosed her, warily. He said vaguely, "Why should we fight? Makes too much noise." He listened. There was no sound from the child's room and he let out his breath. "Good thing *she* didn't begin to howl again. I can't take any more of that."

Nell said, "I know." A flicker of contempt crossed her face. "I understand about the future," she muttered.

"I talk too much sometimes." He was trying to be careful. "What I need. . . . Finish the bottle with me?" He took it out of his pocket.

"Good thing this didn't get smashed in the excitement." He looked vaguely around. "Aw, what's a glass?" He tipped the bottle.

She took it from him with both hands. The notion of drinking out of the bottle seemed to tickle her.

He said, "Say, where did the Joneses go?"

"Why?" Her voice was as careless as his.

"I was wondering how late— Was it theater? Or a party someplace?" He feigned relaxing.

She still had the bottle in both hands. Carrying it, she walked between the beds and sat down near the head of one of them. "I don't know," she said vaguely.

"Shindig, eh? That sounds like a party. Somebody's apartment?"

"Your turn." She gave him the bottle. Her face was full of mischief. She said, "I understand about the future, Johnee. Everybody does."

"I guess so," Jed said.

She took a slip of paper off the table between the beds, where the phone was. She began to pleat it in her fingers. "You think I'm stupid?" she asked, looking sidewise.

"Everybody's stupid sometimes. Looks kinda stupid of the Joneses not to say where they'd go. What if the kid got sick or something?"

"Oh?" Nell said brightly. "You mean they should have thought ahead? About the future?"

"Did I say something about the future ever?" He grinned. He was thinking, I got under her skin, though. Must have. He felt better.

Nell tore the paper idly into fancy bits. When Jed passed over the bottle she let the bits fall on the carpet. Too late Jed saw them fall. He received, in a telepathic flash, the news. What had been on the paper. Why she had torn it. How she had foxed him. And the news of her sly laughter.

He was chagrined. He kept himself from showing it, he hoped, and from anger. They may know at the desk downstairs, he comforted himself, where the kid's folks went. He said, and perhaps this was the result of the damped-down anger, "Say, what was this about a fire?"

"Fire?" Nell smoothed the bedspread. She cocked her head. She seemed willing to talk about fire if that's what he wanted to talk about. It didn't mean anything to her.

"I got a little bit of what your Uncle Eddie was saying."

"Oh, that."

"Was it your house burned? Your parents? I thought he said so." She didn't answer. "Upset you, Nell?"

"That's what they say," she said demurely.

"Who?"

"Oh, doctors. Uncle Eddie. Aunt Marie." She frowned. "Aunt Marie went to the show tonight."

"Where was the fire?"

"Home."

"Some small town, was it?"

"It wasn't big." She curled up her legs.

Small, all right, Jed thought to himself, if they let this one loose. But he said to himself quickly, No, no, there must have been some testing. Yet his thoughts went somberly on. Probably Eddie showed up ready and willing and anxious to take her far, far away. Probably the town would just as soon not face up to it. Nell wouldn't be any of the town's business far, far away.

"So it was an accident," he said, making a statement. "Well, I'll tell you something. The future's one thing you got to look out for. The past is another. Because the past adds up. You know that?"

She frowned.

"This accident. Your father and mother both died in it?"

"It was an accident." He heard the jump of her voice to a higher pitch. He knew it was a threat. It warned, Look out! It reminded him of that screeching tantrum. It warned, Be careful! Danger! Touchy!

"Well, I'll tell you," he drawled nevertheless, "and it's a funny thing. You take one accident, why, that's too bad. Everybody's sorry. Poor Nell." She was curled up as tense as a coiled spring. He tried to fix her gaze, but it was all blueness. He kept on drawling. "But you take *two* accidents, that's different. That's not the same. It's really funny how, after a second accident, right away, the first accident doesn't look so much *like* an accident anymore."

Her face went blank, either because he'd hit her with an idea or she didn't know what he was talking about.

"Good thing to keep in mind," he said lazily.

She said, "They didn't do anything to me." Her face was sullen. But Jed felt a sick wave of absolute knowledge.

He watched her. He said as quietly and steadily as he could, "What

I'm saying . . . the first time is different. But things like that have a way of piling up. It gets harder. Because it counts. It adds. One and one make more than two. They make questions. So maybe you better not get walking in your sleep," he finished gently.

She didn't move. He thought, *I got it over.*

And the bottle was empty. He gathered himself to get up, now, and go quietly.

Miss Eva Ballew believed in many things. One of them was duty. She walked toward the telephone. One of them was justice. She walked back to the chair.

But however strong her beliefs and her conscience, Miss Ballew was a physical coward and knew it and all her life had fought her weakness. Now, she realized full well that she had been prodded too many times . . . three times . . . and she was taking too long . . . much, much too long . . . to make up her mind what she ought to do.

Sometimes, if you take time to decide, the need to do anything passes of itself. . . . Miss Ballew reproached herself with bitter shame and she walked toward the phone.

But. . . .

She walked to the chair. She banged her fist on the chair back and the pain helped her. Justice. Very well. If justice won, it was because this was going to take more physical courage, and she was a coward, and she wished to deny her cowardice.

She went to the dresser and got her purse, not to be naked without it once away from her room. She left the room and, flogging herself, marched around the hollow square of the eighth floor.

Nell hadn't moved. Jed, all the way up, standing, said, "So long." He felt a little pulse of compassion for her, who was lost and had no inner compass to find the way again. "Be seeing you."

Once more, and briskly, somebody's knuckles knocked on 807's door.

Nell was up, lynx-eyed.

"Oh, no," said Jed softly. "Oh, no, my lady, not again! Not this time!"

He faded. Towers faded, the way he had to go, through the door to the kid's room, to 809 . . . and closed it behind him.

Chapter Thirteen

MISS BALLEW rapped again. Because she was afraid, she did her best to be angry. She knew someone was in there. Did they think they could lie low?

The door opened so swiftly it surprised her. A girl in a dark dress, not a very big girl, not very old, looked at her with blue, blue eyes and said, with an effect of stormy anger, although her voice was low, "What do you want?"

"My name is Eva Ballew. My room is across the court on this floor." Miss Ballew's words were as neat and orderly as herself. She tended to begin at the beginning.

"Yes." The girl seemed to listen but not to hear, almost as if she were listening for something else. And it seemed to Miss Ballew that her anger was aimed elsewhere, also.

"Before I call the manager of this hotel," said Miss Ballew more boldly, to command attention, "I think it only fair to ask whether you can explain."

"Explain what?"

"What is going on in these rooms," said Miss Ballew, loudly and firmly.

"I don't know what you mean." The girl was looking at the caller but not seeing her, almost, thought Miss Ballew, as if she were *also* looking for something else out here in this bare corridor.

"There is a child," said Miss Ballew coldly. "Is she your child?"

"I'm taking care of her."

"I see," Miss Ballew's mouth was grim. "Yes, so I imagined. Is there or was there a man in here?"

"A man?"

Miss Ballew longed to cry, Pay attention, please! "I saw the man," she announced, sharply, "so that is an unnecessary question and you need not answer it." She could see into room 807 and no one else was visible, at least. She did not feel physically afraid of rather a small girl. And if the man had gone. . . . Miss Ballew was encouraged. She said, yielding to curiosity, "Who was the man?"

"Listen, you can't—"

"The child," cut in Miss Ballew coolly, "has been crying in a most distressing manner, twice. And I have witnessed certain rather strange scenes over here. I must ask for an explanation."

"Who are you?" began Nell.

"I am someone who will call downstairs if I do not get the explanation," said Miss Ballew dictatorially. "In the first place," she went on, beginning at the beginning in her orderly fashion, "awhile ago, you were at the window with the child?"

"Yes, yes," said Nell impatiently, "what are you trying to—"

"I have already told you. I am trying to find out whether or not it is my duty to call the manager."

"But why should you?" Nell stepped closer, with the door behind her now. Her glance slipped down the corridor to the right, briefly.

"Because," snapped Miss Ballew, wishing this girl would pay attention and not carry on this duel with some invisible thing, "it seemed to me, for one thing, that the little girl very nearly fell out the window."

"Well, she didn't," said Nell carelessly. "While you were at your snooping you must have noticed that."

Miss Ballew bridled but stood her ground. "Snooping or not, I wish to see the child."

"See her?" For the first time, Miss Ballew felt that her words were heeded.

"Yes, see her for myself."

"You've got a crust!"

"Nevertheless, if I do *not* see her, I intend to call the authorities." So much for rudeness, Miss Ballew's eyebrows remarked.

"I don't know what's the *matter!*" Nell said in whining exasperation. "What do you want to see her for? She's sleeping. What are you talking about?"

"Why did she scream so dreadfully?" Miss Ballew narrowed her eyes.

"When?"

"The second time. Come now, stop evading, young woman."

"What?"

"I think you'd better let me in."

"*You* listen," Nell said. "I'm here to take care of her. You're a stranger. How can I let a stranger in? How do I know. . . ."

"You don't," agreed Miss Ballew, "but unless I see her for myself, the manager or the detective here *must*."

"What business is it of yours? I don't underst—"

"Are you afraid to let me see her?"

"I'm not afraid," said Nell shrilly. "But I can't do it. I'm not supposed to. You talk about duty—"

"Now, see here. I am a schoolteacher. I'm sure I look like one. You ought to be able to tell that I am a responsible person."

"You're trying to cause trouble."

"On the contrary. I wish you would realize that I could have called downstairs directly. I felt, however, that it was not fair to cause trouble, as you say, if there is no reason. Therefore, I have taken the trouble to step around here. There may be some simple explanation and if the child is perfectly all right and asleep, then there is no occasion for any trouble at all. Now, is that clear?"

"What would her mother say if I let any old person?"

"What would her mother say about you entertaining a man?" In the same tone, Miss Ballew would have said "about your smoking opium."

"He's gone." The girl's eyes flickered toward the right again. "And she *is* perfectly all right. She *is* sleeping."

"I beg your pardon if I seem to insist in the face of your direct statements, but after what I saw—"

"Saw?"

"Perhaps you don't know that the Venetian blind was so adjusted that I *could* see."

"See where?" Nell's head went back on the neck.

"Into the child's room."

"It's dark in there," Nell said stupidly. Perhaps a little drowsily.

"Not quite. There was a very little light, perhaps through the connecting door."

"Light?"

"And the child did stop her screaming rather abruptly," said Miss Ballew.

Nell's eyes slipped sidewise. "What did you see?" asked she.

Ruth was only half listening to the women's voices. She would have preferred to be in the group of men where the talk, she was sure, must have more meat in it. It could hardly have less. These women, from far-flung spots, had no basis for gossip and, since they weren't even sure who each other's husbands were (except Ruth's, of course) they didn't even have the fun of ranking each other.

Except Ruth. She could have been preening herself, for no woman had missed her rose-colored presence at the Speaker's elbow. But her heart wasn't in it.

There was a faint superstitious element, too, a fear that if she got to thinking herself too darned smart, something bad could happen. She felt, absurdly or not, as if she rode the narrow edge of danger, as if, by standing here among these party-painted women, she was taking a risk. She said, "Yes, indeed," again, and again the sense of danger fluttered her heart.

Peter strode out of his group and snatched her out of hers. Their steps fell together to the music as if they were at home at the Saturday night neighborly. " 'Smatter, hon?"

Ruth looked up with clouded eyes. "Now, I thought I had you fooled."

"Nuh-uh. Worried? About Bun?"

"I'm sure I'm silly."

"No, you're not sure," he said. "Something on that phone call bother you?"

"I don't know." She slid her hand higher on his sleeve. "Probably it's just because I'm a hick and this great big town scares me. Listen, Peter, even if I don't always act it, I am a grown woman. Let me do something. Let me take a cab over to the hotel and see. I'll be perfectly all right, and I'll come straight back and dance till dawn. And I won't *spoil* it."

"We could leave now," he said, guiding her in a turn.

"But . . . the fun!"

He grinned, admitting the fun. "Man from Chicago, I'd like to have a few words—"

"Then do. Please. If you go, I'll feel terrible. *You* can't go."

"My night to howl," he grinned. "Got cab fare?" He would let her go. Peter wouldn't *make* her spoil it.

"Not a penny," she confessed.

He danced her into the mirrored exit, squeezed her, let her go, and gave her a five-dollar bill. "Don't trust any handsome strangers with all this moolah on you, baby."

"I won't." Ruth thought, I don't trust that stranger, that girl. It's what's wrong with me.

She wouldn't let him come any farther than the cloakroom with her. He looked at her little watch from her bag and said rather seriously, "It shouldn't take you long to get across town at this hour."

Somebody said, "Oh, Jones," or was it, "O'Jones"?

Ruth smiled at him. She left the scene. She felt at once much better to have escaped, to be free, to be going.

A doorman found her the cab. The city thought nothing of a young woman in evening clothes taking a cab alone in the night. No look. No comment. The city minded its business.

In the outer night, in the streets, were many, many people, all minding their business. Millions and millions of people, thought Ruth, not only here, but millions of other places, too, who never heard and never will hear of me. She thought, For each of us, me, and every one of them, how few are anything but strangers.

Chapter Fourteen

JED STOOD in the dark. He heard Miss Ballew introduce herself and knew at once *this* was the old biddy from across the way. Through the slats of Bunny's blind he could see her room, still lit.

He wondered if he were going to be able to get around the two of them, out there, without an uproar. Maybe Nell would let her into 807. But if not. . . . He wondered about going around the hollow square in the other direction. He had an impression that one could not. It was only a U after all. Suites across the front, perhaps. Dead ends for the corridors.

He wondered if he could take refuge by knocking at a stranger's door. God forbid, he thought piously. No more strange hotel rooms for Towers. Only God knew what's in them.

He rehearsed his exit in his mind.

And he meant exit. Total exit. There were worse things in the world than sitting the night out at the airport.

The stairs went down, he knew, just beyond the elevators. Well, he could move fast, Towers could, on his long legs. In his mind, he placed all the stuff in his room. Where to snatch up this and that. He traveled light. There was little to snatch. He could be in and out of that room, he thought, in a matter of sixty seconds, and exit, bag and baggage.

Then let her screech her lies.

He had little doubt she'd cook up some lies, all right. If necessary. Or even just if it seemed like fun at the moment. Or if she was mad at him. And, he thought, she is!

Dancing, yet!

Unless he had knocked, with a few words in a few minutes, a totally unfamiliar idea of caution into her head. Of course, he'd been thinking of the kid. He'd been trying to get into Nell's head the danger, the undesirability, of harming the kid.

So that Towers could fade, of course.

Damn it, Towers had to get out of this! A fine mess! Assault, maybe, on account of Eddie in there, and the benefit of the doubt on Nell's side. For long enough to make it a mess, all right. And Eddie, tempted, if not almost obliged, to say something hit him but he doesn't know what. Everything just went black, and so forth. That would be the easiest thing for Eddie to say, wouldn't it? Eddie could even kid himself that it was true.

So there's Towers, in a jam. Jail, bail, telegrams. Would his high-powered new job, his big fat step in the up direction, wait quietly for some judge to let him loose? And would a judge?

Nuts! He ground his teeth. Trouble would breed trouble. He had to get out of here. Never *was* any business of his, the kid and the sitter. Not his kid, for Lord's sake. Strangers. All strangers. If the parents didn't know any better— Probably didn't give a damn what happened to the kid, he thought angrily. Off on a shindig, all dressed up. Probably drunk as skunks by now, and painting the town. Why should Towers care?

Why should he be so angry about it?

And also if Eddie, the elevator boy, stuck *his* neck out and got bashed in the head for it, what was that to Towers? He didn't feel for Eddie. Eddie had it coming.

He still stood, just inside room 809, still listening. He didn't know what he was waiting for. No question, really, but what Towers better move fast. That old biddy had her teeth in it now. Listen to her. "I wish to see the child." Icicles hanging off every word. Sounded like a pretty stubborn old dame. "And she's white," he thought, not quite letting himself know why the word came to him.

Nell was stalling, but he thought that the old biddy would walk right over her. He took a soft step. He better get going.

Have to steam himself up to some fast footwork now. Once out, out of this hotel, he thought, let them whistle for the wind! He'd fade. He was never here. He'd be clear away, on the town, one in millions. Gone, like smoke.

And Towers right back on the track again, on his way up, as he had it figured.

No one would ever know a thing about this. How would they? Why should they?

Kid was asleep and anyhow the old dame out there was going to raise a row. She was hell-bent to do it. No need for him to figure in it. Let her do it. She was the type to do it. Let it work out that way. Why should he duplicate what she was already going to do?

He might drop a word at the desk on his way out, though. He could have heard a commotion over here, from his own room. The old biddy had from hers. Just as well tip the hotel. Then Nell *couldn't* stall her.

His eyes had adjusted to the dark in here. He could see the far bed was undisturbed. On the other the little kid must be asleep.

Funny thing she didn't wake up during his late wrestling match with the wildcat. It hadn't been a silent one.

That bed was awfully flat.

His hair moved with his scalp.

He crept a few steps in room 809. Of course, she was an awfully little girl, probably wouldn't make much of a hump on a bed. He didn't know. He'd—damn it—he'd hardly ever *seen* a sleeping child. He didn't know if they made a hump or not.

There wasn't any little girl on the bed.

He looked at the windows and Towers was sick and sickness was going through him like cream swirling down through a cup of coffee and something thumped on the floor.

He knelt in the dark crevice between the beds. He felt, blindly. Something threshed. He wanted light but he didn't dare. His fingers found a thin chilly little . . . what? Shoulder? Yes, for he touched a soft braid. He felt for the face, the warm lips, and the breath, but touched, instead, fabric.

God damn her to hell, the goddamned bitch, she'd bound and gagged the little thing. Oh, damn and blast her rotten soul! Aw, the poor little. . . .

"Bunny?" he whispered. "Bunny Jones? Aw, Bunny, poor kid. Listen, sweetheart, I wouldn't hurt you for a million dollars." His fingers verified. Yes, her ankles were tied together. Wrists, too. And that cruel—stocking, he guessed it was, in and over the mouth!

"You fall off the bed, honey? Aw, I'm sorry. I'm sorry about this. Mustn't make a noise, though."

Oh, Lord, how would the child *not!* if he ungagged her. It was not possible for her not to cry! He knew this. It would not be in her control. She must cry out, must make sound as soon as she was able.

But she mustn't! Or Towers would never get away.

Now what could he do? Thoughts flashed like frightened goldfish in the bowl of his brain.

Grab her, just as she was? Take her with him? Yeah, and run past the two women at the other door, with the kid slung over his shoulder. A kidnapper, yet!

Fantastic! No, no, better not do that.

He sat on his heels. His hand tried to comfort the little girl, smoothing her hair. He thought coldly, "So you're in a jam, Towers?"

But then his mind went all fluid again and in it those fish flashes and in the panic he thought, Damn it, no! He thought, I've got to fix it for the kid and get out, too!

Look out for yourself, Towers! Nobody else will. It came back to him, in his own words. A guide, a touchstone.

All right! Use your head! Nothing was going to happen to the kid beyond what already had. The woman out there would keep Nell busy. And he, Jed, would tip off the hotel. So, for five minutes' difference, five minutes more. . . .

Crouching near the floor in the dark he could hear the city crying, its noise tossing and falling like foam on the sea, as restless, as indifferent, as varied, and as constant. And he saw himself, a chip, thrown, blown, attracted to another chip, to swirl, to separate, to grow arms and be, not a chip, but a swimmer, and push away.

Once away, who would know? Never see these strangers again. Mess!

He leaned over and whispered, "I'm afraid you'd cry if I undo your mouth, honey. I wouldn't blame you. I'm just afraid you can't help it. We can't make any noise, just yet. Listen, I'm going. Going to get somebody. Get your daddy." His hand felt the leap of the little heart. "Get your daddy," he promised. "Be still just a little while longer. It'll be OK." He didn't lift her to the bed for she was more hidden where she lay. "I am a friend," he said absurdly, out of some pale memory in a boy's book.

He got up and went softly to the door of 809.

Chapter Fifteen

"I SAW," said Miss Ballew in her precise fashion, "the child, as I suppose, sitting up in the bed and a figure approach and appear to struggle with her. The cries then stopped, most abruptly. So you see, I require," said she hastily, "some explanation. I cannot believe," she added vehemently to cover the shake that was developing in her voice, "that any grown person would use force on a child. What, actually, were you doing?"

Nell looked sleepy.

"Answer me," said Miss Ballew angrily. "If it wasn't you, who was it?"

"You said you *saw—*" There was hint of impudence in the girl's face, something saucy that must be crushed at once.

Miss Ballew said, coldly, "I certainly did see *someone,* doing *something,* which has very much alarmed me. I would advise you, young woman, to take me to that child at once." (But she was afraid again. She was dizzy with her fear.)

A door to her left and the girl's right opened and closed very fast. A man was in the corridor and had passed rapidly behind Miss Ballew almost before she could turn her head. Moving with long gliding steps, he rushed on, he vanished around the corner. Miss Ballew staggered in the wind of his passage.

It had been so swift, so startling, so furtive, and there had been a white roll of his eye.

"Who was that!" Her knees felt mushy.

The girl looked as if she could hop with rage, as if she would begin to bounce, like popcorn.

"Explain at once!" cried Miss Ballew and reached out to shake this stupid creature.

The girl collapsed at her touch. "Oh, oh," she said. "Oh—" and bent her arm against the doorframe and buried her face in her arm. "Oh, I was so scared! Oh, miss, whatever's your name. Oh, thank you! You've saved me!"

"What!"

"That . . . man!" said Nell, muffled.

"Why, he must have come out of the next— Yes, I see he did! Out of the child's room!"

"Yes. Yes," cried Nell. "Now do you see? He was in there all the time. He said if I didn't get rid of you. . . . Oh!"

"Oh, dear," said Miss Ballew faintly.

"He said he would—" Nell's body pressed on the wood as if in anguish.

Miss Ballew rocked on her feet and reached for the wall.

"He just forced himself in here. He was so wild!" Nell cried, "and strong." Her face peeped now from the sheltering arm. "I didn't know what to do!"

Silence beat in the corridor while Miss Ballew fought with her wish to fall down. One heard, one read, and all one's life one feared, but not often did one encounter. . . . But the ruthless predatory male was, of course, axiomatic.

"There wasn't anything I could do." The girl's whine broke the spell. "I couldn't—I'm not very strong."

"But he is getting away!" moaned Miss Ballew. For she heard, in the mists of her horrors, the yawn of the door to the fire stairs and the hish-hush of its closing. This, she felt, was outrageous. Outrageous! That such things . . . in a respectable hotel . . . and go unpunished! The anger was starch to her spine. She tightened her mouth, gathered her strength, and bustled past the girl into the room. She threw her stout sturdy form on the bed and reached for the telephone.

Downstairs, Rochelle Parker shifted the lifesaver expertly into the pouch of her cheek. "Yes?"

"This is Miss Ballew," said the agitated voice. "I'm in room—what?" she cried to the girl. "What is this number?"

"Number 807," said the girl quite promptly and calmly.

"Room 807. A man has just fled from here."

"*What* did he do, madam?"

"Fled. Ran. He ran away." Miss Ballew was often forced to translate her remarks. "He was up to no good." She tried to be basic. "Get him!" cried Eva Ballew and reverted. "He must answer for it. He must face his accuser and be brought to book. This is criminal and he must be apprehended."

"Just a moment, *please,*" said Rochelle. She pressed the button that would discreetly summon Pat Perrin to a phone. Almost at once, she plugged him in. "Yeah?"

"807's on, Pat."

"Yeah, what is it?"

"There was a man in here," said Miss Ballew. It was as if she said "African lion." "He is trying to get away, right now."

"What did he look like?"

"What did he look like?" cried the teacher to the motionless girl.

The girl's lips opened and her tongue slipped to moisten them. "He . . . had red hair."

"Red hair!" Miss Ballew's voice both informed Perrin and doubted the information, for this had not been her own impression.

"Very dark red," said Nell, "brown eyes, freckles."

"Dark red, brown eyes, freckles, and tall. I saw that. And I think a gray suit."

"Brownish," Nell said, "and a blue shirt."

"Brownish? Well, some light color. And a blue shirt. And he took the stairs, not two minutes ago. You had best—"

"We'll see," said Perrin. "He intruded, you say?"

"He did, indeed," cried Miss Ballew in ringing tones. It was the very word.

"I'll see if we can pick him up," said Pat Perrin, sounding competent and unruffled. He hung up at once.

Miss Ballew rolled a bit and sat up. She propped herself on the headboard. She was trembling. "This really—" she gasped. "I don't know when I've been— What did happen? How did he—? Who—?"

The girl, who had closed the door, came slowly around the bed and sat down on the other one. Her eyes were a trifle aslant and an odd blue. She clasped her hands in her lap. Unpainted nails. Dark, decent dress. Modest ankles, shabby shoes.

Miss Ballew read all these signs as she was bound to do. "You poor thing," she said. "I don't know your name."

"Nell." Not Sonya. Not Toni. Plain Nell.

"I am Eva Ballew," said that lady warmly. "I suppose you were under such strain. I thought your manner was odd."

"You don't know," said Nell wanly, and Miss Ballew's heart fluttered alarmingly. "Oh, Miss Ballew, I just had to tell you those lies," the poor thing said pathetically. "I couldn't help it. He was in there, and he said he'd listen, and if I dared. . . ."

"Simply terrible!" murmured the teacher. "How ever did he get in here?"

"Oh, he knocked, and of course I went to see who it was." Nell twisted her hands. "And then he just pushed me."

"Didn't you scream?" It was Miss Ballew's conviction that a woman always screamed. It did not, at this time, cross her mind that there was any other procedure whatsoever.

"But he said . . . said he was a friend of the people's," said Nell. "I didn't know."

"No, of course, you couldn't know. Tsk. Tsk. Do you think he had been drinking?"

"Oh, he was!" cried Nell. "Look!" She seemed very young and lithe as she reached for the whiskey bottle. The cheap dress twisted tight to her body. Miss Ballew felt a shiver, rather a delicious one, along her nerves. She gazed, horrified, at the bottle's emptiness.

"And then," said Nell, "Bunny—that's the little girl—she . . . she woke up." Nell put her face in her hands. She dropped the bottle on the floor to do so. Miss Ballew's mind swirled. So odd. Poor thing, so upset, to do such a disorderly thing.

"Now, now," she soothed. "It's all over, now." And then, fearfully, "Isn't it? There wasn't? Nothing?"

Nell took her face out and shook her head vigorously. Her tawny yellow hair tossed.

"Well—" said Miss Ballew feebly. Her heart raced. She felt unwell.

"Anyhow," said Nell moodily, "he only tried to kiss me once. He just kept on drinking and drinking."

"You should have screamed," Miss Ballew said trancelike.

"But I was so scared, I didn't dare. . . . And I thought maybe, when Bunny cried so loud, someone might notice." The girl's eyes rolled.

Miss Ballew felt herself flushing guiltily.

"And she didn't really 'almost fall,'" said Nell with sudden passionate indignation, "at all! He was mad. That's what it was. He thought I was trying to, you know, get somebody's attention out the window like that, so he dragged her away."

"Oh, dear. . . ." Miss Ballew thought how wise one is never to believe too hastily in what one thinks one sees. Always, she noted, wait for the other side of the story. "And when she began to scream so, later? Why was that, my dear?"

Nell looked wildly around her, threw herself face down, and her shoulders heaved, and soon her sobbing shook the bed.

"Now," Miss Ballew struggled to reach over but she felt dizzy herself, and she couldn't make it. "Now," she said, "don't—" She thought, Someone must soon come. She herself was really not in any condition to deal with this any further. It was shameful, but she felt as weak as a kitten. Just hearing about it. The poor girl must have had a violent psychic shock. In fact, Miss Ballew knew herself to be suffering the same thing, vicariously.

"She got scared and began to cry," sobbed Nell. "She just got scared. That's why she began to cry. But he was so mad. It made him wild. He said she had to stop that noise." The head slipped, the face turned, the wet lashes lifted.

Miss Ballew lay against the headboard and her rather long countenance was whitening. "Then it was *he* in her room?"

"You saw . . ." the girl challenged.

"Yes, I saw. But it was too dark. I couldn't clearly see. Oh, my dear, if he has harmed—"

"Oh, he didn't *hurt* her." Nell said and suddenly she sat up again. "He just made her stop crying." A little smile—pitiful, it might have been—worked on her face. "And there wasn't anything I could do because he locked me in the closet. . . ."

"Incredible." The teacher's lips were stiff.

Nell looked solemnly at her. The room fell . . . as if all its emotion-laden air swirled, falling . . . to silence. "You know," she said, "I think he was insane."

Miss Ballew said, "Is there— Could you? A glass of water? Or could you call, perhaps the house physician. I really am afraid I am having rather a reaction. . . ." She closed her eyes.

Insanity was obviously the explanation. For things so wild and wanton, insanity was the definition, really.

In the dim bathroom of 807, on the cold floor, Eddie stirred. His right arm moved as one moves in sleep. He turned a little to his left side. Then he lay still.

Chapter Sixteen

THE HOTEL DETECTIVE, Pat Perrin, put up the phone and crossed the lobby, moving quietly. He opened the door to the base of the tall rectangular tube where the fire stairs ran. He discounted, from long practice, ninety percent of what he had just heard. But for the sake of the other ten percent, he stood and listened. Any sound, he knew, would come booming down to him.

And so it did. Someone was on those bare stairs. His own ears informed him. So far, so much was confirmed. He waited, quietly. He wore a gun.

Jed realized the echoing clatter of his descent in this confined space. Nimbly, he brought himself up against a door, stopped the second or two it took to rearrange his own rhythm, tugged the door in upon himself, and stepped steadily out to the sixth-floor corridor.

As he crossed the carpet toward the elevators a man—just a man—

joined him. Jed took care not to be caught looking to see whether the other was looking. The man pressed the down button and, superhumanly, Jed did not. He set his suitcase down, denying the need of his nervous hand to hang onto it. It occurred to him, freakishly, that he had left a blue tie and a good pair of socks, damn it. His jaw cracked and he deliberately let tension out of it. Without fidgeting, he watched the dial, as the other man was doing, as all elevator awaiters seem compelled to do. The hand was coming down.

Disinterested, strangers, they stepped on in silent sequence as the elevator obeyed the call. And in silent sequence they stepped out, below. Jed, looking to neither side, walked to the desk. His gait deceived. His trunk and shoulders showed no effort, but his long legs drove hard against the floor and bore him more swiftly than they seemed to do.

He said crisply, "Checking out. Towers, 821."

"Certainly, Mr. Towers."

"Mind making it quick?" Friendly and crisp but not too urgent. "Just got hold of a cancellation. I can get out of here tonight if I make it down to the station." Jed looked at the clock in the woodwork back of the man's head.

"Yes, sir." The clerk did not seem to put on speed but Jed was aware that he did, in fact, waste no motion. He recognized the skill in it. He made himself stand still.

Pat Perrin knew when no feet rattled on the stairs. He caught a boy and posted him here, near where the stairs came down, at a door to a narrow passage that was the back way out. He caught another to watch the entrance to the bar, for one could exit to the street through that dim corner room. He himself had a brief word with an elevator boy. Then his skilled eyes ran down every man in his sight. "Tall, light suit." He weaved among the chairs. He moved along the carpet.

"You figure," Jed was asking pleasantly, "about twenty-five minutes to Penn Station?"

"That's close, sir. Might do it. Here we are." The clerk turned the reckoning around. He took an envelope from a box and presented this, too. Jed saw his name before him in a script he knew. A note from Lyn. Lyn Lesley. He stuffed it into his coat pocket. (No time for her now.) He took money out.

Perrin's eye checked Jed's tall figure in the gray suit. *Dark* hair, *no* freckles, *white* shirt. He walked on by, the eye skimming.

Jed put his wallet back, picked up his bag, surveyed the way ahead, the not-very-long distance to that revolving door and out. He was the same as out already. The clerk already counted him for gone. To turn back, to speak again was like contradicting the forward flow of time itself.

But Jed put his palm noiselessly on the blotter and the clerk looked up.

"You'd better," said Jed, speaking slowly and soberly and emphatically to be understood and heeded in this, the first and only time he would say it, "send someone to room 807, right away. Trouble. A kid's in trouble. 807 and 809. A little girl. If you know where Mr. and Mrs. Jones went, call them. It's their kid."

He turned swiftly and went, in that same smooth, deceptive, very rapid gait, in the shortest line to the revolving door and through it without a check.

Then he stood in the air, in the open night, and he was out of it, and it was their kid, wasn't it?

Pat Perrin knew someone on those stairs had got off the stairs. So much was true. Whether he rode down or not was a question. Now Perrin peered through to the street, saw him, tall, dark, and handsome, in the white shirt, harmlessly pausing to light a cigarette. He pushed through and crooked a finger to the doorman, said a word or two. He raked Jed's back with his glance, conscientiously, turned, looped on his own tracks, and went back through the lobby because the other exit would be the one a fugitive would like. He saw Milner at the desk lift a startled hand as if to beckon. He signaled with his own, Busy (no time for him now), and he walked on by.

Jed shook out his match. All right. So he'd established Towers had nerves of iron. And what now? Cab? Bus? Subway? To the airport? His thoughts were jumpy.

A cab swerved in to the curb and braked in his very face. He thought it was querying him. Then he saw that it had a fare to discharge here. He stepped aside.

As the domelight went on, he could see her. Young woman, blond, attractive, in party clothes.

He stood with his bag at his feet and blew smoke out. Here was a cab, emptying before him, becoming available, and in it he would be gone, like smoke. Smoke poured out of his mouth. He half turned his head. He looked (because he was in some way forced to look) up behind him at the checkered façade, the tall bulk, the flat and secretive face of the Hotel Majestic.

The girl from the cab, with her change, bills and all, in her bare hand, got out. She swept her long skirts, aquamarine velvet over rosy silk, up in one hand. Her golden slippers stepped quickly on the gray sidewalk. She went by Jed. Her gaze crossed over his face blankly, and he blankly watched her by, for they were strangers.

Jed saw the doorman prance, and the door spin. The cab door in front of him remained open. It hinted, tempted, invited. Finally it said to him, "Well?"

He moved nearer and put out a hand, ducked his head, brought his bag up in the other hand, and his knee up. . . . Something hit him. It seemed to him that he was struck in the face by a barrier as soft, elastic, and yielding, as easy to pass through, as a cobweb. Something that was no more substantial than the air itself. Only a faint scent . . . breathing into his face from the cab's closed place. A perfume, it was, that stopped him because he knew that scent and it made his stomach turn over. Why, he reeked of it, himself! Of course. It was *on him!* It came from himself.

He barked, "Sorry," and slammed the door. He lifted his hand, giving permission and command. Go ahead. The cab's gears snarled at him. It went away in a huff, saying with a flounce of its back bumper, "Whyncha make up your mind, stupid!"

Jed trod his cigarette out. He felt rooted on the sidewalk and his feet kicked at the invisible chain. All right. He would not shut himself up with that sickening odor. That's all. He'd air himself free of it. Walk, then. Lug your damn bag. But get gone, stupid! He held hard for anger, this kind of anger. His hand came up to brush before his face.

Milner, the man at the desk, leaned over, full of summons, but Pat Perrin was out of range of a soft hail and a loud hail would never do. Milner's still-startled eyes blinked. Towers, 821. Eighth floor, sure enough. Fellow might know what he was talking about. Something wrong in 807? Peter O. Jones, 807 and 809. Mr. Milner didn't know where the Joneses were. He was annoyed as well as startled. But of course he would check. It would never do not to check up on such a warning.

He took up a phone and pivoted, looking anxiously for some reason at the hands of the clock. "Give me 807, Rochelle, will you?"

"Sure thing." Rochelle alerted. She thought, "Oh, boy, something's up!" She thought, "*I* smelled a rat up there hours ago." She was rather pleased. There were long stretches on this job that were pretty dull. She hoped this was going to be interesting. Whatever it was. She said softly, "What goes on, Mr. Milner?"

Since Mr. Milner did not know, he was haughty. "If you'll ring them, please?"

"OK, OK." He heard Rochelle ring them. He stood, holding the phone, staring at the clock as if he could by the willful power of the human eye stay the hand, as Ruth O. Jones went rustling by behind him.

No need to stop for her key, she reflected, since of course Nell was there to open the door. Besides, it would take time. Her feel of time wasting was because she'd been wishing too long to come. Only that. Why, the lobby was just the same, just the same.

Ruthie and the jitters. How Betty would laugh! Betty the city mouse. Betty the louse, who'd begged off. Although why on earth I assume *she's* so darned reliable . . . Betty and *her* system of values . . . Betty who doesn't even know, yet, what a woman's in the world for. . . . It was the blood tie, of course. It was the mere fact that Peter's sister could not be a stranger.

Now Ruth began (for everything upstairs would be just the same) to pick and choose among excuses. One could not say, I came because I don't trust you an inch, my dear. No. But one could say, I came for a clean handkerchief, which would be pretty feeble. Obviously, no shoulder straps to break. Oh, say a pill. Say some special remedy brought from home. For a headache, say. It would do.

There was a man in a brown suit talking in rather an official manner to the elevator boy. He kept on talking. "I beg your pardon," Ruth asked. "Is this car going up?"

"In a minute, ma'am."

"Thank you." She stepped by. They kept muttering together. The boy said, "Never rode with me."

Ruth's foot in the golden slipper twitched. Oh, don't be silly! Surely a minute doesn't matter! (Except on the inner clock of her apprehensive bones.)

Chapter Seventeen

NELL LET the water run. Then she filled the glass. She stood, holding the glass, and twisted the faucet once or twice, on and off. Her face was sullen and a little bored and weary as she looked down at the form of the little man on the bathroom floor, lying as if he were normally asleep, twisted a bit to one side, as if to be comfortable.

The skin around his eyes twitched, as if the bright light affected him. She frowned faintly, and then her whole body seemed to shrug, to lift off the problem and let it go. The hell with it.

She snapped off the light, opened the door that she had so speedily put between her and room 807, and pulled it after her quite deftly as she stepped through. "Miss Ballew?" She was all sweet service.

The schoolteacher, with her eyes closed, was silently reciting poetry. It was a trick to play on the release of the fearful substances to the blood, on the whole panicked interior chemistry. Sometimes, by taking the brain's attention elsewhere, she could wait out, slow down, and defeat the pound of the goaded heart.

"Oh, thank you, my dear. Really, this is so feeble of me." Her teeth chattered. "But I lead rather a quiet existence. I rarely. . . ." The phone rang. The glass was still in Nell's hand. "I'll get it," chattered Miss Ballew and jerked around.

Nell sat down quietly. Her toes turned in, then out, almost imperceptibly. Her finger tips danced a little on the cool damp glass.

"Yes?" quavered the teacher.

"This is the desk. I've had word of some trouble. Perhaps you can tell me?"

"Trouble!" burst Miss Ballew. "Yes, *certainly,* there has been trouble. I spoke to *someone,* long ago! Now, who was that? Really, by this time you ought to have accomplished something. Do you mean to tell me! Didn't you *stop* him?"

"I beg your pardon," said the astonished voice.

"Did you or did you not stop that man! I told you—I described him."

"Who is this, please?"

"This is Miss Eva Ballew. I have 823 but I am now in 807 as you ought to know since you are speaking to me here. Now, I reported this trouble minutes ago—"

"Yes. Yes, I see, Miss Ballew," he broke in. "The house detective must have taken—"

"*Must* have! Are you guessing? Who are *you,* pray?"

"I'm at the desk, ma'am."

"And do you mean to tell me that you do not know! See here. Is anything at all being done?"

"The house detective evidently—"

"Evidently! Are you men or mice down there? Where is *he?*"

"He is evid—He is looking—that is, I see, now."

"You are too late and too slow," she spoke on top of him, "and it has been too long. You have irresponsibly allowed that ruffian to escape."

Milner's spine curled. "But is the child all right?" he demanded.

"The child? Why, yes, I believe—"

Milner, man, not mouse, was delighted to say, disagreeably, *"Do you mean to tell me that you do not know!"* and snap, "Someone responsible will be up there at once," and slam down the phone. But all the same, he was relieved. Pat Perrin knew about it.

Miss Ballew hung up and her eyes were pained. So often this physical weakness had betrayed her. So often it had led her to be ashamed. She knew so well what one ought to do, but the weak flesh was a drag.

"What was it?" Nell said.

"They . . . someone will be up. They seem confused." And I, thought Miss Ballew, am a pitiful, despicable, cowering wretch. And she tried to shift her legs.

"He got away?"

"Evidently." It was no use. Her legs were mush still. "My dear," she said sadly, "hadn't you better see to the child?"

"Oh, yes," said Nell quickly. But she rose without haste, in fact, rather slowly and tentatively. "Don't you want the drink of water?" She didn't seem to know what to do with it.

Miss Ballew received the glass. She was not a fool. Now, as she knew her guilt and realized that someone ought long ago to have gone in to the poor frightened child, the terrified little girl, she began to wonder why Nell had not gone. Nell, whose responsibility she was, had fetched water for a stranger instead. It didn't ring right. First things had not come first. No, it rang wrong. Echoes of their first exchange began to come to her. Nell's rudeness and the odd manner. She could no longer so glibly excuse it. And she seemed, besides, to see in her mind's eye that the man in the corridor had no freckles on that averted cheek and no blue in his clothing.

She looked at Nell. She murmured, "It's incredible, really." The girl seemed to be waiting politely for her to go on and perhaps she didn't understand. "It's hard to believe," translated Miss Ballew. "I've never heard such a wild story. There seems to be no sense . . . not even a mad method to this man's actions. Are you sure?"

"What?"

"Are you sure you didn't encourage him?"

"I haven't done anything," Nell said, looking surprised. "I don't know what you mean."

This was an echo, too, and it rang false. "Come now, of course you know what I mean." Miss Ballew looked annoyed but she checked herself. "Never mind. This is no time for debate. See to the child, my dear, and bring her in here, do. Poor, poor baby. When the detective arrives," her voice faltered from its habitual tone of instruction, "I daresay he. . . ."

"He what?" Nell frowned faintly.

"I mean to say," said Miss Ballew dryly, being fair, "perhaps he's seen more of this sort of thing . . . perhaps more of it goes on than is dreamed of in my philosophy. And of course," she added thoughtfully, "The child. . . . How old is the child?"

"How old?"

"She is not an infant? She is old enough to talk?"

"Of course," said Nell wonderingly. "She's nine, I think."

"Then that is fortunate," said Miss Ballew, "for of course she will be able to corroborate your story."

Nell was just standing there, looking stupid and even half falling asleep.

What a handicap to have so limited a vocabulary, thought the teacher. "Corroborate means to confirm," she explained, "to tell the same story, or enough to prove it, do you see? That's why I point out—"

"And fortunate," said Nell, "means lucky." She was smiling. Why, she was dancing! She stood on the same spot, there at the foot of the bed, but for a moment Miss Ballew had the distinct impression that she was dancing. Even her face had a twinkling, sparkling look. Impish, as if she'd thought of something, had an idea, or knew a mischievous secret. "I know more words than you think I do," said Nell. "And I understand the future." She flung up her hands . . . yes, it was a dance! (Miss Ballew looked on, bewildered.) And then the dark skirt flopped and fell out of the moving arc and reversed. . . .

And the girl was leaning on her two stiff arms, her knuckles white on the footboard, her eyes very wide, very blue. "I . . . I wonder. . . ." The eyeballs turned in slow fear and the slow fear welled in Miss Ballew.

"She's awfully quiet," Nell said, softly, softly. *"Isn't* she?"

Miss Ballew clawed her own throat.

"Don't you think . . . it's funny?"

"F-fun—" Miss Ballew wafted her arm across the air.

Nell's teeth enfolded her lower lip. Now she looked very grave and thoughtful. She walked on soft toes to that inner door. Her hand was slow on the knob and nerves in the teacher's temple turned excruciatingly with it.

The latch fell out. The door yawned. No sound emerged from 809.

"Bunny?" Nell called, softly, softly.

There was no answer.

"Bunny!" The girl's back shook as if with a long shiver. Only quiet answered her. Her eyes rolled as she looked over her shoulder. "I'm afraid . . ." she whimpered.

Miss Ballew was afraid, too. She could *not* move. Her own ears knew that frightening silence was really there. "But you said— But you told me he didn't . . . hurt. . . ."

"He was in there, *afterward*. After you knocked. Do you think. . . ."

"Don't think! Don't even say!"

But Nell's words fell like Fate. "Maybe he remembered . . . she's old enough to talk. . . ."

"Our Father which art in heaven," mumbled Miss Ballew. "Beseech thee . . . from evil. . . ."

"It would," said Nell, glassy-eyed, "be so easy. She's just . . . a little thing. . . ."

"Go see!" screamed Miss Eva Ballew, up on her elbow but paralyzed for all that. "For the love of heaven, girl! Go *in* there and *see!*"

Chapter Eighteen

LYN TOUCHED his arm. He veered away from her touch as if he expected a blow to follow. (Yah! Iron nerves, Towers?)

"Lyn! Oh for—I thought. . . ."

"Didn't they give you my note?"

She was there, and not an apparition, standing beside him and, in the light of the city night, her face was sweetly, soberly wondering why he was as startled as this to see her. Ah, she was sweet and sane!

"Gosh, you look. . . ." He grabbed her woolly blue arm. "What are you doing here at this hour? You been rattling around this town *alone!* It's too damn late. Lyn."

"I'm not afraid. . . ."

"The street's no place—"

"I *haven't* been—"

"I don't care where you—"

"Nobody bothered—"

"You ought to know better!"

"Oh, don't be so—"

"Little fool. . . ."

"Oh, Jed!" she wailed. They teetered back from the brink of the same quarrel. The same damn thing. Jed even stepped backward on the sidewalk.

"I guess this is where we came in," he murmured.

"Where I walked out," she laughed uncertainly. Her eyes were not merry. But they were sweet and sane.

He put his hand in his pocket. "Jed, didn't you read it?"

"No, I. . . . Not yet." He fumbled for the envelope. He felt troubled . . . troubled. Not ready to meet her. She was here too soon. He held her note passively in his hand.

"It's nothing." She tried to take it, gently, but he refused to let it go. "I've been waiting and waiting," she said breathlessly. "In the lobby, Jed. It was safe enough. I was just about to give up and go home. I went into the drugstore . . . saw you . . . I've been calling your room."

He made no reply, no excuse, no explanation.

"I waited the longest time," she said.

"Why, dear?" he asked gently.

Lyn's face looked as if she were touched to tears but she did not weep and she did not turn her face away. "Because I'm sorry, Jed. That's about all there is to say about it. I'm ashamed to have been so stubborn and ornery. I'm sure you were more in the right than I was willing to admit while I was so mad."

"Never mind." He slipped his arm around her. "Never mind. Never mind." He thought, If this isn't like her! This kind of weird, high-minded, overdone fairness, this proud dragging down of her pride.

"I couldn't bear you to go all that way," she said quietly, keeping her own balance, although he embraced her, "and us mad. That's . . . all about it."

"Was I mad at you?" he said, scarcely believing it.

"Where were you going?" She put her bare fingers to her eyes.

"Oh, I . . . was more or less lighting out," he said vaguely. He felt very sad, very sad. He had a sensation in the breast as if the heart would break.

"Could we have one drink somewhere? And would you take me home? Will you make it up, Jed, and get the nasty taste out of our mouths, before you go?"

He looked down at her. "You beat all," he said gravely. "But you're sweet. How come you do the way you . . . ?" He broke off.

He looked up and the stone face on the building above him had no expression, nothing to say.

"I called you things I don't believe," Lyn said in a low voice. "Is it a date?"

Something bigger than he was took him and shook him like a rat. He covered the shudder up by grabbing for his suitcase. "It's a date, Lyn." He let his mouth curve, his voice be as tender as it wished to be, and she smiled like the rainbow.

Jed looked away, off over her head. Why did he feel so troubled and sad? Here was she, stubborn little love, trying to get back where they'd been. And why not? So Towers had his date, after all. Didn't he? Right back where he'd been. Wasn't he? (Episode over. Close quotes. File and forget.) Here's Towers in the evening with his own girl under his arm, and a honey she was, wearing that proud humility, *believing* (his heart sank because it was so heavy), trusting that he was going to match it. That they'd be together again. Be that as it may, the night was young and nothing was lost. Not a thing. Was it? And he could park the suitcase somewhere and on with the dance! March on! Te dum de dee. . . .

Proceed, Towers. From where you were. Advance, right out along the line, the line you cut in your time, the track you see before and leave behind, that goes, if you are smart, straight without any stupid detours. . . .

"Please, Jed, let me have my note?" she begged softly. "You don't need. . . ."

He looked down. He said, "No." He put it back in his pocket. Oh-ho no! he thought. This we look into, in some dark bar. "Just a minute, honey," he went on, sounding to his surprise exactly as if this was what he'd planned to say from the moment she had touched his arm. It came out so smooth and easy. "Something I want to check, a minute. In here."

She smiled. It was all right with her. Anything he said, of course. He thought, What a reckless attitude *that* is! But he touched her and with tenderness pushed her into a slot in the door and pushed the door, following.

What the hell was he going back in for? Curiosity? One thing, he'd surely keep it from Lyn, what he was up to. It was nothing, anyhow. Take a minute. No need to invent a lie, for her . . . innocent, reckless little love! No, he'd just take a quick look around, that's all. He thought he could tell, pretty quickly, if they'd got up there to the little kid, all right. Surely repercussions would sift down to the lobby, which he would be able to feel. Maybe no other guest could notice or catch on at all. But surely he could tell. And rest his mind about it.

That would really close it off. Lyn would never ask. Or, she'd take it, if he gave no answer, if he never explained. There'd be nothing to mention, nothing even to think about, once he knew nothing was . . . dangling.

Towers could then proceed.

In itself, the hotel now knew something was up. The news ran on its nervous system, in the minds of its own people. The guests were unaware and might never become aware of this as the guests had been unaware of many things on many other occasions. But the hotel knew now.

Rochelle sat at her board. She knew. She prepared to be the spider in the middle of the web. All things would eventually come to her.

Milner knew and was nervous behind his front, although his front remained as wooden and polished as the walnut around him. He was about to leave his post. He'd had a quick word with the assistant manager and that one agreed that Milner himself must go up there. He would emerge from his inner place and take over at the desk.

The bartender knew, in his dim barricade in the far corner of the farthest corner. The porter, emptying ashtrays, had a faint knowledgeable air. The bellboys knew. "Some guy got away," they dared say to each other softly, but they veiled their watching eyes.

Perrin was almost resigned to the idea that the man had got away. If he had not, but still lurked somewhere, where was it? No redhead and so forth in the corridors, in any of the public rooms. Not in the bar's deepest recesses, not in the men's rooms. If he was registered and had a room and lurked *there,* it might take a little doing.

Perrin strode up to the desk and caught Milner. "Who we got that's tall, redheaded, freckle-faced, light suit, blue shirt?"

"Nobody," said Milner. "Say. . . ."

They wiped trouble from all their faces. The assistant manager said, "Yes, Mr. Hodges." A guest took his key, made a firm didactic statement about the weather, went away.

"On the trouble in 807?" the manager said.

"Yeah, dame described this man. . . ."

"Just what did he do?"

"Intruded," said Perrin dryly.

Milner said, "It was a man who tipped me. Is the kid all right?"

"Who?"

"Who told me? It was. . . ."

"No, no. *What* kid?"

"Little girl. Jones."

"I'd better get up there," Perrin said thoughtfully. "Nobody told me about a kid."

"That's not good, having a kid in it. I was just going. . . ."

The manager said, "Uh—keep it quiet."

Two of them swung off separately. Milner negotiated his way around the walnut embankments. Perrin met him again, near the elevators.

The elevators knew, although they whispered up and down without telling.

"Couldn't have hurt the kid," Perrin remarked. "All she said, he intruded."

"All she said to me, did we stop him," agreed Milner. "Ran out, did he?"

"Yeah, he's not up there now."

"Nerves?" said Milner hopefully. Perrin shrugged. Whatever it was, they assumed it was all over but, of course, the hysterics.

An elevator whispered down. "Say, that's Towers now." Milner peered. "Fellow who tipped me. Thought he—oh. . . ."

"Oh, what?"

"He's got the girl. She found him." Milner relaxed.

"Eight," said Perrin quietly and stepped on. The boy moved only an eyelash. But he knew.

"Up? Up?" caroled Mrs. McMurdock. "Come, Bobo. Come, darling. Time for beddy-bye." The little dog ran into the elevator and sniffed moistly at Perrin's socks. Milner and he exchanged looks. The car started upward.

"He loooves to ride," said Mrs. McMurdock. "Doesn't he, Bobo? Doesn't he, boy? Loves to ride! Yes, he does! Just loooves to ride!"

She did not know.

Chapter Nineteen

RUTH, AS SHE RODE gently upward, stuffed her change into her little evening bag without looking down at her hands. She kept watching the blank metal door beyond which the floors were sliding by. She was the only passenger. The car made no stop but hers. As it sailed toward a soft landing and went into the little shuffle for the precise level of the eighth floor, she felt a perverse regret for the ending of an ordeal, a resistance to the necessity of shifting from one mood to another.

She stepped out. Behind her, the car stayed where it was a second longer than was normal while the boy listened to the quality of the silence up here. It seemed to be mere silence. Disappointed, he looked at his lights, yanked the lever, and sailed upward.

For Ruth, the corridor was just the same, just the same. She hurried to her left. She turned the corner.

The door of 807 looked just the same . . . as bland and blank as all the others. Prepare to shift. Inside, the girl would be dozing, and Bunny fast asleep, and the debris of her parents' dressing would be strewn about just as they had left it. Shift. The mood now is hushed. It's the mood of— All's well. Naturally. Of course it is. Ruth tapped gently.

At once a much agitated female voice cried, "Oh, yes! Come in! Oh, come in!"

Ruth's mood leaped like lightning. Her hand leaped to the knob. She burst into the room and met the frightened eyes of a stoutish middle-aged woman she'd never seen in her life before, who was half sitting, half lying in a strained position on Ruth's own bed. The woman's black dress was awry over her stout legs and her mouse-colored hair was awry, too. "Who are you!" cried this stranger in a voice that was also awry.

But Ruth put first things first.

Her gold bag fell out of her hand. Without a word, she flew, hands up, across 807 to 809. She batted the partially opened door and it swung wider. 809 was unlit. Ruth aimed herself like an arrow at the light switch. She flashed around.

She saw Bunny's two bare feet twitching on the bed and the girl's dark back bent. Ruth cried out, "What's the matter?" She got one glimpse of Bunny's bound mouth and then saw the girl's face blinking at her over the shoulder, the drowsy evil in the sullen careless glance, and she knew what the wicked hands were about to do.

Making no cry, Ruth simply flew at her. Her hands bit on the shoulders, and with all her might she heaved backward, to get the evil away. Still, she did not scream. Instead, she called out in almost a cheerful voice, "It's all right, Bunny. It's me. It's Mommy."

The shoulders rolled, writhed, and slipped away from her. The girl's body turned with vicious speed. Ruth felt herself knocked backward and the small of her back was wrenched as it slammed against the other bed and she felt her neck crack with the backward weight of her head. She flipped herself quickly over and slipped downward to her knees, hearing silk rip. She fastened both hands on an ankle. She crawled backward, yanking and pulling, out from the narrow place between the beds. *Get it away from Bunny.* This was first. And Nell came, hopping, tottering, kicking . . . and her hands clawed for Ruth's face, hunting Ruth's eyes.

OK, thought Ruth. *All right.*

Ruth had not always been a gracious young matron, a pretty wife, a gentle mother. In her day she'd climbed many a tough tree and hung by knobby knees off ladders with pigtails dragging. And she'd chased the other kids off rafts and over rooftops. And she'd played basketball, too, on a tough team, even in so-called free style, which meant she had pulled hair and bitten and gouged with the rest. And she'd run up and down the playing fields of many schools and been banged in the shins by hockey sticks. She'd had her bruises and given them. The world of direct physical conflict, violent and painful, had not always been beyond her ken.

"So!" she hissed with her teeth closed. There was lightning on her eyeballs as she got her hands in that yellowish hair and yanked and the girl screeched and fell forward, twisting, and Ruth rolled on the hard floor to get from under her.

She felt the teeth in her forearm and pain as claws ripped at her cheek. Ruth's long rosy nails went into the other's flesh, where she could, and with the sharp spurs of her heels she slashed at the other's shins. Her own head thudded on the carpet and hands like wires sank in her throat.

She wouldn't have screamed anyhow.

She pulled up her knee. Silk ripped, velvet tore. She put her sharp golden heel in the wildcat's stomach and straightened her leg and Nell went sprawling. Ruth walked on her knees and dove on her, got the hair, whammed the head to the floor.

But the head bounced. The body in the dark dress was taut and strong. It wasn't going to be that easy.

Ruth heard herself growl in her gullet, now it was free. Fast as the fighting went, she yet summoned with a cold brain old strengths, old tricks, and when they were not enough, she began to invent. . . . She had realized, long ago, that she fought here something wild and vicious that wanted to hurt, that didn't care how. Probably mad, and strong by that perfect ruthlessness.

But Ruth, too, was fortified. She was wilder than the tomboy she used to be. She was more vicious than the girl athlete. She was Bunny's mother and she was easily able to be absolutely ruthless in that holy cause.

She said to herself, *OK. All right.* And she was not afraid.

It never crossed her mind to scream. It seemed her sole and simple duty and even her pleasure to fight with all her body's strength and her mind's cunning. (Outside of any rules, if that was the way it was, and OK, too.) It did not cross her mind to wonder who would win either. She sank her own strong teeth in the enemy's wrist, while she tried with her mind to think just how she was going to conquer . . . what trick would do it . . . even as she was tossed and the merciless elbow was crushing her breast.

Miss Ballew managed to get her feet to the floor but her weight would not balance over them. The column of her leg would not stand, the knee joint would not lock. She knew now she would be forever haunted by remorse and shame if she did not force herself to help in this emergency. But she was not well. Her heart hurt. There was a sharp pain in her side. Her mind knew that her body was lying, and her heart pitied the body's treasonable victory, as her lips prayed cravenly for someone else to come.

Chapter Twenty

THE MOMENT he was inside the lobby, Jed knew that the hotel, in itself, was aroused. The alarm was spread. He saw it in the stiff pose of a different head behind the desk. He knew, too, that there had been, and yet was, a search going on. He saw that in the veiled turn of all the eyes, in the porter's spine. Looking for someone? For whom? For *him,* no doubt.

It came to him that he was taking a certain risk in the mere act of stepping back within these walls. Sure, they were looking. Once more his mind played back its recorded impressions, a glimpse of the fellow in the brown suit weaving among the chairs, and his beckoning hand and the doorman's response, and the doorman's *belated* prance to his normal duties. The man in the brown suit had been looking for someone, all right. For whom, if not for Jed?

All the way across the lobby, he could see that very suit, the same man, over there right now, waiting for an elevator. The clerk to whom Jed had given warning was beside him, and all the way across the lobby, Jed knew when they spoke his name.

What was this?

They were *looking* for him and they, for some reason, were not looking for *him.* He saw himself split in two, the object of their search, and merely Towers who had just checked out of 821. They hadn't put it together yet. They would, sooner or later. And easily. For instance, right over there lounged the boy who had brought up the ice. Who was, all by himself, the missing link. When would his haunting eye catch sight of Jed and recognize?

Jed guided Lyn so that she stood with her back to the elevators and he, bent as if to listen to her, could watch them with an eyebeam over her head. Those two men were authority. Obviously. Were they *only now* going up to see what was wrong on the eighth floor? If so, they were darned late! Wires must have got crossed. It had been a long time.

(A long, long time for a helpless, frightened little girl to wait in the dark for her daddy or his equivalent.)

He ground his teeth. What was going on? Lyn stood obediently, her head thrown back to look up into his face. She didn't know why they were standing here. She trusted there was a good reason.

He said rapidly, "Do you mind? I just want to see. . . . Talk to me. Make some remarks, hm?"

"You're being mighty mysterious," Lyn said lightly. It was so plain she trusted he had good reason. "Mine not to wonder why. Me and the six hundred. Lyn, number six hundred and one."

He felt his jaw crack. "Keep talking."

The elevator took on its passengers . . . two men, one woman, and a scampering little dog.

"Nothing is quite so numbing as to be told to say something. Makes your mind a blank. Just like on long distance. Hm . . . I like raspberry pie very much but the seeds do get in my teeth. I'm very fond of cucumber sandwiches in the summertime. Is this better than the weather? Am I doing all right?"

"You're fine."

Jed was farsighted, been so all his life. He could see from here the indicator moving on the dial. He could not read the numbers but then he knew already where the eight came. He said bitterly, "Why in Christ's name didn't I lock the damn door!"

"If I ask questions," said Lyn placidly, "I won't be making remarks, will I? Cross out 'will I.' "

"The door *between*," he growled. What he was telling he didn't know.

"Oh, between. Well, that's nice. That's quite illuminating."

"If I had any brains. . . ."

"Oh, you have, Jed. I think you have. Good-looking as you are, you must have a brain. I think it's very possible. Lessee, what's my favorite flower. At a time like this, I ought to know so I could tell you. But I like too many kinds, too much. But you take roses."

Although he kept his eyes on that dial, he knew Lyn's face was full of peace. She had no right! His glance flicked down. She had her hands in the big pockets of her coat and her back was bent in a sweet, almost yearning arch, in order for her face to turn up to him, and her eyes were sweet and sane and full of peace because she believed. . . . She was a little fool to believe in anybody!

"You look about nine years old," said Jed with a whipsnap of anger. And he sent his eyes again to the dial.

"Oh, I don't think so. I think I probably look about nineteen and just as if I've got a terrible crush on you, a bobby-socks-type crush. And you look like thunder, Jed. If I knew what the matter was I'd try to help. But you know that, of course." (I even trust you to trust me.) "Mine only to keep talking, eh? Why, then, I'll go ahead. Babble. Babble. Do you care for the chamber music? No, that's a question. Well, I always say it depends. And it does. Everything depends. . . ."

The hand on the dial had stopped . . . must be at about four. It seemed to be stuck there. Was it out of order?

"Come, boy. Come, boy. Ah, naughty Bobo! (Loves to ride!) But this is home, boy. Home! Now, Bobo must be a good boy. Biscuit? Bobo want his biscuit? If Bobo wants his biscuit. . . . Oh, what a naughty, bad doggy! Bobo! Listen to me! No . . . more . . . ride. Do you understand, sir? Beddy-bye, now. Come, Bobo."

Bobo retreated to the inner corner of the elevator and sat down.

Mrs. McMurdock giggled in her throat. "So ki-yute! Isn't that—little monkey! Bobo, boy, Mama will leave you. Biscuit, biscuit?"

The hotel's people stood silent. Mrs. McMurdock was a guest. Bobo was a guest. A guest need not know all there is to know. They wore small chilly smiles, not too impatient, not too amused, either.

Bobo frisked between Milner's ankles.

"Shall I pick him up, madam?" the elevator boy said most respectfully.

"No, no. Now, he must learn," said Mrs. McMurdock. "Now, he'll mind in a minute." The trouble was, Bobo did look as if he would mind, any minute.

The hotel's people cleared their throats with professional patience. It wasn't going to be very pleasant placating that woman on the eighth floor, admitting to her that her wicked intruder had got away.

In the lobby Jimmy said, "Hey, kids, sumpin's funny! See that fellow over there, one with the girl? Say, what was the room again?"

"Room 807."

"Yeah," drawled Jimmy. "Yeah. . . ."

Jed's eyes flickered in his stony face.

". . . partial to rum," Lyn said, "with pink stuff in it. And you sure can get thirsty, talking so much. Filibuster is running down, Jed. Don't elect me senator, anybody. Is it all right now? Can we go?"

In Jed's head exploded the loud NO for an answer.

Her face changed. One second, sweet and pretty, and pleased with the nonsense she was able to spin. The next it had lost all that pretty animation, light, and color. Jed did it. By the look he bent on her he wiped the pretty peace off her face.

He said quietly, "I'm a rat, Lyn. A complete rat. Go home."

"But, Jed, I've been wait—"

"Don't wait anymore. Never wait for me."

He stepped around his suitcase. His face was flinty. His muscles surged. He went across the lobby in a walk so smooth and fast that he seemed to float.

He knew that bellhop straightened with a start.

The hell with that!

He pushed on the door to the fire stairs.

Ah, God, NO!

He shouldn't have run out on that little kid! What kind of rat did such a thing? A rat like Towers. A complete no-good. . . . He was sad, he'd been sad over it a long time. So sad his heart was heavy.

Ah, NO!

A pair of socks wasn't all he had left and lost up on the eighth floor. And left, forever. Gone, like smoke! Yeah. You can't catch it back again, no more than you can a wisp of smoke. Thing like that, you can't retrieve.

And who would know? *Towers* would know.

This trip, all the way down to the lobby and out, wasn't even as good as a detour. There wasn't a way back from this side road to the main track. No way *on* again, *in* again. Rat forever, amen.

But he went up. Went up with all the great strength of his long powerful legs, three steps at once, then two, but pulling on the rail, around and around, climbing the building more like a monkey than a man going upstairs.

Passed the buck. Towers! Let the old lady take care of it. Towers! White! He sobbed breath in.

He thought, I don't know what I'm doing . . . know what I did. . . . Never even thought to lock that door. Could have made sure to keep her out of there. Could have done that much. He and he *alone* (not Eddie. Eddie was out on the bathroom floor) . . . Towers *alone* knew what kind of sitter that Nell turned out to be. Knew the poor little kid was waiting. The old biddy couldn't know *that,* and where was she all this while? Arguing? No reason to think. . . .

No, no. What Towers *alone* knew was that, reason or no reason, there would always and forever be some risk with that Nell around. But a risk for somebody else, of course. For somebody else's kid. A little thing who couldn't do a thing about it. So *Towers* figured the risk to his own six feet three, to his man's hide, to his . . . what?

Now, he couldn't remember any risk for Towers. For *nothing* he ran out. For the sick shadow of nothing at all he'd lost what he'd lost.

This complete revulsion was making him sick. OK. Cut it out, Towers. What's done is done. Take it from here.

Eighth floor?

He must be in pretty good condition.

Yeah, condition!

There was the elevator. And there they stood, talking. Questions and answers, with the elevator boy. The hell with them. They didn't know there was a risk. Or they'd hurry. He couldn't understand why they hadn't hurried. Jed rushed past.

Aw, probably Bunny was all right. Probably. Pray so, and if so, here's Towers heading right back into the middle of this jam, for nothing. Doing no good. But maybe not for nothing. He didn't know. All he knew was, while he could still move for himself he was going to make sure. He was going to bust in there and if the old biddy hadn't found her yet, Towers was going to untie the little kid and the hell with everything else . . . and five seconds more, one second, one pulse beat more was too long.

Room 807's door was wide open. The old biddy, crouched on the edge of the bed, took one look at Jed's wild figure and heaved in her breath and let out a scream to wake the dead!

But Jed was in 809 before it died.

Nell, hair hanging over her eyes, had one knee on either side of the slim body of a woman, supine on the floor. Their hands were braced, hand against wrist, arms against aching arms. The woman on the floor had blood on her mouth and her cheek was torn and her breathing was shallow and difficult. But her eyes were intelligent and they yet watched for her chance.

Jed took little Nell by the short hair of her head. He ripped her away. She came up in his grasp, screeching, and hung from his hand, limp in surprise like a sawdust doll.

In the corridor, Milner and Perrin saw the racing figure and in their startled ears rang the woman's scream. Perrin got his gun in his hand as they began to run.

The door of 807 was wide.

"The man," croaked Miss Ballew, voice thick and hoarse. "That's the man!" Oh, she knew him. By the indescribable. By the habits of motion, the line of the back, the tip of the shoulder, the cock of the head.

"The *one*," she sobbed. "The man . . . the same one!"

Perrin looked toward 809.

He saw a tall man with a face of utter fury drag, by the hair of her head, a small blond girl through that door. Saw him drag her around the wooden frame as if he didn't care whether she lived or died, as if he didn't care if he broke her bones.

"Drop that girl! Let her go!"

Jed's head went back and the eyes glittered down the long straight nose. "The hell I will! You don't—"

Perrin fired.

Chapter Twenty-one

RUTH O. JONES lifted her shoulders from the carpet and pulled her twisted rags and tatters aside to free her legs. She wiped the blood off her mouth with her arm. She combed her fingers through her hair. Some of it, torn out at the roots, came away in her broken nails.

She walked on her knees—there was no need to rise higher—over to Bunny's bed.

She paid not the slightest attention to the gunshot as it blasted off behind her.

She said in her firm contralto, "OK, honey bun? For goodness' sakes, what happened to *you?*" Her cut mouth kissed the temple lightly. Her fingers were strong and sure on those wicked knots.

Jed kept standing, somehow, because he had to keep an eye steady on Nell. She fell on the floor when he had to drop her as if she had been a sack of meal. As soon as he was sure she lay as limp as she seemed to lie, he looked at his right hand. He took it away from his left side and looked at the bright blood on it.

He looked at the men, standing tense and threatening in his path, and he tried to smile. The elevator boy was behind them. Then he saw his girl, Lyn, behind *him* . . . looking, as if she peered through trees in glade, between the men's bodies in at the strange tableau.

Ah, the little fool! "Go home," he said.

Then he heard it. In the other room Bunny began to cry.

Over Jed's face passed a look of peace and thanksgiving. He turned, reeling, because he was wounded and no kidding, stumbled, and made for the big maroon chair. He thought he sat down in it. Perhaps it was more like falling.

"Oh, Jed!"

"But that's Towers. . . ."

"It's the same man. . . ."

Now, he was three. Or maybe only one again. Or nothing. No matter. There was a difference in the way a kid cried. Funny . . . could you write down the difference in musical terms, he wondered. Pitch or timing or what? One kind of crying that gnawed on your nerves and pierced your head. This kind didn't do that. No, it didn't do that at all. It was a thing not unmusical to hear. . . .

Perrin, kneeling over Nell, barked, "What did you do to this girl?"

Jed didn't feel like bothering to say.

Miss Ballew let out another yelp of pure shock. Eyes starting from her head, she reacted to her sight of the little man in the hotel's livery who was standing in the bathroom door, holding his head, looking out mouselike at them all.

"Munro!" thundered Milner. "What—"

Eddie blinked. Silence rustled down, that they might hear his feeble voice. "I guess . . . Nell musta got into more mischief. Did she? My niece? Nell?"

"Who?"

Jed pulled himself from the mists. "Nell, the baby-sitter. On the floor." He braced himself, watchfully. "Nutty as a fruitcake," he said.

But Nell only rolled, drowsily. Her arm fell aside in sleepy grace, revealing her face. Her eyes were closed. The blue gone, her small face was left perfectly serene. There was a long scratch from eye corner to jaw. It looked as if it had been painted there, as if she felt no pain. She seemed to be asleep.

"That's Nell. Yes, she. . . ." Eddie tottered to look. "That's the way she did—before," he said in awe. "After the fire, they say, she slept . . . just like that." He swallowed and looked around at all their set faces. "How can she sleep?" he whimpered.

"Somebody," said Jed wearily, "go see. I suppose it's Mrs. Jones. This one pretty near killed her."

Perrin got off his haunches and lurched through the door. Milner's horrified eye sent fury in sudden understanding where, from his point of view, it belonged. "Munro!"

"I . . . didn't think . . ." said Eddie. "I kinda kept hoping she'd be all right. But I guess. . . ."

"Next time, don't guess," said Jed. "Lyn go home."

"Not now." She moved toward him, drawn. "I won't, Jed. I've got to know. . . ."

He closed his eyes.

When a fresh scream rose up, out there in the other room in another world, Ruth's fingertips did not leave off stroking into shape the little mouth that the wicked gag had left so queer and crooked. "That's right. Just you cry. Golly, Bun, did you see me fighting! Wait till we tell Daddy . . . missed the whole thing. . . ." Ruth held the little head warmly against her battered body. There was comfort soaking through from skin to skin. "Cry it all out, sweetheart. Cry."

"Mrs. Jones?" a man said to her. His hair seemed to her to be trying to stand on end.

"Go away. Hush. Please call my husband. . . ."

She stroked and murmured on. Not until she heard Peter's voice did her wounds and gashes remember pain.

"We're just fine," Ruth said quickly. "Jeepers, have we had an adventure!"

Peter's face was dead white as he looked upon his wife and child.

"She was the crossest sitter I ever saw," Bunny said indignantly. Her arms went around her daddy's dark head where he had hidden his face against her. "She tied my mouth all up, Daddy, so I couldn't cry. She certainly didn't want me to cry awful bad."

Peter roused and looked at those stockings.

"Bound and gagged," Ruth said quietly. Her face said more.

"G-gosh, she must have had terrible ears." Peter's voice trembled. "I expect she's got sick ears, Bunny."

His hands curled and uncurled. Ruth's eyes said, I know. But it's over. Be careful.

For Bunny didn't realize what had almost happened to her and it was better if she didn't. You mustn't scare a little girl who's nine so that all her life she carries the scar. You must try to heal what scar there is. Ruth knew, and deeply trembled to know it, that someday she would leave Bunny again. And with a sitter, of course. She must. (Although not for a good while with a stranger. Maybe never again with a total stranger.) Still, they would go gaily as might be on in time and they would not permit themselves to be cowed, to be daunted. They dared not.

Poor Peter, shaken and suffering right now, and fighting so hard not to betray it. Peter knew all this as well as she. They were tuned to each other. "Bunny's fine and I feel fine, too," she told him. "Really. A few scratches. Did they take her away?"

"They're coming. They'll take her to a hospital," added Peter, for Bunny's sake, "because she's sick, really. She doesn't know how to get along with people who are well."

"Will she get better," said Bunny with a huge snuffle, "from those sick ears?"

"I don't know, pudding. They won't let her be with well people anymore, unless she gets all better."

Bunny's shuddering sobs were becoming like the soft far murmur of the last thunder of a departing storm. "Daddy."

"What, Bun?"

Ruth felt the head turn on her breast. "Did you have fun?"

Peter couldn't answer. But Ruth could. "Oh, Bunny, it was lots of fun. And Daddy made a good speech. I wish you'd been big enough to go." She rushed on. "Daddy stood up and all the people, everybody was dressed up. . . ."

Peter looked upon the condition of his wife's clothing. "Those . . . scratches, hon," he said in a minute, sounding as if half his throat was closed. "There's a doctor out there."

So the doctor came in and looked them both over.

"You know," said Ruth when he had gone, licking the antiseptic in her mouth, "I pretty near had her licked! I think!" she laughed. "I must look terrible but I feel fine."

And she did. Ah, poor Peter with the retrospective horror and the wrath locked in and buttoned down. But Ruth had got rid of it by tooth and claw. And she remembered now, with relish, certain digs and blows. She felt quite peaceful. Fulfilled, she thought, the tigress in me. "Hand me in some of my things, Peter. I'm going to bed in here with Bun."

"OK, girls."

"Maybe we'll order hot chocolate! Shall we? Lets!"

"In the middle of the night!" squealed Bunny and the sweet smooth skin of her face rippled in the warning of delight to come.

Peter O. Jones, with a smile covering (from all but his wife) the tears bleeding out of his heart, went back to 807.

Chapter Twenty-two

EDDIE WAS GONE, damned for a reckless fool, with all the anxious ignorant hope he'd called his caution, dust in his whimpering throat. (Don't worry, Eddie, Marie would say.)

Milner was gone, to harmonize with the walnut downstairs. (Keep it out of the papers, if we possibly can.)

Perrin was gone. ("Sorry, Towers. You can see how it was?" "Sure. That's OK.") He went with Nell.

And Nell was gone. Still seeming asleep, looking innocent and fair. Only Jed spoke to her. Jed said (and it seemed necessary—somewhere once, this he had planned to say), "So long, Nell."

She was asleep so she didn't reply. Yet there was a lazy lift of the lashes. (They won't do anything to me.)

Nearly everyone was gone. Miss Ballew remained, sick in her soul, with the doctor's suggested sedative in her hand. Jed was in the big chair again, bloody shirt loose over the vast bandage. Lyn was still there.

The doctor warned once more that Jed must take a few days' rest before trying to travel with that wound. Then he was gone.

"You'll stay over, Jed, won't you?" Lyn's mouth was stiff.

"A couple of days, at least. I'll see." Jed's side was stinging like the devil now. Telegrams, he thought, but time for that later. Maybe he'd break his cross-country trip and stop to see the family. Felt like it, somehow. Worry them, though, if he turned up shot. "Lyn, will you please. . . . Your family's probably. . . . Why don't you go home?"

"I will soon." She didn't look at him. She looked at her trembling hands.

Peter took Ruth's things to her, came back, flipped up his tails, sat down, put his head in his hands. "Jesus."

Lyn said, with that stiff mouth, "You're terribly upset, of course. Shouldn't we go, Jed? If I can help you to your own room. . . ."

"Or I," said Miss Ballew drearily.

"Don't go. Ruth wants to say good night. A minute."

"Your little, uh, Bunny's all right?" asked Jed.

"Soon be. Kids bounce back. Thank God. Drink with me?"

Jed didn't feel sure. He felt this room rejected him. But he was *fallen* in this chair.

"I ought to go home," said Lyn whitely. "I don't mean to hang around . . . be in the way."

"I ought to go," said Miss Ballew. (To be a worthless old coward and on top of that be fooled and fail in the mind, too!) "I was of very little use."

"Take it easy," Peter said. "Better try and take it easy, all of us."

Jed shifted his stiff side, reached slowly for the pocket of his coat, for the envelope. He managed to open it with one hand. It said, "Dear Jed:" And that was all. No more.

Well. He looked back into dim reaches of time. It would have been enough. It would have been plenty. He crushed it up and put it back in his pocket. He didn't look at Lyn.

Peter passed drinks. "Nonsense, Miss Ballew. You need this. There." He sat down. His brown eyes locked with Jed's gray. "As I understand it, you left Bunny tied up? But you told them at the desk on your way out?" Peter's voice was light, tentative.

"I figured it wasn't my business," said Jed levelly. "I didn't want to get into a mess. I figured to get away."

Well, he hadn't got away. He'd got shot. And Towers was a rat. So, then, he was. The little girl was OK now. Mother, too. Nothing, thank God, they couldn't get over. So . . . if Towers was left in his rathood, that was not too important to them anymore.

Gray eyes locked on brown. "That's the kind of rat I am, I guess," Jed said quietly. "Later, I got a little nervous . . . a little too much later."

Miss Ballew's lips trembled. "I was so stupid," she said. "I was worse than no use. My *fault*. . . ."

Jed's gray eyes met hers. They said, Don't blame yourself too much. They said, I understand. They said, Us sinners—

"Seems to me," Jed drawled, "if you're hunting for blame . . . if I hadn't come over here in the first place. . . ."

"If I hadn't walked out," Lyn said bleakly.

"No. Lyn. . . ."

"You think *I'm* not doing any iffing?" Peter asked. Brown eyes met gray. "If I'd even looked at the girl with half my brain on it. Me and my big important speech! I left it to Ruthie. Of course, she got it. In her bones, the way she sometimes does. If. . . ."

Jed shook his head.

"Ruth knew I needed her. She chose. Even *Ruth* can if. . . ." Brown eyes said to gray, *All us sinners*.

Peter got up to pace. "Ruth says she had her licked. But I don't know. . . ."

"I don't know, either, sir. I couldn't say." Eyes locked again. "Now, don't kid me, sir," Jed said gently. "They weren't two steps behind me. They'd have been on time."

And then he smiled. Because it only mattered to Towers now, and Towers could take it. "Tell you, it isn't often a man says to himself, You ought to be shot, and right away, someone obliges." He moved and made the wound hurt. It was not so bad. It was like a session with the hairbrush, or a trip to the woodshed. He didn't mind.

But then Lyn said, as if she broke, "I'm afraid." Why, she was all to pieces. She wasn't *Lyn*. She looked white and old and sick and she was shaking to pieces. "I'm scared to go home. That's the truth," she wailed. "I'm scared of the night. I'd g-go but I'm afraid. Such t-terrible things . . . I don't know anything. I'm scared of what a f-fool I've been." She wept.

Jed winced. "And you ought to be," he said grimly. But it wasn't *Lyn*. It was sick and ugly.

Ruth said, "Ssssh. . . ." She stepped out of Bunny's room, leaving the door wide. She wore a man's woolen robe because she was cold now, with shock. (And Jed was glad, remembering Nell in the long silk.) But her battered face was serene.

Lyn choked off her whimpering.

Peter held Ruth's hand to his cheek. "Asleep?" he whispered and she nodded. She looked lovely, this little blond Mrs. Jones.

"Drink, darling?"

"Not on top of the chocolate."

"Ruthie, would you be scared if I took this young lady home?"

"Why, no," Ruth said smiling.

"Uh, you see, Towers can't do it. He ought to be in bed."

Jed said, appalled, "Yes, and I'm going there. But listen, get the hotel to send somebody. Lyn can't go alone. But you can't leave Mrs. Jones, sir." She's had enough! he thought.

Ruth smiled at them all. "Don't be afraid," she said gently.

"Here we sit, with our hair turning white," murmured Peter in a moment, but his eyes were shining. " 'Don't be afraid,' she says."

"Well, you *dasn't!*" Ruth smiled. "Or what would become of us all?"

She wasn't long for them. She wasn't all in room 807. She kissed Peter's brow, made her good nights. She didn't say thanks. Perhaps she forgot, or she knew. . . . She withdrew, went back to her sleeping baby, and the door closed behind her.

They sat, sipped quietly. Lyn's face was pink, her eyes were ashamed, her back was straighter. Jed thought, I know her. I know what she's made of. And, he realized, *she* knew more about Towers, the real Towers, than anyone else on earth. Something grew, here . . . never could have grown had they gone, say, to a show. Something known, for better, for worse. He touched her hand. She turned hers and her icy fingers clung. "Put an ending on my letter sometime, honey?"

"How, Jed?"

"The regular ending," he said soberly. Yours truly. That was the way to end a letter.

Lyn smiled like the rainbow.

I'll just have to take care of her, he thought. She mustn't be afraid. His finger moved, humbly, on the soft back of her hand.

Peter said, "Yep. We oughta be scared, all right. Ignorant optimism won't do it. Won't do it. But we've got *not* to be scared, just the same."

"Courage," sighed Miss Ballew. She rose to say good night.

"We are strangers," Peter said darkly. "Whom do we know? One —if you're lucky. Not many more. Looks like we've got to learn how we can trust each other. How we can tell. . . . How can we dare. . . . Everything rests on trust between strangers. Everything else is a house of cards."

Miss Ballew went around to her room, having been drinking at midnight with strangers! Strangers and friends! She was, and not from liquor, a little bit intoxicated. She felt warm around the heart and a bit weepy and quite brave.

Peter came back and sat down, gazed at the two of them, moving his lips. "Damn it," cried Peter O. Jones. "I wish I'd said that!"

"Said what, Mr. Jones?"

"What I just said!" Peter was cross.

Lyn's eye met Jed's and dared be a little merry. "But . . . Mr. Jones, you just *did*. Didn't you?"

"In my speech!" cried Peter. "*Now* I have to think of a better ending." He glared at them.

The Dream Walker

Chapter One

THE CRACKS in this ceiling are too familiar. There is one like the profile of Portugal up in the corner. It makes a king with a crown; his long scraggy nose has a wart on it. I am tired of seeing first Portugal, then a king, then Portugal again. But even I can't read any more. I can't listen to the radio, either, and be dragged by the ears the raggedy journey over that dial one more day. Makes me feel as if I were disintegrating; the strands of order and purpose in my brain seem to be raveling out to a fuzz like a tassel.

It's a revelation to me that I can't—let me record this while I am practicing—cannot stare at the ceiling and wonder and worry and brood about life and death. I am to wait? Well? Meantime, what am I to do? How shall I be occupied?

So they brought me a tape recorder, which I think is a fine appropriate tool for telling this story. All I need do is talk. Some clever girl can punctuate and place the paragraphs later, if it turns out that I'm not able.

Yes, my voice plays back crisply, as it should after all my studying and teaching, too. The girl will have no trouble. Will you, my dear, whoever you are?

Enough practice. I therefore (as Ben Jonson said) will begin.

This is a story you know already. But I'm convinced that it has been told the wrong way. The attack has always been the same. They've told you, first, the fantastic appearance of things; and piled up evidence of the marvelous. They have brought you up against what looked like proof of the impossible, until you were properly amazed. *Then* they say, "But of course it was nothing but a hoax and this is how it was done." And all the storytellers run downhill. They must recapitulate. You cannot follow it. Or rather, you don't.

I guess I know as much about it as anyone in the world, having been in the thick of it, and in a position to hear what all those concerned have had to say. You'll remember me from the newspapers. *Olivia Hudson: dramatic teacher in fashionable New York City Girls' School.* You'll know my face: thinnish oval with nothing distinguished about it but high and too prominent cheekbones and one crooked eyebrow. *Olivia Hudson, thirty-four.* Place me? I'm going to tell the whole story into this machine, the other way around. The scene *and* the backstage machinery, all as it happened.

Oh, it's called a hoax, now that it has been uncovered, but I'd rather call it a plot. A meticulously planned and almost flawlessly executed plot, with one strict purpose. It was all designed to damage one certain man.

It *has* damaged him. That's why I think, if I tell it my way and you follow it, there may be some gain.

It was the old power of the Big Lie. Even now, when you don't have to believe the lie anymore, it's hard enough, isn't it, to believe that anyone would have gone to so much trouble? Such a crazy business! Therein lies its wicked power. I hear people still saying, "Oh, I never believed that stuff *but* . . ." They are still talking. People drag out the same old saws. "More things in heaven and earth, Horatio." Also, ". . . smoke, there's fire." And some say everything didn't come out. "There must be more behind it than we know." The lie was so weird and wild that it is hard to believe in the liars. So it all makes for argument . . . talk, talk, talk . . . as anything that smacks of the supernatural makes for talk and argument. (See flying saucers.) People delight in challenging reason with the marvelous, anyhow. It's all the talk and the inevitable tinge of doubt that remains and still, I'm afraid, hurts him.

Of course, we didn't know where the plot was going. We had no idea what it was designed for. It rolled up to such a size, before we knew it had to be exposed, that our difficulty was . . . and still is . . . to explain. Who these people were and not only how but *why* they did it.

Very well then. It was a plot. There were four people and (as far as I know) only four, in the plot. And one of these worked simply for her hire.

The plot was directed against John Paul Marcus and only him. The rest was buildup.

I have the good fortune to be related to John Paul Marcus. I call him Uncle John, although he is my grandmother's brother-in-law, and the relationship is remote. He is seventy-seven years old now. He has never held political office but everyone knows he has served his country better and longer than most people alive. He is rich, having found it rather easy and not particularly important to make and keep money. He is influential, not because he is rich but because he is as alert today as when he was thirty and, by the sum of all the alert days of his long life, he is wise. This wonderful man has such balance and insight that he knows how to be steady in the dizzy dance of crises and confusions all around us. So he has been like a wise and beloved Uncle John to the entire United States of America. No use for me to go on about Marcus. You know how often men in responsible places have listened to him.

This is the man they wanted to pull down.

There were two men and two women in the plot. It was expensive. There had to be money, not so much in the execution of the plans—this was comparatively cheap—but to pay those who made and executed them. The man with the money had a motive. The man with the brains had a kind of motive, too. He was to get nearly a half a million dollars besides. The women—one with her kind of motive, and the other simply for her wages—cost, as usual, much less.

The man with the money was Raymond Pankerman. His grandfather made the money. His father used it productively and increased it fabulously, and in the endeavor lived to a healthy eighty-four. But Raymond just got it. He was a flabby creature—balding, with bad posture, with a pout to what was once a rosebud mouth. Fifty-two years old when all this began, married for the fifth time, no more successfully than the first. Childless, without occupation. He'd had a doting mother who had always thought he could pick up the business side soon enough. She didn't think there was much to it. But when papa died, at last, the great complex of industries continued to be run by men who knew better than to let Raymond throw ignorant decisions into an intricate and delicate structure that grew and changed as flexibly, in a real and fluid world, as a living tree that bends to the wind and drinks the rain. And is as perishable.

So there he was. Shut out. With the income, to be sure, but

understanding nothing about its sources. Raymond's education, I can guess, was the most superficial gloss. He seemed to have nothing to do but spend money he never made.

He got to spending his money in a strange place.

Probably they flattered him. Probably *there,* he got what he thought was respect. Who knows? The money was useful to *them* for *their* purposes. Anyhow, Raymond Pankerman had bought himself a secret that sustained his tweed-scented ego when all busy men, and most women (especially his wives), found him dull and negligible.

But he had the primitive reactions of a spoiled baby. Rich and world-weary, with ringside tables and third-row seats wherever he went, fifty-two years old, who would imagine he would react like a four-year-old? "He spoiled *my* fun; I'll spoil *his.*"

It seems that John Paul Marcus, one day, one spring, said softly in the appropriate ear that it might be wise to look into the possibility that Raymond Pankerman's money was going into strange channels. This was something that rose to the top of Marcus' mind because of nothing in the world but experience. The long boiling and testing of the ingredients of life were in the kettle. This suspicion rose up and became visible. He skimmed it off and offered it for what it was, a mere suspicion. And lo, when it was investigated it turned out to be the truth.

Raymond Pankerman was caught—shall I pun and say redhanded?

So the Law began to move toward the long cautious prosecution.

Now there are jackals and small men for hire who will scurry and poke about. So Raymond Pankerman *knew* (as the public, by the way, did not know) that he was in a bitter mess, he had been caught financing what amounted to a spy-ring, he was due to be dragged through the courts, he was suffering and would suffer more, he was in fact ruined, because John Paul Marcus had seen what was invisible, heard what was silent, sensed what was hidden. So, as Raymond was bound to see it (Raymond never having taken a long hard look at Raymond or anything else), Marcus, and *Marcus alone,* was to blame.

(I doubt whether Pankerman's underground playmates even knew of the plot. It was certainly not devised by them. Its objective may have pleased them. But the methods would have seemed to them the sheerest nonsense. No, it was, as far as anyone knows, a strictly private plot. For revenge.)

All right. There had to be money and there was money because Raymond Pankerman had a lot of it. But there had to be brains, too. It was no easy matter to cook up a way to damage Marcus. And this is where Kent Shaw came in.

When they met the plot was engendered. You take a spoiled baby, too old to spank, with plenty of money, giving him power, and the reckless blind and angry wish to destroy that which has thwarted him and no wisdom and not much sense, either—bring him together with that other diabolical brain. . . .

Kent Shaw hasn't been thought of as a brain for many a year but he was born an infant prodigy, just the same. He was one of those who got through Yale at something like fifteen. He always had a flamboyant quality that attracted attention. He burst into the theater and, as a playwright-director in his twenties, he did some very exciting things. But somewhere along the line, Kent Shaw lost the thread. Or perhaps he never really had hold of it. He grew progressively farther and farther away from any relation to ordinary life as it is lived, day in and out, by ordinary people. So he lost emotional connection with his audiences. They didn't know what he was talking about. He ceased to excite them.

So he had a series of dreadful and even ludicrous failures. He grew desperate and denied his own convictions, and did cheap sensational things, contemptuously. And they failed. At last, he went abroad and shook the dust of crude America from his feet. But the war drove him back, 4F and miserable. He hung around New York. Sometimes his high-pitched voice snapped through radio bits. Sometimes he briefly caught onto the coattails of people flying into TV. He wrote a book that nobody bought. He wrote a second one that nobody printed. He developed a very nasty tongue. He lived in some cheap depressing den and wore shirts proudly darned to indicate both fastidiousness and poverty. He was down to earth, at last, and might have made use of his real talent, except that he, too, was a spoiled child. And bitter. He was a broken, bitter failure, at thirty-nine, and seemed to have survived himself by a hundred years.

But the brain, you see, was still in that head, the brilliant fantastical brain. Furthermore, Kent Shaw hated the whole world, and particularly, I suppose, America, which would no longer praise him or, worse, pay any attention to him at all. And he wanted money so that he could soar. He must have known that to pull John Paul Marcus down with a brilliant lie was blackest treason, whatever the Law would say about it. But Kent Shaw didn't care.

I will tell you how these two men met because for a long time it was a great mystery. No connection between them was apparent. Raymond Pankerman and Kent Shaw inhabited two different worlds. No witness was ever found, but the one, who had seen them together.

It happened in Mamaroneck on the nineteenth of August. In the midst of a heat wave. At four in the afternoon. Raymond had spent the morning sweating with his lawyers. He had spent his noon hour wrestling with the press. He had fled to the modest apartment of a nephew of his current wife. This was in Mamaroneck, near the water, and he thought he would be hidden and comparatively cool there. He had to be in the city the following day to hear more lawyers view his situation with deep alarm. But his flight had not been entirely successful since one young newsman in an excess of zeal had trailed along and was lurking outside the door.

Inside, however, Raymond was all alone.

The apartment adjoining belonged to some friends of Kent Shaw's who were on vacation and who had soft-heartedly given him their key. He had fled the heat wave. He was alone. Kent was not an alcoholic. That particular illness wasn't his. But he had a bottle of gin and some lemon and lime and the ice gave out.

Kent Shaw heard sounds next door. He opened the dumbwaiter and rapped on the door across the shaft with a broom handle. Raymond opened the door on his side. Kent asked for ice, recognized the heavy pink face that had been on front pages, introduced himself. Raymond had vaguely heard of him. I don't know the exact sequence that led to the happy thought that neither should drink alone. But Kent Shaw, who was small, only five foot six, and all skin and bones, took it into his head to climb perilously through that dumbwaiter shaft. So they joined forces.

There they were in the little apartment, unseen by anyone, and they mixed some drinks and they talked.

Raymond denied, of course, everything that was just then coming out in the papers. He was a wronged man. Kent Shaw agreed soothingly but he was not fooled. I don't know how soon Raymond spoke the magic sentence. But he did, saying, "I'd give a million dollars to pull that John Paul Marcus off his high perch."

And Kent Shaw said with a glittering eye, "For a million dollars, I will do just that." Startled, Raymond was cute enough to bargain. It ended up a half a million for the "package."

I wish I had heard the dialogue. I can imagine Kent Shaw, who never could sit still, flashing up and down the room. I can see Raymond's jowls quiver with the desire to believe that this strange feverishly excited little man could help him to his revenge.

But what *could* they do to John Paul Marcus? You look at a man's life that is sweet and sound from the beginning, and to hurt him (unless you shoot or use a knife) you must lie. But what lie?

It was no good to try anything to do with women. Marcus was seventy-odd and it was ridiculous, and even if they could have successfully lied about women in his past, there would be no uproar. "Be a dud," Kent Shaw said. "The powder's damp. Who, in these Kinsey days, would get excited?"

It was no good to try anything to do with money either. Marcus had always had money. His business life was an open book. Besides, Kent Shaw knew as little as Raymond about business and money. They couldn't lie convincingly. They didn't know enough.

They thought of pretending that Marcus had committed a crime, a killing or a vicious assault. They had some nasty ideas. But any such scheme would require a good quota of witnesses, all of whom must lie, and they didn't dare trust too many people. For of course, it was their dream that the plot would never be discovered. No, crime was not good. The law is too tough. You need proof.

Then Kent Shaw thought of the effective lie. Marcus must be involved, as Raymond was, in treason! *This* was the lie to tell. Easier, much easier. Doubt was enough. No one could prove a negative, not even Marcus. Suspicion and apppearances would be enough. Needn't prove it in a court. Taint was enough. Because such a taint would strike at his whole function, at the root of his meaning. Who (if they succeeded) would listen to Marcus, ever again? That was the one cruel way to get revenge.

Kent Shaw must have paced and bounced and talked and in the excitement both of them forgot the pretty convention that Raymond Pankerman was an innocent man.

"*You* can taint him by association," Kent Shaw cried.

And, Raymond, who knew he was guilty, knew he was fallen, forgot to pretend he wasn't and resolved, then and there, that he would not fall alone.

But how could this be arranged? No good for Raymond to get up in some courtroom and simply lie. *He* was tainted and a man like Marcus couldn't be pulled down as simply as that. So there was the problem of evidence, some evidence. Forgery perhaps? Forgery isn't easy, science being what it is today, and it involved the risk of a hired expert, too. Then a suspicious meeting? Overheard talk? No way for Raymond to get at Marcus. If they met in the park it would hardly seem suspicious or secret. Especially as there was certainly no way to tempt Marcus, himself, toward any foolishness. He *wasn't* foolish and they couldn't expect him to be. And he lived surrounded by devoted people, none of whom they would dare to try to bribe. Kent Shaw thought he might use that very loyalty against the old gentleman. (The public would think they'd lie *for* him, he pointed out.) "But it has to get out, to the public," Kent Shaw said, putting his finger on the key of the plot. "It has to ring from the roof tops. Plenty of stuff ends up being filed in triplicate. And forgotten. This bomb has got to go off in the marketplace. At high noon. We have to get it around, call in the pressure, print it, talk it up. I know something about publicity, Mr. Pankerman."

Then, the glitter. "There was an idea I had once. . . . It would have been a sensational publicity stunt. I never could see enough profit in it, never bothered to mention it. But I happen to know a pair of women. . . ." Kent Shaw began to see the shape of the fantastic lie.

Raymond Pankerman wasn't impressed with the basic outline at first. He looked very sourly upon the supernatural element. Shied away. Felt he had been talking to a crackpot. But Kent Shaw, pacing, talking, gesturing, wild with excitement, gradually sold him. "The one thing that *will* make talk," he said. "Of course, you are right. No sensible person is going to *believe* it. But he won't be able to *explain* it, don't you see? And there are plenty of people who will be awed and impressed and glad to believe because they wish such things could be. And they'll argue with the other kind. And it can be rigged so that the evidence falls out of this other thing, as if it were casually. . . .

"It will work," Kent Shaw said, swearing whitely by whatever gods

he had. "It will take time, some money but more time, and it must be perfectly done without any stupid mistakes. But it will work." Then he told Raymond what it was he, personally, must finally do and it clicked. Raymond saw the delicious irony. He tasted already the sweetness of his revenge.

They knew they would have time. Raymond was in for a long slow siege with the Law, months of it, before he would be entirely helpless. They roughed out the plot and discussed how the money was to be paid. They arranged another secret session together, there in November. There would be, after that, the putting up of the stakes. In the meantime, Kent Shaw was to develop all details, prepare the script, line up the cast (many of whose members would never know they had been in a play). Raymond gave him expense money. Kent crawled back the way he had come. They swore utter secrecy. Who knows what they swore on? Blood perhaps, like Huck and Tom.

What they wanted to do was from coldest vanity—narrow and bitter and mean. But money and brains will serve any master. You don't think the deluded, emotional, immature can make an effect on the real and solid world of affairs, because you don't remember King John or Benedict Arnold or Adolf Hitler.

When Kent Shaw left the apartment that evening, his head was full, I'll warrant, of his masterpiece. He would pull off the biggest show he had ever staged and no one would ever know it. He could gloat in secret, meanwhile possessing the only tangible thing that a dirty, grubby, contemptible world really respects. The long green, the money.

Of course he had to line up the women. He could buy one. The other, he thought, would play. Kent Shaw had his outline and he could see much of the detail already. There were some contingencies he could not foresee. If he had, I wonder if it would have mattered.

Chapter Two

I REALIZE that I have been cheating. Very well. I can't resist telling the first incident from the outside. I can tell it as an eyewitness. I was there.

It happened on a Sunday afternoon, the sixth day of December. Charley Ives called me, about one o'clock.

"You going down to this gathering at Cora's, cousin Ollie? In a cab, I hope?" I admitted I was. "Pick me up?"

"Oh, Charley. . . ."

"You'll be going by. Why not, Teacher?"

"Because it's so much simpler for you to go in your own cab and such a nuisance in traffic," I sputtered. Charley often made me sputter. I had a deep long-seated impatience with him. I didn't *want* to pick him up.

"I'll be on the sidewalk," said he coaxingly.

"So easy to miss you. . . ."

"Most unmissable fella in the world. Two o'clock sharp?"

"If you're not on the sidewalk, Charley, my boy, I'll just have to go on."

"Aw, Teacher," he said, "school's out."

I could see him grinning as if his picture had been projected on my dark-green wall.

I went on getting ready. (I don't live at the school but by myself in an apartment nearer the river. I may as well say that I live well, and not on my salary. I've always had quite a lot of money.) This was going to be a ridiculous way to spend a bright December afternoon, watching Cora Steffani's latest TV effort. But she'd asked her friends to come and view some filmed half hour or other.

My old friend, Cora (born Stevens) was in the plot.

I can realize, now, that I never did entirely trust her. I knew she didn't mind lying, when she could see a profit in it. In fact, I suppose I knew she was pretty much a phony. But I was her friend. You don't

choose a friend for his high moral integrity. You really don't. I'd
known Cora so long. We'd gone to dramatic school together. We'd
been young together and—if you keep in touch—that holds. Then,
years ago, she'd been briefly married to my cousin, Charley Ives, and
I suppose it made another bond.

I remember surveying, that afternoon, the split kind of life I was
leading, since I'd been seeing so much of Cora lately. Days of earnest
endeavor, doing the best I could with my girls and loving the work
more than I ever admitted. (You grow shy; you don't want to be
too vulnerable; and the great sin, these days, is taking yourself
seriously.) So, days of good hard work, and nights and weekends,
running down to see Cora and certain other less than upright characters. Oh, I had fine friends in the theater, too, people whose endeavor was just as earnest and far more significant than mine. But
Cora and the raffish crew that turned up around her. . . . Well, I
had known her so long. And rascals are vivid, sometimes, and that's
attractive.

Cora and I are the same age, much the same size, both brunettes.
I had a bit of gray showing. Cora's black hair was blacker and glossier
than ever. It was her livelihood to look as young as she could. My
job would let me grow old.

We took different turns, long ago. I dropped away from Broad-
way. The fact is, I never really made it. Cora said I hadn't the guts
and she was right. I hadn't the nerve or the skin for it. The sad thing
is that, for all her courage, somehow she never really made it, either.

Cora Steffani. The name turned up once in a while but all the small
parts she had played indifferently well didn't add up to very much.
But she still, at thirty-four, seemed to think that next year she'd make
it. *That* I admired. As for Cora, I knew she thought I had feebly fallen
back on an unearned income and was dabbling. But she had known
me so long. . . .

In a way, we were each other's habit. We had a curious pact of
plain speaking. We didn't have many secrets one from the other. The
secrets we did keep, each to herself, were the deep ones.

Charley Ives was on the sidewalk. He got in and *filled* the cab, the
way he does. Charley is a big man and he takes space, but why does
he seem to take all of it?

"Hi, Teach."

"Charley, my boy, how long have you been standing on the sidewalk?" I sputtered.

"Oh, twenty minutes."

"You could have *been* there. It was silly to wait for me and five minutes' ride."

"With contraptions like those on your feet in the dead of winter," said Charley morosely, "you're going to talk sense?" I bristled. I was wearing black satin, without so much as a button's worth of ornament on it, and it needed frivolous shoes. "Silly, she says," brooded Charley. "Lay off, or we'll fight, Cousin Ollie. I'm in no mood for this clambake, anyhow."

"Why must you go?" I said.

"Ask me no sensible questions, I'll tell you no silly lies," said Charley idiotically.

Charley Ives was Marcus' grandson, which made us more or less cousins. Long, long ago, in the days just before the Second War really broke upon us, Charley and I had a fight. I don't like to remember it, but I do, clearly. I, stamping and howling that art and truth and beauty and understanding and being sensitive to people's infinitive variations, all this was important, Hitler or no Hitler. Charley shouting that all that mattered—all—was to stand up with your kind and kill your enemy or be killed and dramatic art was for the birds. It was a very young and very stupid argument. Charley went to war and was gone a long time. When he came back, long after the peace, he wasn't young any more. And neither was I.

He, too, was thirty-four that December day. He'd taken to calling me Teacher. It made me feel elderly and stiff and ridiculous. So I called him Charley, my boy, and God knows whether he minded.

He brought out the very worst in me. When I was with him I *was* the teacher. The stereotype, I mean. Something waspish and preachy. The truth was, he mystified and therefore irritated me.

After the wars, Charley had bought into a publishing house. (Everyone in our family seems to have money. Perhaps we bask in the golden glow around Marcus. I don't know.) But it seemed to me that Charley (of all people!) was doing no work. The money did the work, for all that I could see, and Charley was window-dressing. He was so big and he looked relaxed and knew how to be charming and he turned up everywhere seeming to have no pressing duties on his mind.

(The young woman who had shouted Hooray for art and sentiment and dainty understanding, she had learned to keep quiet. She hid in a shell that was poised and calm and she never shouted anymore. But the young man who had been so willing to get killed . . . where was he?)

Charley stirred. "You going down to Washington for Marcus' birthday next month? How about flying down together?"

"I can't go until the last minute. Classes."

"I can go anytime," Charley said easily. "So it's a date."

I sat there thinking, Of course you can go anytime. Why *don't* you have something that limits you?

"What are you going to give him for a birthday present?" Charley wanted to know.

"A book," said I.

"He's got a book. I send him crates full. I had an idea. Want you to help me pick it out."

"Why me?" said I. Why fly down with *me?* I was really wondering. Why wasn't he taking Cora? I knew he had taken Cora to see Marcus while they were married and that Marcus hadn't cottoned to her. Marcus is ever gentle, but you are not left in doubt about his feelings. Now, I didn't know whether she and Charley Ives were engaged again or what. I thought, grimly, it was probably "or what." The fire and flame between them had died away abruptly, long ago. Yet Cora acted as if he belonged to her and Charley, amiably, let her do it. I knew Charley worshiped Marcus. For all I knew, he'd split with Cora because of Marcus. If now, at the age of thirty-four, Charley, my boy, was torn about marrying his ex-wife all over again against his grandfather's advice, he didn't confide in me. I was afraid he would. It was none of my business. I didn't understand a thing about it. I didn't want to know.

"I like your taste," Charley said. "In fact, I defer to it."

I'd lost the thread.

"Do you know you're about as absentminded as a full professor?" Charley teased me. I didn't answer or we'd have fought.

Cora's apartment, on the fringe of the Village, had one really good room. It was full of people that day. Only two of them mattered. Kent Shaw, faintly bouncing with tension, as usual, was sitting in a corner. And Mildred Garrick was there. A large woman with a cherub face, a crown of braids on her head into which she had a habit of thrusting feathers or flowers according to her fancy. Today she had a fat maroon velvet rose over her left eyebrow. Mildred wrote a column. She looked surprised to find herself where she was. And, since she could—an' she would—print one's name, Mildred was Queen-for-a-day in that company.

"Olivia, beloved," gushed she. "Do you know, the older you get, the more absolutely distinguished you become?"

"You're just being kind," I said as dryly as possible. "Do you know Charley Ives?"

"Of course. Of course. Of course." Mildred pulled me aside. "What am I doing here?" she asked me with round eyes.

"Oh, come, Mildred, don't be such a snob."

I saw Cora put one arm around Charley's neck, pull him down, and kiss him on the cheek. She then sent him to tend bar and he went, wearing her lipstick.

"When is this program?" demanded Mildred. "I have an appointment . . ."

Somebody said, "It's just about two thirty now."

Cora was wearing tight black-and-white checked pants and a black blouse. Her thick-rimmed glasses rode on her head like a tiara and the cord attached to the earpieces hung off the back of her neck. She was too busy to greet me. She knew she needn't bother. She was swaggering back and forth, hands flying, gesturing people onto cushions. "Kent, darling," she said in her affected way that by now was her only way, "is the little gadget hooked up? Kent's going to take this off on a tape for me. For the voice. Isn't he a sweet?"

I craned my neck and saw Kent fussing with a recorder. "I'm ready," he snarled, "to make you more or less immortal." Nobody bothered to resent Kent Shaw's snarls anymore.

"Somebody tune in CBS, then. Now, kids, I don't say this is high holy art. . . ." Cora's eyes flashed mockery at me. She suddenly crossed her legs and sank swiftly to the floor. She pulled her glasses down to position, put her elbows on her knees, pushed fingertips into her cheeks, and was absolutely still.

The screen filled, music played, a title flashed on.

I was watching Cora's face. She was not at all a beauty. The face was thin. She had a rather long straight nose with a most distinctive tip to it. The nostrils flared back; the very tip of the nose made a sharp little bony triangle. That nose was the most arresting feature, gave all the character to her face. The effect was inquisitive and a bit mischievous. I was thinking that no makeup could change it. I was thinking, also, that Cora had this much skill. You did not know what went on in the head. The face did not need to tell you.

Somebody said, "Hey, Cora, I thought. . . ."

"Oh, no!" she cried tragically and clutched her forehead. "This is the wrong film! I'm not on! Oh, no!"

So she rose. The slim legs were supple and strong. She got up from that cross-legged pose like a fourteen-year-old. "I'm so sorry!" she cried, desolately, and walked to the far end of the room and flung herself upon the window bench.

People exerted themselves to be good sports about the fiasco and a great hubbub arose, very loud and jolly. Even Mildred Garrick tried not to make her intention of getting away as fast as she could too obvious. Everyone let Cora alone, assuming she was upset and embarrassed. In the corner, the tape recorder ran, apparently forgotten.

It was Charley Ives who said quietly in my ear, "Is Cora all right, do you think?"

So I looked at her. She was lying on her back on the narrow bench, her head crooked on a cushion, one leg bent so that the foot was on the floor. Her glasses, hung around her neck by that thick cord, seemed to catch a little yellow light, although draperies had been drawn, to protect the TV screen, and where she lay it was dim.

"Can't be asleep," I murmured. I thought Charley hesitated to go himself to rouse her or comfort her or whatever. I thought he wanted me to do it. So, of course, I went.

She wasn't asleep. But she couldn't be roused. Now others noticed something odd. Somebody rolled up one of her eyelids. She had not fainted. She seemed limp. Her pulse was fast.

People said not to crowd, to let in some air. Someone drew the curtains open and she lay, just as limp, in full daylight. Somebody wanted to call a doctor. Somebody asked what time it was. Somebody answered.

Cora opened her eyes and sat up.

Charley said, "What ails you?"

"I don't know. I went away."

"Fainted?"

"I don't know. I was walking on a beach," Cora said in a perfectly matter-of-fact voice. "In my green summer cotton."

"Dreaming? You couldn't have been asleep."

"Wait," she said sharply. "Wait. . . ." It was as if she were catching a dream back that might fade. "Josephine Crain was there. I walked up to her. I said, 'Josephine, please tell me where we are.' She doesn't know me. Then I remembered what I've read. I said, '*You* are in Florida. But where am I?' Then I was frightened. I was terrified. I walked very fast, hard to do on the sand, in my white sandals with heels. . . ." Cora looked down at her feet in black heelless slippers, and I know I shivered. "What"—she began to rub her head—"what happened?"

"Must have had a dream," said somebody soothingly. Somebody brought her a drink. Cora sat huddled together. I thought she looked all of thirty-four. "It was the strangest kind of dream," she muttered. "I think I will crawl into bed, if you will all excuse me."

"Do you feel ill?"

"I don't know."

Mildred Garrick said to me, "Now, what was all that?" She pranced out. People left, awkwardly and at a loss for an attitude. It was just awkward, just odd. Kent Shaw waited until nearly last. "I'll leave the machine," he said. "Don't make a mistake and erase it."

"Erase what?" said Cora. "What do you mean, Kent, darling?"

"The thing was running the whole time. You might want your analyst to hear it."

"I don't want to hear it at all. Take it away."

Kent shrugged and took it away. Charley and I were left with her. He took her hands. "What happened, now . . . really?" Charley can be very sweet and gentle. Some big men can.

"Just what I said. I can't tell you more than that." She pulled her hands away. "I thought I was on a beach."

I said, "So long, you two."

But Cora said, "No. Charley, you go away. There's a dear man. Let Ollie stay with me." (We had known each other so long.)

So, Charley left and I stayed. Cora didn't go to bed. We lounged, talking quietly, not about her dream or whatever it was, but gossiping a bit. Cora didn't seem to bother to put on any act for me. I thought she had suffered some queer mind lapse and it had frightened her. I thought she was toughly assimilating whatever the sensation had been. I let her be. She finally said she felt all right. I knew she meant that I could go.

She had the grace to thank me, in a phrase that was pure Cora. "Your ivory tower has made you a nice peaceful type to have around," said Cora.

"No questions asked," I said lightly. "Have a snack and go to bed, why don't you?"

"Ollie, I will." She kissed me. Then just as I went through the door she said, "Ollie, you know Josephine Crain, don't you?"

"Um hum."

"She *is* in Florida?"

"Miami. Yes."

"When will she be back?"

"The twentieth, I think. She's going into rehearsal."

"Sometime," said Cora, "ask her."

"Ask her what?"

"If I was there."

Josephine Crain is one of our truly great. She came back to town, as planned, and the day after, right in the midst of the Christmas rush, Cora called me. "Ollie, do something for me? I know you will."

"I might if I knew what it was."

"Go and see Josephine Crain. You know what to ask her. Kent Shaw's promised to go with you."

"Oh, Lord, Cora, she's busy. I can't bother her."

"But I've got such a bad thing about her. Please. Meet Kent at the theater. He says they are reading this morning. They'll break around two."

"Meet you and Kent Shaw?"

"Not me."

"Why not?"

"I can't go, Ollie. I'm too scared."

I was her friend, wasn't I?

Josephine Crain is a great and gracious lady. She led us into a bare dressing room, me and Kent Shaw and that tape recorder.

"Jo," I said, "I've got a funny thing to ask you. Can you remember anything about where you were or what you were doing on December the sixth, in the afternoon? Can you place it?"

"I must have been on the beach," she said. "I always am after lunch."

"Did—?"

"Wait," said Kent Shaw. "Miss Crain, may I turn this recorder on?" Jo's lovely eyebrows moved. "I want to record what you say. You'll see why." He was terribly excited, must have been. He hid it fairly well.

"Is this all right, Olivia?" Josephine had amusement in her warm rich voice. Her eyes asked what I was doing, traveling with Kent Shaw. "I'm not going to be sued, am I?"

I said, "I think perhaps it's a good idea. It will settle some foolishness. I'll explain later."

"If you say so." She smiled. So Kent Shaw plugged in the machine.

"Now, Jo," I said, "please try to remember December sixth, around about two thirty in the afternoon. You were on the beach, you say. Did anything the least bit odd happen?"

"Odd? December sixth was a Sunday, wasn't it?"

"Yes. It was."

"What do you mean, odd, Ollie?"

"I don't want to suggest anything."

"You don't mean the woman in the green dress?" said Josephine Crain.

I was stung with surprise and then immediately by unsurprise, by suspicion. I heard Kent's breath whistle out. "Go on," I said.

"Well, that was certainly odd. This perfect stranger came plodding along. Spoke to me. Called me by name, in fact. Asked me to tell her where we were."

"What time was it? Can you quote her exactly?" *I* asked the questions. Kent Shaw didn't speak. Perhaps he didn't dare.

"It was . . . oh, middleish. Between two and three, I would say." Josephine's voice changed to one sharper and harsher than her own. " 'Josephine, please tell me where we are.' "

"What did you do?"

"I goggled, naturally. Then she said, '*You* are in Florida. But where am I?' So I said, 'You are in Florida, too, for heaven's sakes. What's the matter?' But she went away very fast. She vanished."

"Vanished?" I gasped.

"I mean, of course, she just disappeared." Jo gestured impatiently.

"Disappeared!"

"She left the beach, to be perfectly literal. What is the matter, Ollie? She went between two buildings to the street, or so I suppose."

"Describe her, Jo?"

"Brunette. Slim. Not as nice a figure as yours, but not bad. Green cotton dress. White sandals with some kind of heel. Nothing to say about the face except a longish nose with a pulled-over flattened tip to it—"

"Oh, me," I said, "Oh, my! You don't know a Cora Steffani, Jo?"

"No."

I reached for a clipping from an old theater magazine. "This face?"

Josephine's eyes narrowed. "That is the nose. I don't think I'm liking this, Ollie."

"No. You won't like it," I said.

"I'll play back the other piece of tape," said Kent Shaw in his shrill voice.

Well, of course, it was all there. The time, too. Verified by the fragment of the TV program and somebody's questions. Josephine Crain didn't like it one bit. "What is this supposed to be? A trick?"

"Very like," I said, feeling stunned.

"*Yours,* Mr. Shaw?" Josephine lifted her brow, in that instant divining what we weren't to know for a long, long time.

He bared his teeth. "I think I've been used," he snarled. "I don't appreciate it."

"What made you bring that machine to Cora's?" I demanded.

"Someone had borrowed it. I'd picked it up to take home. Cora spied it and insisted." His dark face looked intent and angry. "Only how could she *know* I would have it?"

"The whole thing is ridiculous," Jo said. "If it is a trick, why? This woman is a friend of yours, Ollie?"

"Let me play the tape for Cora Steffani," I said slowly. "I'd like to see what she does about it."

"We can always erase it," said Kent Shaw boldly and as if he had a mind to do it, then and there.

But we didn't erase it. Kent Shaw and I, and Charley Ives and Mildred Garrick (who'd heard about this somewhere) all watched Cora listen to it. Watched her cut off a scream and fall to weeping. She hung on to Charley's sleeve and wept on his jacket. She wouldn't talk. She seemed terrified. After a while, she begged *us* not to talk about it. Mildred Garrick pinched her lips together.

How could a woman be in two places at once? How could she walk in a dream? How could Cora lie on a bench in her own room surrounded by people, and walk on a beach in Florida, too? No sensible person could believe such a thing. Mildred was suspicious and had no comment.

Nothing, apparently—happened. Oh, there was some talk in Cora's little circle. Cora seemed to try to squelch it. She put the tape away. Did not destroy it. Jo Crain refused distastefully to answer questions. Nothing seemed to come of it.

Kent Shaw acted as uneasy and suspicious as anyone else. He must have been throbbing with triumph and excitement.

Because it was a brilliant beginning. Almost flawless. Josephine Crain was above suspicion. Josephine Crain needed no sensational publicity, of course not. So the incident was just odd. Hushed up and very odd.

But the tape and the unimpeachable witnesses, one of whom was myself, to prove a woman had dreamed in New York and walked in Florida—this existed.

Now I will tell you about Darlene Hite, and how she did it.

Chapter Three

SHE WAS the fifth child in a family of seven. (Darlene! Lord knows what they named the other six!) The family was poor. It hadn't gone in for education, either. Darlene had to meet the world on her own, with no help, financial or otherwise, from her background. She was born in San Diego, California, and she was bright and not badlooking. She left home at sixteen and made a try for the movies.

Any girl who launches herself toward any form of show business runs into difficulties. Nobody ever made it easily. If she is like Josephine Crain, *both* sensitive and tough, *both* delicate and indestructible, she isn't hurt and she makes the top. If she is like me, just sensitive, she draws away from pain, does something else. If she is like Cora, just tough, she fights tooth and claw, never admits she is hurt or a failure. If she's a Darlene Hite, she is either toughened or destroyed.

Darlene Hite never knew the world to be anything but a jungle and everything that happened to her made her think she was alone in it. She was cool and clever, but she was limited. When she needed help, she didn't know where to turn for it. Darlene was betrayed and cheated and had no recourse. What she learned by "experience" was what she had already expected. *Darlene,* she believed, had to look out for Darlene. She was toughened.

She went to work in a third-rate nightclub, still show business, although she was only intermittently a performer and most often a kind of Johanna Factotum. She was a lone wolf. The loneliest of wolves, living a cruelly underpaid and defensive existence with iron control, until Kent Shaw came after her.

Darlene by this time was thirty, a somewhat artificial blonde, but slim, medium high, and gray-eyed, like Cora Steffani. Her face was not as narrow. Her eyes were, in fact, larger and lovelier. The mouth was not the same either. But the nose, the long nose with that distinctive tip to it, gave all the character to her face. And it was Cora's nose.

Kent Shaw had seen her during his Hollywood phase some years ago. Now he approached her with what must have seemed like perfect candor. He had a scheme on. She, and only she, could help him work it. Therefore, she could name her price and he expected it to be high.

Darlene listened. Wouldn't you?

It was a publicity stunt, he told her. He was going to raise a certain actress into a blaze of light. Darlene vaguely understood that this other woman had a wealthy protector who could pay. To accomplish what he had in mind, Kent Shaw said, he needed Darlene for a series of performances over a period of months, which he would devise and which must be played exactly as he directed. She was cool and clever and could do the job. But it wasn't her cleverness he wanted to hire. Many girls were as clever. She, and she alone, was qualified. Because of the shape of her nose.

How much would it pay? Darlene wanted to know. He told her. Darlene did not ask if she was going to go against the law or do harm. She asked what she had to do. The money must have looked like a shaft of sunlight cutting down into the jungle. When Kent Shaw swore her to secrecy, Darlene understood that, too. In Darlene's world, secrecy was natural. Of course one kept one's business to oneself, and especially a Good Thing.

If she had known the true objective of the plot, would she have agreed to work for wages? I don't know. Maybe Darlene would not know. She had narrow horizons. The meaning of a man like Marcus might not have been visible to her, from where she struggled alone down in the dark thicket.

Kent Shaw invented the scenes, chose the costumes, picked the sets, wrote the lines, set the timing. Darlene had, as Cora had, a tiny sheaf of narrow paper slips on which, in a kind of shorthand they well understood, this script was written. Such an *aide-mémoire* was necessary. For it was a long drawn-out show. The scenes were to be played weeks apart. But time and sentences had to be exact, to the word and to the minute. Communication with the director, once the curtain went up, would be (almost) entirely cut off. Darlene hid her script in the same place Cora's was hidden, a place always close about her person, that no one ever suspected.

She got into Miami the night before the sixth of December and went to a modest rooming house, appearing quietly dressed, not too prosperous, not too young, not very interesting. She wore on her dyed-black hair a small hat with a nose veil. The veil had a fancy edge that nicely obscured the tip of her nose. She used a name that I've forgotten and implied that she had come to town to take a job and would seek permanent living quarters on the morrow.

She stayed close in the room until after noon the next day. She left, then, wearing a cloak of darkness. It was a lightweight garment, something like a duster, with loose sleeves and a belt. Darlene already had her hair piled high with a comb like Cora's but she covered this with a scarf. She walked to the quiet little hotel on the water where Josephine Crain always stayed. She went into the ladies' room and slipped out of the duster. It hung inconspicuously over her arm and hid her handbag into which went the flat-heeled dark shoes and out which came the white sandals. Now she appeared in a duplicate of Cora's green cotton dress. In fact, she was close to a duplicate of Cora.

She walked out upon the beach and spotted Josephine. Darlene checked the time, to the minute. She was a very cool and competent person. She walked on stage, said her lines, and fled.

Going between two buildings, Darlene slipped from white to dark shoes, pulled the comb from her hair and let the hair hang to her shoulders. She was inside the duster and buttoned up in a matter of seconds. The woman who stepped into the street would not even have been shouted after by any pursuer of the woman who had left the beach. Thus, she vanished.

She went quickly back to the room, burned the first little slip of instructions, paid her bill, left town by bus immediately. Nobody noticed her. Why would anyone?

The whole thing, of course, rested on the invariable habit of Josephine Crain, who was "always" alone under her umbrella on the beach in the early afternoons. The gamble was that she would be there on the sixth day of December. If she had not been alone, it wouldn't have mattered much. But she had to be *there*.

She was there.

Kent Shaw had done brilliant research. He chose for his unconscious cast and took his gambles on people with routine habits. They were people above suspicion and therefore of good repute. Well-known people, who had set themselves in patterns. He had combed the nation for such people. They were all middle-aged or older. They were all successful people who did as they pleased, who had developed routines which were respected. There are more of such people than you would think.

The gamble was the weakness of the plot. Ah, but when it paid off, it was the plot's wicked strength! None of these people could possibly have been bribed. Their testimony was truthful and unimpeachable.

The first incident went off beautifully.

Still, the result was meager, for all the planning and all the trouble. Why weren't they discouraged?

Kent Shaw, watching, delicately prodding in his own person the course of events, playing for the biggest stake of his life and having planned it this way, was simply absorbed. To Darlene Hite, it didn't matter. Placidly, she, the employee, could go on, win or lose, to the next part of her job. Cora Steffani was, after all, on stage, even though so far the stage was very small and obscure and the audience merely her own circle of quite insignificant people like me. Still she had the role and must henceforth play it to whatever audience.

But Raymond Pankerman could have seen and heard nothing at all for his money (since Kent Shaw was ruthless that they communicate in no way whatsoever). Still, Raymond was surrounded by harassments of his own. And, after all, the bulk of his investment in this strange affair was not to be paid out except for value received. The big money lay in a shabby old safe which stood in a run-down, cheap-rent, one-room office, taken in Kent Shaw's name. But Raymond held the combination to this safe. Kent Shaw couldn't get into it . . . yet. So, Raymond could afford to shrug and be patient.

There was, as I said, some talk. I remember the first *argument* I heard. One Saturday, after Christmas, I ran into Charley Ives, down-town, and he begged me to come and look at his idea for Marcus' birthday present. He took me to a jeweler's and showed me a letter cutter, gold and steel, an exquisite thing.

"It's beautiful," I said. "Of course, Marcus *has* paper cutters."

"Marcus has everything," Charley said lightly, "but a token of love is a token of love. I wasn't sure of the design."

I don't know what took me by the throat. I said to myself it was outrageous that a man, a big strong healthy intelligent man like Char-ley Ives should be fussing over a little bit of a birthday present; should have the *time* for such fussing, however exquisite the gift or beloved the recipient.

"I know I'm no artist. What's the matter?" said Charley innocently. "I kinda like it. You tell me if it's all right, Ollie."

"Of course, it's all right. You *know* it's all right."

"Gosh," said Charley.

"Gosh what? Charley, my boy."

"I don't know why you're cross with me, Teacher. I'm being a good boy."

I might have blazed out at him if he hadn't turned to tell the clerk that he'd made up his mind. Then he grabbed my arm. "Don't apolo-gize," he said cheerily. "Come on, let's have lunch."

We wheeled into the nearest restaurant and there was a man Char-ley knew, another big man, named Bud Gray. Somehow, this Mr. Gray attached himself and joined us and I was glad.

One of these days, Charley and I were going to have another fight. The truce between us had gone on too long. When Charley came home, at the war's end, so briefly, I was fighting the battle of Broad-way, and Charley, worrying about postwar problems in Europe, had no time for mine. Besides, I avoided him, knowing and feeling guilty about it in my soul that all civilians fight a war in safe soft places. When Charley came home after his spell in occupied Germany,

I was teaching. We met at Marcus' house and Charley seemed mildly surprised that I wasn't trying to be a great actress anymore.

I told him, to put it simply, that I had failed. "I didn't have what it takes," I remember saying.

"What does it take?" He'd seemed amused.

"Among other things, courage," I'd told him.

Charley said to me, "Doesn't everything?"

"Cousin Charley," I'd said, "let's not fight. I withdraw the word 'courage.' Probably I don't know what it means. I know I haven't got it."

"Whereas, I'm as brave as a lion but I 'don't understand,'" Charley had said coldly. "Okay, Teacher. No fight. So be it." The truce had set in.

It wasn't long after that that he met Cora Steffani and there was fire and flame and they ran off. Two months later, she went to Reno and Charley went to Japan.

That was just as the Korean affair broke out, so he was gone again quite a long while. Then he came home and became (of all things) a publisher and we began to meet (of all places) at Cora's.

I'd seen a lot of him. (He'd seen a lot of her.) And sooner or later I was going to tell him how I thought he was wasting himself and I was going to sound like Teacher, sure enough. When I announced that I thought there was an awful lot of man to waste, when I told him to his teeth that I knew he was no boy. When I asked him why . . . why . . . why . . . was *he* hanging around, playing the playboy?

And I didn't *want* to fight with Charley Ives again.

To get back to the restaurant . . . pretty soon Kent Shaw came in, saw me, came over to ask me how Cora was. He said he hadn't seen her in a couple of weeks (and no more had he). This led to Kent's sitting down with us to wait for his date, and all of us telling Charley's friend, Bud Gray, about the strange dream or trance Cora had gone into, and how it seemed as if she had been in two places at once.

Mr. Gray said he'd call such a thing impossible because, in human experience, it was unknown.

Kent Shaw said, "That's where you're wrong. It's not unknown. What I can't swallow is that it could happen to Cora Steffani."

"When has it been known?" Charley wanted to know.

"Why, there was a Saint . . . Anthony, wasn't it? Don't remember the details, but *he* managed it. Then there was Maria Coronel. You never heard of her? A lady of Spain who would fall into such trances and wake up, claiming she'd been busy converting Indians. No doubt they thought she was off her sixteenth-century rocker. Only thing, when some Spaniards got into Mexico somewhere, they kept hearing from the Indians about a mysterious lady in blue who had come around preaching. Point is," Kent Shaw grimaced, "such a thing happens to a saint or a religious type. *Not* to an aging and not very successful actress who has no religion at all."

I waited for Charley Ives to resent this. "You're talking in terms of miracle?" inquired Charley with an interested air.

"What else?" Kent said. "Now, if it had happened to Olivia—"

"Oh, for pity's sakes!" I said.

"I don't say you are a religious," said Kent, as if he apologized for calling me a dirty name, "but just the same, you've got a dedicated air about you, something as honest as the sun," said Kent Shaw solemnly (That little fake!), "a little bit out of *this* world. Whereas Cora Steffani. . . ." His whole face was a sneer.

"Charley and I are both very fond of Cora," I said stiffly.

Kent Shaw drew back his lips in that smile that was so unpleasant. "Still, I think I've made my point."

Charley sat, looking at him. Charley has long tan eyelashes. He keeps his face tanned, I don't know how, and his eyes are so vivid a blue that they startle you, framed in those lashes in that browned face so near the color of his hair. Charley's not a handsome man. But he is not one that goes unnoticed. He *filled* that chair. Kent Shaw looked back, as saucy as a terrier.

"In the case of this Cora," said Mr. Gray soothingly, "at least there is evidence that isn't mere legend."

"Evidence!" scoffed Kent Shaw. "Oh sure. A tape recorder beats the word of a saint. Naturally. Naturally."

"A legend is not the same thing as a record."

Well, they argued until a newspaper man named Ned Dancer came in and Kent whistled to him. As Ned came over, Kent dropped the subject, but this Bud Gray was full of unused ammunition. "I still say," he said, "that if this Maria of yours had had a tape recorder and a flock of affidavits from those Indians, then you'd have a comparable basis."

"Affidavits!" scoffed Kent. "You can have them. I'm willing to believe in Maria Coronel because it's charming. But in Cora Steffani I am not willing to believe."

"What was it then? Coincidence?" asked Gray. "You're willing to believe *that?*"

"Or was it prearranged?" asked Charley.

"What was *what?*" Ned Dancer wanted to know. So he was told. Perhaps he thought his leg was being pulled. He shut his mouth and refused comment. But, of course, now he had heard about it.

Charley asked me, after Kent Shaw had gone, what *I* really thought. I said I tried not to think about it and I must go.

I didn't want to answer if he asked me whether Cora was a liar. I was trying so hard to mind my own business.

The second incident happened on January 4 or January 5, depending. . . .

Chapter Four

LAST NIGHT I stopped without finishing a sentence. I thought my voice was failing. Come now, my voice will not fail if I use it properly and I can't stop. I don't know how long I will have.

On the night of January 4, a group of us had been to a preview. We drifted back to Charley Ives' place for the necessary chewing over of our impressions. I suppose there were ten people, Charley, Cora, me and a beau of mine who doesn't matter, and others. Kent Shaw was among those present. I don't know how he inserted himself but we were all used to Kent's turning up and tagging along. What seemed more important, Mildred Garrick was there.

Cora sat in one of Charley's big fat chairs. Half past midnight, which brought us, in New York, to January 5, she put aside her glass. I saw her give a little sigh. Mildred, who had been pumping me for my opinion of the play we'd seen, soon nudged me. "There she goes! Look! Look at Steffani!"

Charley was already bending over her.

"Wait a minute," cried Mildred. "Let her alone, everybody. Who's got the correct time? Ah, there, Kent darling, I suppose you just happened to bring your tape recorder?"

Charley gave her a chilly glance. "There is no tape recorder here."

"No?" said Mildred mockingly. "Well, well."

Kent Shaw got all the implications, bared his teeth in a voiceless snarl, went far across the room and sat down, looking venomous.

"Who here takes shorthand?" Mildred demanded. A girl named Helen said she did. "All right." Mildred had taken over. "Now Cora is going to come out of it, and mark the time, somebody, when she does. And you, Helen, dear, take down everything she says."

"Why, Mildred?" asked Charley.

"Because," said Mildred, "if this is a stunt, it's a damned good one, is all as I can say." Mildred had a row of pink seashells mounted on a comb thrust behind her crown of braids. She wore a pink crepe evening dress and she stood belligerently, with her feet apart, the crepe clinging to some bad bulges along her hip bones. Charley turned his back on her.

He lifted one of Cora's very limp hands, very gently. I went near. Cora's head lolled on the chair. She looked completely out. She was wearing red, a dress that came up high around her throat and was topped with a necklace of jet. She wore tiny jet earrings. Her lipstick looked cracked and raw on the limp silence of her mouth. I looked down on her with nothing but bewilderment.

Charley said softly, "Don't worry, Ollie. We'll wait a little."

It lacked a few seconds of 12:40 when Cora came to herself abruptly, as before, in a ring of watching faces. This Helen sat on the floor with pencil and paper.

"Dreaming, dear?" said Mildred with a nasty little edge to the question.

Cora swallowed and the jet choker gleamed.

"Don't say a word if you don't want to," I said. "Maybe we should get a doctor."

But Cora paid me no attention. Her gaze went through me to the wall. "I walked into a restaurant," she said, "with dark walls, hideous oil paintings. I had on my brown broadcloth suit and my beaver collar. I seemed to be standing there alone. People at the tables. Then I saw one face I thought I knew. I walked up to his table. . . ." Her face showed us a flash of fear. "I said, 'Pardon me, sir, isn't your name

Mr. Monti? I know I've seen you. I'm Cora Steffani. I seem to be confused. Where is this place?' "

Cora stopped talking.

"And where was it?" snapped Mildred.

"The Boar's Head Tavern," Cora muttered.

"Where?"

"In Chicago." Her voice rose. "In *Chicago*."

"What did the man say?" asked Charley Ives calmly.

"He . . . didn't know what to make of it." Cora raised her hands as high as her shoulders. Now she looked at our faces fearfully. "I don't either."

"What happened?"

"They wanted to help me," said Cora impatiently. "But I ran. I went through a revolving door. It was cold. And then it was over."

She began to shake.

"Who was the man?"

"His last name is Monti. He's a cellist. Plays with the Mannheimer Symphonic. I don't know the man. I know who he is. Why should I dream about him? It *wasn't* a dream." Cora's thin hands, that betray more age than her face, were clenching and twisting.

Mildred Garrick and some of the others pressed her with more questions but Cora only shook her head and would not answer. She looked on the verge of hysteria.

Charley said to me, "I'm going to get rid of these people and call Doc Harper. You stay, will you please, Ollie? I think she ought to go to bed, right here. Help me, will you?"

Of course I said I would. So Charley picked her up out of that chair and carried her back through a long hall into his bedroom and I trotted after. Charley went to block people out. I helped Cora undress and got her into Charley's huge pajamas.

I said, "Cora, if you need to talk you know you can talk to me."

"Oh, Ollie, it's gone," she said. "It goes just as a dream goes. I think there were several other people, but it fades. It's gone, now. All I sharply remember is as much as I said out loud. You know. Didn't you ever tell a dream, at breakfast? You can't tell *any more of it,* ever. Only this *isn't* dreaming. There's something wrong with me, Ollie. It's a relief when everything fades. . . ." She kept up that shaking. But when I touched her, she wasn't cold.

I got her into Charley's bed and she turned her face to the wall.

When the doctor came, I left them and went back to the living room.

Mildred was still there. She turned from the phone. "Got them. A milk plane, or something."

"Got what?"

"Seats to Chicago. Charley and I are going to fly out, right quick."

"What *for?*"

"To talk to this man, of course. This Angelo Monti. He's in Chicago, tonight, all right. I've checked that."

"You don't mean you are going to all that trouble?"

"Somebody," said Mildred, putting her finger on it, "is going to a lot of trouble to fool us, if that's what it is."

"Well?" said Kent Shaw from where he still sat in the corner. "You're willing to be fooled?" His little dark face was furious.

"Sure. I'll be fooled in a good cause," said Mildred. "If this checks out like Jo Crain did, what a darling story!"

"Ollie, you'll stay here with Cora?" Charley said to me, looking as if even he might be on the verge of getting worried. "Keep her doing whatever the doctor says. Tell her where I'm going and why."

"You tell her," I said. "I don't know."

Kent Shaw said, half screaming, "Why? Yes, why are you two fools going to bite on this bait? Spend your money? Go roaring off?"

"None of your business," said Mildred indifferently, "is it, little man?"

"I don't want any part of it. I want out! You're never going to make me believe any cheap second-rate—"

"The way out is straight ahead of you," said Charley Ives.

Kent pranced nervously the length of the room to the foyer. He looked back. Couldn't resist it. "Angels and ministers of grace," he began to declaim. Then he seemed to choke and ducked away.

"You know what?" said Mildred. "I think the little fella is scared just about sick. Superstitious. Well, well."

I said lightly, "That or he's mad with jealousy because somebody *else* cooked this thing up."

Then I was sorry. I hadn't meant to say "true" or "false" about Cora Steffani. I saw Charley let his lashes down. He was going to fly off, affording the time, affording the money. He wouldn't say "true" or "false."

"Which is what Kent Shaw *would* think," I amended lamely.

I, too, would stand by.

We forgot Kent Shaw. Actually, he had just stepped off stage and that was his exit line. It took control to walk out before he knew if he'd won the second toss. But he had written it that way. Now he had played all the bit part he had written in for himself.

Dr. Harper, classmate and friend-of-old to Charley Ives, found nothing apparently wrong with Cora. He gave her a sedative on some kind of general principle. Three of them bustled off. It was after 2:00 A.M. Charley's spacious apartment, a whole floor of an old house, was silent. Cora seemed asleep in Charley's bed. I prowled the silent place. I lay on the couch in my slip with a blanket over me. I looked at the dim tall ranks of Charley's books on the walls. I, as they say, tossed.

Charley was out in the town getting checks cashed by friendly bartenders, picking up Mildred, making that plane.

What did I honestly think, at that time? Why, I had no doubt at all that it was a prearranged trick between Cora and someone. I couldn't see how it was done. But I didn't think it was supernatural. I thought it was a slick silly trick and she'd get her name in the papers and I didn't mind if she did. Or didn't. I wasn't losing sleep over that.

Cora was resting easy in Charley's bed in the bedroom I'd never seen before that night. On his dresser stood a photograph in a chaste and narrow golden frame. It was a photograph of me. And I was a little bit upset. I didn't like it.

In the case of the Chicago incident, Kent Shaw hadn't taken much of a gamble. The proprietor of the Boar's Head Tavern happened to be no Englishman, but one Gallo, boyhood chum and compatriot to Angelo Monti. If the Mannheimer Symphonic Orchestra played in Chicago on the evening of January 4, as it had long ago contracted to do, it was certain, barring serious illness or death itself, that Monti would be at the Boar's Head after the concert. Not to have appeared there would have shattered a long sentimental tradition and broken an unwritten law with its roots in two warm hearts. Which was un-thinkable. So it was very close to a sure thing.

It paid off. Angelo Monti was in his place when the curtain went up on Scene Two.

Darlene Hite got into Chicago about noon that day (she spent the intervals taking quiet and lonely "vacations" in various country places) and went to a small obscure hotel in her decorous way. When the time came, she got into costume, the suit like Cora's, did her hair up in Cora's fashion, put on another long loose garment, this time a coat with a hood. It was cold in Chicago.

She walked into the restaurant at the appointed time, with the coat over her arm, and she said her lines. Angelo Monti struggled to extricate himself from his position among his friends at the center of the banquette. His kind heart was at once anxious to help the strange lady if he could. But the lady fled.

There came into the show at this moment, however, an extra scene, a bit added by that old reviser of all the best-written scripts of men.

From another table, as Darlene fled, a strange man rose up. He came swiftly over to Monti, who stood, napkin caught on his paunch, staring after the woman in brown. This stranger was tall, blond, and baldish, with a florid complexion. He asked if the lady was in trouble and what her name was.

Monti said helplessly, "I don't know her."

The stranger said, "Maybe I do." So he threw money on his own table and he hurried through the revolving door.

He caught her in the act of slipping into the coat and pulling up the hood. So he touched her arm. "Darlene! Say, what do you know! Doncha remember me? Ed Jones from good old San Diego," and brayed in the cold street, "Sa-ay, long time no see!"

Darlene had to recognize him because she had to move away from this spot without argument or delay. He wanted to know if there had been any trouble. She told him she'd made a mistake of identity. She made up a reason for being in Chicago. Darlene was competent and quick. She amiably made a date with him for the following day and let him take her "home" to the wrong hotel.

Through it she walked to another exit.

But Ed Jones was unlucky. It occurred to him that he must change the hour they had set for the morrow. He went in and discovered that she was not registered and someone had seen her walk through. So Ed Jones went to that side exit and while he stood, fuming, the cab returned. By sheer bad luck, Ed Jones found out where she had gone. In the morning, when Darlene checked out and started for the bus, Ed Jones fell in beside her.

He was a stubborn and an unlucky man. A part for him had to be improvised.

On the morning of the fifth I put on my beige-and-gold theater dress again. Cora was awake, looking lazy and well. I thought her fit of nerves, faked or not, was over. I told her I had classes and she let me go without protest. So I hurried uptown to change to sober clothing and go to work.

Ten o'clock that evening, Charley called. "We got the dope. Cora's still here. Come on down."

I'd been waiting, waiting for this call. Yet now that it had come, I didn't want to be disturbed. "Tell me on the phone, Charley, my boy," I said. "I'm tired."

Mildred had taken along a stenographer and they had Monti's remarks on paper. He didn't have the ear for lines that Jo Crain had. The correspondence was not perfect. But the time checked, the description checked, the nose had been noticed, Cora's photograph had been accepted. The bit about the strange man was, of course, extra. Monti said the mysterious stranger had never returned to the restaurant.

"I suppose she vanished," I said, "and it upset him."

"Ollie, Cora's pretty upset. She—"

"Charley, I think I'd better not."

Cora had grabbed the phone. "Ollie, what can I *do?* Ollie, stay by me? Everybody is going to think I'm a freak! Please, Ollie, don't *you* leave me!" I could hear she'd been crying.

Charley took the phone. "Coming down?"

"Do you really need me? Isn't Mildred there? What can *I* do? I work, you know."

"I'm going to take Cora home," Charley said briskly. "She can't stay here."

Why not? I thought.

"She wants you to stay at her place."

"Stay? Move in, you mean?"

"She wants you, Ollie. Rather have you than anyone. Says you're her oldest friend. She shouldn't stay alone."

"Oh, me," I sighed. "Oh, my. . . ."

"You won't do it?"

"Of course, I'll do it," I said with foreboding. "But no point in coming there where you are. I'll go directly to Cora's."

"Thanks, Teacher," said Charley. "I'll be just as glad there's some responsible—"

"Glad to oblige, Charley, my boy," said I heartily and he hung up suddenly. But I had the foreboding. I couldn't do this and teach, too.

When I got to Cora's there was more uproar. Mildred Garrick had left Charley at the airport at 9:00, treacherously saying nothing about her immediate plans. She had gone directly to Cora's apartment, bribed the maid, and searched the place. The only thing of any significance she had found was the tape. She'd made off with it.

I said it was plain burglary, which, after all, is a crime. But Cora only wrung her hands and said she couldn't fuss. That would only make it worse.

So, on January 6, Mildred ran a whole column about Cora and her dreams of being elsewhere and the strange "fact" that people did indeed see her elsewhere, although she was here. Mildred invented the phrase *The Dream Walker*.

Well, Josephine Crain was fit to be tied. Angelo Monti was also annoyed. *They* were above suspicion. Their annoyance and reluctance rang very true. It helped a lot.

The story was not exactly believed, of course. It was discussed. People got into arguments over such things as the relation between a supernatural manifestation and a time zone. These, however, were people in show business, a flamboyant few. Not the general public.

Yet Ned Dancer, no theatrical gossip columnist, he, was quietly asking some searching questions.

From this time forth (although we didn't know it) Cora was carefully watched. Mildred had permanently bribed the maid to look at her mail and listen to her conversations. Ned Dancer had bribed the switchboard operator downstairs to listen in on her phone calls. But nothing suspicious came in the mail or turned up in her conversations or transpired on the telephone. Kent Shaw was smart when he cut off communication.

Now he had dropped out; he'd washed his hands of the whole thing. He didn't come around anymore.

"If this is a stunt," Mildred said to me, "it's a dilly, is all I can say."

Cora wasn't ill, of course, and if her nerves twitched she bore up well. With callers who wanted to be told all about this business, Cora was terse, tense, and subdued. With me alone, she didn't discuss it at all. We were a pair of old acquaintances who had our secrets and were at once a little hostile and a little relaxed together.

On January 9, she rehearsed and performed in a radio drama, going about her business as usual. So I went home. Cora didn't need her hand held. Or, if she did, Charley Ives was underfoot enough, hanging around, big and rather taciturn, watching us both, and suffering Cora to tease and command him. I pleaded my job. I was glad to get away.

But I was disconcerted when my girls began to ask me questions. "Miss Hudson," one said, "if *you* tell us all those statements are accurate, we'll have to believe them."

"They are accurate, as far as they go," I said, "but of course there is a great deal that's unknown."

"Miss Reynolds says it's a publicity gag."

"It may be," I said and kept smiling.

"And that it's cheap and dishonest."

They waited for my judgment to be pronounced. I said, "A publicity stunt may get an actress noticed. It can't make her a better actress. Only work can do that." (Always the teacher.)

"Cora Steffani must be pretty good," one said didactically, "or else *you* would see she was faking. Maybe you do, Miss Hudson."

Those kids can really get you into a corner. "I don't easily accept the supernatural," I said. "Let's leave it at that."

But then, of course, one brought up extrasensory perception. And another spoke solemnly of one's duty to keep an open mind.

I had to say that we weren't there to decide between such alternatives and could not, without more knowledge. I reminded them that what you kept your mind open for was not idle amazement, but more knowledge. "Don't open your minds so wide that they hold nothing," I told them severely. "And don't be sheep, either."

"We aren't sheep," one said.

"Then why is every girl in this room wearing her hair short and brushed upward all around her head?"

"Because *you* do, Miss Hudson," one said sheepishly.

"Then I'm a poor teacher," I said.

Next day their heads were riotously different, each from the others. Oh, I suppose it's a backwater, it's unimportant, this work of mine. I did enjoy them, my innocent imps, my frivolous angels, my worried ones, my sly ones, and the few with shining eyes.

Chapter Five

THE FIFTEENTH of January was Marcus' birthday. We flew down that morning. I wouldn't let Charley Ives call for me but it seemed perverse of him to make the airport at the last minute. As we went aboard, bearing gifts, Charley said if he'd thought of it he'd have brought me an orchid.

"You are thoughtful," I said, "but since I think an orchid is a floozy, it's just as well."

He said that, offhand, he couldn't think of an intellectual-type flower. Could I? I flounced onto that plane. I had plenty of physical room in my seat, next the window, but Charley *filled* that plane, of course. I felt barricaded by his body from all the near world and on my other side the world fell far. I watched the city go by under and then there was New Jersey. "I'm going to doze," I said firmly and wedged the little pillow under my neck.

"Cousin Ollie," said Charley. I was wide awake. "A question will have to be asked. I don't want to fight, mind you. But what do I *do,* that you haven't any patience with me?"

I said, "Nothing." A look of long-suffering came upon his face. "I mean that," I said indignantly. "What do you do for a living?"

"For a living?" he drawled. "Why, nothing much."

"So I've seen," said I. My heart was pounding. I didn't want to fight.

"Where did *you* get this Puritan idea?" asked Charley after about a hundred miles of earth had turned and put itself behind us.

"I'm no Puritan."

"About work. Work, for the night is coming."

I got it from *you*, I thought, outraged. But I said wearily, "I suppose I've found out there's no other way to be even moderately happy."

Charley said, after pondering, "You may be right, Teacher." Then he grinned down, the maddening way he does. "You mean to say, whenever I got up the nerve to ask you this, you'd have answered?"

"Let's not have questions and answers, please. Teacher's tired."

"Doze," he said. "Doze, by all means."

I couldn't even shut my eyes.

"If *you* made a promise," Charley said to the plane's ceiling, "*you* wouldn't break it."

"Not if I could help it."

"Hard work and high principles," he muttered. "All this and Art, too."

Now I shut my eyes tight because they were stinging with the start of tears. "You make me sound like a prig," I said. "All right. Maybe I am."

"There are those who would say so," said Charley Ives, and I had a distinct vision of Cora Steffani's mocking face.

"Have you promised to marry Cora again?" I said loudly, to my dismay.

"Uh uh," said Charley. His eyes flashed blue.

"Why not?" I cried idiotically.

"Now, really," drawled Charley with an eyebrow cocked.

"Sorry," I said, looking out at New Jersey or whatever it was. "Just vulgar human curiosity."

Charley was as quiet as a mouse. After a while he stirred in the seat. "You've got everything hindside forward," he began. "You always had."

"Charley," I said in something like panic, "truly, I can't be your confidante."

In a moment he asked, "Why? Are you Cora's? Just in a spirit of vulgar human curiosity, has Cora told you this trance business is a fake?"

"No. She has not." I was all prepared to be a little bit hurt.

"Nor me either," said Charley. "But, Ollie, you *know* it's got to be."

I looked at him and sighed. We both smiled. "She'd do it," he said, "just for the hell of it."

"I know. But how can she be working it?"

"Beats me."

"She'd have to have a double," said I. "They could have figured that Jo Crain would be on that beach. But I can't understand that Chicago business." (We didn't know about Mr. Gallo at this point.) "How could they figure out that one?"

"Couldn't," said Charley, "without signals. What signal is instantaneous over a thousand miles?"

"The common ordinary household telephone, for one."

"True. True. But there was no phone call. Was there?"

"Not that I know."

"She may go on with it and pull another one."

"No telling when or where, either," I said.

"Well, I suppose the sky's not going to fall if Cora gets a little newspaper space."

"It isn't hurting anyone," I agreed, just as ignorantly.

"Interesting character, my ex," said Charley lazily.

"Of course," I said.

"Do you like rascals, Ollie?"

"Some."

"Energetic ones, eh?"

I looked out the window.

"I expect *you* wouldn't hurt anyone," Charley said after a while. "Scruples, you'd have." I stiffened. "But don't you ever get tangled up among your principles?" he teased me. "Loyally, you come when Cora calls. Although you're pretty sure she is a fraud."

I started to say, I came when *you* called. "We've known each other a million years," I said instead. "Once, we were young—"

"Poor . . . old . . . thing," said Charley softly.

"Charley, my boy," I said, "will you please not needle me all the way to Washington? I knew I shouldn't have got on this plane with you."

"I'm just a grasshopper, trying to get along with an ant," said Charley cheerfully. "Though it seems to me, once it was the other way around."

"It *never*," I began indignantly. Then he kissed me. "What—!" I sputtered.

"Go to sleep," said Charley Ives. "Improve the shining hour." He settled back, looking pleased with himself.

I rode the rest of the way with my eyes closed but my mind was frantically trying to figure out what promise he had made to whom, and if not to Cora, then why did he let her act as if she owned him? Isn't it a strange thing that you can get to be thirty-four years old and presumably mature, and still catch your mind carrying on as if it were in high school? I was *consumed* with vulgar curiosity. I *couldn't* ask.

When we got to Marcus' big, gracious, and delightfully shabby house, the clan had gathered, sure enough. Charley promptly disappeared. Since he fills a room, the big lug, by the same token when he isn't there he leaves an awful space. He didn't turn up again until dinner time and he didn't explain. Marcus seemed to know where he had been. But then Marcus seems, sometimes, to know everything.

God bless him, dear Marcus. He's not a large person physically. He is rather slight and rather small. Whatever his features were when he was young, handsome or otherwise, by now, in the years of his life, he has carved his own face. And it is beautiful. I suppose that's true. Every thought and every feeling that seems to run through the brain and the body so swiftly and briefly still leaves the mark of its passing. Just as water drops that have long reached and disappeared in the sea, each and all made the riverbed through which they came. It's a terrible true thing.

It did you good to look at Marcus. His face was his biography.

He was pleased with the gaudy brace of thrillers I'd brought. He said only Charley catered to his sneaking passion for blood and detection. "Charley!" I was surprised. "Tries to keep me supplied," Marcus said, "but it's peanut reading. You can't stop till they're all gone."

Marcus isn't grim. He's easy. He's tucked into life as if he enjoys it, just as it is. So, while Marcus can talk to you about any subject at all, still, when you are with him—I don't know—the wind blows wider.

The puzzling business of a woman who seemed to be able to be two places at once fell out of my consciousness until Charley Ives, after dinner, chose to tell about it. The company (oh, there was Charley's mother, Virginia Ives, and his sister, Joanna, and Sally Davies, Charley's first cousin, and her husband, Sig Rudolf, and my parents, Millicent and George, and Charley's brother, J.P.; and there was the help, Johnny Cunneen, Marcus' secretary, and the little sub-secretary, Ruthie Miller, and his stately housekeeper, Mrs. Doone) *all* of them, it seemed to me, began to argue.

Those who scoffed and wanted to dismiss an unimportant bit of nonsense met a stern demand for a reasonable explanation. Whoever tentatively got wistful about ghosts ran into hard-headed laughter. That was the way it worked, of course.

Marcus himself said little. He did say that if it was a trick, it must have been planned for a long time and it must cost something (money and brains). "Is publicity of that kind worth so much, Ollie?"

"I can't see that it is, Uncle John."

(But of course Marcus sees clearly. Money, brains, *and a purpose*. Yet nobody, not even he, could have guessed, in January, what the purpose was.)

Sally and Sig Rudolf flew back with us and she bent my ear all the way with what she calls problems. They dropped me at my apartment. Marcus was safely seventy-six, and it had been a good day.

I suspect I ramble. The plot. The plotters.

I suppose Raymond Pankerman, seeing Mildred's column, was gratified as the plot sprang to life. Cora was probably hugging herself with wicked joy. Kent Shaw, however, must have been devastated by anxiety.

Who was the stranger who thought he recognized Darlene? And had he recognized Darlene? Or *Cora?* It made a difference. If he recognized Cora (and Darlene got away) well and good. But, in either case, if Darlene *hadn't* got away, then there was someone who had seen too clearly into the hocus-pocus backstage. Kent Shaw, that dark, bitter, driving little man, exiled by his own cold cleverness from the middle of the excitement, hard-headedly keeping away—how he must have suffered! For Darlene, who could have communicated (since they had a device arranged for an emergency) did not.

Darlene, in fact, was having a difficult time. This Edward Jones had conceived the perfectly sound idea that Darlene had tried to brush him off. But, stubborn and perverse as he was, hard-to-get meant had-to-get to him. And Darlene knew, even better than Kent Shaw knew yet, that Ed Jones certainly could blow up the machinery

of the trick anytime he chose. So she knew it had been a mistake—
it wouldn't be smart at all to brush him off.

She let him follow her to the ranch in Texas where she was taking
another of those "vacations." In fact, she teased him and tried to
keep him near. She was worried. It was all right, so far, because he
hadn't seen Mildred's column, not being interested in her kind of
gossip, and no discussing was being done in Texas. Yet. But Darlene
knew that if all went as planned, there would soon be pictures, pictures of Cora Steffani. What could prevent Ed Jones from popping up
to say not only that he knew the same nose on another woman's face,
but that he knew it was the other woman, Darlene Hite, who had
been in a tavern in Chicago, *saying she was Cora Steffani.*

Darlene finally made a decision on her own. She was forced to do
so. The third incident nearly ran them into disaster.

Chapter Six

KENT SHAW was really clever. I had already heard some
people say that it seemed significant, how Cora dreamed in a crowd.
"Makes sure she has an audience, doesn't she?" some said.

So when she dreamed and walked in the dream for the third time,
she dreamed in quite different circumstances.

This was not solely for variety's sake. This time it was a wild
throw. The risk of failure was great. Even with success, the timing
could not be exact. It had to be left somewhat vague so that there
would be a safe margin. Therefore, this time no tape recorder and
no shorthand could be allowed and no witness, either, who would
have any idea what was supposed to be happening. The two witnesses
were unimpeachable, just the same. A cabdriver drawn from the
traffic's grab bag, and a cop who happened to be by.

Two solid citizens, then, who thought they had a fainting woman
on their hands. Who exchanged glances when Cora sat up suddenly

in the cab, early in the afternoon of February 10, took paper from her purse, and began to scribble on it.

The driver had gone to the curb and hailed the cop. The cop had opened the cab's door. *They* wanted name, address, and diagnosis. Scribbling they couldn't wait for.

"Lady," the cop said, "if you're okay, the driver will take you home. If you want a doctor . . . Lady . . . Listen, ma'am . . ."

"Don't speak," cried Cora, scribbling.

"Don't get mad," the driver said. "You was out. So what was it? A fit or something? Hey, lady!"

Cora, of course, stopped her scribbling exactly when she chose to stop. The cab took her home. She called me. The maid heard her and called Mildred Garrick. The operator downstairs called Ned Dancer. I called Charley Ives because Cora asked me to.

So there we were.

Cora was still huddled in her camel's hair topcoat. "Happened again and it's gone," she told us. "It's lost. I tried to write it all down but they were so impatient. Maybe it doesn't matter. Maybe it's just as well. Only I'd rather know." She seemed to be in a state. While Charley comforted her, I took the piece of paper. She'd scribbled on the back of an old script and the writing was big and agitated.

"Snow," I read. "Everything white. Cold. Galoshes, Blue ski suit. Mittens and cap. Wild country. Empty. Man on the path. Bundled up. Dark clothes. White hair. Long, long jaw. Gray eyes. Said, 'Is there anything at all I can do for you?' Irish. I said, 'I'm lost. When did it snow? Which way is New York?' He pointed. I ran. Slipping in snow. Trees. A mountain. Voice calling after me. . . ."

"That's all there is," I said. I sorted out those disjointed words and made a scene of them in my mind.

"What did the voice call?" Charley wanted to know. I thought his question was an odd choice out of all the possible questions.

Cora just shook her head and wailed. "I've told you and told you how it fades."

"Where did this happen?" asked Mildred.

"I took a cab down from NBC. I must have passed out. I don't know where."

"When?" Ned Dancer demanded.

"Don't know when, either. I suppose you could find the driver.

But I can't tell how long I'd been out before he noticed. I came to and there was a policeman. You could ask."

"Don't think we won't," Ned Dancer said.

"I meant," said Mildred, "where's all this snow and stuff? Where did you think you were?"

"I'd been there before," said Cora in a low voice. "I think it was Aspen. Aspen, Colorado."

Charley got up jerkily and began to walk around.

"Come now," said Mildred gently.

"*Don't* believe it!" Cora cried. "*Prove* to me it isn't so! I *want* you to! Please!"

Ned Dancer went to the telephone. Charley said slowly, "We can fly out. . . ."

Ned said, "I intend to."

Charley said, "To prove anything, Cora, you'll have to go, too." She looked terrified.

"That's quite right," I said. "You can't go to bed and hide your head. That is, if you want to prove anything. The man with the long jaw, if you can find him, will have to see you face to face. And so will Josephine Crain. And so will Angelo Monti."

Cora made moaning sounds. "Ollie, can you come?" she whimpered.

"Ollie has work to do," said Charley Ives quickly.

"That's true. I couldn't possibly go," said I.

Cora looked up at Ned Dancer, who is a slim smooth-faced man with the coldest eye in the world. "Do I have to go? Mildred, are you going?"

Mildred stood there, sucking a tooth. She had on a gray suit and a sharp black feather stuck at a jaunty angle in her hair. Mildred's eyes were cold, too, and shrewd.

"No use for me to go to the mountain," she said phlegmatically. "Neddy, here, is going to have it on the front page before I could use it. I'll have to sob about it, later. Cheer up, dear," she said to Cora. "Charley will protect you. And how can you lose? If you weren't walking in Colorado, why then you'll feel better, won't you? If you were, you'll only be slightly notorious."

Cora was crying and carrying on and clinging to Charley. Dancer was on the phone. Mildred slipped out to speak quietly with the maid in the kitchenette.

I sat with that piece of paper in my hand. For the first time, I was frightened. It seemed *too much,* somehow. Too elaborate. I suppose my mind was following the hint from Marcus. Expensive. Who could pay? Not Cora. She was always a lap behind her bills. (Certainly not Kent Shaw. Everyone knew how poor he was.) If it was a trick— *someone* was paying. And how was all this to be worth what it cost? What could be its purpose?

They flew to Colorado. Charley Ives, Cora Steffani, and Ned Dancer. I taught my classes.

Charlie told me, when they got back, that the first thing the Reverend Thomas Barron, clergyman, of Denver, said to them in his Irish lilt was this sentence, "Is there anything at all I can do for you?" Of course the dear man said it a thousand times a week. He had said it to Darlene Hite. Cora, in New York, had *quoted* him. You can see the power in that.

Charley said to me, "Coz, do you realize that, up until now, there was no direct quotation from the other side? What Cora said, yes. But Cora never quoted directly a word Jo Crain said, or this Monti, either."

"I hadn't realized," I admitted. "But of course, you are right."

"This man in Colorado says it to everyone," Charley explained. "What gets me is how could Cora Steffani *know* that?"

"I don't see how she could know it," I said gravely. "She must be frightened."

Charley looked down at me with a sharp turn of his head. But I was shriveled in the cab's corner. We were on our way to hear the tape recording that Ned Dancer had made in Colorado.

The thing was, I'd been tossing while Cora and Charley were away. One night I sat up in my bed. I'd been *seeing* Cora tucked in against a plane's window and Charley's big body barricading all the world away. I sat up and had a session with myself in the dark. None of *that,* Olivia, I said to myself. Don't be a snob, of all things. Cora was in the family once already, and if she is going to be in it again, remember it's not up to you to wince. What's the matter with you? You're practically living vicariously. Tend to yourself. Live as *you* must. Be what you ought. So I had got myself in hand.

"Ollie, *you're* not beginning to think she walks in some astral body?" Charley looked incredulous.

"No. But I don't *know* what's going on," I said, "and I've decided that until I do *know* more, I'm going to stand by. We've known each other a long time. Most people are going to draw away from her. I won't be one of them, yet. I don't think I want to talk behind her back, either." I didn't add that I thought it was outrageous that he did. I tried not to think it. That was his business.

"Okay, Teacher," said Charley in a stunned way. And then we were there, at Ned's office.

Cora wasn't along. (Neither was Kent Shaw and nobody gave him a thought.) Yet Ned played the interview back for quite a group of us that evening. The affair was getting less and less private.

"Dr. Barron," Ned began on the tape, respectfully, "since we want to get this on record, today is the eleventh of February, is it not?"

"It is." (The moment I heard those two syllables in that rich voice I knew that *here* was a witness farther above suspicion than the Rockies are above the plains.)

"You are the Reverend Thomas Barron of Denver. We are now in Aspen."

"I am and we are. Go ahead, lad."

"Now, yesterday, you were out for a walk, sir?"

"I was."

Charley's voice came in. "Pardon me. You go for these solitary walks pretty often? As a regular thing?"

"I do. I come here, see, for the two weeks every winter. I'm not spry enough for the sports, long is the day, but I can still walk, praise God. So I do a good bit of walking alone and looking about and breathing the good air. Then, by night, I'm jolly with the younger ones around the fire. It all does me good, I believe, both the one and the other."

"Yes, sir." Even Ned's cold voice was softened. "Now, you met this lady yesterday on the path. Had you ever seen her before?"

"I had not. What is it," Dr. Barron said blithely, "the amnesia? Now, my dear, don't you worry. It's a prevalent thing, that, it seems to me, but no one the worse for it that I ever heard of. What is it you want me to say now?"

"Just tell us what happened, sir," Ned said resignedly.

Charley prodded. "And the time."

"The time? Now, I was heading *to* the Lodge, so it would be near my noon meal. I can't say closer. I was a mile off and coming up. This young lady was coming down. I don't know if she stopped me or if it was only the look of her that stopped me. I had not seen her before in my life. I said to her, 'Is there anyting at all I can do for you?' I said."

Gasps came into the recorded sounds.

"What is it? Eh?" No one answered so the minister went on. "And she said to me that she was lost. I think she also spoke of the snow. Then she wanted me to say where New York was lying. Before I could get my wits together—"

"Did you point, sir?"

"I may have pointed but I doubt it. I haven't the head for geography. But she didn't stay, see. She ran away then."

"Did you shout after her?"

"I don't remember that I did and I don't remember that I didn't. I did wish she had stayed so that I could find out what was the matter."

"You didn't follow, sir?"

"I'm not so fit for haring after a young woman in the snow, which is a pity. All I could do, I watched, and her running down that path. Then the man leaped from a bush."

"What man?"

"How should I know what man? A big man, it was, although too far for to see clear. He took her roughly with his hands and I didn't like the look of *that* and I would have gone down. But he stopped it and they slipped their arms around each other's backs, do you see, and off they went. And it was a friend, my dear, and you're all right now?"

"You didn't mention a second man, Cora?" Ned's accusing voice.

"I know," Cora's was a terrified croak. "I can't remember . . . not now. . . ."

"Now whatever it is," Dr. Barron said chidingly, "you mustn't be pestering her."

"You will swear that this is the young lady you met on the path yesterday?"

"I don't know that I'll swear at all," the minister said.

"But you—"

Charley's voice interrupted. "Can you tell us what she was wearing?"

"Why, the very clothing she is now. The blue trousers and all. But she'd a scarlet cap on her head and very becoming, too."

"It's at home," Cora's croak.

"Now, I've said all I'm going to say." Dr. Barron's charming voice was stern again. "This young lady is in some trouble and it's scaring the voice into her throat, and you'll tell me the trouble and we'll do what we can."

"We are all her friends, sir," Ned Dancer said tensely. "If you can swear, one way or the other, it will put her mind at rest. Is this the same young lady?"

"Maybe it is and maybe it isn't," Dr. Barron said, "but it's plain to me she's more upset today than she was yesterday, and until you'll tell me what's the matter, I'll do no swearing and that thing listening."

That was the end of the tape.

I asked them what Dr. Barron had thought of Cora's side of the story. Charley smiled. "The old gentleman didn't turn a hair. Said the Lord would make it all clear if and when He felt like it, and in the meantime, people should not pester each other." I had to smile, too.

"But did he swear it was Cora?" demanded Mildred.

"No, he never did swear."

"This second man," I mused, "surely he should turn up once he sees the papers."

Mildred Garrick said sourly the second man was no doubt Cora's demon lover.

He didn't turn up.

The story was in the papers, all right, but it was, at first, treated gingerly and briefly. The news magazines picked it up for an oddity. Then came Mildred's column, making the most of it. Sobbing, as she'd promised. *Dream Walker in the snow!* Finally, Ned Dancer plastered it, complete, over two pages of a Sunday supplement, with dialogue and pictures. The captions were impressive. "First lady of the American theater, Josephine Crain."

"Well-known musician, Angelo Monti." "Beloved Clergyman, Thomas Barron." "New York Publisher, Charles Marcus Ives." And even, "Olivia Hudson, 34, teacher in fashionable girls' school." Oh, plenty of class this story had!

And Cora Steffani couldn't have swallowed a gnat without it being known, so closely was she watched after that.

I went down to stay with her again because she said she was afraid to be alone. Charley Ives wanted to hire a nurse, or the like. I said she needed a friend. He said impatiently that he was her friend as much as I was and he'd see she was taken care of. I said she'd asked for me. He said, "You don't want to get mixed up in it." I said whether I wanted to or not, I seemed to *be* mixed up in it. We almost fought.

But I had to go.

Oh, I should have known, if I hadn't been so busy with *my* conscience, that Cora asked for me, and mixed me up in it, and wanted to use my unimpeachable testimony to hurt a dear old gentleman I adored, for much the same reason I had to let her do it.

Chapter Seven

IT WAS February. The plot was working up splendidly.

Was it?

The trouble was, Darlene Hite had to tell Ed Jones. She had hoped to slip away from him to do the Colorado bit. She knew something would have to be done about him, but she was caught by the appointed day, and she thought she could get back to the Texas place before anything broke. But he followed her. He was suspicious and had nothing to do but indulge his suspicions, and he was in a mean mood. Been teased, I suppose, more than he could bear. Although he was a mean person, I should think. So there was that scene in the snow. And she told him.

She said, "Don't, Ed. It's only my job. I'll tell you all about it." And she slipped her arm around his back (as Dr. Barron said). "I'm not supposed to tell a soul," she said, "but I'll tell *you*."

She told him it was a publicity stunt because that's what she thought it was.

Ed Jones knew at once that he was in a position to spoil the fun.

Darlene knew he knew and faced up to this as one does in the jungle. She gave him money. She said her boss would realize what a good idea this was. She said if Ed would be quiet she'd speak to her boss and see if she could get him a job, too.

Ed Jones had a little money—not enough, of course. He was a drifting person, not steadily employed. He thought he'd stumbled into an easy job, "helping" Darlene. He must have known perfectly well that it was blackmail of a kind. He rather liked being backstage. He was interested in money, but he wasn't reliably devoted to money and Darlene knew this. She had to manage as best she could.

The two of them started for San Francisco in his car. The whole scheme now rode on whether Ed Jones would stay sober or be able to bear reading the papers without boasting that he knew a thing or two. Darlene managed him, somehow.

Now, possibly Raymond Pankerman was pleased at what he read and heard and thought it was going well. Maybe he sat among his lawyers, fighting his paper battles, and out of the side of his eye he watched his chance of revenge, as it grew. And maybe Cora simmered inside with mirth and excitement. But Kent Shaw must have been frantic!

What *about* that man in Chicago? Who *was* that second man in the snow? Kent Shaw was the writer-director-producer. Not to know must have driven him wild!

On the fifth of March, Darlene Hite called, at a prearranged hour, the assigned number of the phone in the booth of the mediocre little bar where Kent took care to be every third evening. When he stepped into the booth, nodded to the barman that this call was his, he must have thanked whatever gods he had to hear her voice.

Darlene told him the San Francisco incident was out. George Jocelyn, the writer, had taken off unexpectedly on a trip. What they had planned with him couldn't be done. Kent Shaw would tip Cora? . . . Yes, yes, but what about this *man?* . . . So Darlene told him all about Ed Jones.

"*Told* him!" Kent shrieked. And pressing for an end that Darlene didn't even know about, the ruin of John Paul Marcus, he must have rummaged for and found the inspiration. How he could save his beautiful scheme, that was going so beautifully well. How he could not only save it but improve it. And gamble everything. All in the world Kent Shaw had left to put on the table.

So he said, "Give him more money. As much as you have to. Tell him, if he opens his mouth, there will be no more money. For you or for him. Keep him close to you and quiet. Skip San Francisco. But meet me in Los Angeles earlier. March twenty-fifth." He told her where. "I'll have a job for him. In the meantime, lie low somewhere. Fly to Honolulu. It's a quick flight from where you are. You can have a nice time in the islands. No matter what you do, keep him quiet and tell him nothing *more*. I'll see you myself in L.A. The twenty-fifth of March."

So Kent Shaw hung up and now the brain had to gather the wavering shadow of his solution and bring it out of nothing into solid plan. He had to incorporate Ed Jones usefully into the plot. He did it brilliantly, I suppose. Certainly, the one thing Kent Shaw could not bear was to see his work spoiled now. Now that the plot was rolling, it had gone this far with such success. Impossible for Kent Shaw to accept exposure and defeat, now, in the glow of achievement. For an Ed Jones? A man who had happened to be in a tavern in Chicago? A character rung into the cast by that bad playwright, coincidence?

It was too bad. But perhaps it was not necessarily bad, at all. Perhaps it was good. Perhaps it supplied a missing element of strength, of depth. Why, yes, it did. It could.

Kent Shaw saw ahead. But I wonder how far.

Los Angeles is murky. It is still murky. But first I can tell you how Cora and Kent Shaw had a conference. Kent Shaw managed this by, outrageously, breaking a taboo.

I was living with Cora through February and into March. I went back and forth to my school. But she gave up working almost entirely. So far the affair had not helped her employability. Perhaps because those who employed her saw as yet no fierce public curiosity. The strong interest, the lively talk, was still more or less within the trade. Therefore, there were too many interruptions in the studios and too much time lost because of the curious who wanted to speak to her or anyhow look at her. The role she played lasted twenty-four hours a day. Every evening people came in.

Sometimes I think the ones who would not talk kept the talk alive. Josephine Crain refused to see Cora and to speak of it at all. Even Angelo Monti's good nature had its limits. He saw Cora and rather reluctantly identified her and thereafter would not discuss it. Dr. Barron became, I understand, sweetly adamant and not a word would he say. I didn't talk, Lord knows. And Cora found a masklike look, very sweet and sad and meek, a pawn-of-fate look that she put on. She wouldn't talk very much. Just enough.

Charley Ives would turn up some evenings and sit there in Cora's big room for an hour or two, keeping his eye on. Oh, Cora was watched from all sides. *I* watched her. So there was argument and speculation and baffled curiosity around the town, but nobody watching saw anything.

February went into March and March went along. Nobody noticed that Cora went to a certain tea roomish eating place not a block from her apartment in a kind of pattern. She'd go Monday and Thursday. The next week, Tuesday and Friday. The following week, Wednesday and Saturday. This had been going on since December and the pattern was inconspicuous. The place was convenient and a habit. Yet, if Kent Shaw were to come in while she was there, and if he made any occasion to tuck his napkin into his collar, it was a signal. It meant that the next planned incident must be discarded.

On March 8, Cora and I were in this place, having a bachelor-girl kind of evening meal. When Kent Shaw came in, I saluted him, and Cora nodded, but he simply glowered. He didn't come over to speak to us. I thought he was still either superstitious or envious and didn't bother to decide which. Kent Shaw seemed to me to be the same shabby relic of himself he'd been for years. Oh, I saw him put the napkin up and tuck it around his collar and pick up the supremely dry and unjuicy bit of fried chicken in his fingers. I didn't wonder. It meant nothing to me.

"Kent's an odd one," I said to Cora. "I'd have thought he'd have been right in the thick of all this dream life of yours, spouting theories. You?"

Cora shrugged. "Sorry little man. Burnt himself out, years ago."

"Speaking of getting burnt, are you giving up?" I asked her.

"Giving up what?" She peered over her glasses.

"Theater?"

"Never."

"I don't notice you running around to see who's casting."

"Ollie, I can't. You know that. I mean, not now."

"For how long can't you?"

She pulled her glasses down to hang around her neck and looked at me thoughtfully. "Oh, this will die down," she said lamely. "I may never have a dream again."

"If you do, I advise you to see some doctors," I said. (I don't know why.)

Cora took hold of her glass of water and her fingers whitened. "At least you can see it's an affliction," she said angrily. "Most people think it's a great joke. I've got a notion to go ahead and get married again and the hell with it."

I was startled. I know my mouth opened. Then I knew that although she stared at her plate which was probably a blur to her without her reading glasses, she was really, by nerve and ear and eye corner, watching me. I felt a wind of malice.

"You think if you get married again you'll stop this dreaming?" I asked her in my most detached manner.

"They do say it's the end of dreaming," she murmured facetiously.

I could have asked her if she'd found it so. She'd never talked to me about Charley Ives, nor told me why she had so soon divorced him. But I didn't ask. I never had.

Kent Shaw got up, then abruptly sat down again, studied his check. A signal. Cora's head turned slowly. "Why haven't you ever married, Ollie?" she cooed.

"I'd rather dream," said I.

"Of course, you do have your work," Cora grinned nastily. "I suppose the high-brow temple of fine art where you serve couldn't do without you."

Kent Shaw was now arguing with the cashier. He paid, with an air of anger, and he left the place.

"It better not do without me tonight. I've got some grades to figure." I could always pretend her cracks didn't hit me. "So shall we . . . ?"

"In a minute," said Cora, swigging coffee. "No offense, huh, Teacher? Excuse me, Ollie?"

She went to the "Ladies." And I sat, wondering whether I was fond of her or not. Whether she hadn't become more like a relative with whom I was involuntarily entangled. Whether she would soon become a relative (in law) again.

Meanwhile, Kent Shaw nipped around the corner, went in a side passage, and broke a taboo. He rapped on the "Ladies" and Cora let him in. The door was in nobody's view, back in a warren of interior partitions. I didn't suspect a thing. I'd seen Kent Shaw go out of the building. I didn't even know there was that other way in. When Cora came back, we paid and walked home. Me to my work, to sit remembering my girls and assessing their progress and being too generous, I suspect. (And beating down that question. *Who* wanted Cora to marry him, again, and had been refused, so far? And *how* had I gotten it hindside forward?)

Meanwhile, Cora sat before the TV set, swinging one ankle, smoking, looking lazy, but inside the dark head, the brain was busy memorizing new instructions.

Kent Shaw told her there would be no San Francisco episode because Jocelyn, the writer, had gone away. Therefore, he thought it wise to move the Los Angeles episode ahead in time. Iron was hot, best to strike, and all that. But he said he was leery about Patrick Davenport's eyes. Davenport, that famous movie director, was an eye-minded gentleman and as smart as they are made. "This Hite kid," Kent said, "just hasn't got it. Her walk, for instance, isn't yours. She doesn't carry herself as you do and I can't teach her. Now, Davenport might get that. He could catch on, too fast, to what's going on because *he's* reading the papers. Don't think he's not. And I'm afraid of that eye. In his own house, too. I'm nervous about it. We can't wreck this thing now."

He was nervous, all right, ready to jump out of his skin. But he did not tell Cora what really made him nervous, or anything at all about Ed Jones. He said he had changed this Los Angeles bit to a device he considered safer. So he told her what she was to do. He told her it depended on his getting in touch with Darlene. So he would signal. He told her how he would do that. If he gave the signal, she was to use the revised version. If not, then they would have to stick to the original, because they must coincide with Darlene, if she went through with it. So Cora made a note or two on her script, which was always with her. *He told her the title of a certain book and described its jacket, which she noted.* After that, she saw that the coast was clear for him, and Kent Shaw left the way he had come, and Cora joined me.

And if I suspected nothing, I truly believe, *neither did she!*

Kent Shaw flew off to Los Angeles. On the twenty-fifth, he met Darlene. She was as disguised and inconspicuous as ever. He congratulated her on her finesse, said he'd even raise her pay, said the scheme was going like wildfire and everyone was pleased with her. He must have been probing shrewdly into Darlene's emotions and sensibilities. The praise braced her but she remained cool. More money, of course, she approved.

He told her that the one unforgivable thing would be exposure of the plot, ever. He said it must remain the mystery of the decade, and never revealed. He said there had been only four people in the world who knew, four who would be forever silent. He was one, she another, and Cora, and one more. But now there was Ed Jones. Oh, he said she had done well to tell Ed Jones. He understood that. But now, he, Kent Shaw, would take over. This Jones liked money? Darlene said that he did, but he was vain and he was after *her*.

"You don't want him, do you?" Kent Shaw asked her outright. Darlene said placidly, "No." So Kent Shaw told her not to worry. This Jones would follow her no more. She probably wouldn't see Ed Jones again.

Darlene sighed relief. It had been a strain.

Kent pried into the past. Who was Ed Jones? Darlene said she had known him in high school, where he'd never paid much attention to her.

"You don't mind what I tell him about you?" Kent asked. And Darlene said no. "New leaf?" Kent Shaw had asked suddenly and shrewdly.

"When I get the end pay," Darlene had said.

"You'll have to be careful. Remember, don't let any tax man start wondering."

Darlene implied that she'd thought of that long ago, not having been born yesterday. Then Kent Shaw, perceiving once more her relationship with law and authority, told her he had changed the script and what she was to do.

She was to do nothing in Los Angeles.

He was taking a risk with Darlene, but he had to. She left that city on the night of the twenty-eighth of March. She wore her little veil, her inconspicuous clothing. She spoke to no one on the bus, caught nobody's eye. She changed to a train in Reno, went east, then south, and by a round about route to New Orleans, where she checked in at last for a "vacation."

But by this time she knew what, I do believe, *she* had not suspected, either.

Chapter Eight

SO MARCH WENT ALONG and the Dream Walker affair seemed to be dying down. Some people pointed out that the dreams had occurred in December, January, February, and one should happen in March and Cora was watched. But nothing happened until March was nearly gone.

The night of the twenty-eighth, there were people in Cora's apartment. Mildred Garrick (who by now took a proprietary interest toward the whole thing and came as frequently as she could) was there. Charley Ives, of course, and four or five other people who do not really count. It was a gloomy Sunday. The weather was dull. People were in some kind of depressed state, longing for spring, which would tease us for weeks before it really came. The evening wasn't jelling socially. Mildred was restless and glum. She wore a black-and-silver buckle in her hair and told Charley Ives, who was kidding her, that she knew it was not a success. Mildred had a blind spot, a certain lack of humor about her famous idiosyncrasy.

Charley was sprawled all over a sofa big enough for two.

A couple of guests were quarreling bitterly without saying a word to each other, using the rest of us as way stations for nasty cracks. One other was getting as drunk as he could, all by himself. Cora seemed irritable and almost on the point of throwing everyone out. How I wished she would!

She was wearing a violet velvet jumper with a white silk blouse and she looked very handsome. She'd put it on after I had turned up in salmon silk and we clashed so dreadfully that I couldn't sit in the room near her. So I was on the window bench, withdrawn. I was tired of living with Cora. I wished I could read. My tongue was hanging out for a book.

Cora swished over to her TV set and somebody groaned and said, "Oh, no, have we come to this!"

"Don't complain," said she. "You're not being amusing." It was her house and her set and no one could stop her. She clicked around the channels and we got a snatch of one commercial after another. "What was *that?*" she said and turned back.

A panel. Everyone groaned. "Wait a minute," said Cora in a bright interested voice. "Look who's on!"

It was Kent Shaw. There he sat, hunched and tense and bouncing ever so slightly. The camera wheeled along the faces and steadied on the so-called contestant. That panel show was an imitation of its betters, originating in Hollywood, making heavy hash of a stale idea. People in Cora's room began to make wittier remarks in criticism. The great boon of television! Sometimes the wit and nonsense that flies among friends during a B-movie is more entertaining than an A-movie in a politely silent theater could possibly be.

The camera came to Kent Shaw and he put his thumb in his mouth, a most unfamiliar gesture, something I'd never seen him do. How could I know it was a signal?

Somebody had just made a crack about the unfortunate contestant that to us in our low state seemed hilarious, and there was laughter in Cora's room for the first time that evening, when she slowly toppled over from where she'd been sitting on a cushion. Cora, in violet velvet, was out on the floor.

"Is this one of *those?*" a guest said, awed and delighted.

Charley was kneeling beside her. For a big man, he can move as fast as a cat. I knelt, too, as he worked the cushion gently under her head. She was in no faint. Her pulse was quick and jumpy. It occurred to me that Cora was excited and the blood was telling us so. I could not believe in her. I had tried. I'd done my best to give her all the benefit of every trifle of doubt. But I knew she was faking.

"Where do you suppose she *is?*" a girl said shrilly.

"Be quiet," said Mildred. "Eleven thirty-eight, E.S.T. Who is going to take this down?"

The man who had been drinking too much looked remarkably sober and said he could do it. Mildred's cold eye didn't trust him. There was a muted dispute going on over our heads while Charley and I knelt there and Cora was still.

She was relaxed. That took control. Most trained entertainers know how to do it. I can do it, myself. I teach my girls the trick of letting every muscle go. The heart will quiet. . . .

But Cora didn't stay out for more than five minutes. She rolled her head, opened her eyes, and the whole room became utterly still.

"I was walking in a street or a road," she said. Charley's arm held her sitting up. "No one . . . no one was there. I could tell there were high banks or hills on both sides. The street was like a ditch, deep down. I saw a sign by a street lamp, next to a palm tree. Cameroon Canyon Drive. I crossed the crossroad. I could see lights, very high up, to my right and left. But I was down in a kind of slot. I was scared. I'm always scared." Her lips trembled. No one else in that room so much as breathed.

"I kept walking," she went on. "There was nobody . . . nobody to ask. I saw a pink house, with white frosting, number 11880 . . . 11880," she repeated. Then she screamed. "Look in the ferns! Look in the ferns!" she cried out. "In the ferns!" And she put her face into Charley's coat. She put her arms around his neck, her fingers clutching, her body shaking. I felt sick.

Mildred was bending over. "What else? Now, come on, Cora. Never mind the hysterics."

Charley said, almost absentmindedly, "You shouldn't pester." And how he did it, I don't know, but he got up from the floor with Cora in his arms. He put her on the couch but she wouldn't let go of him. I saw him gently prying her fingers loose.

"No use to get a doctor," Mildred said disgustedly.

Cora turned. Now, her back was to the room and her face was in the upholstery. She wasn't making a sound.

"Cora." Mildred shook her shoulder. "Is that all, for heaven's sakes! Cora?"

Cora said the one word she shouldn't have said. She said, "Dead."

"What did she say?" No one could make anything of it and Cora lay silent with her head buried.

"Oh, let her alone," I said.

"Ollie?" She made the faintest whimper of my name.

"I'm here."

Charley got up from the edge of the couch, poker-faced, and I sat down. The salmon of my dress against the violet of hers was enough to put your teeth on edge.

"Palm tree, eh?" Mildred said. "South, then. Florida again?"

"With lights up high and a road in a canyon, it sounds like California," Charley said.

"Sooner or later," said Mildred grimly. "Oh, sure. Southern California. Beverly Hills, I presume. Well, well. Let's see."

Somebody argued for Palm Springs but Mildred, rummaging in drawers, found a street map of Los Angeles. On the TV screen, Kent Shaw, with sour brilliance, was guessing something or other, when somebody finally turned it off.

Mildred Garrick got on the phone. The rest of us sat dumb and dazed and listened to her.

"This is Mildred Garrick, in New York City. A funny thing just happened here. I want to ask you to make a check on it. Can you get a man up to number 11880 Cameroon Canyon Drive? It should be a pink house somewhere in your city. . . . Yes, I know. I've been there. It's quite a city and I've seen the colors of your houses. . . . Sure, I understand that in a polite way you're saying I've got a crust. . . . Listen, I called the police because I'm a law-abid . . . I work for the newspapers. . . . Because I want somebody with authority. . . . That's right. To go to this address right away and look in the ferns. . . . 11880 Cameroon Canyon Drive and how should I know what ferns? What trouble can it be? Pick up one of your telephones. . . . Nope, I can't explain. You wouldn't like it. . . . Doesn't look like Beverly Hills to me and I've got a map here. . . . Even so, don't you people speak to each other? . . . No, I *won't* call Beverly Hills. I can call a newspaper and get somebody right out there. . . . Okay. They can print the result I got out of this call, too. . . . Look in the ferns. That's right. . . . No, I'll call you back in about thirty minutes. . . . I told you, I run a column. . . . Okay."

"What could be in the ferns?" someone said.

"We may find out." Mildred looked grim and powerful. "Cora, if you want to make this really good, kid, better tell us from here what you saw in those ferns."

Cora wouldn't answer. She couldn't. I will always believe she did not know that the policemen, three thousand miles away, were finding in the ferns the dead body of a man named Edward Jones.

I've said Los Angeles was murky. It still is. I don't know, and no one will ever know, how Kent Shaw did it. *That* he did it isn't open to much doubt.

Ed Jones was killed by poison from a hypodermic needle, not a noisy way to kill a man. One could manage it in an automobile, for instance. How and when Kent Shaw got the body into the huge decorative mass of tall ferns on the front corner of Patrick Davenport's wide lot we do not know.

When Mildred called Los Angeles back in thirty minutes, even she let out a yelp. She stammered and stuttered and promised to explain. But first she turned around to tell us. "A body!" she said. Cora was still lying with her back to all, and she did not move. "The house belongs to Patrick Davenport," said Mildred, "and there is a dead man in the ferns!"

I *then* saw the ripple of shock go down Cora's violet back. So did Charley. Our eyes met.

Mildred left the phone hanging and yelled at her. "Did you see a dead body? *Did* you? Now listen, Cora, this isn't funny!"

"I . . . don't . . . remember . . . anything . . . at all . . ." sobbed Cora into the upholstery. "Go away. Everyone go away." Now she shook and when I touched her she *was* cold.

And no wonder. Now, if never before, Cora Steffani knew her role had to be played *forever*. Kent Shaw had told her he would put an animal in the ferns. He told her not to say what kind, because he wanted to make it as bizarre as possible. A monkey, if he could find one. But he might, he said, have to make it a dog. Oh, I believe she did not know the dead animal would be man.

Kent Shaw took a risk with Cora but he had her in a terrible position. She'd made it too good. She'd said that word, "dead." And no one would doubt she'd meant a dead man.

I could tell she was really terrified and I had a vision of the uproar that was coming. It was Charley who said thoughtfully, "When this breaks she has got to have some seclusion. I'll call Dr. Harper."

"Now, wait a minute, Ives," Mildred said. "The cops are going to want to talk to her and you can't hide her."

"I'm going to get her into a hospital," Charley said. "Cops can talk to her there can't they?"

"Oh, please!" Cora rolled over and pulled herself up. She was green with fright. "Yes, a hospital. I'm scared. I can't stand this. Take me to a hospital. Help me, somebody! There's something terribly wrong."

"Couldn't agree more," said Charley Ives, rather grimly. So he got her admitted. Charley Ives put her in that hospital. He had reasons, some of which I didn't divine. I thought it was wondrous kind.

So did Cora. I wonder how far Cora could see ahead.

Darlene Hite read all about it. It didn't occur to her to go to the police and tell all she knew and guessed. In the first place, to go to the police wasn't a thing she'd been trained to think of as either a duty or a pleasure. In the second place, once the police succeeded in tracing the recent whereabouts of Ed Jones and found out about a female companion who had been acting so modestly furtive that she used false names, it couldn't take them long to wonder whether she had some motive for getting rid of Mr. Jones. If the whole great hoax came out, no matter who told them, Darlene was in for it, because Ed's knowledge of the plot was a nice fat motive for her. Finally, Ed Jones had died between 8:00 and 10:00 P.M. and while Darlene had left L.A. at 8:00 P.M., she had done it inconspicuously. She'd come a long way round about. She couldn't possibly prove an alibi. And saddest of all, she had no faith that anyone in the world would help her.

What she had was a cool head. Then and there, *she* looked thoughtfully far ahead. She knew Darlene had to take care of Darlene.

Chapter Nine

BRILLIANT! And what an improvement! (If you can stand where Kent Shaw stood.) Now there was publicity, all right. Now, as Mildred Garrick put it, it wasn't funny. Now there was talk. How *could* a woman surrounded by witnesses in her own apartment in New York City discover a body in Southern California?

But she had!

So how do you explain it?

If you insist it's a trick, she's mixed up in a murder and surely that's pretty drastic. Who would go this far to get her name in the papers?

And if it isn't a trick, what then? She dreams, and dreaming, walks? She travels in a trance with another body at her disposal? She can be two places at once? Why, then, she is at the least a witness in a murder case. Legally? The *Law* is going to allow that she was in Southern California and New York, both places, on the night of March 28? Has she an alibi for this murder, or hasn't she? What's to prevent a woman of her talents from murdering or stealing or committing any other crime? If she's not subject to the laws of time and space, what can a judge do to her?

Cora was in the hospital, incommunicado.

Who was this dead man, the papers cried, and answered. He was a man named Edward Jones. Born and raised in San Diego. Navy. Then a drifter. Seattle, Chicago. After Chicago, had dropped out of sight. Then he might have been the man in the tavern in Chicago. *Was* he the man in the snow in Colorado? The hint of violence there was remembered and quoted. AH HA, people cried. Then Cora Steffani, in her trance state at least, had reason for violence against this Jones. And she had killed him! But she was in New York, the tavern was in Chicago, the snow was in Colorado, and the body was in California.

How it bred talk! I don't suppose there was a hamlet in the land where the inhabitants did not ask each other's theory about the Dream Walker. And the answers!

Cora was in league with the Devil. Cora was a witch. Modern science is always rediscovering truth in old wives' tales. There *were* witches, after all. And this settled it.

Nonsense! Cora was insane. She had an insane capacity for telepathy. Science could swallow and digest that, somehow.

Nonsense! Cora was a criminal. The whole series had been only to cover up this crime. Alibi before the fact, of course. Ever read thrillers?

Nonsense! Cora Steffani had never, as far as could be discovered, even met this Edward Jones. Never been in San Diego. Or Seattle. Only briefly in Chicago. She was just an unfortunately gifted mystic, possibly a natural yogi. She was to be pitied. *She hadn't done it.*

Nonsense! She had a twin sister, unknown to herself, and there was this famous correspondence between twins. *And the twin had done it.*

Nonsense! *Cora did it.* Because she was really a Martian, and Ed Jones had known that, and we are all being watched by Beings from Outer Space.

Nonsense! The whole thing is just a publicity stunt.

Murder? *Oh, nonsense!*

Miss Reynolds called me into her office. "Miss Hudson, you've been close to this Cora Steffani? I believe you've even been staying with her, have you not?"

"I've known her for seventeen years, Miss Reynolds."

"She's in a hospital, now, I understand."

"Yes, ma'am."

"Do you go to see her?"

"Of course."

Miss Reynolds pursed up her mouth until little vertical wrinkles made a mustache. "My dear, is it wise?"

"If wisdom comes into it," I began slowly.

"Oh, but surely it does. Olivia"—she didn't often call me Olivia and this was ominous—"I'm sure you must know that your influence with these girls is considerable."

"I know there is responsibility."

"You have a certain gift," she said. "They are drawn to you. Now I have thought of you as a fine influence. I've congratulated the school for having on its staff a real lady. An old-fashioned term, but I can't think of another that comes so close to expressing the quality of graciousness and kindness and devotion to ideals."

"Thank you," I said, knowing perfectly well where all this buttering-up was going, "but if I abandon an old friend because she is in some rather sensational trouble, I'm afraid I wouldn't begin to deserve all that you are saying."

Miss Reynolds frowned. Then she broke down. "What's behind all this nonsense?" she wanted to know.

"I wish I could tell you. I can guess that she's gotten herself into a mess she didn't foresee. I know she is very much frightened. And I know that hardly anyone looks at her without seeing a freak, one kind or another. I don't know what to believe, Miss Reynolds, beyond that. The fact that she really is frightened. Of course, I could drop her. Let her be afraid by herself. It sounds as if it would be easy. Like drawing your skirts in close and walking away from someone who had fallen down in the mud. Maybe you wouldn't get physically dirty. I'm talking to myself, don't you see? I know I am in a strange position and I'm not entirely sure what's right to do. I'm quite aware that a teacher is an example. Perhaps you can help me, Miss Reynolds?"

She was looking more and more uneasy.

"Suppose," I said, "an old friend had done something very silly and it goes too far and something wicked enters in, and she is frightened and asks for you? Do you say, 'No. You got yourself into this mess and I wash my hands'?"

Miss Reynolds said, "I may have to fire you." But she used the slang term and her smile was warm, although somewhat rueful.

"I realize that you may," I said.

"What do you tell the girls?"

"I try to be . . . steady," I said. "I tell them that you needn't be blindly loyal, but you mustn't be blindly contemptuous either. And when you don't really know enough to understand thoroughly, perhaps you should take the risk on the side of kindness." I could feel my occupation slipping out from under me. "I don't think that much will contaminate you, really," I said.

Miss Reynolds leaned back in her chair. "We are committed to sobriety and security, here," she said rather grimly, "but if you can hold it steady, as you put it, let's not be committed to cowardice." And she sniffed. "For a gentlewoman," she said, "you are a creature of some force. I was going to preach to *you*."

"Miss Reynolds," I said, "I love this work beyond almost anything else in my life. The trouble is, all teachers preach. If I don't practice, then I should resign. I'm groping along. I confess I do think Cora Steffani is something of a fraud. I think she has been lying and I'm sorry that it's so. But I don't think she is a criminal."

"And if one day you do?"

"Why," I said ignorantly, "I suppose I will still be sorry that it's so."

(What an ivory tower I was in! It makes me squirm to remember. The world can't do without kindness. Or *anger, either*. And live and learn and, if I live, I will have learned.)

But I wasn't fired, that day, and I kept on seeing Cora.

Knowledge of the plot was now confined to the original four. Darlene was busy looking out for Darlene. Raymond Pankerman may have been shocked, but he was helpless. If he exposed Kent Shaw he, himself, was probably an accessory, for after all he had financed his murder. And his revenge, so close now, would be out the window. He kept silent. The thing was out of any control of his. Kent Shaw was running the show. And *he* lay low. By some definitions, at least, he was pushing madness. Perhaps he gloated. The publicity was a deluge.

All the past was dragged out, tapes, interviews, witnesses. Hysterically by the papers. Soberly by the police. Maybe it was significant that comedians didn't touch it, based no gags upon it. People were somewhat afraid.

Cora was examined and cross-examined. But all the police got from her was the same impossible story. Dr. Harper had admitted her to the small hospital on the West Side where she was to be "observed." They kept people out. She would see no one but the police, when she had to, and me when I could come. And Charley Ives, of course. (When I went to pay her hospital bills I found that Charley was taking care of them.)

I know something about her thoughts and guess more. Cora was horrified because a dead body was a plain and simple horror that even she could see. (Whereas, a dead, a murdered *reputation* was only part of the game she thought life was.) While she shivered in the dread that Ed Jones' death was just what it seemed to be—murder, and cold-blooded, too—still she tried to imagine that it could have been an accident. She had cut herself off from the communication point, that tearoom. Kent Shaw was still in Los Angeles, anyhow. So she waited.

What was she to do? Destroy herself? She had already hesitated too long. It seemed to her that the secret must be kept. But was that possible? There were three others who must never tell. Darlene, Cora did not know, had never seen in her life. But Darlene was being silent and Cora could guess *her* reasons and find them at least as powerful as her own. Raymond Pankerman was being silent. But she knew he wanted results, and she must have wondered if, failing his revenge, he would forever keep silent. Kent Shaw also wanted results, or he didn't get paid. Now she *knew* Kent Shaw. She knew that if she did not go on with the next step of the plot, Kent Shaw, in rage and frustration, might very possibly, in one grand gesture of self-destruction, broach the secret and destroy her, too. It looked to her as if "results" were indicated. Yet it would take tremendous nerve to go on.

I think she wavered. She began to feel fairly safe, protected as she was, with no assaults upon her nerves but those that came in print. And I was standing by, and Charley Ives. . . . Why not leave off, neither tell nor continue? Simply stop, now, and let there be no more of it? For the buildup was over. The next step was the big one, against Marcus. And Marcus was dearly beloved of Charley and me. She must have weighed the benefits of our partisanship against her fear of what Kent Shaw might do. I know when she decided which way to take the risk.

This Bud Gray, this big quiet man I'd met once before, became very much interested in the whole affair. One day I was in the tiny shop one could enter from the ground floor of the hospital, a convenient little corner where a visitor to the sick could find a gift, a magazine, or a snack. Charley came in with Mr. Gray.

Charley and I had been avoiding most gingerly any discussion of Cora and her behavior. I'd said I wouldn't talk behind her back and Charley scrupulously respected my decree. But Bud Gray had no such inhibition. They climbed up on stools on either side of me. "She let you in, too, eh?" Gray said to me. I nodded. "Have you tried to get her to talk?"

"No. I haven't."

"Don't you think you should?"

"Cousin Ollie thinks Cora needs a friend who won't ask questions," Charley said.

"Who doesn't?" Bud Gray remarked. "But we'd like to know who killed a man." They both looked down at me.

"If she wants to tell me anything," I murmured, "she knows she can."

"Would you respect her confidence?"

"Why, not if it was murder," I muttered.

"Then she won't tell you it was murder."

"She won't because she certainly didn't murder anyone," I said. "I was *there*."

"What *do* you think is going on, Miss Hudson?"

I shook my head. I'd been feeling trapped and miserable for days.

Gray said, "I'll tell you what I think. I think she's got an accomplice and the accomplice put the body in the ferns. I think that's obvious. Cora could tell us where to find her. Not telling us constitutes accessory after the fact."

"That's right," said Charley.

"Not telling *you*," I exploded. "Are you policemen?"

Gray smiled. I was looking at his face. But I could tell that Charley's eyes were flicking messages over my head and I nearly fell off the stool. Suddenly I was sure that Bud Gray *was* a policeman in some fashion and I thought it must be some very secret fashion, too.

"Let's say this crazy affair has got me fascinated," Gray said. "And murder, to coin a phrase, is everybody's business, isn't it?"

I'd been having a soda. I gnashed my straw.

"Now, look here, Miss Hudson. Somebody has got to break that woman down. You wouldn't condone a murder, or so you said."

"Of course I wouldn't," I said. "But I don't *know* that Cora had anything to do. . . ."

The two of them were silent for a moment.

"She has to know," said Charley.

"Did you know your friend Cora was pretty pink some years ago?" Gray asked rather tartly. "How do you stand on that sort of thing?"

"Where I think I should," I said haughtily. "What did she *do*? What is she *doing* now? I'd have to know quite a lot about it and see some evidence before I'd take a stand."

"You see, my cousin Ollie never, never judges people without full knowledge," Charley said gently. His voice had an undertone that made me turn and his look made tears of humiliation start in my eyes.

"Are you a policeman, Charley, my boy?" I said in my most teacherish voice, to cover what I was feeling. Charley said nothing, but I felt light bursting and searing me, too.

"Charley gets around," said Bud Gray very lightly. But it seemed to me that they had told me, these two big men who *worked* at something while I, and so many others, slept. I was crying to myself, Why haven't I known! Charley in Europe after the war, Charley in Japan wasn't in the front lines all that time. *Of course,* he was a policeman, in some secret way, and couldn't tell. (He must have promised!) I was ready to weep that I'd been so stupid.

"How p-pink is she?" I stammered. "What is it? Tell me."

Charley leaned his head on one hand. "Bud thinks he can needle you. He doesn't know you. About Cora, I can give you an opinion. She was fashionably pink, in the old days when that was fashionable. So much you probably remember, too. But in my opinion, Cora never really held a political thought in her head and never will. She belongs to a profession that doesn't always have much connection with reality. She thought it was the smart thing. Then when the style changed, she changed her ideas just as she would have changed her hem line. I will say that at one time she was acquainted with some who weren't so superficial. But she doesn't see them anymore."

I felt *furious* with Charley Ives, just as you would feel if you'd scolded a person for lying abed on a sunny day, and then found out he hadn't mentioned his broken leg. And I resented his crack about the profession. I believed that theater prople, like any artists, had to be *more* alert and *more* informed about reality than anybody else. At which, of course, *I'd* failed, not to know that Charley Ives was up to something! *Everything* was humiliating.

"Put it plain, then," said Gray. "Do you think Cora Steffani would talk to you?"

I suppose, to keep the silly tears from spilling over, I made my face proud. With some effort I considered what he was saying. I shook my head. "We are not confidantes, as you can see. Besides, I'm not cut out to be a spy."

Charley said, "It's not high-minded, is it, Teacher?" His big shoulders heaved. (We were fighting.) "Acting, on the stage, you see, Bud, that's art. But in real life, it's something sneaky and low."

"Everybody acts, in real life," I said. "And sometimes it's sneaky and sometimes it's self-control. And nobody's talking about art."

"Let's not be sneaky," he said as if he hadn't heard me. "Let murder go."

Gray said, "We *were* talking about murder, weren't we? Well, Charley, I guess I was wrong. I thought she might help us. Never mind," he said to me. "It isn't any job for a lady schoolteacher."

I was so mad I could hardly see. "You were married to Cora once, Charley, my boy," I said coldly, "and might as well be now. Aren't *you* in her confidence? Why can't *you* break her down? *You* should know how."

Charley's face wasn't saying anything. "Maybe you're right, Teacher. Maybe I better go up," Charley said, "and in my own crude way do what I can."

He left us, not so much as looking backward, and Mr. Gray and I sat side by side.

"I suppose he's very good at it," I sniffed forlornly.

"Who's good at what?"

"Charley Ives. At this secret kind of police job."

"What job? I don't know what you're talking about." Bud Gray wasn't going to tell me anything. He moved his soft-drink glass in slow circles. "Charley's a good citizen, shall we say?"

"Oh, certainly. That's what we'll say," I said from the depths and blew my nose.

"It's the bizarre, the time-and-space angle, that fascinates me about this business," Gray said ruminatively.

"Practically makes a Federal Case out of it." He grinned. "But the other woman must be plenty smart."

"The other?" I made myself stop thinking about Charley Ives.

"The accomplice. The one who does the walking, on schedule, and then vanishes. The one people see. Her job isn't easy." He spoke with a good deal of sympathy. I suppose he's had experience and knows what it means to turn up on schedule, and to vanish, too.

"How could there be such a person? How can they do all this?"

"Ah," said Gray, "we wish we knew."

"And why?" said I. But I wasn't really wondering why. I was worrying only about my own position. How could I turn away from Cora? And how could I not? What should I do? Now, I can understand that nobody expected me to be superhumanly wise. But me. Which was pretty vain and foolish, but there I floundered.

When Charley came down in about five minutes, he wore his poker face. They both went away, saying only polite good-byes. I felt cast out.

I went up to Cora's room and found her in a weeping rage. Charley Ives had made her so. Who else? So I proceeded to be patient and soothing toward the furious woman whom I even tried to forgive for taking some of her anger out in sullen unresponsiveness to me. But whom I neither knew, nor understood, nor even deeply cared for. No harm if, passively, in suspension of judgment, I stood by an old friend, said I to myself, compulsively.

That's when she decided to go through with it. She had compulsions of her own. Marcus says the difference between us was only that she didn't take the risk on the side of kindness. But I think Marcus is kind.

Chapter Ten

THE WHOLE MONTH of April went by with Cora barricaded, everybody baffled, hue and cry. Nothing more happened until that fifth day of May.

Darlene, meanwhile, was going about her business. Kent Shaw stayed out West. He was not seen about, and certainly not thought about by me. Raymond Pankerman was in the throes now, and his case competed with Cora's in the headlines.

And Cora remained in that hospital, acting, acting. Doctors came and went. Policemen came and went. Before all of these, she remained stubbornly baffled, herself, afraid of her own mystery, and unable to remember (*that* neat device that saved her so much trouble and risk) any more than was on record already about her dreams.

And I came and went, in the delusion that I was aloof but kind, and I found Cora listless, playing prostration. We would speak idly of other things. I must have been restful. But Charley Ives came no more. I did not see him anywhere.

Now a day or so after Cora's stormy time with Charley Ives, she had a jeering little note from Kent Shaw. I brought her mail from her apartment. She let me read the note. It said:

> CORA, DARLING:
> Dead bodies, aw-ready! Come off it, why don't you? Next time you get on your broom, keep away from Los Angeles. This kind of town, a man takes too much dope some night, they clean the streets. Me, I don't believe all I read in the papers. When I do, send me rue, send me rosemary.
>
> KENT

I made nothing of that. Maybe Cora saw both a reassurance and a threat in it. And took rosemary for remembrance. She *wanted* to believe Kent Shaw was not a killer. And she knew nothing about Ed Jones, except what had been in the papers. Nobody *knew* he was the man in Chicago, or in the snow. That was only guesswork. Maybe she could believe that Kent Shaw, looking for something dead, had found a body. Just any body. Maybe she swallowed that. In a way, she had to. Anyhow, the public uproar continued.

It was bad for the hospital. Cora thought it was a fortress, but it was her prison. Charley Ives had put her there to keep, and the hospital, resenting it fiercely, was nevertheless stuck with her. So she spread herself out in that room-and-bath, bringing her own things, becoming cozy. But newspapermen crept about the building, trying to get in and the open pressure they put on was enough nearly to buckle the walls. Cora kept refusing to see the press.

On the fourth day of May, she capitulated. She agreed to talk to one and chose Ned Dancer for that one because she knew him. He could relay the interview or not, as he pleased. (He'd better please, said the rest.) She would see him tomorrow, at 2:00 P.M., if Dr. Harper and I would consent to be present.

So then it was the fifth of May, and at 2:00 P.M., Ned was ceremoniously admitted, and along with him who should turn up but Charley Ives.

"Mind?" he said.

Cora said wanly and sweetly, "Of course not, Charley. Please do stay." If there was a glitter in the eyes, the lids were heavy and hid it. I didn't sense the malice. I was busy taking care to be calm and detached in my chosen position, standing by.

I will not forget that fifth incident. The scene exists somewhere indelibly in my brain as if it were a film in a can. It actually does exist on a piece of tape, for anyone to hear again. Ned Dancer had brought the inevitable recorder. Cora made no objection. Ned said there were some people who didn't trust him, as he plugged it into the wall and set the microphone on the table.

Cora was propped high on the bed, having climbed back in to play invalid for this occasion. She wore a rose-pink woolly bed jacket and careful makeup. Set among her froth, which could not entirely conceal the hospital white and hospital austerity, she was rosily and frivolously pretty, except for the pawn-of-fate mask on the face and the nervous slide of the hands along the edge of the sheet, back and forth. Ned Dancer stood up to the right of her and asked his questions in his unemotional voice. The doctor, a tubby little man with graying hair en brosse, rimless glasses, and an air of harassed goodwill, was silently standing behind him.

Charley Ives was sprawled in the low visitor's chair, overflowing it, not so much physically as by the very quality he has of being noticeable. I had refused that chair or any. I was literally standing by, on Cora's left. I remember my dress because I wore it for days afterward, a crisp taffeta with white at neck and cuff (which white I laundered in some odd places).

Cora answered Ned's questions patiently and without ire. There was nothing new. We'd heard these answers all before. The interview went drearily as the tape rolled relentlessly on the spool. At half past two, Dr. Harper shifted position, as Cora's eyes closed tiredly. "About enough . . ." he began.

"One or two more," Ned begged, "and then I'd like to talk to *you,* Doctor."

"Nothing I can tell you," Dr. Harper said, quickly putting up his defenses. I was listening to this exchange.

Charley rose from the chair. Cora's head had slipped sideways. I stood there and saw the flutter of her heart expressed in trembling pink wool and I thought, appalled, "Oh, no, no, no! Not again! Not anymore!"

The doctor stepped closer. Ned Dancer said, "What?" Then sharply, "Is that a trance state, Doctor?"

Dr. Harper touched her. Her lips tightened. He lifted a hand to slap her cheek and Ned stopped him. "Wait," he begged. "Let's just see what happens. This is giving me a break." His bleak eyes commented: Break, yah! No doubt my presence was arranged. He looked around at the spool of tape still turning. "How long do these things last?"

Charley said, "Can you tell she's faking, Doc? What about it?"

Dr. Harper licked his lip. When he spoke he must have had the turning tape in mind, because it was a fine screen of obscuring syllables, sounding calm and judicious, but with no meaning. He didn't even commit himself to saying he didn't know.

Ned said anxiously, "That's an hour's tape and there's about twenty minutes left. What do you think? Shall I turn it off? I want to *get* this and I'd rather not stop it. How many minutes do these fits run?"

"You want a prophecy?" said Charley, somber and resigned.

Dr. Harper forgot his caution. "I can bring her out of that, I think." I knew at once he had pain in mind.

"No, no," said Ned. "Wait a minute. Listen . . ." he wanted the story. (May he be forgiven.)

"Sit down, Ollie," Charley said to me. "You don't have to stand there, for gosh sakes. You look like you're going to fall down."

"I'm all right," I said, trying not to fall against his arm. But I wasn't all right. I did need supporting. I was tired to death of the whole business. How long could I stand by while this went on? How long was Cora (my old friend Cora) going to keep it up? At first I was weary. Then, I was afraid. It seemed too long, too much, too elaborate. She'd got all the publicity possible already. She was in a mess about a murder. What more did she want? How *could* it go on?

What if, I thought, Cora really was helpless, was ill in the sense of being abnormal, supernatural? Then, was it a shell, lying there in pink, and did Cora herself, clothed in a spare body, like a second suit of clothes, walk somewhere? Speak somewhere? To be seen and heard somewhere else, not here?

To believe that *all this was contrived* seemed just as mad as to believe it wasn't. For the first time, really, I, Olivia Hudson, tasted belief in the appearances. It was the first time and the last.

The clock and the tape rolled on and on with our heart beats, Charley's, where the back of my head was resting, mine near where his hand held me. Time played tricks with me, being very long, very short. It was actually twelve minutes before Cora opened her eyes and straightened her neck and stiffened her back.

Ned glanced at the tape, still going, and was about to speak when I said (may I be forgiven), "Don't interrupt. She forgets, if you do."

Cora said in that brisk way she had of speaking her part, so effective, because it sounded like simple reporting with all her emotions postponed. "I was walking. I was in a park. Wearing my gray coat. I stopped to . . . see where I was. There was a man on the path who said to me, 'Beg pardon, could I ask a favor of a stranger?' He wasn't young, wasn't old. I *knew* him." Cora pressed her temples in her palms. She had the stage. Not one of us moved. "He said to me," she went on, "'Would you give this envelope to an old gentleman around the corner, sitting on a bench, over there? Just tell him it's from Ray.' 'I'll be glad to,' I said, 'if you will tell me where I am.' 'You are in Washington,' he told me. 'Just do this thing for me?' So I walked around the corner and there was an old gentleman and I gave him the envelope. It was pale blue. And I said, 'This is from Ray.' And he thanked me and put it away. So I. . . ." She hesitated.

Charley's hands hurt me. Charley said in a quiet voice but one that vibrated through my whole body, "Who was the old gentleman?"

"Marcus," said Cora at once, staring into space. "John Paul Marcus."

"And this Ray?"

"I've seen his picture all over," she said. "I think the name is Pankerman. So I. . . ."

"What's this?" Ned's eyes jumped.

Cora looked bewildered. Her eyes changed focus. "I don't know," she faltered.

"That's all for now?" said Charley in that same voice.

"It fades," she whimpered.

"The hell it fades—" Charley threw me aside and went over and jerked out the cord of the tape recorder.

"Let it alone," bellowed Ned Dancer. "Wait a minute. Cora, *what did Marcus do with the envelope?*"

Cora opened her mouth but didn't speak. Charley was stuffing the cord into the recorder's case with violent haste. He discarded the microphone. He shut down the lid. Ned said, "Hey, that's mine."

Charley said, "Dancer, if you breathe. . . ."

Ned said, "I got to."

"Come to Washington. You can't print this kind of stuff without checking."

"No," Ned said.

"And you won't." Charley wasn't asking.

"I will, if it checks," Ned said. "I got to."

Charley said, "Doc, keep quiet and shut her up. Don't let anybody in here."

"Nurse. . . ."

"Keep the nurses quiet." Charley yanked out Cora's telephone. The doctor yelped. "The woman's a devil," said Charley Ives. "I'd strangle her, gladly, right now. If it would do any good. Which it wouldn't. You, keep her quiet." Cora began to wail and moan. Charley now had the tape recorder in one hand and Ned's shoulder in the other. "Cousin Ollie," he barked at me. "You better keep her lying mouth shut."

"Get out of here," the doctor said wearily.

Ned Dancer opened the door. The doctor was bending over his writhing patient with his ear close. We didn't hear it. We were not meant to hear it yet. But she told him, then or a little later, one thing more.

I didn't hear it because I went out the door behind the men. "It's all lies," I said in the corridor.

Charley sucked air in through his teeth. I'd never seen him so angry, not even the time we had fought so long ago. "Raymond Pank-erman passing secret papers to *Marcus!*" Charley made a sound of such deep disgust that I thought he had spit on the floor.

"It's going to check," Ned Dancer said. "Marcus himself is going to tell us there was this dame in a gray coat. . . ."

"That he accepted an envelope from some stranger? From some Ray? Naaaaah."

"And put it away. Yes, and it will be found."

"Can't be."

"No? Dead body couldn't be in the ferns, either. This thing is built."

"Over my dead body will they get away with this one," Charley said.

I said, "Tell me what I can do."

Charley herded us both down the hall into Dr. Harper's office. He

closed and locked the door and got on the phone. Ned stood there biting his thumbnail, his cold eyes bleak. I stood against the door.

"Ruthie? . . . Charley Ives." Now Ned moved and listened to little
Ruthie Miller's voice from Washington. "Where is Marcus? . . . Oh,
yes, I see. . . . Anybody with him? . . . Cunneen, eh? No, nothing I
can tell you. Just ask Marcus not to talk to anybody outside the household. Tell him I'm coming right down."

"So he's in the park?" said Ned.

"Yes, he's in the park. It's a chilly day, but he goes if it isn't actually
storming." Charley was quoting. His mouth drew down bitterly.

He dialed long distance again. Maybe you've seen a man fight with
a telephone for his weapon. Charley argued, insisted, demanded, and
finally, although it had taken him twenty minutes, he got a number
out of someone that gave him the man he was after.

"I want to talk to Raymond Pankerman," said Charley for the
sixth time. "I'm told he's due there. . . . This is Charley Ives and it
is important. . . . Oh he did? Put him on. . . . I don't care what he
wants to know. Tell him who is calling." Charley hung on.

Ned Dancer lifted his head. "He's been in the park?" said he
lightly, like the flick of a rapier.

"Yes, he's just come across the park," said Charley's bitter mouth.
He was hunched over the phone with one foot on the recorder. I stood
tight against the door. Ned moved up and down like a man in a cell.
Then once more he put his ear where he, too, could hear the speaker
on the wire.

"Pankerman? My name is Ives. You crossed the park just now?
. . . As a matter of fact, I *am* interested. You met a woman in a gray
coat? . . . No, I *don't* need to tell you what it's all about. Did you
give her anything? . . . What's that? . . . *Go to hell!*" shouted
Charley and hung up and held his head. Ned Dancer said something
crude and unfit for my ear.

"What did he say?" I quavered.

"He said he didn't have to answer," said Charley in a voice of
loathing. "Asked me if I'd ever heard of the Fifth Amendment."

We stared at each other's faces.

(Oh how deep was Raymond Pankerman's prankish laughter?
How much did the ego expand under the tweeds? How sweet was his
revenge?)

Charley jumped up, pushed me aside, and unlocked the door. He herded us out, seeming as big as a mountain and about as lazy and easygoing as a volcano.

"Tell me how to help," I cried. "What shall I do?"

Charley had no hands. He hung onto that recorder and Ned's shoulder again and Ned was as shifty and nervous as a race horse at the barrier. "You, Teacher?" Charley was thinking about everything but me. "I got to get hold of Gray. Ned and I are going to Washington, right quick. Find the accomplice. Get the whole damn scheme out by the roots. Prove exactly how they are working this." He spun around.

"I'll try," I said.

Charley gave me one blue flash through his lashes. Then they were off, taking the stairs, looking for an escape from what other newsmen might be lurking in the lobby. They went too fast for me to follow.

I knew, as well as Charley did, how this could hurt Marcus. What, *he* had any furtive truck at all with such as Pankerman? If such a thing were rumored, the whole country would wince and ask an explanation.

Rumored! But the *way* of this rumor was so fantastic! There was no explanation of Cora Steffani, the Dream Walker. No way to understand how she could have done what she said she did in that park. But, oh, there would be people to swear that Pankerman was in the park, at the exact right time. And Cora had done it before, as the whole world thought it knew. There was a dead man in the ferns, wasn't there? So some would dismiss this for a ridiculous falsehood, and some would not. But fraud or no fraud, not one cranny of the nation could fail to reverberate with the *story*. Marcus would be in the white heat of publicity, defensive, trying to prove a negative, denying.

Denying what? We didn't even know yet what was supposed to be in the envelope, but I quaked to think of it. Ned Dancer must be right. There would be an envelope. The devilish scheme would include a real envelope, somehow, somewhere. It wasn't all clear in my head, but I *felt* that here was the reason for the whole scheme. I felt they meant to injure Marcus and this purpose was important enough for all the trouble.

Charley Ives was right. The one thing to be done was expose. Get it out. Open it. Find out who, how, why, and tell, on our side, with fact, fact, and fact. We could not sit smug and say, "Why that's ridiculous. Untrue. Who could believe such nonsense!" People didn't have to believe the nonsense. Doubt was enough. Doubt, for most, is exactly the same thing as condemnation. Those who are really able to suspend judgment are not in the majority. Even they aren't getting anywhere, but only preparing to get somewhere.

I saw all this. I could no longer stand around piously maintaining that I hadn't enough to go on, so I wasn't making up my mind. *Harm* was being done. You can't just tolerate cruelty, *un*kindness. You have to *find* something to go on. I gave up being inhumanly detached. I was just as human as anybody else. I took some things on faith. I chose my side. That's not enough, either. I must go *find proof* that the Dream Walker was a wicked fraud.

I went downstairs and talked the hospital into cashing a big check. I wasn't a policeman. I had to do what *I* could do.

I called on Josephine Crain.

Chapter Eleven

"Jo," I said, "I'm here to beg you to help me prove that Cora Steffani is a fraud and this business a hoax."

"Well!" Josephine's lovely eyes were amused. She drew me down on a quaint little sofa in her sunny room. "What's happened, Olivia? I thought you were her little soldier." (I hoped she'd never have to know what had happened.) "Not that I don't agree with you," Jo added. "She's used me and I don't like that. Never did."

"Tell me about the woman on the beach. She wasn't Cora, of course. How was she *different?*"

"I don't like to talk about it and don't quote me, Ollie, or I'll scream." Jo looked at me thoughtfully. "But there was one thing that nobody seems to have noticed. In her little scene, *I had no lines.*"

"Charley Ives noticed that."

"Bright lad. Look, Ollie, my dear, I saw her for the briefest moment. I hardly got my attention out of my book. She resembles this Cora, of course. It's the same nose."

"I want a difference."

Jo said, "I've seen this Steffani on TV, you know."

"Go on, Jo. You did notice something."

"The woman I saw on the beach didn't use her hands. Whereas Steffani is the handy kind," Jo made with beautiful accuracy one of Cora's flying gestures. "That's a deep habit, a mannerism like that." She looked at me sideways.

"Doesn't help much, unless you're ready to swear."

"*I'm* convinced," Jo shrugged. "But what would it mean if I did swear?"

"Was she excited?"

"Not very. A cool customer, I'd say. I think she intended to seem upset and confused. But her hands didn't move, Ollie."

I sat thinking of Cora's hands, acting out annoyance, anguish, bewilderment, anything, everything.

"Every hair on your head says this is important," Jo smiled. "Don't tell me why, if I shouldn't know."

"I need some proof. I need it bad. Tell me this, Jo. You do go to the beach as a regular thing? People could expect you to be there?"

"I go South for the sun and I insist on it. Yes, I sit on the beach and read or study every day that it is possible and nobody disturbs me. Yes, it's regular. I daresay I am as good as a sundial."

"That's why they used *you*," I said.

"It seems to me they've used you, too," she reminded me.

"Jo, if you think of anything. . . ."

"If I had proof," she said tartly, "I'd have trotted it out long ago."

I rose and she was willing to let me leave her as abruptly as I wished. I was thinking that surely Josephine Crain's opinion would have some weight. Josephine Crain's conviction would convince. Then at her door she said, "Wait a minute. There was a ring on her right hand. A narrow dark stone."

My hope ebbed away. An observant woman, an honest woman, who was an expert on gesturing hands, who understood the tyranny of a deep habitual mannerism. So what? It was the ring that would count. Cora Steffani wore on her right hand a ring with a narrow stone.

Angelo Monti I tracked down (learning from Charley Ives) by

wrestling for an hour over the telephone. He was in town and at rehearsal.

"Miss Hudson," he said, reluctantly, "I can tell you only that I saw the woman. I saw Cora Steffani. They looked like one to me. I am shortsighted. My vision is not all that it ought to be. Perhaps I am not a good eyewitness. I hope not."

"They are two women and I must find the one you saw in Chicago."

He didn't argue with me. He had soft brown eyes, and whether they could see well or not, they were sympathetic. "I wish I could help you," he said. "You are very determined, for some reason."

"Any smallest thing. . . ." I thought to myself he was a kind of expert, too. "Her voice?"

"Her ordinary voice," said Monti, "is a little bit nasal. Not bad. Not good."

"*Cora's* isn't."

"Is that true?"

"But did you never hear Cora speak?"

"I hear her on the air. Then it is the actress voice. Too high in the mouth to my taste. I think it is like some singers who have the worst dreadful speaking voice in this world. They do not use their expensive education for every day, eh?"

"*Cora* does," I insisted.

"Ah? But this woman spoke to me in Chicago with a nasal voice. Oh, very faint, but unpleasant to me. If she was lost, you know, to be unhappy will change the voice." He was getting vague and confused. I wondered if he were superstitious.

"But you'd be willing to say the voice in Chicago is not the voice Cora uses on stage?"

"That much I would say. My ear is good. Does this have a meaning?"

"Wait," I said. "You saw Cora herself, here in New York. Didn't she *speak* to you?"

"She did not," Monti said. "It was in a studio. I was arriving and she leaving. I did not speak much myself, only to say her name. What does one say to someone you have met in her dream? It is awkward. She looked quickly very unsteady and her friends led her away. Perhaps it was odd that she did not speak *at all*." He looked at me hopefully.

"I think it was odd," I said.

"My eyes can be fooled. My ear, no. I guess you are pretty, Miss Hudson. I *know* your voice is charming and I would recognize it in the dark twenty years from now."

"I'm sure you would," I said warmly. He was such a nice worried kind little man. "But the problem is to find this faintly nasal voice." He shrugged, looking helpless. "Tell me this, Mr. Monti. Could it be predicted that you would be in that tavern that night?"

So then he explained about his friend Gallo.

"I see. I see. Yes, that's helpful. You were bound to be there and nowhere else. They could count on it."

"This helps you believe there are two women. But does it prove so?"

"No. No, of course not."

"The man," said Monti, "I have identified in a picture." He shivered delicately.

"What picture?"

"A picture of the dead man in Los Angeles. Of course, I don't trust my eyes. I cannot hear his voice again, unhappily."

"The dead man *was* the same man! The police have talked to you?" I cried.

"Have they not." He sighed.

"Did you mention the woman's voice to them?"

"No one asked. I did tell them one more thing, not in the papers."

"What was that?"

"She wore a pin. Gallo, my friend, he agrees to this. It was a small golden horse pinned on her shoulder. Gallo has eyes."

"Yes," I said, my excitement fading. "I mustn't keep you."

I left him. There it was again. An expert, a man with a delicate ear. But who would trust these experts of mine? And their intangibles? Cora's golden horse, for sale in department stores everywhere, it was solid. It would count.

I called Miss Reynolds and begged a leave of absence. I suppose my urgency was as obvious over the phone as it was in Jo's sitting room or the bleak rehearsal hall. She let me go. I caught a cab, all luggageless as I was, to the airport. There are not many seasons when a single person, both flexible and determined, cannot get a seat to where she wants to go. In an hour I was on a plane for Denver.

I had two little details about the second woman. She did not use her hands much when she talked and she talked in a voice that was faintly nasal to a very discriminating ear. What, I asked myself, would Dr. Barron of Denver be an expert about? I found out very soon.

It was dark when I got to Denver and late by the time I had myself dumped on his doorstep. In one of Denver's inevitable brick houses, I met the gentleman whose voice I already knew.

"Is there anything at all I can do for you?" he said to me.

"My name is Olivia Hudson. I've come from New York. I need your help."

"Why, then, you'll surely have it," said he, and he took me in and the first thing I knew I was sipping hot tea while the good man's wife, who was a little bit of a dumpling with snowy hair and merry young eyes, would not listen to any tale of having been fed on an airplane but prepared to give me nourishment as if I were starving.

I told Dr. Barron all about the Washington incident. He reminded me of Marcus. Although he was a foot taller and perhaps a foot wider, too, he was just as solid all through.

"It's a dirty business, then," said he. "Bearing false witness like that. Now, how shall I help you, my dear?"

"Think of something," said I once more, "that distinguishes those two women. To help me find the other one. Did the one on the path use her hands much?" I made Cora's gestures. "Like this?"

"Maybe she didn't." Dr. Barron's beautiful clear gray eyes were intent on the memory of what he had seen.

"Or the voices. Were they different?"

"It's possible. I never swore they were one. After a while, I was not satisfied."

"Why weren't you, sir?"

"Now, the one that met me on the path," said he, "*that one* was making out to be lost." He looked me in the eye. "But it was all put-on," he said.

"You mean she was acting?"

"Put-on," he repeated. "It wasn't true. If ever I saw a young woman who'd know where she was, and all, it was *that one*. She was not a bit scared and she didn't think she was doing wrong."

"What do you mean?"

"A fellow in my line of work, he meets more of sin and sorrow than the baker's boy," said Dr. Barron, "and she wasn't sinning and she wasn't sorry. She was cool as a cucumber and it might be that she was doing her duty. But the young lady who came the following day, oh, she was mad."

"Cora was *mad?*"

"Full of the anger and the hatred. And the weeping and the gnashing of teeth," he said. "Oh, but that was put-on. And me trying to comfort her when they turned the machine off, and she tickled to death about something all the time. Indeed, she was."

I realized his field in which he was an expert. Soul states, you might call it. I gasped. "You mean Cora was triumphant? But of course, she might have been." I began to turn in my mind my own memories of Cora's states. I'd known her for seventeen years. All I remembered sensing under the mask was a bit of malice now and then. But of course Cora was malicious. Always had been. I was just used to it.

"Oh, she wasn't so easy," Dr. Barron said, "until I had said my say and she was sure it pleased her. Oh, that weeping and that wailing and that gnashing of teeth, it was put-on all right." (And he'd know what was put-on. I couldn't doubt it.) "Sorry," said he, "*she* was not. But she was sinning. For I count it not a good sound thing to be full of hate for another. Now, the young man, Charley. He was one she's mad at."

"Oh?" I said faintly. "You mean my cousin, Charley Ives? Why, I guess they quarreled. But Cora doesn't hate Charley. They were married once, but it was a friendly divorce."

Dr. Barron looked at me kindly. "Did you think there was such a thing, my dear?"

"But *tell* me. . . ."

"Now, my dear, what am I to tell you? That young woman would enjoy the clawing of his bright-blue eyes out. And if she plays she wouldn't, it's only put-on. How can I know why that is? But here we're doing no better than gossiping and we're no farther."

"It's hardly proof," I said, feeling very queer. I pulled myself together. "Dr. Barron, did the police ever show you a picture of Edward Jones?"

"He that leaped out into the path, the day, and grabbed her? They did, indeed, show me a picture but I was too far. If he's the man who's dead, I should be sorry I did not swear it was *two* young women, at the time."

"I don't know how much good it would have done," I murmured.

"It's kind of you to comfort me," said that darling man. But he needed nobody's comfort. He was *tough,* my Dr. Barron, in the most wonderful way.

"Now, here's Jane," he said, "and you'll have the dish of soup she's fixed and the bite or two on top of that and you'll spend what's left of the night on the couch which I'm told is fair comfortable."

"I can't spend the night, thank you. I requested a seat to Los Angeles, and if they've got one for me, I must go. I haven't much time."

Mrs. Barron said, "Ah, dear, can you sleep on them planes so up in the air as they are?"

Dr. Barron said with the most wonderful smile, "Why not? I see, my dear, you mean to find out what is behind it all. You are very angry with these women."

"Yes," I said. "I am very angry."

"Good," said he.

But I wasn't going to put on anything. "I don't know . . . I don't care if it's good or not," I said, nearly in tears. "If I can I'm going to stop them."

"I thought I would tell you," he said gently, "it's not always a bad thing to be angry. For I can see you are not used to it. Eat now, while I'm thinking if there is anything at all that I can do."

He hadn't remembered anything more before I found the airline had a seat for me and I left them in a rush, but feeling as if I were tearing myself away from my home. While I was borne in the dark over the mountain snow and over the desert cold, I had the deepest conviction that their prayers rode with me. So I lay in my seat and I cried a little bit. And I felt better.

Although all I had found out about Darlene Hite was her hands, her voice, and the businesslike state of her soul.

Chapter Twelve

MUCH BEDRAGGLED, I got to Los Angeles in the morning, took the airport bus to a hotel downtown, and checked in, but not to rest. I washed my travel-dingy collar and cuffs which (being nylon) dried while I washed myself.

There was nothing in the papers about Marcus, not yet. I didn't call Washington or try to tell Charley Ives where I was or why. I had nothing very solid to offer. I considered where to begin here. As I dressed, I thought of renting a car and driving out to Cameroon Canyon. But I realized there was no point in talking to Patrick Davenport. He hadn't, according to all accounts, seen or heard anything whatsoever outside his house the night of the murder. I knew he was a lean, dynamic man who dominated, wherever he was, talked very fast, and was impossible to interrupt. I didn't think it would help to tangle with him.

So I went to the police.

I was put into the presence of a sober, spruce young man, Sergeant Bartholomew. He had a plain face, a steady eye, a clear soft voice, and he seemed to carry responsibility quietly, as a matter of course, although I soon felt him to be both sensitive and subtle. He repeated my name politely and I knew at once that he recognized it and me and had placed me. I told him I'd come from New York to talk about the murder of Ed Jones. "I want you to tell me things," I said. "I don't suppose you will, unless I tell you some things first."

"It might be a good idea," he said with a smile.

So I told him all about the fifth dream, in the hospital, and Cora and Raymond Pankerman and the blue envelope. I knew I'd have to and I knew it was safe to do so. I didn't have to argue the implications. His plain face grew stern.

"Marcus is my great uncle," I said, "but you know Marcus, too, and this weird lie they are telling must be exposed. I don't know what's going on in Washington. I've been talking to Josephine Crain and Angelo Monti and Dr. Barron, so far. Now, I want to find out from you. . . ." I couldn't state what I wanted to find out.

"We want to find out, too," said he. "Did those people tell you anything useful?"

"There are *two* women, Mr. Bartholomew. There must be. And all these people think so." I told him what I had gleaned. So little. "No proof," I ended.

He was smiling over Dr. Barron. "Oh," he said easily, "there are two women, all right. The other one is the one we are looking for, too."

"You think she killed Ed Jones?"

"We think she'll know a lot about it."

"Angelo Monti identified Ed Jones, didn't he?"

"He more or less did. We have to be careful about a single identification from a photograph by a man with poor eyes."

"I suppose so," I said somewhat dejectedly.

He looked directly at me. "This Cora Steffani wasn't in any trance state on the night of March twenty-sixth, was she?"

"No. Why?"

"Ed Jones was seen in a bar with a woman that night."

"Here in Los Angeles? Was she like Cora?"

"The description's not very detailed. She probably was the right height and coloring."

"Nobody saw a woman on Cameroon Canyon Drive, the night of the twenty-eighth, when Cora *said* she walked there in the dream?"

"Nobody."

"Patrick Davenport didn't?"

"He sure wishes he had," grinned the sergeant. "He's called me up six times with queer noises to report that he's just remembered and so on." He shook his head. "Nobody saw her, Miss Hudson. She wasn't there."

"Of course Cora wasn't there."

"Neither was her double. I don't think any slight five-foot-four woman—that's your own build, Miss Hudson—dragged a big man's body out of a car into those ferns." (I suppose I shuddered.) "I wouldn't be surprised if the accomplice had an accomplice," he said, watching to see what I would make of this.

"Do you know anything about this double?" I pleaded.

"I don't know whether I do." He gave me that direct and thoughtful look again.

"Did you show the people in that bar Cora Steffani's picture?" He smiled and I said hastily, "I mean, what did they say, when you did?"

"They can't be sure. Don't want to be sure." I could tell he was hesitating; there was something he could tell me. I just sat across the desk and stubbornly waited for him to do so. "We get what you might call rumors," he said. (I knew he was still trying to make up his mind about something else.) "This Jones may have been seen in Texas. May have been seen in Nevada."

"Does that help?"

"If he was in Texas, it was with a woman. In Nevada, they think he was alone."

"Who *was* Ed Jones?" I asked.

The sergeant rubbed his chin. "You know Cora Steffani very well, I guess."

"Very well. For seventeen years."

"I'd like to show you something." He had made up his mind. He reached inside the desk. "More or less my own little idea," he said, "but a check is being made, just in case. I want you to look at this page and tell me what you see."

He had a brown imitation-leather book, a high school annual. He showed me a group picture, class of 1939. "Now, this"—he tapped a face in the back row—"is Edward Jones."

I looked at the glum, self-conscious young face. It only slightly resembled the rather horrible newspaper pictures of an older Ed Jones in death. I'd never seen the face alive, I knew. I glanced up at Sergeant Bartholomew. He was stubbornly just waiting. He wanted me to see something of my own accord.

So I looked back at the page and my eye ran through the ranks. All these lost, no longer existing faces, so young and so self-conscious, each so convinced that all the world was watching him. When I gasped, the sergeant handed me a magnifying glass so quickly it was as if he had pulled it out of the air. The last girl in the first row was looking off haughtily to the right. She had Cora Steffani's nose.

She seemed to be a blonde. The chin was not too like, nor the brow. "That nose!" said I. And looked among the names and found, for the first time, and seared it into my memory, her name. Darlene Hite. "But that would be the *one!*" I cried. "*She* must have known

Ed Jones. And it's Cora's nose, exactly! What are you doing about this?"

"Checking," said he.

"It hasn't been in the papers."

"A nose isn't a lot to go on. You have to stop and think, Miss Hudson. It's not our business to injure innocent people. Suppose this Hite girl was married and had a few kids and lived quietly someplace? The publicity in this thing is murder, you know. I'll tell you this, though. If you recognize that nose as easy and quick as you did, well, it sure must be like." I thought he seemed pleased.

"Do you know anything about this Darlene Hite?"

"Comes of a big family. Fifth child, two younger than she." (His grammar astonished me.) "No money. Darlene came to Hollywood and found some motion picture work." (People in and around Hollywood speak of "motion pictures" not "movies." Just as a pilot speaks of an "airplane" not a "plane.") "She lost out, I guess. She was working in a nightclub, up until last fall."

"Where is she now?"

He looked at me with a light in his eye. "She's missing," he said with a certain amount of satisfaction.

"Missing!"

"Dropped out of sight. Left the job. Said nothing to anybody. A misleading postal card is all the sign of her."

"Since last fall!"

"That's right."

"You *are* looking for her?"

"We sure are."

"Then, she's *not* married with kids and all that," I reproached him.

"She is not. We turned up that much so far. But still a nose in an old picture isn't much to go on and we don't know enough."

I seemed to have heard this before. "But it's so important," I cried. "Marcus is going to be crucified. The publicity will be murder for him. Wouldn't the newspapers, the public, help you find this Darlene Hite? Shouldn't you let them try?"

"It's a question, all right," said the sergeant judiciously. "But if this Darlene Hite *is* the double who's been in on these stunts, then the general reading public isn't going to notice her around because she'll take care. Whereas, if Darlene Hite has nothing to do with it, then we should be able to locate her pretty soon and easily, without excitement. Follow me?"

"I guess so," I said reluctantly. "But. . . ."

"Oh, we'll find her. It's not up to me to release her name and description but I can tell you this. If it seems best, then they will be released." He was proud of his job and his colleagues, I could see.

"Are you asking me to keep quiet?"

He said, "I wouldn't have told you, Miss Hudson, if I hadn't thought you were a reasonable and balanced person. I don't expect you to go hysterically to some tabloid. I know you're pretty anxious, but we'll find her."

"How soon? It has to be soon. Could I make a long-distance call on your telephone? I'll pay. I think . . . don't you? . . . we'd better know what's going on in Washington."

"I was wondering how I was going to find out," he said and shoved his phone over.

I called Marcus' very private number. Johnny Cunneen answered. "Where are you, Ollie? Charley's been having a fit."

"I'm in Los Angeles. How is Marcus?"

"Oh Lord, Ollie, it's a mess."

"Is it?" I wailed. "How?"

"Look, Ollie, I was *there* in the damn park. Not a soul spoke to Marcus or gave him a *thing*. There *was* no dame in any gray coat."

"But that's good. Isn't it?"

"Nobody believes me."

"What do you mean, nobody believes you? Why not?"

"Because I'm Marcus' boy, that's why. The idea is, I'd die for him. So naturally, I'd lie for him."

"*Who* doesn't believe you?"

"Ned Dancer, for one. He practically called me a liar."

"Is he *there?*"

"He got away," said Johnny in a voice of despair, "and all hell's going to break loose. . . . Wait. Here's Charley."

Charley Ives barked across the continent. "Ollie, for God's sake, where are you and why?"

"I'm in Los Angeles, finding things out. What's happening there?"

"That damned blue envelope—"

"Oh, no!"

"Oh, yes! Ned called the hospital back this morning and I, like a fool, let him do it."

"You had him there, at Marcus'?"

"We practically had him in chains. But listen. Cora, damn her eyes, told Doc Harper after we left, and she told Ned Dancer this morning, that she saw Marcus put the envelope inside the jacket of a book. Said it was a lurid-looking jacket and the title had the word 'stranger' in it. I'll bet she deliberately saved that bit for Ned's ear, so I couldn't suppress anything. Well, of course, when Ned hung up he poked around on Marcus' shelves. How could I stop him? *And it was there.*"

"Oh, no," I moaned.

"Thriller *I'd* sent him in a big bundle, *two months ago.*"

"Oh, Charley . . . How *could* they?"

"Yeah, how could they? Those books were wrapped in our own shipping department. Thin little envelope, seemed to be stuck to the binding. Ned got it out. We may be able to prove it was glued. As if a little glue was enough to stop this thing." His voice faded.

"Did Marcus have that book with him?"

"In the park? Of course not."

"Then. . . ."

"And how's he going to prove he didn't have it? Everybody thinks Johnny and Ruthie and all of them would lie for Marcus."

"Was the envelope bad, Charley?"

"Pretty bad," he said so quietly that my heart stopped. "We've got the envelope, but Dancer read the note. And what's worse, in the turmoil and confusion, he got away."

"How is Marcus?"

"The same," Charley's voice fell in descending tones of sorrow.

"Wait, Charley. Hang on, please." I repeated much of this rapidly to Sergeant Bartholomew. "I'm going to tell him about this Darlene Hite. I want you to agree. You see. . . ." I began to flounder and bite my tongue. "There are . . . I mean, there must be . . . may be other kinds of police organizations that could help find her." He nodded. "She *has* to be found. Please, won't *you* tell him?"

Sergeant Bartholomew said briskly, "No. You go ahead, Miss Hudson. I'll want you to talk to my boss." So he left the room and I told Charley Ives about Darlene Hite.

I heard him sigh. "Teacher," he said much more cheerfully, "you revive me. I'll get Bud Gray on it. Of course, she may not be the right one."

"Of course," I repeated, "she may not be." But our hope pulsed on the wire, just the same, that she was.

"Let me talk to your policeman. Wait. What are you going to do now? Come back here, will you?"

"There?"

"Marcus would like to see you. I have an idea you can be useful."

"How?"

"I want you to help me get the truth out of the one we know has got it. The one we know where to find. It's got to be done, Ollie."

"Cora?" said I.

"How soon can you get a plane?"

"I don't know."

"Hurry. And don't go near Cora. Come here first." Charley's voice got sharp and stern. "Don't let her know that you're not still standing by. Maybe you don't like that, but it's damned necessary."

"I'll see you," I said, "probably by morning."

"Coz, you heard what I said?"

"I heard. I want to poke about L.A. a little more."

"Ollie," said he, "I hate to tell you this but the Los Angeles Police Department is on the telephone. I can even talk to them anytime I want. You don't need to get their information by a personal interview, you know. Now come home, coz. All is forgiven."

"Charley, my boy," I said, nettled, "expect me when you see me."

I gave the phone to Sergeant Bartholomew, who had come back. Afterward, he and his boss and I talked for an hour. (I never did pay for that phone call.) After that, the sergeant and I went to the ratty little nightclub where Darlene Hite had been employed.

We found a girl singer and a man who played in the band, both of whom had known Darlene. For an experiment, I turned myself into Cora Steffani. I'm a pretty good mimic. I spoke in her affected voice and I lit a cigarette in her exaggerated way, with the eyes squinted against the smoke, with the wide flapping of the fingers to shake the match out, with the arm moving full length from the shoulder to flick ashes in a receptacle placed that far away. I not only used her flying gestures, I used what I knew of her inner attitude. I became alert for my own advantage, slightly mischievous, inquisitive, and full of schemes and yearnings. "Darlene Hite was about my size?" I asked. "Was she like me?" I let my hands plead, as Cora's do.

"Darlene had blond hair," the singer said. "What do you want to know all this for? I told you, she's in Vegas. I got a postcard."

The sergeant said quietly, "She's not in Vegas."

"Do I remind you of her?" I said in Cora's bursting manner.

"She isn't *anything* like you," the boy said distastefully.

I raised my brows and slid my eyes to the corners as Cora does.

"Darlene isn't so *nervous,*" he said. "She don't keep waving her arms around."

"Does she smoke?" asked the sergeant.

"Yeah, but not like that. Darlene, she sticks a cigarette in her face and that's it. She don't make a big thing out of it." He stared at me with a kind of stolid disgust.

"She doesn't talk like that," the singer said. "Not so Eastern and fawncy. Darlene isn't trying to make herself so damn glamorous," she blurted. Evidently they didn't like me one bit.

"What's it about?" the boy glowered.

I changed. I let my hands fall and be heavy. I spoke a trifle nasally. "More like this?"

Now, they stared indeed. "What goes on?" the boy said suspiciously. "Darlene's okay. Minds her business. I don't feel like answering questions."

"She works for a living," the singer said severely.

"I'm trying to find her, that's all," I said in my own voice. "Tell me anything you can about her. How does she walk? Does she turn her toes in or out? Has she any pet gesture?" I worked on it as I sometimes work on a characterization with my girls. I got them to say that Darlene walked, bent forward from the hips, and carried her head forward. That she smiled with her lips closed. But it was so slight. Almost nothing. The shadow of Darlene Hite against the mists of nothing was very thin.

Nor was there anything they could tell us about Darlene's departure. Nobody had come. No letter. No phone call had been noticed. Darlene had not said what her new job was or who had hired her. They despised us for not believing she was in Las Vegas.

I said to the Sergeant when we left, at last, "I may have overdone it, acting Cora Steffani. But was it just coincidence that they mentioned the hands, and the voice, and the businesslike attitude?"

The sergeant said, "It was very interesting, Miss Hudson." And our eyes met and both of us privately believed that Cora's traveling second body was Darlene Hite, all right. I've never seen a better demonstration of the difference between belief and knowledge.

Well, I went back on my tracks, hotel, airport. When I got on the plane for Chicago, one of my fellow passengers was Kent Shaw.

Chapter Thirteen

WHEN I GOT on the plane at 8:00 P.M. a late Los Angeles paper had the story, printed cautiously in a small box, full of hedges and alleges, about Marcus and Raymond Pankerman, *Dream Walker carries mystery message?* Ned Dancer had got away and the story was out and the fierce light was going to beat on Marcus and the jabber would begin and I felt sick.

Kent Shaw saluted me with appropriate surprise. He got out of his aisle seat and peered down the plane's length for two empties, side by side, assuming that we would so travel. But I quickly sat down in the aisle seat opposite his. I was tired, having had no real sleep in something like thirty-six hours, and I wasn't going to stay awake and talk if I could help it—not to hear his sour comments. I was feeling failure; time had run out. I wanted to be alone.

Just as soon as we were all buckled in and the door locked, Kent Shaw inclined his head. "What are you doing out here, Ollie? I thought you taught school nine days a week."

"Flying trip, obviously," said I. "Business."

His eyes were jumpy. He looked as tense and bouncy as usual, as if only the seat strap held him down. "What do you mean, business?" he demanded.

"My business," I said, making a big bright smile as rude as possible.

"Excuse me, I'm sure." He subsided with a grimace of his own. We lumbered in mysterious figure-eights over the field. After a while,

Kent unfastened his belt and leaned over. "I see your friend, Cora, is at it again." He looked moist at the mouth, almost as if he licked his lips over this. "Notice the paper?"

I felt revolted. He was to me a symbol of the pawing and fingering, the terrifying curiosity of millions. And I was exhausted, but he *would* talk. He was bursting with talk. "Excuse me, Kent," I said. "I've got to do my laundry."

"What?"

I fled to the tiny washroom where the roar and the rattle of flight is so loud. Conquering my sickness, pulling myself to numb but anyhow calmer acceptance, and taking what comfort I could from the homely chore, I washed out my collar and cuffs once more, while we bounced a little over the pass and streaked out above the desert land.

When at last I went back to my seat, Kent Shaw was humped over, apparently dozing. I softly asked for a pillow and a blanket and spread my laundry, nearly dry already, to hang over the edge of the seat pocket before me. I went to sleep.

I've wondered. Did I save my life by doing my laundry? Would I have been enticed into telling Kent Shaw that I had heard of Darlene Hite? Would he then have thought I knew too much? I suppose not. After all, he couldn't get rid of the Los Angeles Police Department. And I didn't talk. I didn't tell him. But would he have taken fright, if I had? Did I save Cora's life, for then, by doing my laundry?

Now I can guess he was panting to know what I, so close to Marcus, was thinking and doing. But he tried to seem, of course, less eager than he was.

Anyhow, stupid with sleep in Chicago, I changed planes for Washington, and since Kent Shaw stayed on for New York, I got away. I had no paraphernalia. It was only a matter of slipping on my coat and walking out with the leg stretchers. If Kent Shaw had been working at some cautious way to pump me between Chicago and New York, he was disappointed.

The morning paper had a bigger, juicier story. Oh, it was out and it would soon be roaring.

Marcus was just the same, just the same. I hadn't wired. I took a cab to his house. Charley Ives grabbed me with both hands and smacked my cheek. "What, no suitcase? Come in, coz. There's a council of war." He was kind, but I suddenly felt very feeble. What had I been doing that was any good?

Marcus has a room full of books and papers, deep in the house, and there I found him and embraced him and he was just the same. Not a man who bewails cruel fate or cries, Oh, why have they done this to me! He looked his usual blend of spryness and serenity. And if he was hurt in his feelings he didn't bother to express it. "Well, Ollie, I hear you've done some detective work, too."

"Not much, Uncle John." I looked around.

Bud Gray was there, calm and alert. Johnny Cunneen was there, miserably angry. Little Ruthie Miller's nose was pink with woe. Sig Rudolf was there. (He is a lawyer and an in-law.) His broad face, and even his scalp where the hair recedes, was mottled red-and-white, as if his effort to suppress distress and rage were only skin deep. Charley Ives, however, looked easier than I had last seen him. He'd been in action. He and Bud Gray were men of action. They understood fighting, and the waiting involved, too, and all sorts of real things. I could feel I was in the presence of professionals.

As I told them all I knew, I could see that over and above what a real detective had discovered it was scarcely anything. I don't think they were impressed by my wispy bits of description. All of that seemed feeble and feminine and fairly useless.

They began to tell me what they knew. They had already dug up three people who had been in the park at half past two, day before yesterday, on the fifth of May. Who all admitted they had watched Marcus, he being a celebrity. Two of them had seen no one approach him. The third one said he had seen a woman in a gray coat speak to Marcus and hand him a piece of paper.

"He did not," Gray said. "He's the kind of witness who doesn't even know he is lying. Remembers, to suit what he thinks the facts are."

Charley said, *"He's* talked to reporters already. *He'd* be the one."

"Oh, there'll be more such witnesses," Gray said. "Some of them will have seen it all in a dream."

Johnny Cunneen said, "I was on the next bench, keeping an eye out, as I always do. But me they don't listen to." He held his head.

"Pankerman admits to being in the park," Charley said to me, "and all three witnesses say they saw *him*. We don't doubt he was there."

"Did you see him, Uncle John?"

"Neither Johnny nor I saw him," said Marcus. "I suppose he kept around that corner, behind the trees."

"Does Raymond Pankerman admit he asked that favor of a strange woman? Does he admit he gave her an envelope?"

"Oh, no. No, indeed. Not at all. For the rest, he stands just as he said he would, on the Fifth Amendment." Gray looked disgusted.

"So as not to incriminate himself," Charley said. "And that's devilish. Because he does incriminate himself, and Marcus, too."

"He has been behind this entire sequence," Marcus said.

"Pankerman!" I was astonished.

"Of course." Charley ticked off points. "In the park at the right moment. Lying, by this damned device of keeping suspiciously still. His name, his handwriting on the note in the blue envelope. Of course, he's behind it."

"Why?"

Then Marcus told me how his own hunch had been Pankerman's fall.

"Just for *revenge?*" cried I. "Why, that's . . . that's. . . ." I had no words for what I thought it was. Personal revenge seemed pitifully small and out of place against the scale of this affair. Personal revenge has been almost outlawed by doctrines of "adjustment" and self-analysis. The whole battery of popular psychology is trained in the opposite direction. Even violence, even war, is no longer thought of as revenge. But it *is,* I thought. Revenge is *exactly* what heats the blood. We *want* revenge. We *want* to punish. Oh Lord, I thought, who can be wise? What human being—when his blood, his glands, the motivations of his energies are so designed? I knew Marcus would say, as Dr. Barron would say: Anger is ours, built in our blood, to move our bodies. We can't deny it. It's just that our brains must tell us what shall make us angry.

"What was in the envelope?" I asked. God knows *I* was angry.

"It's locked up," said Charley, "with a couple of handwriting experts. Purports to be a windup, in Pankerman's handwriting (and I'll bet that's genuine, myself), of some secret and damnable dealings between him and Marcus. Winding up, because Pankerman is going to be incapacitated. There's enough implied, and just enough, to be damned cleverly convincing."

"Convincing?"

"Some people are going to think I am a traitor," Marcus said and

I, thinking of all the stainless years behind him, thought my heart would break.

"No, they won't," I cried. "We'll stop it. How did they get the envelope into the book? Charley, you should know that."

Charley said, "I've had our place turned upside down. It would have been too easy. Anybody, dropping around, could have wandered into the shipping department. Anybody with the slightest cover of a reason to see me, for instance, or any one of the editors. Or it could have been a boyfriend of a clerk. Even a fake inspector of some kind. *When* it was done, we can roughly guess because we know the shipping date. March tenth. But I send Marcus books every month. Not hard to know."

"The envelope was glued in?"

"We think it was. They didn't want it to fall out, of course. But it was done by gluing a corner of the gummed strip on the envelope itself and who can prove it didn't *happen* to fold out, *happen* to stick?"

I was silent, appalled.

"Pankerman is in it and Cora Steffani is in it, and this Darlene Hite is very possibly the other woman."

"I'm sure she is," I said.

"And the whole thing," said Charley Ives, "has been working up to this."

Ruthie Miller, with her tiny hands clenched, said, "They are just fiends!" I saw Marcus smile at her.

"I can see, vaguely," I said, "why Pankerman might do it. I suppose he had to use Darlene or somebody else who looks as much like Cora. What I don't understand—why would Cora Steffani want to hurt Marcus? Or . . . or you, Charley? Or . . ." I floundered, "or *me* for that matter? She knows how we feel about Marcus. Is she doing this to me and to you, just for the notoriety?"

Charley said impatiently, "Teacher, she *is* doing it."

"But I thought you and she were . . . almost together again. I know you're fond of her. You *like* a rascal. I understand that. And I've rather liked her myself. What motive overpowers that . . . well, call it fondness?"

Charley looked at me with pity. Gray said, "Guessing why isn't going to help us find this Darlene Hite. Which is what we've got to do. An awful lot of people are looking for her, right now. But if she killed that man in L.A., believe me, she could be out of the country."

"I wonder," said Marcus. We all listened. "Tell me," said the old gentleman, "if these people worked out this plan, as they must have done, far in advance and in great detail, could such a plan include this killing?"

"No," I said. "Of course not. Ed Jones happened to recognize the other woman in Chicago. So they had to keep him quiet. Of course, they couldn't have planned on killing him from the beginning. I don't think even Cora—" I stopped. (Why *even* Cora? Did I think Cora was blood-driven, then? Cora would take revenge? For what?)

"How did this woman, Cora, *know* he'd be dead in the ferns on March twenty-eighth?" asked Marcus.

"Perhaps she didn't," I said. "She *was* shocked. I remember. Don't you, Charley?"

"She expected something dead," Charley reminded me. "But I agree. I don't think she expected it to be human."

"Then," said Marcus, pursuing his own lucid line of reasoning, "there was a change in plan, and the question is, how were these two women in communication?"

"A change, sir?"

"Isn't it too much to suppose that they had for many weeks planned for something to be dead in those ferns so that when it became necessary to kill a man, he fitted right in?"

"Ned Dancer had the switchboard operator bribed and Mildred Garrick was paying the maid," Charley said, surprising me, "and Ollie was there all along. Kept there no doubt to observe that there *was* no communication."

"I observed none," I said unhappily.

Marcus gave me a swift loving look. "But they changed a plan. They did communicate. Now, I would like to suppose there had been no Ed Jones. What was the original plan, before they changed it?"

"Oh, I suppose more stuff," said Charley. "A few more well-known people, until they had drawn enough attention."

"Would it have been quite so violently publicized," said Marcus, "without that dead man?"

"I see what you mean, sir," said Charley. "That dead body is the one thing that really put this show on the road. But that was an afterthought. A revision."

"Yes. So I wonder," said Marcus, "if they had been left with the original scheme only, would they not be planning yet another of these . . . occurrences. A capper incident, to sandwich me in the middle and help the excitement along?"

We considered this. It seemed *right* to me. A deliberate anti-climax. A good showman faking a show not to look like a show might do that.

"They don't need it now," Gray said.

"But when you suggested that Darlene Hite has left the country," Marcus turned to him, "I began to wonder if her job is quite over. Somebody very clever has designed this thing."

"How, in the name of heaven," cried Johnny Cunneen, leaving off worrying his fingernails with his teeth, "can you *guess* what they'll do, if they *are* planning another one? It may be anywhere in the whole country. It can happen to any one of thousands of people. It lasts about five minutes. You can't set any trap."

Charley said, "But if you could, Darlene Hite would walk right into it."

Gray shook his head. "She's too smart," he said didactically.

"Just the same," said Charley, "on a bare chance, I think we'll try to be ready."

"How can you?" cried Ruthie.

"Have a plane set to go. Do that much. It only costs money. First sign of any trance, we can take off, and with luck. . . . After all, this Hite woman does not really vanish into thin air."

"She does about as well," said Gray.

Charley looked stubborn. Sig Rudolf cleared his throat. He was about to say something ponderous. But I said, "Charley, my boy, I hate to tell you this. But wherever Cora may walk in a dream, there'll be folks, and if folks, then probably a telephone. We're not getting anywhere. We can't just wait and hope Cora does it again and chase around in airplanes . . ." (which was absurd for air-worn me to be saying). "That's so feeble," I sputtered. "While Marcus is going to be hurt." (*Is* being hurt, I thought.) "What *are* the reactions?"

"Grim faces," Gray told me, "around the Capitol."

"Everybody knows," said Charley, and now he was up and walking around, "that Marcus is no liar. But, damn it, the thing has got to be explained."

"But we *can* explain it, can't we?" Ruthie said. "It's just a plot against him."

"Baby," said Charley Ives, "we have to explain with bells on. We have to do it down to the last hook and eye. We got to get confessions and tape recordings and cross-examinations and witnesses and breakdowns and the works."

Sig Rudolf said, "Certainly. Then you can sue, and get it into the courts, where there is some orderly machinery. In centuries of struggle, we've figured out the best way men know yet to get at the truth, expose the guilty, protect the innocent, and if we now bypass the work of these centuries and accuse and convict and sentence a man by gossip and rumor—"

"Sig," said Charley patiently. *"We know.* Unfortunately, there's no law that I ever heard about which says a woman *mustn't* be in two places at once, if she can manage to do the trick. We can hardly drag Cora into court for that. Let's get on, shall we? Now that Ollie's back."

"Tell me what I can do?" I said.

"Pankerman is sitting behind a mass of lawyers, three deep. Darlene Hite is not available. But Cora Steffani is in that hospital where I was smart enough to put her and keep her handy. So Cora Steffani is our bird-in-hand, and she has got to be broken down until she tells us. Now, you, Ollie, are going to stand by Cora for auld lang syne. . . ." I began to shake my head. "Even the lie about Marcus," continued Charley, "while it upsets you, still can't wean you from your high principles. Can it? You have no proof that Marcus didn't do it. You don't believe in condemning people."

"No," I cried. "No."

"Ollie, you're going to have to."

"I *can't* pretend to be that stupid," I flared. "Cora's not that gullible. She knows what I think of Marcus. The whole world knows."

"Loyalties," said Charley, "conflict. Yeah. Well, somehow or other, you've got to keep on being her only friend. I don't care how you handle it."

"How can I pretend to be her friend when she's lying about Marcus? There's a limit to what's plausible."

"I'm telling you what you can do to help," he said. (Charley Ives and I were going to fight.) "You asked me. Act, why don't you? Use your art."

"You don't even understand what it *is*," I cried.

"Make-believe, isn't it?" he snapped. "How have you managed to stick around being loyal to her since Ed Jones died? Keep *that* up."

(I couldn't imagine how I'd managed. I didn't know.) "I was wrong," I cried. "Absolutely stupid and wrong. But what I'm trying to tell you, for me to step out of character. . . ."

"Just be yourself, Teacher," said Charley. "Just be a kind of unshakable saint, sweetly naïve, nobly aloof, devoted to principle, and stubborn as an ornery old country mule."

"Charley, my boy," I began, "your childish ideas—"

"Shut up, coz, and listen to me. You've got to be tolerant and kind and loyal and understanding."

"Who says so!" I raged. "And what are *you* going to be?"

"Me, I'm going to be so unnice and caddish and ungentlemanly," said Charley Ives, "that you and she will quite agree. I'll rile her up. She'll turn to you."

"You're a dreamer," I said. "She'll never confess to *me*. Charley, you're a fool!" I was so mad at Charley Ives that I'd forgotten there were other people in the room.

Bud Gray said, calmly, "It's an old police trick, Miss Hudson. The mean cop and the mild sympathetic one, working in a pair."

"I'm to be a policeman, then?"

Marcus said placidly, "You're not a bad actress, Ollie. You're a pretty good one."

I looked at him and the wind blew wider. "Of course, I'll try," I said. "*Anything,* Uncle John. If you think it might work."

"I imagine," said Marcus, "Charley can make her pretty mad if he wants to."

"I don't doubt *that,*" I said. "It's just—"

"It's the only. . . ." Charley put his hands in his pockets as if to keep himself from shaking me. "What can we do but try to upset her and trip her up? She's safe with her mouth shut, so far, and she knows that and all the or-elseing in the world isn't going to make her forget that. But if she gets good and mad at me, I should think she might blurt out something to a female chum." He looked me in the eye. "Yes, it's dirty."

"I don't *care* how dirty it is," I cried. "That doesn't worry me. I'm touched by your little character sketch, Charley, my boy, and your faith and all. But I don't think it will work. You never have understood how it is between Cora and me."

"Likewise, I'm sure," he snapped. "And it's got to work. Come on, let's get going. Try doing what I say." Charley looked dangerous.

"Yes, sir," I said, as humbly as I could which wasn't very. He threw my coat around me. Sig begged a ride in the plane Charley had waiting. Gray was coming, too. We said good-bye to Marcus. Good-bye and good hope.

Chapter Fourteen

CHARLEY AND BUD GRAY sat together and talked while I, beside Sig Rudolf, listened and did not always hear his oratorical fuming. We would be in New York soon after noon, although I'd almost stopped noticing the days go around.

The papers were sniffing at the story now, much more boldly. By nightfall, they would be in full cry. Whoever believed that Marcus would not lie would be wearing graver faces as the uproar increased, ink spilled, tongues wagged. We could deny, deny . . . deny. We could tell all the truth we knew until our faces were blue, and it wouldn't be enough. It couldn't still the voices or stop the ink flowing.

Charley Ives was right. We had to have a fully detailed explanation on our side.

We were nearly in when Charley came over. "Where will you tell Cora you've been?" he asked me crisply. "Better decide."

"Denver, Los Angeles, Washington."

"Why not just Washington, for two nights and a day. You can't explain Los Angeles." His voice became rather gentle. "Ollie, don't you understand? You're going to have to be lying to her."

"I presume," I said stonily, "that when you lie you should try not to get caught at it. Kent Shaw was on the plane out of Los Angeles. Who knows if he's seen her, or seen someone who's told her?"

"I beg your pardon," Charley said. "Kent Shaw have anything to offer?"

"If he did, I didn't take it. I went to sleep."

"You must be tired." He was being cautious and gentle. "It was good of you to go."

"Not much good," I said. I don't like kid gloves.

"Ollie, let's not fight."

"Charley, my boy," I said wearily, "the opposite of fighting isn't, I hope, buttering each other up with patronizing praise. I realize that I am the rankest amateur at this police business, although I must say you're not very good at acting, either. Don't worry about me. I'll try to do as you suggest."

Charley's face was pink. "Sometimes, I can't understand how you can make such thoroughly nasty remarks, while looking as if you were after the Holy Grail," he said. "You scare the life out of me."

"Why?"

"If I didn't know you were a petty thief, I'd be telling myself you *could not* tell a lie."

"Thief!" I squealed.

"Well," he said, cocking a blue eye, "it was more or less my property."

"What was?"

"At least I didn't steal it from you. I stole it from somebody else."

"Charley," I bounced upright, "you are the most exasperating . . . !"

"Well," he said, blotting my sentence and my whole train of thought out, with his sudden deep sadness, "put up with me, Ollie. Let's put up with each other, shall we? For Marcus' sake?"

I was shocked. "There must be some misunderstanding," I murmured.

"I think so," he said. "And I'm a better *actor* than you think. Never mind. Lie your head off to Cora, will you, coz?"

"It'll be lying," I said. "It won't be art, though."

"Do you think," he said through his teeth, *"you're* not exasperating? That fight's thirteen years old."

"Truce. Truce," I said. "I'll be her only friend, the best I can. It's a lousy role, Charley." Tears started in my eyes.

"Aw, Teacher," said Charley softly and touched my hair lightly.

I shivered violently. I couldn't, thereafter, move or look. In another moment, I knew he had gone back to talk with Gray.

I streaked uptown to my apartment and peeled off that detestable blue taffeta dress. My rooms looked like an archeological exhibit, and all my things were relics of a former era.

I hurried out of there to the hospital. I could not . . . could not solidly imagine my role. It was unprepared, undigested, unrehearsed. I knew I was stepping on stage to do what I warned my girls never to do. I was not secure in the part. I didn't understand the woman I was about to present.

Charley was there already. Downstairs, he pounced on me. Bud Gray, he told me, was already hidden in the room next to Cora's, with some listening device against her wall.

"Go first," said Charley. "Establish yourself."

I sighed. "I'll have to try it my own way," I warned him.

"Any way that does it." He was all policeman.

So I went upstairs and tapped on her door.

Cora was wearing a gold-colored robe of silk, embroidered with black dragons. She was sitting in an easy chair, talking to a strange young man. "Why, Ollie! Where have you been!" she exclaimed. But she was more wary than cordial. She knew she had offended me beyond all forgiveness. How could I make her believe otherwise?

"You'd hardly believe where I've been," I said grumpily.

She introduced the young and rather pink-cheeked man as a henchman of Mildred Garrick's. "Press?" said I. "Oh me. . . ."

"In a friendly way, Miss Hudson," the young man said. "Message from Mildred, that's all."

I went over to the high bed and lay myself upon it. "I'm exhausted," I said. "Go on with whatever it is."

"It's nothing," said Cora. "Mildred sends this young snoop around from time to time. Mildred's been . . . kind." (Mildred had been making the most of her inside track.) Cora got up and swished about, the long folds of golden silk boiling about her quick feet. "Ollie, where *have* you been? I thought you'd gone forever."

"I've been detecting," I said.

"Oh?" Cora lit a cigarette in her exaggerated way.

"Where have I not been?" said I. "I've been to Denver, Los Angeles, Washington."

"Since day before yesterday?" she cried prettily. Maybe she hid alarm.

"What's the news?" said the little boy from the newspaper.

"No news." I closed my eyes.

"Then what are you here for?" asked my old friend, Cora. Her voice was ready for weeping or for rage, whichever way the cat would jump. (I was the cat.) "I suppose you want a piece of my scalp," she challenged.

I said, "No."

"No?"

I opened my eyes. "Cora," (I suppose I had on what Charley Ives would call my Holy Grail look) "swear to me that you don't understand this thing. You only know you dream."

Cora looked queer. "Ollie, I swear." Her voice trembled very nicely.

"Two impossible things before breakfast," I misquoted. "Either you are a wicked liar. Or you have strange dreams. Choose one, I suppose."

"Miss Hudson," said the pink-faced lad excitedly, "you think John Paul Marcus *may* be mixed up with Pankerman and that crowd?"

"No, no, no," I said quickly. "I wonder if Pankerman isn't *using* Cora's dream."

"Hey, that's an idea!" he cried. It wasn't much of an idea. "But . . ."—he looked around at Cora in apology—"you do," he said to me, "believe she dreams?"

"What else can I think?" I said. "She might want publicity. She might want notoriety. But to get it by wrecking Marcus . . . I cannot believe she'd do a thing like that to"—I let a beat go by—"people she loves."

Cora chose tears, of course. "Ollie, darling, how can I tell you? I was afraid I'd lost you. Nobody . . . nobody else knows what all this does to me." She was all broken up. "I should have known," she quavered sentimentally, "that *you'd* be fair. You've always been the fairest person I've ever known."

The pink boy went away, all agog.

The moment he was gone, Cora said, suspending her tears. "But I don't know whether to believe you. . . ."

"Don't then," I said. There would be no more tears. We never had been sentimental.

"Why did you tear off all over the country?" she demanded.

"I wanted to know. Talked to Jo Crain, Monti, Dr. Barron."

"Isn't he a lamb?" she cried falsely. (Put-on, I thought.)

"And people in Los Angeles," I told her.

"Davenport?"

"No. Bartholomew. Police."

"Well?"

I shrugged and threw my hands out. "You just are not that clever," I said and the line rang true. Her eyes flickered. "So I don't know what it is," I continued, "and since you swear to me. . . ."

She swished herself around and sat down. "Don't gimlet-eye me, Ollie. There's no way to understand it. I'm sick of trying. *We* don't need to talk about it, do we?"

Silence.

"What are you going to do?" I asked after a while.

"Go abroad, maybe. Run away."

"No vaudeville turns? No confessions?"

"I've had offers."

"I'm glad you're not taking them."

"Bad enough, as it is," she said, playing forlorn.

"Cora, can't the doctors help you?"

"They don't seem to." She accepted this implication quickly. "And I am so tired of this cage. Do you know how long I've been in this hospital? I can't leave it. I feel as if I wouldn't get across the street with my limbs still on."

"No more would you," said I.

Cora sighed deeply. "It's good to have you back. I've been lonely." She looked sideways. "Where is Charley Ives? Do you know?"

I didn't have to produce an answer because Charley Ives was rapping on the door. He came in and the walls bulged. I guessed he'd been next door and had heard much that had been said. I pulled at my skirt and sat up more primly and somewhat defensively.

"Ah, girls," said Charley. "Letting your hair down?" He looked at me as if he'd like to throttle me.

Cora's lids fluttered. Otherwise she was motionless.

"You," said Charley to her with no more preliminaries, "are a liar and a louse. And you," he said to me, "are a fool."

"Well!" said Cora brightly. "This is charming. Do go on."

"Do you think I won't?" Charley put his hands in his pockets. "Cousin Ollie sees no evil. But I never did wear rose-colored glasses. It's Pankerman's money that pays for this prank."

"It doesn't cost anything," said Cora plaintively.

"It will. You're implicated up to your neck in slander and fraud and homicide."

"Am I?" She looked sideways at him. "Why aren't I in jail, then? Wouldn't they have to prove all this, Charley dear?"

"Ah," he said easily, "Darlene Hite can prove it."

Cora was good. Very good. She didn't startle. She was braced, of course. She'd been ready for thunder and lightning from Charley Ives. She didn't even make the mistake of saying, "Who is Darlene Hite?" She said nothing.

I said it. "Who is Darlene Hite?"

"The other one," Charley answered. "The astral body. A real woman with Cora's nose."

"Somebody wants to get in the act," said Cora with superb ennui.

"You're not ill," said Charley. "I'll pay no more bills here. Why should I keep you?" She narrowed her eyes. "Besides," he continued, "since you and Darlene Hite together killed a man, your next stop is jail."

"How could I kill anybody in a dream?" she said mournfully. "Who's this Darlene? Somebody wants her name in the papers, too? What a name! Why don't you bring this Darlene? Before you make corny threats, Charley, dear."

"I'll bring her."

"When?"

"When I'm ready." But Charley just wasn't convincing.

Cora laughed. "Trying to save your precious grandpa?" she mocked. "What did you do? Hire somebody? Are you blaming yourself, Charley, dear?" Now her voice was pure poison. She enjoyed it. "Are you thinking that if only you and I were still married, why, I'd have cut my tongue out, wouldn't I?"

"You'll wish you had," he said, and it looked to me as if he was the one who was going to be enraged.

Cora said, "Oh, Charley, go away. Leave us. Make him go, Ollie." Then, pitifully, "I can't take much more." But she could. She was enjoying it.

Charley said, "I'll tell you what you couldn't take. A man having the guts to say he didn't want you." Muscles tightened in her neck. In mine, too. "Fell for each other, in a big way, didn't we?" Charley said. "All of our dreams came true. Only trouble was, I wasn't quite so deep asleep, and I proceeded to wake up. And had the nerve to say so. Being unwilling to spend the rest of my life in hell, for one mistake. And we had pious speeches, didn't we? About being good friends. And, oh, we were so gay. And lust," said Charley Ives, "for a dirty indirect revenge in your filthy little heart."

Cora was getting angry, now, all right.

"Did you think," said Charley, "that I, who'd had my eyes opened years ago, wouldn't *know?* You're so small you'd get into a scheme like this, just for your name in the papers. But it's peachy-keen, it's jolly fun, isn't it? . . . to ruin John Paul Marcus, while you're at it, for the oldest cliché in the book. The woman scorned."

"You may go," said Cora loftily.

"When you turned on the—shall I say?—full personality," said Charley and, oh, he was insulting, "even then I wouldn't stay married. And you had to play civilized—"

"Get out," said Cora in a voice that was thick and ugly.

Then Charley was calm and smiling. "Poor . . . cheap . . . mean . . . little thing . . ." he drawled. He left us and closed the door softly.

He'd done his share. She looked as if she'd explode. Now it was for me to catch her reaction. To receive the indiscretions born of this rage. But I, I was so absolutely flabbergasted at Charley's tactics that I could hardly pull myself together. I didn't know the role. It was impossible. "Why . . . the . . . conceited . . . ass!" I muttered. It wasn't good. It was dreadfully bad. Put-on, as Dr. Barron would say.

Cora turned around. "Get out," she screamed at me. "Get out, Ollie, darling darling Cousin Ollie. Get out, Teacher!"

I slipped off that high bed. "I shouldn't have heard. I can forget."

"In a pig's eye you'll ever forget," she screeched. "It's water on the desert to you. Think I don't know? You're mad about Charley Ives. You're crazy for him, yourself!"

So I took up my bag. "Call me, if you like," I said as quietly and stolidly as I could. "When you are feeling better. And don't worry about the bills," I said over my shoulder. "I'll stop at the desk and take care of them."

Cora said chokingly, "Just let me alone, you and your noble charity."

"Oh, I will," I said, "whatever you say." (But I tried once more.) "I haven't anything to do," I said, "since I've lost my job, standing by you."

She screamed at me, "Get out!"

So I left her.

Charley Ives met me at the elevator and we rode down silently. In the lobby he said to me, "I was wrong, Teacher. And you were right." He said it straightforwardly with his blue eyes steady.

I wanted to look everywhere but at his face. But I said to his unhappy eyes, "Maybe she'll call me. I think she may."

"Do you?" he said respectfully.

"Because she can use me," I said. "She has, already."

"How, Ollie?"

"Olivia Hudson, Marcus' kin, on the wrong side. And that boy gone running to tell what he heard." Charley winced. "It doesn't matter," I said. "Marcus knows."

Then Bud Gray joined us.

"Anything?" asked Charley.

"Not a sound. Doesn't talk to herself, apparently. Good try." Both of them were sober in defeat.

"What can we do now?" I asked nervously.

"Find Darlene Hite, I guess," said Charley. "Shall I take you home, Ollie?" He was sober and sad and all the thunder and lightning was gone.

"I better go up to school and resign."

"Must you?" Charley was troubled.

"It's a part of the act, I think." I took pity on him. "Now, Charley, my boy, don't look so distressed. You were about as nasty as anyone could possibly be."

His eyes sparked. "Thank you," he said.

"That Cora," said Gray, "sure wasn't having any comfort from you, Ollie."

"She had to scream," I said, "and accuse *somebody* of *something*. Oh, I suppose I irritate her a thousand ways. It's not as if we were together or alike, you know. We began together but we went different ways. We still check each other as if we were each other's measuring sticks. Hard to explain." I stopped mumbling. "I'm not excusing that terrible performance. I was bad."

Gray said, as so many people will, "You did your best."

But Charley said, "If she had, she'd know it."

I wanted to bawl. But I said, "They do say them as can, do. And them as can't, teach. Don't they? Sorry I muffed it." So I got away.

Chapter Fifteen

I WAS PERMITTED to resign without protest. I think I would have been discharged, anyway. Miss Reynolds couldn't understand my position, of course, and even if she had, there was just too much publicity.

Cora did use me. The news went around that I refused to call her a liar. Which implied, no matter how you twisted it or turned it, that I (of all people) thought Marcus might be the one who was lying. So Marcus was being hurt and I was helping. Although my bit was hardly significant in the flood.

Questions were asked in official places. Usually reliable sources and unidentified spokesmen hedged and hinted. Politicians puffed up with loud cries that the people be told. They didn't say what. Committees were rumored. Columnists recapitulated and among them there were the "objective analyzers," the angry partisans, staunch defenders, witty scoffers, and sad reluctant viewers with alarm. Everywhere, the eye met the printed suggestion that there must be more than met the eye.

It *was* released, on our side, that there existed a Darlene Hite, and now the entire nation was looking for her. That high school annual picture and a theatrical photographer's highly retouched version of her grown-up face were printed everywhere, side by side with Cora's. Nobody found her.

Charley Ives went to Washington the following Monday. Bud Gray stood by in New York. There was a plane ready. A forlorn hope.

Cora stayed, secluded and protected, in that hospital. I paid the bills (a fact that got out and hurt Marcus, too). She kept to her story. What else was she to do? She was safe as long as she did. She could read. She knew from the newspapers how we had heard of Darlene Hite. She also knew we couldn't find her.

Raymond Pankerman (although he was in the toils, personally) must have been gratified. Marcus was being hurt.

As for Kent Shaw, he was seen in his usual haunts and he joined, naturally enough, in the endless discussions. But we gave him no thought. Why should we?

Happy little man. Swelling to the point of madness, scurrying shabbily about, with the great secret of his masterpiece, his swan song, bathing his veins with joyous self-congratulations. Reading and listening and swelling, swelling with that poisonous pride!

I was right. Cora did call me. The mere existence of a Darlene Hite, acquainted with Ed Jones, had done us some good. At least, it was fuel for theories on our side. So maybe Cora felt she needed to flaunt me. Maybe she was thinking of those bills. Anyhow, she called me, on Monday, and I went.

She made an apology. Said she'd been upset.

I, groping for my part, said that Charley obviously had been trying to upset her. And Charley had been nasty.

"I loathe him," said Cora.

"Naturally," I said.

Cora looked at me oddly. "But Charley's psychology wasn't bad," she said airily. "If a woman did want a man she couldn't have, she'd protect herself."

"How do you mean?" said I.

"Why, she'd cover it up. She'd seem to . . . dislike him. Don't you think so, Ollie?"

I shrugged for an answer, while Cora watched and licked her lip. Then, in mutual relief, we left that subject. It almost seemed that we were back in the old arrangement. We were as we had been, old acquaintances, neither of us altogether fond or trusting, but still each other's habits, and able to stay in the same room, part hostile, part resigned.

So I was there when Kent Shaw turned up, to call. (Perhaps he took care to see that someone should be. It was no time for him to be seeing Cora alone.) He came glumly, that afternoon, and hadn't much to say. It was, I thought, a concession to pure curiosity, which he resented in himself. This is what he did say. "Cora, dear, why don't you go to Spain? Or Rome? Very pleasant in Spain. And Rome is charming."

"I very well may," she told him.

"Book passage, then," he urged. "Ten days ahead, at least."

Cora said somewhat impatiently, "I know."

"Doesn't cost too much and well worth it to get away. You can afford it, can't you?"

"I expect so," she murmured.

"Tell me when to send the usual basket of fruit." Kent rose to go. Cora grimaced. "Oranges? Dates?"

"No lemons, dear," Kent said. (This seemed to me to be somewhat inane.)

"Sugared fruit, Kent darling," Cora said, "if you really want to please me."

"Of course," Kent said, "we want to please you. Don't we, Ollie?" And Kent went away.

I thought it was feeble persiflage, chatter, nothing. What they were really saying to each other, I didn't hear. I can hear it now.

HE: It will be over soon.

SHE: Yes.

HE: Ten days from now.

SHE: I know. I remember.

HE: Then you will be rewarded.

SHE: I expect to be.

HE: I expect to pay.

SHE: I know the date.

HE: Don't fail. No lemons wanted.

SHE: Just be ready with the sugar, the money.

He agreed. And I sat by, her old friend who knew her well, and asked her when he had gone if she really thought of leaving the country. She said she had really thought of it. She said she was weary of all the public uproar. It occurred to me to wonder how she could afford it. But that was all.

So time dragged on, ten more days of it. And it was a dreadful time. Hard-headed investigators, of course, took no stock in the supernatural. But they could not find Darlene although hundreds of women with noses anything like Cora's had been crucified for a day. And now the gags began. Wisecrackers called Darlene Hite a white herring. Marcus was being red-washed, some said. And this frothy stuff hurt him and cheapened him, and broke my heart.

Worse, of course. The envelope had been in Marcus' house, and none could explain who had put it there or how. Unless it had been handed to Marcus in the park, where Raymond Pankerman had been, at the right time. No one could explain how, if Pankerman was behind it all, how . . . how . . . how could Cora Steffani in New York know what she had known.

. . . What Dr. Barron would say on a given afternoon in Colorado . . . the look of the book that Marcus owned . . . and always the dead man in the ferns . . . that hardy haunt would rise.

Even so, I didn't know how bad it was for Marcus until the day Charley Ives came back, the twentieth of May, and met me in the little snack bar at the hospital.

If Marcus went to the park, Charley told me, knots of people tended to gather. They would keep their distance but they stared without pleasure, uneasy, doubtful, hideously curious. That was the public. Marcus no longer went, every day, to the park.

What was happening to him privately, Charley said, was hard to define, impossible to prevent. A thing as uncapturable as a breeze. The withdrawing of respect and confidence. Softly, without proclamation, people withdrew. They did not cry angry disillusion or even cut him dead. But it was not the same anymore. Secrets were not spilled out to him in perfect flow. Problems were not opened before him, pro and con, in full detail. His advice was not asked for. His store of wisdom and experience was not drawn upon, but rested, unused, unregarded. Charley said it was a spiritual punishment that could kill a man. So Marcus read a lot, kept by himself. Those of his household, Charley said, were in an agony of surface cheer and helpless grief.

Well (although because I am so much smaller, it only happened to me in a smaller way), I knew what it was. From me, also, people drew away. They did not understand me. (At the hospital so much, with this freak of a woman. Did I *believe* in her supernatural powers? An educated modern person like me? Or did I *know* something?) They shunned me for an unknown quantity or despised me for a traitor to Marcus. Washed their clean hands of someone so freakish and incomprehensible. Oh, I felt it. It hurt. How precious a thing it is to meet everywhere an assumption that you are most probably decent and normally intelligent. If this is lost, you are left in the loneliest kind of place, a world without any fellows where you find no peers and don't belong.

Charley himself was clearly in anguish over Marcus. He said he wished he could figure out how to put Cora over some kind of rack and wring the truth out of her. But he said ruefully that racks don't wring truth, unfortunately.

I said regretfully that I, in my part, wasn't getting anywhere. I said she used me gladly, even cynically. But she would never confide in me.

"Just the same," he said, "try to hang on and stick to it, coz. May help us yet. We never know what'll help."

"Oh, I agree," I said. "And nothing matters now but to help Marcus."

He looked at me with a tiny curl of the old teasing light in his eye. "What, nothing?" said he.

"Nothing at all," said I.

And I thought to myself, someday, somehow, I may find the role for me, the one I can play-act for Cora Steffani that will strike close to the bone and shake her heart and upset her defenses. I will find the rack on which to stretch her.

Bud Gray came in. We looked at him hopefully.

"That Darlene," he said, gloomily, climbing on a stool at my other side. "She's the clever one. I sure could use a dame who knows how to get invisible the way she does."

"What would you do with her?" I asked idly.

"Use her in my business. Have her steal the papers . . . out of the black portfolios of the bearded strangers," said Bud in bitter jest. "And then vanish."

"Charley, my boy," I said suddenly, "speaking of stealing, what on earth did you think I ever stole from you?"

"Photograph," he said absently, "from my dresser."

"Oh?" I said, stunned. "That?"

"I'd have given it to you," he chided gently, "if I'd known it offended you. No matter." (His mind wasn't really on me. It shouldn't have been . . . I knew that.) I asked no more questions.

Why he'd had my picture there, I'd never know. But I was thinking that *Cora* must have stolen it and taken it away. But why? Because she was jealous? Jealous of me and Charley Ives? How could that be? But of course she was. She had let that out. "Cousin . . . Teacher." It was possible. After all, I had thought he cared for her and was drifting back to her. Although he did not and was not, or so he contended. She could have made the mistake the other way around. We were a triangle without a base, Cora and Charley Ives and I. Jealousy. Well then, thought I excitedly, how can I use it? Small . . . human and small . . . but such a thing as jealousy, compound of love and hate, that moves the blood. How could I fit it into a role?

The girl back of the counter said, "Aren't you Olivia Hudson? Dr. Harper wants you. Room 862. Right away."

"Oh?"

"He says Miss Steffani has gone into a trance." She rolled her eyes. We flew for the elevator.

Chapter Sixteen

ON THE AFTERNOON of the twentieth of May (ten days after Kent Shaw's visit), Cora went through her trance performance for the sixth time. It was much like the rest. At four after 3:00 P.M., she opened her eyes and told us where she had been walking.

On a golf course, she said, that lay high on a headland projected into water. She had been wearing her dark red jacket, a gray skirt, and a gray-and-red paisley scarf around her neck. She had spoken, this time, to a golfer, an elderly man with a pure white mustache and slanted white eyebrows. "But it can't be real," she whimpered, clutching the black silk collar of her Chinese jacket. "There *is* no such thing as a *red* golf ball."

"What did you say to the man?" asked Gray with quiet intensity.

She had said her usual lines. Where am I? and so on. She threw in the usual flat statement that she had felt afraid.

"Where was this?" asked Charley Ives softly.

Why, she had been in Maine. Where in Maine? Castine.

At this word, Charley Ives and Bud Gray oozed out of the room. I think Cora was shocked to see them so swiftly slip away. She was about ready to go into the weeping part, the hysteria, and she cried my name for a beginning. But her performance had become a most superficial reading. I thought she was working against a certain lassitude. But I didn't intend to stay for the aftermath.

I said shrilly, "Can't she have a sedative, Doctor? Don't let her suffer. Stop this, can't you?"

"Don't leave me, Ollie. . . ." Her wail was mechanical.

"I can't stay in this room," I said to the doctor. "It scares me. . . ."

I must have given a good performance because he responded helpfully, snapping, "Better go put your head down."

So I ran out of there. I ran in the corridor. I jittered in the elevator. I raced across the green carpet in the lobby. I was about to hurl myself through the revolving door when Charley and Bud came along *behind* me. I found myself flying through the door in my own compartment as if I were a badminton bird.

"You can't come," said Charley sternly in the street, but I scrambled into Bud's car with them, just the same. They had no time to argue with me. Any hope of catching Darlene Hite lay in speed, of course, so the car roared northward, to where the amphibian and its pilot waited at a small airport in Westchester. Now flying is no gypsy business, any more. But Charley and Bud had certain mysterious connections upon which I did not spy. (They had, for instance, a way to get in touch with each other through some third relay station.) Through this channel they could and did insert our sudden purpose into regulated patterns. They arranged permission to land on water, as they had foreseen might be the way to come down closest to an unknown destination.

Yet it had taken us more than an hour to become airborne and the amphibian was no jet. We would not get to Maine for hours more.

Yes, *we*. Oh, they hadn't got rid of me. It was a four-place plane. There was room. I was stubborn.

Once we were sitting still in the sky watching time turn, the flurry died and we caught our breaths. Charley said, "Cousin Ollie, why didn't you stay with her?"

"She wouldn't have said anything helpful. She just goes into a silence. You know how she does. I'll bet you one thing. This is the last stunt. She was let down, and relieved too. I think her dreamwalking is all over."

"Could be," Bud agreed. "But Maine's too far. We're not going to make it, kids. This will be what is known as a wild goose chase." He stretched his legs as far as he could and sighed. His nice undistinguished face was soberly unhopeful.

"Be thankful it isn't Arizona," said Charley Ives. "And if it's our last chance, all the more reason for taking it."

"Darlene's too smart," Bud said. "She's not going to hang around."

Charley had himself draped with radio connections. "If the police get her, we'll hear," he told us.

"The police in Castine?" said I. It seemed they had phoned, downstairs in the hospital. "Why, they *will*." My hope revived. "Castine's not a big place and out on a point of land the way it is. . . . I've been there."

Gray was wagging his head negatively.

"If they don't," I asked, "what shall *we do?*"

"Beginning to wonder," said Charley grimly.

"Talk to this golfer, whoever he is?"

"Not a lot of use. He'll only confirm, like all the rest."

Gray roused himself somewhat. "You know, I wonder why they take the risk. Darlene, for instance, is certainly smart enough to know damn well the risk of getting caught gets greater every time and it's about maximum right now. Could be in the contract, of course, that she gets no pay until the finish of the series. Must be some such motive."

"It may be in the contract, exactly so," said Charley. "Cora took the risk, didn't she? We'll come down on water, close to the middle of town. And Ollie, I don't know what to do with you." I felt like excess baggage. "You shouldn't be seen. You're known. Picture in the papers. Darlene Hite would recognize you."

"You, too, Charley, my boy," said I.

"Not me, though," said Bud with relish. "So *I'm* the one to track down Darlene Hite." All along he'd been keenly interested in this name.

"Suppose I go see this golfer," said Charley nobly. "Pick up what I can and no harm done. But Ollie, how *you* can lie low I do not know because we'll fly in about as secretly as a zeppelin. Better tag along with me. What are you doing here, anyhow?" Charley was exasperated.

"I know more about Darlene Hite than either of you," said I. "She won't answer her official description, for goodness' sakes. But I know things about her she may not trouble to conceal. Her walk, her hands, way she holds her head. . . ." They looked at me kindly, with only a little pity. "You may take no stock in my methods, my dear Watsons," said I, "but *I* do."

"Well," drawled Charley, "we can't throw you out."

"This hope's so damn forlorn," Bud said, meaning to be sweet to me, "let Ollie try."

"By the way, boys," said I briskly, "amateur though I am, may I ask if it's discreet to be seen chatting cozily in that snack bar? Cora's probably getting full reports on the hospital grapevine. I betcha the betting's about even among the help as to *which* side I'm spying on. How can I make her believe I am an ally when I'm hobnobbing with the enemy downstairs?"

"She's right," Bud said. He was smiling.

Charley said, "Forlorn hope. *You* can never fool Cora." He grinned and I could have slapped him. "I doubt if you could fool anybody, coz. You've got a certain transparency, and I'm not being derogatory."

"That chap, Shaw, said it pretty well," Bud put in. "A dedicated person, honest as the sun."

"Oh, pish tush!" I cried. "Little do you reck, Charley, my boy."

"Now, she's offended. There's a female for you," Bud chuckled. "Tell a lady she shines with integrity. What happens? She's just annoyed. You've maligned her femininity." He was teasing. His nice face smiled upon me fondly. Charley was silent in a thunderous kind of way.

"You forget," I said in a thin aloof voice. "I am not only female, but I *teach* the art of make-believe."

Charley murmured, "For the Lord's sweet sake, let's not get into that."

"Marcus," said I. We shut our mouths, both of us.

Bud Gray's thoughts went back to the job. "If I can only just cross, just once, the trail of Darlene Hite, and dig up the slightest indication to go on, I'll guarantee I'll track her." Now he seemed to be taking, if not hope, at least resolution. He and Charley began to discuss methods, how to inquire of places of lodging, depots of transportation, what ways there were to find a moving person. They were all-policemen.

I suppose we made very good time indeed. It was too slow. By six we were still two hours away from Castine. The radio spoke to Charley. Round and about, through channels, the news was sent. Police in Castine knew of a man who actually used red golf balls. A certain Judge Ellsworth. They had gone to the golf course atop the hill and found him playing there. No incident. Nothing had happened there at three o'clock that afternoon. Nothing at all.

"A failure!" cried Bud Gray. "Darlene defaulted. Too smart, like I said. Bet she's a thousand miles away from Castine now." He was completely deflated suddenly.

"Proves they are faked," I suggested feebly, "doesn't it, Charley?"

Charley was in touch with New York. He wrestled with the air waves for twenty minutes. Meanwhile, the plane droned ahead and Bud and I looked bleakly at the subtly failing light.

Charley wrenched at his gear. "It's out," he said angrily. "Through people in the hospital. Sensation," he stated bitterly.

Bud said, "What now?"

"We aren't far. . . . Shall we go on?"

"Let's go on," I urged. I couldn't bear to think of turning back into the seething, the publicity. "Suppose this Judge Ellsworth is ducking, just not admitting—I wouldn't blame him. It's been ghastly for the people like Jo Crain. There may be something we can find out."

Nobody told the pilot to change the course. We flew on. We were peering ahead for the magnificence of Penobscot Bay when the radio spoke again.

"*What!*" yelped Charley. Bud and I nearly climbed into the earphones with him. Charley lit up with energy and surprise. "Here's a twist for us! The incident *happened!*"

"Happened? Did the judge admit . . . ?"

"The judge reported to the police at five twenty. Woman stopped him . . . but it happened *at five o'clock!*"

"Five! Not three, but five! Two hours late!"

"Golfing! At five P.M.?"

"The old chap lives the other side of the course and *plays his way home to dinner,*" said Charley.

"Slip up?" Bud Gray looked as if he would here and now *jump* the rest of the way.

But we knew, whatever it was, it gave us a chance, it cut down the margin.

"She did it," cried Bud. "Darlene Hite. *She is there.*" He yearned at the horizon.

Dusk was creeping in at the day's edges as we came down on the stretch of water inlet from Penobscot Bay that (and for the life of me, I'll never understand why) they call the Bagaduce River. We were certainly not inconspicuous. A boat, divorced from the shore by sheer curiosity, came out and fetched us. So we stepped up on the dock at the base of the center of town. Charley Ives loped off, straight up the hill. Bud Gray started for the police station. I pulled my dark tweed coat close in the sharp air. I'd found a scarf in my pocket and tied it around my head. I walked away from the boatman's stare. Suddenly, all alone.

Ah, but that town is an enchanted town. Castine. Time and space conspire to give it distinction. But the long fascination of its history, the magnificence of its situation, do not entirely account for the enchantment. I knew Castine.

I turned to my left on the street at the base of the hill, thinking to myself that I had my methods. There is a store. I don't suppose any tourist ever missed it. I knew no better place to begin to look for someone who might have seen Darlene Hite. I doubted if much escaped Miss Beth, for all her professional pose of vague sweetness.

Miss Beth's Variety Store is distinguished for being a place of confusion and disorder. I've exchanged notes with people who, years after, tell about finding a box of chocolates among the overshoes, or a string of beads under a frying pan, or woolen socks in a glass lamp chimney. I bought a blue silk nightgown there, I think *because* I found it in a keg of copper paper clips. The entire store is a place where the customers root happily for hours among the wares, stirring them (with no protest from Miss Beth) into even more startling juxtapositions. I don't know how Miss Beth stumbled into her peculiar way of shopkeeping, but I'm sure she is shrewd enough to know its charm and never change. Something is answered there, some vacationing rebellion against classification and discipline. Some feeling for luck unearned. The place is always crowded with people digging and hunting and uttering cries. There, everything one buys has been discovered, like treasure.

As I well knew, Miss Beth didn't close shop at any strict hour, but drifted with the human tide. As long as people came, she kept the door open and herself remained, aloof and faintly smiling, never nagging a body to buy or even tell her what he was looking for, seeming to assume that naturally, he would not know until he found it.

I came to the shop and went in. It was its own glorious mess. There were perhaps ten people in the place, glazed of eye, just as I remembered, pawing happily in the poor light which only enhanced the mysteries. I sought Miss Beth and said to her, "Please help me. I'm looking for a woman, about my height and weight, one who would be a stranger, but who certainly was in town today."

"I don't know, dee-ah," said Miss Beth, putting on helplessness.

"She walks," I bent from the hips forward and pulled my neck out of line with my spine, "or stands like this."

Miss Beth said, "You can't say what she'd be wearing?"

"No." She shook her head and I said, "I know it's almost impossible but I'm very anxious to find her."

"Good many women in today, dee-ah," she said with a faint air of disapproval.

"When she smokes she puts a cigarette in her mouth and smokes without fuss, without gestures." Miss Beth smiled blankly. "Her hair would be dark but she'd have it covered." It was no good. Miss Beth, if anyone, would be able to catch at these wisps of mine. I felt if she couldn't, no one could. I began to think it unlikely, anyhow, that a wily Darlene Hite would have been tempted into this store.

I looked around me helplessly. What a romantic I was. Me and my wispy unsubstantial description. What could I do? Prowl the streets? Go up the hill? Try a hotel? Professionals would be working.

"Her nose," I said with no faith, and tried describing that. But Miss Beth had lost interest and looked at me as if I didn't belong. Behind the mad tangle of a high counter, I heard a woman cry, "Look what I *found!* Henry, come look at this!" I couldn't help smiling. A word came to me. Serendipity. It's been getting a bit of use lately. I said it aloud.

Miss Beth's smile was not vacant enough to fool me. She'd know the word for that happy quality of being able to find something you want but weren't really looking for. I then had a peculiar experience.

I suppose I was strung very tight and vibrating, and there I stood having been transported so suddenly, so far. Stood in this store dedicated to serendipity. And I was, besides, in that enchanted town that for mystical and inexplicable reasons had always seemed to me to be a place to *find* things. What I felt was a surge of absolutely unwarranted hope. Surely if there was magic, it would work for me, I thought, very well. One had only to fall into the rhythm, the joyful expectancy of the unexpected, a mood in which one does not push anxiously or narrowly. One opens and becomes ready for luck. One lets it happen.

I don't know yet. I still think it was the nearest thing to supernatural I've ever known. I smiled at Miss Beth and said to her placidly, "I'm not quite sure what I want. May I just look around?"

It was an unnecessary question. Her business was built on it.

So I turned and felt hope stir. Anything . . . anything might be hidden here, mixed in somewhere. As, indeed, anything may be hidden in the great world itself, confused and roaring as it is, upon which men spin and invent their feeble lanes of plan and purpose. But the great globe is a buzz, a throbbing, swiftly shimmering fabric of intermeshed acts, and it cannot be all charted. How do you know what you want until you find it? thought I, in that strange reverie, and turned my head and saw Kent Shaw walk by in the street.

Chapter Seventeen

SERENDIPITY? I was struck stock still. *Kent Shaw!* Why *here?* He couldn't have heard about Cora's latest dream and beaten us here. He couldn't have come, *having heard.* So did he know in advance? Or was he visiting relatives? Coincidence? No, no. I'd found something!

I slipped quietly out of Miss Beth's and looked to my left. Kent's topcoated figure was moving rapidly along the street. I followed him. You don't quarrel, you don't question. I'd got into the mood to be led, and so I followed.

The street becomes what you would call a road. The road follows the water. The hill went up to my right, across the way. On the water side there is a little museum, old Fort Pentagoet. I followed Kent Shaw along that road until, before the museum itself, closed of course at this hour, he stopped walking. He was obviously disposing himself to wait.

Deep dusk had by now fallen on this side of the hill. I slipped behind a huge shrub, twenty yards away, and stood still, tingling. Was it a rendezvous?

Kent Shaw, here! In Castine, Maine? For the first time, there came into my mind the question I'd never asked myself, although I had heard Marcus make the remark that demanded it. "Someone very clever has designed this thing," the old wizard had said. The question should have followed. *Who, then?* Who had invented this plot? Who devised it? Who masterminded it? Not Cora Steffani. I'd been right when I said she wasn't that clever. Darlene Hite was an unknown quantity, of course, but obscure. And Raymond Pankerman and his money were not in her ken. Nor could he have designed the plot, pudgy-brained Raymond. Where had he acquired the experience or the imagination or the skill to devise such a scheme and direct it and make it work? But Kent Shaw! He *was* capable. In fact, the whole thing was just like him!

I had found something. I had found the brains. I was convinced without any proof. I shifted from foot to foot behind that shrub, wild with excitement.

And Kent Shaw waited by the museum door. I could just see him. I could sense that he, too, danced with anxiety. I could see his arm whip out and strike at the small hedging plants beside the museum entrance. Those movements in the near dark expressed a furious impatience.

I didn't know what to do. A few cars drifted by, their headlights froze him momentarily to something still and anonymous. But there were no pedestrians. Yet he was waiting for something. Some*one,* of course. I felt sure it was Darlene, who, in a plan, was going to meet him there. And I, Olivia Hudson, thirty-four, teacher, female, amateur, was watching, all alone.

This, however, wasn't so for long. Something said my name so softly I thought it was a dream. Said it again a trifle more robustly. I became aware of Bud Gray standing close behind me, sheltered, also, in the lee of that bush. He had called my attention skillfully, without alarming me. In a moment, I was clutching his coat and whispering joyfully into his bending ear.

"Shaw? That him? Okay. We'll see."

I had much excited putting of clues together that I could not possibly whisper then. But, oh, I was glad that he had come.

We waited. The night air was chilly, but it had, as air has in that place, its own peculiar invigorating clarifying quality. Every breath seems to soothe and rearrange the very cells of the brain. I *knew* I had found something.

Meanwhile, the figure of Kent Shaw moved restlessly in a tiny orbit. He kept hitting out at those shrubs, as if pressure inside needed the relief of the gesture. We stood there what seemed hours. Hours. No car stopped. Nobody walked by.

"She isn't coming," I whispered, cramped, stiff, and beginning to despair.

"Doesn't seem so." Too smart, Bud was thinking and I knew his thought.

We could tell Kent Shaw was on the point of giving up and I was wild. "She isn't coming," I repeated. "Oh, pity . . . pity. But we can't miss a chance like this, Bud. Listen, why don't *I* go? I think I can fool him for a moment, anyhow. If he thinks I'm Darlene Hite, maybe he'll speak. It could give us something."

"Careful," said Bud Gray, holding me.

"It's all right. You can watch, or come behind. Then you can hear if he does speak. Bud, let me try to fool him, for even a second or two. Otherwise, he's going to leave and we won't know anything."

"Try it," Bud said abruptly and shoved me a little.

So I tried to put myself in Darlene's skin. I didn't know the role very well. I had such wispy clues, such slight indications. All I had, I tried to use—to walk carrying my head as I'd been told she did—to think of myself as cool and businesslike. I had ready in my throat the syllable of his name. I hadn't taken ten steps around that shrub when Kent Shaw saw my figure moving toward him in the dimness and his restlessness jelled to motionless attention.

I thought, It's going to work!

Then I saw the woman crossing the road. I don't know where she came from. I wished I could wait until she was by. She was a hulk in a coat that bloomed at the hips like an old-fashioned dolman and she walked splay-footed. I hadn't far to go. I tried to slow my steps and stall my approach until this lonely figure should pass me by, for she crossed on a diagonal and would come walking toward me, between me and Kent Shaw. She wore a decrepit felt hat pulled down on her brows.

We would pass. Then I would hear what Kent Shaw might say to

Darlene Hite. I thought, Surely Darlene would stall as I am stalling, so it will work. It will be all right.

But just as she came abreast of me, and we were not thirty feet from Kent's silent shape, that woman whipped out a flashlight and threw its beam full into my face. She said in a Down East twang, "Tain't smart to walk here alone by night, dee-ah. Don't you know no better?"

"Don't do that," I murmured, blinking, exposed. I grabbed for her wrist and turned the beam. It fell on her face. Her eyes were shrewd little slits. Her hair was white, her brows disorderly and pale. So much I saw, when she let go the button and the light went out.

"Should know better," she said severely, "Git back where there's folks."

I could have scratched and bitten her! I muttered something and swiveled around her. The light had ruined my vision. But I knew, bitterly I knew, Kent Shaw had gone.

Then Bud Gray was pinching my arm. He took out a flash of his own and lit it. "Oh damn!" I was almost crying. "*Damn* that old busybody! Do you see him, Bud? Where did he go?"

Bud said, professionally undismayed, "No telling, Ollie. Too bad." He turned his light on the museum door.

"He can't be in there!" I cried. "I thought I saw his shadow. Didn't you? Maybe he ducked up the hill. Can't we follow?"

Bud tried the door. It was locked. He turned the beam of light. "What would we say if we caught up with him? He can be found, Ollie. That's no problem."

"Damn, damn, damn old biddy!" I raged.

"Maybe you were lucky," Bud said.

"What?"

"Look there."

I saw the small hedge, then, in the light. Saw how the low shrubs had been cut and mutilated. I remembered the slashing of Kent Shaw's hand. I said, "What do you mean?"

"He had a knife, I'm guessing, aren't you?" Bud said. "And a darned sharp one, at that."

The night was very cold. I hadn't noticed the cold so much before. Bud put his arm around me and I was grateful for the warmth and the shelter of it. We began to walk back toward the shops. It looked a long dark chilly way. No one was abroad. The dwelling houses were smug and tight, with blinds drawn. The old biddy who had swung that light into my face was not to be seen ahead of us. No doubt she was safe from the hazards of the night behind the blinds in one of the houses. Neither was Kent Shaw to be seen behind us, or anywhere.

Bud said, "I must get on the phone. You'd better be someplace warm."

"Kent saw my face," I said through chattering teeth, "and ran away. Do you think he knows I knew *he* was there?"

"No telling."

"Where did he go? What will he do?"

"No telling that, either. Can we go a little faster?"

"Go ahead," I said. "You need to hurry. I'm holding you back."

"Don't like to leave you," he objected.

"You'll start a hunt for him? Try to catch him?" I stumbled along as fast as I could beside him.

"No use to catch him. But I want him watched."

"Darlene didn't come," I panted. "Why didn't she?"

"Because she's smart."

"He had a knife for *her?* That's what you think? And she'd guessed he would?"

Bud said, "If he *is* the brains and made the plot then he is the killer. I didn't think Darlene Hite killed Ed Jones. I dunno, I never could believe that. Kent Shaw suits me a lot better."

"But he would have *killed* her? *There?* In front of that museum? A corpse with Cora's nose—wouldn't that . . . ? I can't understand what he meant to do."

"The water is near enough," Bud said. "And a knife is not only quiet, but handy for remodeling."

I was so shocked and revolted I nearly fell and he had to hold me up with both arms. Footsteps rang on cement. We could see the shape of Charley Ives coming in his characteristic lope out of light and shadow ahead. "You all right?" Bud said. "Sorry, I said that pretty brutally."

"I'm all right. And here's Charley. You hurry." I thrust his arms away and tried to stand by myself.

"Anything wrong?" asked Charley.

"Take her other arm," said Bud. "Get back to the police station. Hurry."

So they almost carried me. My feet did not seem to touch the ground. While I was being whisked along, Bud told my cousin Charley, in quick short sentences, what had happened.

"Wah . . . !" said Charley. I seemed to rise a foot above the earth on the impulse of his excitement. "Kent Shaw! This is our break! Good girl, Ollie. How did you get on to him?"

"Serendipity," I giggled, impelled toward hysterical mirth by my ridiculous rate of progress and the aftershock of danger.

"The whole damn scheme has practically got his signature on it," Charley cried. "His style, eh?"

I remember saying, tearfully (hysterically), "Why Charley, my boy, that's pretty arty talk for you."

He paid no attention.

"You can see why he's got to get rid of Darlene," Bud said. "Now that it's over, he's scared she'll talk. And if she does, he's in for it, for Ed Jones. Darlene must know that."

"She knows all right," Charley proclaimed joyfully. "Listen to this. Judge Ellsworth meets this dame on the golf course. She wants to know where she is and he tells her. Then she says, 'My name is Cora Steffani and somebody wants to kill me.' Then she runs away."

"What!" Bud's excitement made him stop still and I was stretched between them like a rag on a washline. "Why?" yelped Bud.

"Why *say* that?" Now Charley stopped and Bud moved and I fluttered in the middle. "Because Kent Shaw has also got to get rid of Cora. Darlene is warning her. He's a killer and those two women both know it."

They then plucked me up, with no more pretense that I was in any way walking, and ran up the steps to the police station.

Chapter Eighteen

WE DIDN'T LEAVE Castine until late the following morning. Darlene Hite had not been found.

Judge Ellsworth, who was seventy-three, retired, and the real thing in a golf fanatic, used red balls because he often played so early in the northern spring that sometimes there was still snow on the ground. He played whenever he felt like it, which was nearly always. But the one inflexible thing about it was his habit of playing four holes, always alone, on his way home to his six o'clock dinner.

He was a bit confused when we talked to him that evening, refusing to identify *me* as the woman he had seen. When we straightened that out, he still refused to identify Cora's pictures. He said it was nonsense and a great nuisance and he didn't want to hear any more about it.

He did tell us that when the woman spoke to him he recognized the scene (since the police had already asked him whether it *had* happened). So he was, he said, suspicious. But all alone. And very much annoyed at becoming one of Cora's victims. He had not pursued her when she ran away. He had marched on home to this phone and simply called the police.

CORA WALKS AGAIN, the papers shrieked. DREAM WALKER IN MAINE. The time discrepancy was fuel, that's all, for heated argument. The red golf balls were "color." But the sentence the woman in Maine had said, that the woman in New York had *not* reported (Somebody wants to kill me), that was *sensation!* The story rolled . . . nothing could stop its momentum now.

But we, of course, pondered these details.

Kent Shaw. Who, we said to each other, had turned up in the very beginning and seen to it that the very first incident in the series had been carefully recorded before witnesses for future reference?

Who had somewhat unnaturally withdrawn and taken care not to be seen with Cora anymore?

Who had written her a cryptic note from Los Angeles, which I tried frantically to quote? Who had *been* in Los Angeles at the time of Ed Jones' murder? Who had the chance to signal, on TV?

Who had told Cora that she could go abroad in ten days' time, ten days ago?

Who could have known both women? Who had the fantastical imagination, the genius, the half-mad brain for the job? Kent Shaw. Kent Shaw. He answered *all* of this.

And who, finally, had turned up in Castine—with a knife? Oh, we were convinced, and afraid to be convinced. We had no proof of any kind whatsoever.

The three of us, exhausted, were sitting in the air being carried back. "Why did he want to meet Darlene in Maine?" I asked.

"Thought it was safer. Couldn't guess *we'd* get there that fast. Safer than a meeting in New York would be." Charley was ready with suggestions.

"Why did he make it so long after the golf course bit?"

"Wasn't so long after five o'clock."

"Then you think the bit on the golf course was *supposed* to happen at five?"

"I sure do," said Bud. "Because that's the old chap's one invariable habit. And that's when he'd have no spry young companion."

"How did Cora make a mistake?" I wondered. "If it were *written down,*" said I, "a five and a three are not always unlike. They must have had it written down. How could they remember the tiny things, exact words, clothes, everything? Did you ever search . . . ?" They looked upon me with kindness. "Nothing?" I queried. "Did you look *everywhere?* In the hospital, too?" They looked upon me with patience.

"Got to blow the lid off the entire thing," said Charley, "to explain the one detail that matters."

"The blue envelope," said I.

"Exactly. That's the one."

"Kent Shaw put it in the book. Heavens, Charley, he's always mooching around trying to sell his stuff."

"If we can prove that. . . ." This was our hope. Charley would try.

"What will Kent do now?" I worried.

"We'll watch and see."

"Can't let him really kill anybody."

"That's right. Neither woman. For Marcus' sake, if no other. Guards already on the hospital. Don't worry."

"You think," said I, "he arranged this rendezvous a long time ago. Did he know *then* he'd want to kill her? And set the time after dark?"

"He'd want it dark enough not to be seen," Bud said, "in any case."

"But why a rendezvous at all?"

"For the payoff?" Charley said.

"Now she knows it's dangerous, but how is she going to ever get paid off?"

"Aaaah," said Bud Gray.

"She must *expect* to get paid," I insisted, "or she wouldn't have risked that golf course bit and finished the job."

"Aaaah," said Bud again and drew his head into his collar like a turtle and fell to thinking.

Charley said, "Much as I'd like to lay about me with Kent Shaw's name, I think we'll first have to see what we can get by watching him. We are supposing, aren't we, that he would like to kill two women? One of them is where we can watch her. And he may yet lead us to the other one." Bud sighed.

"No need to be downhearted," said Charley. "Our position shows a lot of improvement."

"If it hadn't been for that chaperone type," I fretted. "If I could have gotten one word out of him, if he had called me by Darlene's name, even . . . that would really have been an improvement."

"If he'd stuck his knife in you," said Charley, "better yet?" Then he exuded a kind of deep and dangerous silence.

"Why, Bud was there," said I. (But, oh, Kent Shaw could have killed me and I quivered to think of it, coward that I am.)

Charley stretched like a big cat. "Might have expected something of the sort. Had you thought of it, Bud? Did you let her take the risk, blind?"

"She'd have taken the risk," Bud said firmly.

"I don't doubt she would," said my cousin Charley, "She'd get carried away by the part."

"I doubt it," snapped I.

Bud said, ignoring me, "You make choices in this business."

"I agree," said Charley Ives stiffly, "but I can't admire taking advantage of Ollie's dramatic instincts."

I was annoyed. "I don't *believe* Bud knew he had a knife. I'm *sure* I didn't."

"You better stick to your trade," he said. "Stay around the hospital. Cora's going to be under pressure and possibly. . . ."

"Indulge my dramatic instincts there, you mean?"

"Uh huh."

"Make-believe?" said I, getting madder.

"That's right," said Charley Ives.

"I think you're jealous," I cried. I was thinking that I, the amateur, who had the luck—but not the sense to keep my mouth shut.

Charley said. "That I deny. Jealousy is a rotten—" He shut up suddenly.

"It sure is," I murmured, thinking of Cora. "If Cora was a 'woman scorned,'" I blurted. "Oh, Charley, you shouldn't have kept on hanging around her."

"Teach me," said Charley, in muted anguish.

I bit my tongue and tasted blood.

"You are right," said Charley evenly, "and I was wrong."

Gray said something about some department and they began to use quick names and expressions I didn't know. They were being professional over my head.

I shrank in my seat, feeling miserable. Me, the blundering amateur, who had the luck—but not the sense to keep my mouth shut. Of course, Charley blamed himself, and why did I have to be the detestable type who pointed things out and was "right"? I pretended to sleep.

When we got back to town, my escorts left me flat to go set up the machinery. They were calmer than I. They knew that patience and effort would turn up something useful. They were trained to take a hypothesis, like the involvement of Kent Shaw, and go to work to test it.

I knew some of the plans. People would try to find a connection between Kent Shaw and Raymond Pankerman. (They never did.)

Try to find out if and when Kent Shaw had got into Charley's place while the book in which the blue envelope was found was lying there waiting to be shipped to Marcus. (They found nothing like evidence; only the possibility.)

Inquire in Los Angeles about Kent Shaw on the night of the murder of Jones. (Nothing.)

Investigate his finances, check on his long-distance calls, his travels. (Too long, too late.)

Go back in his career to see where his path had crossed Darlene Hite's. (And this they found, but what was it but another possibility?)

Of course, possibilities pile up, but it was going to be a long slow swell, and meanwhile Marcus could only deny any knowledge of the blue envelope. But he couldn't *explain,* and the story roared, frothed, spit. . . .

I went home. I let myself into my own place and looked at my books and my records, my paintings, my bric-a-brac, my ivory tower. I prayed that in some way, I, from my isolation, in my feebleness, had yet a use. But all my ideas were, I sadly recognized, strictly theatrical.

This was the twenty-first of May. I called the hospital. Cora would take no calls, see no one. I spoke to Dr. Harper. He told me that they were in a state of siege and that the board insisted that Cora had to be kicked out of there. "Disrupts our work, hurts our reputation, name suffers, people are upset. Can't go on. Charley Ives sold me a bill of goods in the first place. Had no idea what we were in for." He was fuming.

"You can't just throw her out into the street," said I, alarmed, thinking of Kent Shaw.

"She claims it's all over because wild horses couldn't drag another word from her lips. If she ever has another dream nobody will know it. Oh, she's a fraud, Miss Olivia."

"Where can she go?" I was worried.

"She's got an apartment. Oh, she's in a panic. Doesn't want to go there. We've got guards here, as a matter of fact. And it's intolerable."

"She has to be safe, for Marcus' sake."

"I suppose so," the doctor admitted gloomily. "She speaks of going abroad as soon as she can get the money."

"The money?" I pricked up my ears.

"I've half a mind to give her the money to get rid of her."

"Oh, no. Don't you do that. Remind her of *me.*"

"If you want to get in to see her," he growled, "I'll see that you do."

"No. I'd rather *she* let me in," said I.

Staunch old friend. It was a phony characterization.

When I called Marcus, he was cheerful. He knew all that Charley knew. So I told him about my strange experience in Miss Beth's store. "It was odd, Uncle John. What I'd like to know . . . did I feel prophetically hopeful because I was going to see Kent Shaw? Or did I see Kent Shaw because I felt hopeful?"

"Good girl, Ollie. You saw him because you felt hopeful, I should say."

"But wasn't it a coincidence?"

"Coincidence means only a connection that's not seen. Roots meet underground. And hope is creative. Look at it this way. Suppose you'd stood there without hope, bewailing a stone wall. You'd have been blind. He could have walked by without your noticing."

"Hope is creative?" said I. "How can that be?"

"I don't know how," said Marcus. "I only perceive that it is."

So he passed me some courage. While the papers bled ink, the talk careened dangerously, giddily on, and Marcus was being soiled and stained and disrespectful words cannot entirely be eaten, ever. Respect is a kind of Humpty Dumpty. All the king's horses can't put it all the way up again.

Please, if I am making this clear at all, please do read the fine print and the follow-up and all the hard, dry parts in the news. Don't let your mind jump onto the next sensational headline. Oh, it's more fun to float along, enjoying the high spots. The new murder. The latest scandal. Today's clash. But afterward, people have to live. And if all you remember is a vague impression of some nasty mess, and the thing that remains is only your notion that this person once fell away from the clear and unquestioned way—and to know what truly did happen is a task too dry, too hard—ah, please. It isn't fair.

Secretary, whoever you are. Delete the paragraph above, I mustn't bleat. I don't think I'm feeling very well. . . . Tomorrow, if I have tomorrow . . . I can finish this. Start a new chapter. . . .

Chapter Nineteen

I DON'T MEAN to drag you through all the anguish we suffered, being ignorant. So I will try to follow my original intention and go backstage, and tell how the four who were in the plot were moving in what to us was darkness.

I will go back to Darlene Hite. Once she realized (after the discovery of the body of Ed Jones, on March 28) that Kent Shaw was a killer, Darlene saw ahead. She saw what was written on the wall because she was smart. And because she had been in the jungle. Kent Shaw, who had killed a man just to save his beautiful scheme intact, would not hesitate to eliminate her, either, once her job was finished. So Darlene considered her position.

She was not required to do anything in Washington on the fifth of May. (This incident, she knew nothing about.) Her script called only for an appearance in Castine on May 20. That would be the end of it. She was to meet her boss afterward and collect her handsome reward and live happily ever after.

But Darlene, having read the papers and well-considered the future, wished to take care of Darlene. So she left New Orleans early in April, went to Toronto, and there, early in May, she found a surgeon and had her nose remodeled.

Now the doctor in Toronto read the papers, too. When, after I'd gone to Los Angeles, after the fifth of May, we broke forth the suspicion that a certain Darlene Hite might be involved in Cora's huge hoax, and when we published her pictures, you would think he'd speculate about this patient. Maybe he did. But the pictures were old and, as I say, retouched for glamor, and furthermore, *he believed the third witness in the park in Washington.* The doctor thought Darlene Hite had been seen in Washington on the fifth of May. So how could she be his patient, whom he was even then attending? He didn't even mention it. She had another name, a cover story, and plenty of "expense" money. He did not wish to embarrass her.

So Darlene lay low and healed. She read what was supposed to have happened to Marcus and knew it hadn't. She may have dimly recognized the crux of the plot. But Darlene, as I think I've said before, had a narrow view and the meaning of John Paul Marcus was neither apparent nor important to her. She was looking after Darlene, and doing it very well, too.

In good time, she "vanished" from Toronto. She evolved a new character. Bleached her hair back to its original blond or even whiter. Bleached her brows. Took off assorted supporting garments. Practiced a new waddling walk. Bought elderly oxfords, those dreadful shoes that are offered to women over fifty as a matter of course.

She went to New York and foxily smoothed out a future way there. She took off for Castine two weeks early. On May 20, at 5:00 P.M. (the figure Cora took for a three in the script, after all this time), Darlene used a black fringe of artificial hair under the scarf and very easily vanished to a prepared identity after that stunt was over.

But she had ad-libbed. She had warned Cora Steffani, as best she could, for she knew that Cora's elimination was also written on the wall.

Now Darlene's problem was to collect her wages and live to enjoy them.

She had kept the rendezvous with Kent Shaw before the museum. But we interfered. She'd seen us. She was hoping Bud and I would go away. She was watching, when I stepped out from behind that shrub. She could tell as well as I that Kent Shaw had been fooled, for a moment. *She* knew he was dangerous. She may even have known he held that knife, for she could expect a knife. So Darlene acted. Stepped out from some ambush of her own, crossed the road, and threw that beam of light in my face to save my life.

Darlene Hite, of course, was the old biddy in the dolman. But her nose, as we had been able to see so plainly when I turned the light on her, was no longer anything like Cora's nose. I did not recognize her. (Me and my methods! Me and my vanities!)

But she didn't get the key. Key to some deposit box where her money lay hidden and waiting for her. The key Kent Shaw was promising to deliver that night in front of the little museum, in the dark and the cold.

Darlene had guessed easily enough what he'd rather deliver. She had a gun under that dolman. She'd hoped to surprise him, to take the key away, and vanish, as she was so skilled in doing. Then conquer the problem of safely reaching that box—thereafter to disappear forever.

But she had found herself saving my life instead.

Darlene was no killer, nor did she want to see anyone killed. When she saw me on that dim sidewalk, living, and so close to dying, it was no abstraction, either. Darlene was shaken. For the first time, she glimpsed the fact that taking care of Darlene might mean taking care of other people, also. And not letting murder go. But she skipped out of Castine in her own invisible way. There was her pay.

She came to New York, where she had deep-laid some alternate plans. At that time, she was wondering how to expose all but herself, thinking in terms of anonymous letters. She didn't want to appear. She wanted her well-earned money. She'd better get that first, she thought. She would try for it once more.

None of this did we know.

Now Raymond Pankerman, watching the big impossible lie stir up the country to a frenzy, must have been laughing. I suppose it was the bright spot in his days. Yet I wonder whether he had the imagination or the sensitivity to know what had been done to Marcus. I wonder if he was satisfied. At any rate, he paid off. The combination to Kent Shaw's safe was to be forwarded, lacking a countermand, by relays through innocent people. Kent Shaw knew where it lay ready for him. But he was either too smart or too preoccupied to go near it. If he had, he might have been pounced upon. For he was watched.

He had been picked up at Boston airport, on his way down. He'd come back to his rooming house. He did not seem to move.

I can imagine how he was preoccupied. Now he saw himself and his beautiful hoax at the mercy of his fellow conspirators. He could understand the pressure upon them, especially the women. He wanted them silent forever. But he could not murder a woman he couldn't even locate. For Darlene he could only wait, holding the only lure he had, her money. The other woman, however, was very conspicuously located. He knew where Cora was.

So Kent Shaw, in the shabby room among the clutter of his souvenirs, kept to his surface poverty and brooded, schemed, thought. How was he going to murder Cora in the well-protected hospital room? Especially since the whole world had been told somebody was going to try?

He was very clever, that mad little man.

Now, about Cora. She was terrified. She was in a terrible spot. She knew Kent wanted to kill her. She could no longer duck or dodge the fact that he *had* killed Ed Jones. If, to save her own life, she broke down and revealed the plot, she herself was an accessory to that killing. How could she meet Kent Shaw and collect *her* money, fearing him as she did? Even if she had *her* key, how could she go for the money, since her face was as well known to the public as any face alive? The thing had gotten out of hand. The hospital threatened to throw her out. She was afraid. She wanted to run to another continent and hide. What could she use for money?

I'd divined that money was the crux of her problem. Pressure was on her to call for me.

Nevertheless, on the twenty-first, nothing moved. Everything seemed to have come to a stop.

On the twenty-second there were some ripples. Mildred Garrick came to see me. Oh, I'd been seen by the press. The white light that beat on all concerned did not skip me. I played my poor part, said foolish things. I had to. I sent most of them away puzzled or sad. But Mildred had something to tell me.

"Cora's been writing letters. Did you know? Did you advise her?"

"I haven't seen her since—"

"She wrote this note to Jo Crain."

I read the copy she handed me. I blazed. It was as if Cora thought she could get out gracefully by the exercise of just a little charming politeness. She was like a child putting on manners. "Look how good I am being now!" Sweet words, brave apologies, daintily done. I was furious. She didn't, as Charley had said, have a political thought in her head, or a moral one, either. She didn't know the meaning of "accessory before or after the fact" or of "shalt not bear false witness" or any other rule connected with her fellow men. All she knew was that Marcus was famous. She didn't know why. She herself wanted to be famous, period. She hadn't cared why. Greedy for attention, money, and a bit of revenge, she knew not what she did. She couldn't even conceive that the affair of the blue envelope would live after her. She said in that note, oh sweetly, that she intended to go away and surely it would all be forgotten. She didn't even consider that her countrymen would need to know *and must know* what the truth was about Marcus.

Oh, I raged. I walked up and down my carpet and let fly with a good deal of this. Mildred patted the thing in her hair, today, that looked like a huge amber teething ring to me. "Well, well," said she. "All as I can say is, you look like you're changing sides and getting over to the unpopular one again."

"What do you mean?" I yelled at her.

"It's edging around," said Mildred. Her eyes looked tired suddenly and I could see the fine lines under her hearty makeup. "I printed this letter in my column this morning."

"You didn't!"

"Did," Mildred shrugged. "It's a job, honey."

"Jo Crain gave you that? What is Jo thinking of?"

"Nobody's going to know what Jo is thinking without Jo wants them to know," said Mildred vulgarly. "I wanted to know what you'd think and I guess I got it. Kinda hope it will make a few more folks mad."

"Don't quote *me,* please." I was alarmed.

"Boring from within, huh?" said Mildred cheerfully. "Listen, Ollie, I hold no brief for Cora—that little twerp of a half-baked Duse, believe me. But I got a job and I got an ear and I'm telling you, sympathy is edging around."

"How can it?"

"It stuck to Marcus longer than you'd expect. People don't want idols kicked over. But their sympathy is a jumpy thing. You know what's doing it? The hospital threatening to throw her out."

"Oh me," I mourned. "Mildred, leave me out of your column and out of your vocabulary for a little while? I'll . . . maybe I can give you a scoop," I offered feebly.

Mildred grinned. "You're quaint. Well, something has got to give pretty soon," she announced with great good sense. "Cheer up, Hudson. I've been known to keep my mouth shut. Boy, is this a mess!" she added with glee.

I tried to call Charley after she had left. I couldn't reach him. (He and Bud Gray never had given me, the amateur, that mysterious phone number of theirs, through which they could be reached, it seemed, about any time.)

Only a ripple. But Mildred had printed Cora's letter to Jo Crain. And Kent Shaw had read it in the paper. We didn't . . . couldn't . . . see the ripple as it enlarged.

Charley called me that evening, of the twenty-second. Kent Shaw had come to the hospital late in the day. He had been watched, avidly. But he had paced the lobby a little while, looking nervous and un-decided. He had gone away without even trying to get upstairs to the eighth floor.

Actually, he was checking on a point of hospital routine. This foray was a consequence of Mildred's column. We didn't know.

But I will tell you. He watched the florist's boy. Saw how an offer-ing for Cora Steffani was stopped at the desk and looked into. Saw that the boy then put it on the elevator. And knew what to do.

On the twenty-third, Darlene moved. She placed a classified ad for the Monday morning paper.

On the twenty-fourth, Kent Shaw moved. He knew as well as I did that Jo Crain was both thoughtful of her friends and an extremely im-portant and busy person. He knew that her florist had her cards and was used to her ways. So, since Kent Shaw wasn't a bad mimic, him-self, on Monday the twenty-fourth, he used Jo's secretary's voice to order red gladioli, in a basket, to be sent at exactly 4:00 P.M. to Cora Steffani in the hospital.

On the twenty-fourth, then, Kent Shaw came into the hospital lobby a little earlier than 4:00. Again he jittered, paced, and then he seemed to decide. He stepped into an elevator. Got off at the eighth floor. Bit his fingers, looked left and right, swung on his heel and rode down again, without having tried to get into Cora's room.

The guards, who had watched prayerfully (Let him try!), thought he was scared off, perhaps having spotted them or sensed tension. Did not imagine what had happened between floors, in the elevator. And the glass jar of candy that Kent Shaw had carefully saturated with the same poison that had killed Ed Jones rode into Cora's room in the midst of the blood-red gladioli in their open basket, under Jo Crain's card.

But the ripples from his act went a little differently from his expec-tation. Cora was put in utter terror by the news of those two visits, the second one closer than the first. (Which news she received, of course, on the hospital grapevine.) And Cora was in no mood for candy. She wasn't poisoned yet, at 6:00 P.M. on the twenty-fourth, when she called me on the phone.

Chapter Twenty

I'D BEEN FEELING like a cat on a leash, alone all the weekend and alone the Monday, that twenty-fourth of May. When I hung up on Cora, called Charley Ives and got him, I was about to pop with the release of something having happened.

"I'm convinced she's going to ask me for a loan," said I excitedly, "so what shall I do, Charley? Shall I promise to lend her the money?"

"To run away with? She can't be let go, coz."

"I know," I said, "but there's such a thing as the torture of hope. If she thinks she's escaping and then can't. . . ."

Charley sounded amused. "Spanish Inquisition has nothing on you."

"Charley, my boy," I bristled.

"I don't think it matters," he cut in.

"It matters this much. If I refuse she'll, sure as fate, throw me out right away and then what use would I be?"

"Tell her anything you want," said Charley indulgently. "Except one thing. Don't twit her with Kent Shaw's name. He was up on the eighth floor yesterday. Didn't see her. But if we get Darlene tonight, we may be able to bring them all three together and I'd just as soon—"

"Get Darlene! What do you mean?"

There was a silence that shouted surprise. "Didn't Bud call you?" asked my cousin Charley rather cautiously.

"Nobody has called me for days and days," I cried indignantly. "I might as well be unconscious."

So Charley told me about the ad in the morning paper. It was addressed to K.S. and it was signed by D. Charley didn't doubt who had placed it. Neither did I. It asked K.S. to bring "key" to Biltmore lobby, 9–10 P.M. It added, "Uncle anxious to hear."

I suppose I squealed like a teen-ager.

"K.S. is going to have to go," Charley said with satisfaction.

"Are you going?"

"Not me and not you, coz," Charley said, reading my mind. "Kent knows us too well. Bud's going."

"He's met Bud."

"Once. Bud won't be very noticeable. I figure on getting into Shaw's room while he's safely out of it. What occurs to me . . . the very last thing he'll take to any rendezvous with Darlene is that so-called key. Once she got that, she'd really vanish. He'd never have any easy moment thereafter. She wants him in a public place and she may threaten. You see the threat in that ad, don't you?"

"Uncle Sam?" said I.

"Exactly. So he'll give in, agree, but say the key has to be fetched and he'll want her to go some other place where it's lonelier."

"She won't *go?*"

"It won't matter. But we'll move in as soon as they meet. Point I'm making . . . who knows what I might not find in his room?"

"Can I come there?"

"Nope. You're going to the hospital and play games with Cora."

"Charley, if you get Darlene you'll come *there?*"

"Sure will."

"All right," I said. "I'll stay in the audience. I hope there's a show."

Charley said, taking pity, I suppose, because I sounded so forlorn, "Have you talked to Marcus today? Do you know he says Darlene has had her nose bobbed?"

"He does? But Charley, how could she? When would she have time? And with everyone looking for her, wouldn't that be suspicious? I don't see. . . ."

"Marcus just says Judge Ellsworth isn't an old fuss-budget defending his privacy, but an honest and accurate man. And if the judge says the woman on the golf course didn't look like Cora, then she didn't."

"But . . . does that help us any?"

"They are rounding up reports on every nose-remodeling job done over the country in the last couple of months. Can't be too many. May help." (Eventually, of course, it did.)

I said, "Thanks for all the news, Charley, my—" I stopped myself in the middle.

But Charley said, and he sounded a bit miffed, "Oh, I'm your boy, Teacher. *I* don't see why you shouldn't have the news."

He saw, I guess, later.

When I went down the corridor toward Cora's room it was 8:00 P.M. I'd made it as late as I conscionably could so as to be around if there were going to be fireworks. I was trying to put myself into the staunch old friend pose, but when I opened the door she threw me a cue for a better role.

Cora was dressed neatly in gray jersey, had her glasses on, looked very businesslike. She said, "Ollie, how are you? Will you have one?"

She had a small glass jar in her hand and she was twisting the top open. "One what?" I said and she turned it and let me read the label. OLD-FASHIONED HUMBUGS, the label said. I looked up, at her face.

"Or shall we be honest, for a change?" she said.

"By all means," said I. I thought for a moment she was going to confess to me, then and there.

But she said, "I appreciate your 'standing by,' Ollie, darling, even if I do know you belong to the unbelievers. You think I'm a humbug, don't you?"

"And you think *I'm* a humbug," said I slowly. "Well, that should clear the air."

She put the candy down. It had been a prop for her little scene, but now the bit was over, we both forgot the candy. She in her purpose. I in the glimmer I then had of a role I might play that would drive her wild. I wanted to turn it over in my mind, taste it and test it. At the same time, I found myself laying a foundation for it.

I sat down quietly. "What do you want?"

"I want some money." (I said nothing.) "And you have plenty of money," she said a trifle waspishly.

"You want me to finance your departure from these shores?"

"You must see that if I leave the country all this will be a nine days' wonder and then die down. Isn't that a good thing?"

I held on to my temper. "It won't help Marcus much," I said, very flatly.

"Charley Ives seems to blame *me*. But he most certainly can't blame *you*, Ollie. Now can he?"

She seemed to have Charley Ives on a salver and be handing him over. I thought she looked gray in the face.

"You're scared, aren't you?" I leaned back.

"Of course, I'm scared. I want to get away. They won't keep me here and I'd go out of my mind if they did. I *can't* go stay in my apartment. I'd be . . . I'd be at the mercy of the curious. . . ."

"They have no mercy," I muttered, thinking we both meant Kent Shaw.

"Ollie, will you help me? I know no reason why you should. But I ask you to and I need to know."

I didn't meet her eye. (I felt, in spite of everything, like a dirty traitor.) "Oh, I already have," I said carelessly. "I can get you a seat on a transatlantic plane tomorrow morning. You can be in Paris with modest funds—I don't say I'm going to support you forever—by the day after."

Then she sat down. I saw tension draining out of her. She thanked me in that businesslike way, and she told me I would be repaid. But I could tell that she was wondering *why*.

So I talked idly. "You realize you may be hounded, even there? Your destination will be no secret. How are you going to get to the plane? Do you mind an escort of news hawks? Because you are sure to have it."

"I don't mind," she said, and indeed she didn't. The thought cheered her up. It should be safe. "Once I get to France," she said confidently, "I can manage to disappear."

"Like Darlene Hite," I murmured.

She said, "Ollie, whatever you believe, believe this. Never again. No more. And once I am gone, it *will* all be over."

"You think it will die?" said I. I suppose I sounded queer. I felt so angry at her conception of a universe that revolved around Cora Steffani. I hurried on. "And you'll disappear? Have your face remodeled, I suppose?"

"Perhaps," she said. There was a movement of her eyelids, a flaring. It was an idea. "Ollie, can't we drop the whole subject? You do mean this? I can pack?"

"You'd better," said I. "Will you need to go back to your apartment at all?" She said no, she would travel light, and she began, then and there, to organize her possessions. And I to help her.

(In fact, I searched, rather carefully, for something written down. I didn't find it.)

So there we were, two women, folding clothing, speaking of what one needs to wear, both playing the scene, nothing honest about it. She was, all the while, puzzling, wondering why I was being so very helpful, so ready to get rid of her, so easy. And I thinking to myself, I am a humbug, am I? Can't I use that?

"Want to pack these?" said I coming to the candy jar.

"Too heavy," she objected and put it aside.

By ten o'clock, I'd had enough. The nurses were fretting. Nothing had happened. No one had come. And I could bear no more. When I left her, she was still baffled by me.

There was nothing for me to do but go home. So I did. And I waited. No one called me. I thought bitterly that I wasn't even going to be told. But five minutes after eleven Charley Ives came in my door.

"What happened?" I burst.

"Nothing." He cast himself down on my sofa and begged piteously for a drink.

"Did Kent Shaw go to the Biltmore?"

"Oh, yes, he went."

"Darlene?"

"No Darlene."

"What now?"

"Dunno. See if the ad runs tomorrow. Try again."

"*Why* didn't Darlene come?" I cried, impatient with that elusive character.

"Tell you, coz," said Charley, accepting liquor gratefully, "a man wants to murder her and she knows it. I don't think she is going to walk up to him in any kind of place, public or private. I don't think he'll ever lead us to Darlene Hite."

"Charley, what does 'key' mean? Is it a real key, do you think? Key to a box or something?"

"Sure. A box or something. Somewhere in New York City. Or the world." Charley just looked tired. "Small matter which. I didn't find any key. Worse, he's tipped off we're watching him, I'm afraid."

"Oh, me!" I said. "How?" I sat down beside him. I wanted very much to comfort him because he looked so tired and that's not like Charley Ives.

"We've corrupted the landlord, if you must know," he said. "Didn't take much to corrupt him, either. What a dump that is! So I got in, easily enough, and left the door ajar, relying on Bud's man to tip me if Shaw showed in the street. Well, some damn woman from across the hall has got to put her head in and get neighborly. Am I a friend of Kent's? An artist, am I?" Charley dared me to comment.

"Is she a friend of Kent's, do you think?" I said instead.

"I wouldn't be surprised. She looked like something out of Greenwich Village in the 'twenties."

"Couldn't you have warned her not to mention . . . ?"

"Sometimes you make your own trouble," Charley said. "To warn her might set up more importance in her mind than she will naturally give it. I don't suppose it matters. I've got a mind to grab him anyhow and stop this fooling around. Bud is right. Darlene's too smart."

"Arrest Kent Shaw?"

"We've got absolutely nothing," Charley said heavily.

"Couldn't you bluff? *Say* you've got something?"

Charley closed his eyes wearily, and with the blue gone out of his face, it looked like something cut in age-darkened ivory.

"Charley," I said, "Cora thinks she's squeaking out of it. I gave her carfare. I told her she had a plane seat. Thinks she's skinning out of the whole business tomorrow morning."

"She won't," he said dispiritedly.

(I can't help the way my mind works.) "Look, what if Kent Shaw were to find out she's going tomorrow?" I heard myself saying. "Then, if he wants to get rid of her, I mean, *kill* her, and if he thinks she is getting away, wouldn't that stir him up, maybe?"

"And we nab him with the knife at her throat?" said Charley. "I don't want him within ten blocks of her. We can't risk losing Cora. Or any one of them. We need them *all*."

"To explain the blue envelope," I murmured. "But Charley, my boy, hope is *creative,* Marcus says. So—"

"And hope's all I've got," said he, "and that's running low. Excuse me, coz. It's restful here. A man could fall to pieces."

"Ivory Tower. I'll fill your glass." I bustled. "Where is Kent now?"

"He headed for home about ten. Bud's tucking him in. Bud will be here in a minute."

"Oh?" said I.

I brought him a freshened drink and sat down again. I didn't know what to do for him.

"Maybe I need a little sermon," said Charley. "Would you, Teacher?"

"All right." I braced myself. "Any special text?"

"Darkness before dawn? The shower that clears? Anything."

"Let us sit upon the ground," I murmured, "and tell sad stories. . . . We needn't, Charley. Marcus is *tough*. I saw it in Dr. Barron. It's not at all connected with muscles or guns or money or power. I just doubt if it's for the likes of me, or even you, to fear for *him*."

Charley said judiciously in a moment, "Y'know, Teacher, I think you are right."

And I began to cry on Charley's shoulder.

"Cousin Ollie," said Charley, stroking my hair, "what's the matter?"

"Just because I can preach," I sobbed, "and I think I know what one *ought*, doesn't mean I *can*. I'm just a poor female, Charley, and too feeble and I never had any guts, really, and sometimes I wish somebody'd take a little pity. . . ."

"Now, now," said Charley soothingly.

"I don't want to sound 'right' all the time," I wailed. "*Nobody* likes that kind of person. They ought to know that most preachy people are only preaching to themselves really because they need it so bad."

"I'm sure," Charley said gently, "anyone you'd like to like you is going to do it." He held me off then. "You strike me as being fairly tough, you know," he said.

"It must be a pretty good performance," I bawled.

But he wasn't going to soothe and pet me or even tease me out of it, as I suppose I hoped he would. I began to feel foolish. His face was so sad and he so rigid. "I'm *inflicting*," I snuffled. "All against my principles. Excuse me, Charley, my boy. Us old-maid schoolteachers get these spells. We're lone lorn creatures. I don't have a more convenient shoulder."

"Perfectly all right," said Charley. "Here he comes now, I think," he added with relief.

"Who?"

Charley was letting in Bud Gray.

Bud said, "Hi, Teacher." He didn't even notice I'd been bawling. "Bad news, tonight, eh? Well, try, try again."

"*You* don't look discouraged," I said smiling.

"Same routine tomorrow night, if the ad runs?" said Charley rather briskly. "Well, then, since I need my rest. . . ."

"What's your hurry?" Bud said, surprised. So Charley hesitated. "One thing we've gained"—Bud took his drink—"Kent Shaw did go to the Biltmore. Did see the ad. Did respond."

"We're 'way ahead of that, aren't we?" I said. "His being in Castine was no coincidence. Marcus says a coincidence only means that the connecting roots are underground. Am I preaching? I'm only trying to be cheerful."

Charley said with a look almost of pain, "Ollie's cheered me up. Now you cheer her up, Bud, why don't you? I am positively folding for the night."

"Cheer *her* up?" said Bud fondly. "Our little Teacher?"

Charley lifted his hand and grinned good night and went away. It's strange how the space between my dark walls became wider and more bare, more bleak, when he had gone.

Bud said to me, "You don't feel low, do you? Believe me, Ollie, we are going to get them."

"I believe you," I said.

"And speaking of coincidences, as you so intelligently were," (I liked Bud) "you know I thought I saw our Maine friend in the Biltmore Hotel?"

"Our who?"

"Your chaperone. May have been a relative of hers, at that. Younger getup, that's for sure. Green whatchamacallit." He made circling motions of his forefinger around his head, "and big round jiggers from the ears. I learned one time always to look at bone structures and not hats. I sure saw a likeness." Maybe he was babbling to entertain me, because I seemed to be crying again. But I stopped that.

I said, "Oh, Bud . . . oh, Bud . . . oh, what a *fool!* Oh, Bud. . . ."

"What's the matter?"

"Bones *can* be changed. *Noses* can be changed. Marcus said so. It wasn't a coincidence, not at all! Not at all!"

Bud was looking at me but soon he wasn't seeing me.

"And, oh," I moaned, "I thought I was so smart. But all she did was turn out her toes and waddle and she fooled me."

"Darlene Hite," Bud said in awe.

"We *saw* her. You and I. She saved my life."

"Darlene Hite," he repeated.

"That old biddy," said I (at last), "was no Down East personally appointed chaperone for lone women at night *at all!*"

"I think I can describe her," said Bud licking his lip, "as she is now."

"But she was in the Biltmore!" I cried. "If you saw *her,* probably she saw *you.* Maybe she saw you in Maine, Bud. Maybe you scared her off tonight."

"Maybe," he said grimly. "If so, done. Never mind. I think you are right. I've got to get word out. Description. Hey, you know this can result in something?" So he kissed me a loud smack on the forehead and rushed away.

He'd been gone about five minutes when I knew where else Darlene Hite had been tonight and might still be.

Coincidence it was not! I began to think there was no such thing. I meant to *know.* I sat on my phone and called Charley's number. No answer. It was 11:25. He'd left about a quarter after. If he was on his way to bed, as he had said, he'd get there in another few minutes. But no answer. No answer. I couldn't reach Bud, now. I didn't have that mysterious number of theirs.

What I did . . . I called Kent Shaw. It seemed a good idea at the time.

"Kent? Olivia Hudson."

"Oh? And how's life, dear?"

"And you?" I said politely. "I thought you might like to know Cora's flying to France in the morning."

"You thought I might like to know?" he said.

"That bon voyage you promised her."

"So I did," said Kent. "Thanks very much. How early in the morning?"

"Not so early the press won't be there," said I, "more's the pity. The flight's at nine."

"I do thank you," he said rather shrilly. "Mustn't forget our manners, must we?"

I hung up and I thought *Oh, what have I done!* I called Charley again, in somewhat of a panic, and this time he answered.

"Charley, tell me quick," I cried, "that woman who saw you in Kent Shaw's room . . . did she wear a *green turban* and *hoop earrings?*"

"Yes."

"Then she was Darlene Hite!" It took a surprisingly short time to explain to him how this could be so. "Don't you see?" I babbled. "She's *smart*. She figured just as you did. She saw him into the Biltmore and hurried back. She wanted to get her hands on that key. She thought he'd leave it behind just as you did. Oh, Charley, has she *got* it?"

"Seems to me I was still rummaging around too close to the time he'd get in. Believe me, if she could find anything in that rat's nest, she *is* smart. Teacher, are you right this time? The woman I saw *lives* across the hall."

"It really doesn't matter," I said, "whether I'm right. If only I *might* be, we'll have to go and see."

"I'll go see. Not you."

"Can you reach Bud?" I squirmed. I wasn't going to sit home.

"I can relay a message. He'll get it pretty fast."

"What if you don't get him, Charley?"

"So?" He sounded suspicious.

"Don't you see, you *need* me?"

"Don't you remember this Shaw is a killer and nobody for you to tangle—?"

"Maybe he went out. I . . . I . . . I think he has."

"What!"

"Well, I . . . I called him. I told him Cora was leaving early in the morning. Maybe he'll go . . . try for her, now. I did it to get him *away*. So we could get Darlene. Charley?"

Charley groaned. "Cousin Ollie, will you keep out of this?"

"No," I said. "I'll meet you there. You can't get along without me."

"I can't?" he said.

"I saw her in Maine and you never did, you goop!" Silence. "So, shall I pick you up, Charley, my boy?" I quavered.

"I'll be there before you, Teacher," he snapped.

So I slammed down the phone joyfully and dashed into my camel's hair coat, and ran for the elevator.

Charley, of course, first called and left the word for Bud Gray.

Then (of course) he called the hospital. He meant to alert the guards over Cora, lest Kent Shaw turn up. He couldn't risk losing *her*, for Marcus' sake.

How . . . how can I explain the things that happened that dreadful night?

Chapter Twenty-one

BUT I must try.

In the first place, consider Kent Shaw. Half mad, maybe three-quarters mad with disappointment that Darlene Hite had not kept this second rendezvous. Maybe oppressed, besides, by what he may have sensed, the watching, the searching of his room. Feeling on the verge, the absolute teetering verge of a great crashing. Then I call and say the other bird is flying out of hand. What would Kent Shaw do but call the hospital (while Charley and I were talking) to see whether or not he had yet succeeded in getting rid of Cora Steffani?

The hospital let the call go through, on instruction, and someone listened in. So a record of that conversation exists:

"Cora, darling, I hear you are going away in the morning."

"How did you hear that, Kent, darling?"

"Oh, somebody told me. When shall I see you to say good-bye?"

"Good-bye, now," Cora said to him gaily.

"But I wanted to send you a little something for bon voyage. You remember?"

"Mail it, Kent, dear."

"How will I know where to mail it, Cora, darling?"

"Because I will tell you," she said. "I will write. I will be gone a long time, darling, and it is possible nobody will ever see me again."

"Is that so?"

"I shall buy me a new face, don't you see? Then I won't be bothered anymore. Will I?" She was gay. And she was threatening. "But, of course, I can write a letter. To anyone I used to know."

"How clever of you," he said. "What an idea! I will surely mail you some token. Candy? Could I see you tonight if I came?"

"Don't bother. I wouldn't take candy on the plane, darling, because of its weight. Although something sweet. . . ."

"Mayn't I come tonight?"

"No, darling," she said rather indistinctly.

"Ah, too bad."

"It will taste as sweet afterward," she rumbled. "But promise not to forget."

"Oh, I swear . . ." he said.

"Help me." Silence.

Kent's ear must have been lacerated by the phone.

A nurse's voice, distantly, sharply, said, "Miss Steffani?" Then the nurse's voice, in the phone, "I'll have to hang up. I think she is fainting."

So Kent hung up and didn't think she was fainting. And no more was she. She had reached for something sweet to pop into her mouth as they were talking.

Therefore, when Charley Ives called the hospital at 11:38, they were able to tell him that Cora seemed to have been poisoned in some mysterious way.

Charley Ives did what he had to do. He rushed for the hospital. A dying statement could save Marcus. It was no choice really. He had to go.

Consider Bud Gray. He called that relay number, as in duty he must, and received Charley's message at 11:40. He was only five minutes away from Kent Shaw's place. The name of Darlene Hite was like a beacon. And he hurried. So, at about 11:45, Bud Gray spoke quietly to the man watching outside, and he went in. He proceeded up the stairs, heart in his mouth with hope that at last . . . at last. . . .

He listened to the silence on the dingy second floor. He tapped on the door across from Kent Shaw's. Nobody answered. "Mrs. Thompson?" said Bud softly, reading from the card tacked on the door. No answer. "Mrs. Thompson, may I speak to you? Please?"

Nothing.

So Bud said pleadingly and subtly in threat, "Darling? You'd better let me in." And again, "Darling?"

When no answer came to this either, he reluctantly retreated to go

down to the basement and roust out the landlord and get in at that
door.

And now think of Kent Shaw, who must have been at first exultant.
One down! One woman gone! Then wouldn't he realize the terrible
pressure that would descend now upon the other one? If Cora died,
Darlene might be so terrified as to despair of the money, as to tell.
Now he *must* get Darlene Hite. But how? He didn't know where she
was.

He would have been flat against the inside of his own door, listening. He'd have heard Bud Gray say, "Darling?" And it was just as
close to her name as Bud had meant it to be. In the wrong ear.

Darlene didn't answer.

Perhaps Kent cracked his door and saw Bud going away and knew
him for Charley's friend, or perhaps for what he was, a policeman.
Kent would be jumpy to the point of madness, desperate to seize
upon any chance whatsoever. Surely he began to wonder what woman
lived in that room, had rented it two weeks ago, and had not been
seen.

Or, if he had seen her, still I had put into Cora's mind the notion
of remodeling a face. And she had put the notion into his. And none
of us could have known that Kent Shaw, in the course of some romantic skirmish with a former tenant, retained a key to that door.

Darlene Hite, who had boldly decided that safety was actually right
across the hall from death, did not know this either. When she heard
Bud's voice, she crept from the bed, looked at the windows, turned
on no light, made a mistake. . . .

Consider me, knowing nothing of all this, taking a taxi, stopping it
correctly three doors away. Then, hunching myself along the shadows
in the correct movie-spy manner, going up the stoop, passing the man
on watch who didn't know me and didn't stop me, ringing the wrong
bell and getting into the house by this classic method, all the while my
heart beating high with pleasurable pretending to myself that I was in
danger.

I inspected the dirty cards on the downstairs wall. One clean one
said Mrs. Miles Thompson. I found Kent Shaw's name in a kind of
decadently elegant script, with his room number penciled on in red. I
walked up the stairs. The house smelled old and hopelessly encrusted,
as if nothing could ever get it sweet and clean again.

I had only to choose the door across from Kent Shaw's. I expected Charley Ives to be there, of course. My function, as I saw it, was to lay eyes on this woman, and if she was the one from Maine, to say so. Then we would accuse and discover. At that moment, I had put aside my play-acting about danger. I three-quarters believed that Kent Shaw was not in the building. So I went blithely up and when I found the door of Darlene's room swinging, although the room had no light in it, fool that I was . . . I rushed in.

The dark hit me, as if I came up against a wall. But someone was waiting in the dark. Then, in what light came through the blind, for the dark was soon not so black, I could see a glitter, a shine. I knew him by the knife in his hand. Kent Shaw was in there waiting. I could almost sense the turmoil and the evil in his soul.

But, you see, I thought that Charley Ives was at least coming soon. I was almost sure he was already there, somewhere, and I knew that Bud would not be far behind. In the teeth of danger, I didn't even think of danger. When I saw the knife, at once I wondered if Darlene was dead. It sickened me with fear for Marcus. If Darlene was dead, if Kent had got her, and if Cora never broke and told, why then we were beaten.

So I thought I must, therefore, do something for Marcus' sake. *Somebody* had to crack and tell. Lacking Darlene, there was Kent Shaw. Something must be done about him. Oh, I could have turned quickly in my tracks and gone back down the stairs, but I swear that it didn't even occur to me.

By a kind of instinct that wasn't courage—for where is courage when you haven't the sense to be afraid?—I did the only thing I knew how to do. I play-acted. I jumped into another skin. Yet (because this was for my life, as I somehow also knew, as well as for Marcus) I knew it had to be good. I had to make him *believe*. So I chose the character I'd studied for seventeen years. I became Cora Steffani.

There was no light on my face but some light in the hall behind me. I drew myself into the high-bosomed, chin-flung-up, hip-tilted posture that was Cora. I let my hand and arm move, flowing from the shoulder, as I softly pushed the door nearer closed. Now we were in a darker place, but I had no doubt Kent Shaw could see my outline. I said in Cora's voice, "Kent, is that you, darling?"

Now you must know that the hospital was a long way uptown on the West Side, whereas I'd had a straight run down from my apartment.

It had taken me fourteen minutes. Oh, I didn't know that Kent had just within minutes called the hospital, that he knew Cora was there, poisoned, dying.

So when he said in a hoarse voice, "Darlene?" all I thought was, Ah, this is something like it! And I hoped that Charley Ives was close enough to hear.

But I couldn't play Darlene. So I said, in Cora's voice, with one of her flying movements of the hand, "No, dear. Cora. I came for what you promised."

He said, "Go away. Go back. Go back."

"But I need it, darling," said I in Cora's coaxing manner. "I'm going abroad. Didn't you know? I thought I would come for what you owe me. It's only fair." He didn't speak. I strained to *make* him speak, for evidence. "Where is Darlene?" said I, with Cora's suspicious jealousy. "Have you paid her before me?"

He couldn't have been able to see my face. Of course, he did have in his mind the notion of plastic surgery. He may have expected Cora to look other than like herself already. I knew he was confused. I didn't imagine that his masterpiece, his beautiful hoax, was turning over in his brain.

He said, "Darlene, I'm glad you are here. I'll give you the key. That's what you want, isn't it?"

But I had to stay being Cora. So I laughed Cora's high affected laughter. I wanted him to go on saying revealing and incriminating things. I thought Charley Ives had probably come on soft feet and was listening in the hall by now. I wasn't afraid. I said, "Kent, don't you know me? It's Cora Steffani, darling."

"Cora is in the hospital," he said.

"But, darling, I'm the Dream Walker—the lady you've taught so cleverly to be two places at once. . . ."

His thin shrill voice that lacked only volume to be a scream, said, "No. She got the poison. You got to be Darlene."

The word "poison" staggered me. I saw his knife lift and make ready. I'd thought if he ran at me to run into the hall. Now I thought, Where is Charley? I hadn't the time to be much afraid. With a vague notion that I could delay him or appease him, I said, "Oh, very well. I am Darlene."

But I couldn't play Darlene. All the negatives I was using—the voice Darlene couldn't mimic because she wasn't trained well enough, the posture that he had never been able to teach her to hold, because she hadn't the control, the gestures—these were Cora's and never Darlene's. All my wisps of knowledge had an inverted power. I had made him believe I couldn't be Darlene.

He let out a yammering sound. He cried, "Cora!" in a shriek of terror. And the knife flew at me through the air because he believed I was Cora . . . walking.

It struck me in the breastbone. I may have staggered slightly. I did not fall. I hadn't thought of his *throwing* that knife. I seemed to myself to stand there, stupidly surprised. But I stood. I knew I was alone. Charley Ives was not here. Nobody listened at the door. I had rushed in and taken the role of the victim, and nobody was going to cast me for the heroine. I thought with dumb sorrow, "Teacher, thirty-four." Naturally, no hero. . . .

The knife wasn't causing me pain. It was only dragging and heavy. But I knew Kent Shaw could at any moment leap and press the knife deeper and then I would die. So I stood still for my life. I said, in Cora's trill, "Why, of course. I am in the hospital, too. You can't hurt me, darling. Not now, that I've got on to the trick of being two places . . ." and I laughed Cora's laugh. So his whole design turned in his brain.

He began to whinny, a high, sick sound. I knew he was afraid. I knew I could die . . . if I ran. So I took a step toward the faint light that crossed under and through the flimsy blind. The knife tip was wedged, in flesh or bone, and held there. I didn't touch it. I wasn't bleeding. Kent Shaw whinnied and drew himself against the wall.

"You should keep your promises," I said reproachfully. "Darlene and I did all the work. You mustn't think you can kill us. *We* aren't Ed Jones."

He made a most horrible sound.

I shifted my course. I thought I could drive him to the window. I thought if he went through it, then I wouldn't have to die. I could see his face now. He didn't look at mine. With bursting eyeballs, he stared at the knife protruding bloodlessly from my breastbone.

"Ed Jones was mortal, Kent, darling," said I in Cora's saucy, slightly malicious voice.

He fell on the floor and rolled, out of all control, with that high whinnying sound coming steadily out of him.

The light came on. I didn't turn around because I was staring at a pair of hands that came from behind a dirty flowered curtain across the corner. The hands had a flannel sash in them and were ready to bind Kent Shaw to harmlessness. But they weren't Charley's hands.

A voice behind me said loudly, "For God's sake, Ollie!" It wasn't Charley's voice. It was Bud Gray.

He floated in two strides all the way to the corner and flung the curtain aside. He looked piercingly at the woman who had been hidden there. He took the sash out of her hands and bent and secured Kent Shaw, who made no effort of any kind.

The woman said to me, "I guess he would have found me in about another minute and I left my gun in the bed. I guess you saved my life, Miss . . . Hudson, isn't it?" Her voice was not particularly nasal to my ear.

Bud said, "Sit down, Ollie. Don't touch that thing. What in hell has been going on!" He took those giant strides without waiting for an answer, and laid about him with commands, speaking to other people in the hall.

I sat down on the edge of the bed, keeping very erect, and the knife shook so I thought it might be loosened and fall of itself. I said, in my mind, Where can Charley be?

Darlene Hite, in her nightdress, stood quietly.

Bud Gray said to her, "You saved *her* life in Maine. I think you don't like this much anymore. Am I right? Don't be afraid, Miss Darlene Hite. I've wanted to meet you for a long time. Need you on our side."

She looked at him. Her eyes fled, returned. "I've got to be, I guess," said Darlene Hite with her usual clear-headedness.

The rooming house had sprung to life all around us. I sat with the knife quivering, Darlene dressed behind the curtain, while Kent Shaw still steadily went on like a whistle that has been stuck open and the noise begins to rub on the raw of one's nerves. Then police came and soon the ambulance, and a cool and imperturbable young man pulled that knife away. And Bud Gray watched Darlene with glowing eyes and talked and slowly she seemed to respond, to go toward him. So there I was, very numb and calm, sitting with my blouse in tatters and nothing but a wad of gauze to make me decent, when finally Charley Ives walked in.

His face was stone. His eyes were porcelain.

"My hero!" said I idiotically. "What kept you?"

I saw his eyes blaze and, dizzy with a great revealing sense of utter relief . . . I fainted.

Dr. Harper said, "That wound's not much. You're all right, Olivia." I was in the emergency room at the hospital. He was better than reassuring. He let me talk and sort out my own impressions of the immediate past. I finally got what I was afraid to ask out of my mouth. "Cora?"

"Worst possible place to try any poisoning is a first-class hospital," the doctor said complacently. "We got at her with everything in the book. Cora's all right."

"How did it happen?"

"Candies. Humbugs, they call 'em." I let out a startled wail. "How the devil they got to her we still don't know," he said.

"Is she telling . . . ?"

"She couldn't very well talk while we worked on her, believe me. She's back in her bed, playing too sick to speak, thinking it over, I suppose. Charley Ives is fit to be tied."

"He was *here,* then?"

"Hanging over her, with a tape recorder running."

"Of course," said I. "Did they bring Kent Shaw here?"

The doctor shook his head. I didn't like what I saw in his eyes. "Sit up. You're fine. You're also lucky. I better see if Charley's around."

A nurse was helping me put my clothing back together over the bandages when Charley came bursting in. He cast one glance at me and my latest immodesty. The bright blue of his eye was not exactly sympathetic. He spoke briefly to the doctor. He marched over. I understood.

I burst into apology. "Oh, Charley, I was *wrong.* And *you* were right. I shouldn't have done anything I did."

"True," Charley said gently but firmly.

"And you *had* to be with Cora. I didn't mean to reproach you. I was just scared, Charley."

Charley blinked. His face turned wooden.

"Is he really clear out of his head? Kent Shaw?" I cried. "So nothing he says can be evidence? Charley, is it that bad?"

"He's pretty much gone," Charley said.

"Then I've wrecked everything."

"Anything could have sent him off the deep end," Charley said impatiently. "Don't beat yourself, now. Darlene thinks she'd have been gone. . . ." Then he relaxed and looked amused. "You know, a little ordinary human cowardice, and you could have yelled for help. Bud was in the basement."

"Oh," said I stupidly, "then I had a hero after all." Thunderous silence. "I'm sorry for what I said," I was nearly bawling. "For what I did . . . everything. . . ."

"Never mind, coz. Bud has Darlene. But why he didn't jump a little faster into that room I'll never. . . ."

"Oh, no, Bud was wonderful," said I, thinking of Darlene and how Bud had projected to her, somehow, in those impossible circumstances, his friendliness and his admiration and his hope for her. "But it's all right," I cried, feeling reprieved, "if Darlene is talking."

Charley said, "It'll be all right," in a manner just a little too soothing.

I was alarmed all over again. All I could think was that I'd hurt Marcus. "Charley, if Bud was there soon enough to hear what was said, how Kent kept calling me Darlene, and all that . . . won't it help?"

"We've got Kent Shaw," said Charley. "Don't worry about that."

"And Cora?"

"Uh huh," he said. "So now you get home to bed. Walking around with knives . . . of all the . . . !" He turned his back abruptly. "Bud said it was a top performance, in fact, it fooled *him*. Had enough, coz? Better go home, hadn't you?"

"Charley, my boy," said I tartly, "you're a lousy actor. I've said so before. What I did is even worse than I know, isn't it? Tell Teacher, come on."

Charley turned around again. "Okay, Teacher," he sighed. "It's this way. Kent Shaw is in no shape to tell us how he put the blue envelope in the book. Darlene doesn't know anything about that. She wasn't coached about Washington. She wasn't there. And *she* can't tie in Pankerman. She never heard of his being in it. Now, lacking Kent Shaw, only Raymond Pankerman can tell us about the blue envelope, since he wrote the letter that was in it, and he must have given it to Shaw. The problem is, get Pankerman. Him and his Fifth Amendment."

"But Cora can tie in Pankerman," I said slowly, "can't she? She'd know Kent Shaw had no money. And she'd make sure where the money was coming from."

"I should think so, too. But you see, Cora isn't talking. Yet."

"But you've *got* her. For Heaven's *sakes,* Charley!"

"Sure. Sure, we've got her."

"Don't you think you can make her talk?"

Charley said with false cheer, "Maybe. Maybe I'm just pessimistic." We looked at each other. There was that hard stubborn fight in Cora, that long-practiced clawing and scratching for her advantage. There would be no repentance, no aching conscience, no intolerable pain of guilt, to break her down. She didn't even understand what, indeed, she had done.

"Bud's got Darlene upstairs now. Going to try. We're waiting on the Boss," Charley told me. "We can tell her we've got Kent Shaw."

"She doesn't know . . . how he is?"

"No."

"But you haven't got him," I said sadly, "because Kent Shaw *isn't* anymore. Will he recover in time, Charley?"

Charley just shook his head.

"Then," I said, "it's not going to be easy to make Cora talk." And then I saw headlines, pictures, heard arguments . . . and I could see months and months of it, and Cora cast as the lone, the underdog . . . and some woolly-headed sympathy edging around . . . and a long, noisy, damaging struggle yet before us. Unless she confessed, too.

"You don't have leverage," I said, "and she's got nothing to lose."

Charley sat down suddenly on a chair next to mine and he took my hands. "Coz, do you know how to make her talk?" I shook my head. "I forced you to try acting my way," he said. "Maybe I don't understand. . . ."

"I . . . I did have a silly idea," I said. "It's wild and foolish. It's only play-acting."

"We've got to have her story. If we can't smash all of it, in one blow. . . ."

"I know," I said.

"*I* don't know how to deal with her. I've made nothing but mistakes since I met her. Thought I found something I'd been missing—gaiety, spice of life. Ran into something too tortuous and unprincipled for . . . well, for me. Tried to get out of it and made a mess of that, too. I can make her angry, coz. But I'm never the one to know how to make her talk." Charley frightened me, being as humble as this.

"Unless," I said, "you touch a feeling that's true, you won't do it."

"She hasn't any feelings," he said bitterly.

"Yes. She has," I said.

"Coz?" Charley seemed to be listening hard as he could to my very thoughts. "Had you better come along upstairs?"

The doctor said, "Now, just a minute. She's had about enough for one night. Came damned close to being killed."

"Twice over," I said. "She offered me a piece of candy and I was too stupid to ask where it came from."

Charley said to me sternly, "No good to Marcus for you to bewail how stupid you are."

"Why, that's so," said I, bracing up.

"If you even think you've got the least idea how to help."

I felt better suddenly. "Wait and see," I said, "and if she's too tortuous for you. . . ." I suppose I grinned.

"Uh huh," said Charley, sounding more cheerful. "Takes fire to fight fire. You better tag along. What will you *do?*" he demanded.

"Nothing, I hope. If I have to, I'll . . . tell her some truth." (I knew I had to say this.) "She'll never *believe,* unless I do, you know."

Charley said under his breath, "Teacher, you terrify me."

"Let me go," I said, "in a wheelchair, I think." I looked down at my blouse, which was bloodstained. "Just as I am."

"Hold on to your hat, Doc," said Charley Ives grimly.

Chapter Twenty-two

THEY PUSHED ME in a wheelchair down the familiar corridor on the eighth floor and into Cora's room, where there was a crowd. She was lying abed, pale, her lids languorous. They lifted at sight of me. "Why, Ollie?" she whimpered in surprise.

I made *my* lids languorous and sick and said nothing, laying foundations.

"What happened?" she asked weakly.

Nobody answered her. A man I'd never seen before said quietly, "All in order? Shall we begin?" He was a stocky individual with very large eyes over which flesh, beneath his brows, seemed to fall in a fold. Bud Gray was standing near him, exuding a kind of possessiveness over Darlene Hite, in the easy chair. Her almost white, very pale hair was caught back neatly. Her gray eyes were serious. Her hands were quiet. Her attitude was subdued and businesslike. Yet I could imagine that something about her was leaning, leaning with pitiable relief and trust, on Mr. Horace (Bud) Gray. They made a pair. I saw Ned Dancer being a mouse in the corner with his ears out.

Cora's black-and-yellow robe was thrown around her shoulders and the long folds, that should fall to her feet, lay like a long splash above the white coverlet. She was keeping still, in seventeen languages. Oh, I knew her! I prayed I knew her now. Her eyes disdained Darlene Hite, skipped over Charley with a flicker of scorn, but when they shifted to me they were not satisfied.

I touched the floor with my toe and rolled the chair ever so slightly that light might fall on my bandages and my blood.

The Boss began, in a cold monotone, to outline the plot. He began to ring in Darlene's testimony, by his questions and her answers, her firm, precise, untinted answers. It rolled out, sounding complete and damning.

Finally he said, "Now you had a certain written memorandum of all this, Miss Hite. The times, places, and the words you were to say?"

"I did." Her voice was untrained, to be sure, but the nasal quality was really very slight and it was not unpleasant.

"You have it still?" she was asked.

"I have only the instructions for Castine. The others I burned. It is in a kind of shorthand but I can read it for you."

"You think Miss Steffani had a duplicate?"

"Yes, sir."

"May we see yours?"

Darlene took a pair of eyeglasses out of her bag. They were hung on a cord by means of short rubber tubes slipped over the earpieces, just as Cora's also were. Darlene pulled off one of the rubber tubes and produced from its interior a tiny scrap of paper.

Bud Gray now raised his hands and we saw that he had Cora's glasses. He did as Darlene had done. But there was nothing hidden, nothing there. Cora had managed to destroy it all. Her mouth twitched.

Charley Ives said, "No matter."

The Boss said, "That about tells the story. We will move into court. Miss Hite can give her side of it. Raymond Pankerman is available. Kent Shaw is in custody."

Cora said, "Am I in custody?"

"You are."

"Then I am," she said and shrugged. (I almost saw her legs crossing on some witness stand.)

Charley tried very hard to look relieved. "Pretty clever," he drawled. "Why don't you tell us your side of it, Cora?"

Cora said, "Why should I tell you anything? You all think you know everything." Her eyes jerked to me. "What happened to Ollie?" she asked irritably.

I said broodingly, "Kent Shaw and I disagreed, that's all."

Cora bit her lip. Her eyes traveled from side to side. She was shrewd. She leaned back. "Well," she said petulantly, "I should think the doctor might explain that I ought to be asleep. I was *poisoned,* you know."

"I know," I murmured. (It puzzled her.)

"I'm ready to take down anything you have to say," said Bud Gray. (Dancer was, too.)

"Why, bless you," said Cora impudently. "Then take down this. That woman doesn't look one bit like me. You say she's had an operation. *I* say she just wants in on my publicity."

Charley said, "Won't do, Cora."

"No?" said Cora. "Where is Kent Shaw? That pip-squeak mastermind. Why haven't you got *him* here?" Oh, she was shrewd.

"They are examining him downtown," Charley lied placidly.

"Where?" said Cora. "In the morgue? Ah, ah, mustn't fib, you know. If Ollie got hurt as bad as that, surely she was well avenged by all these big strong men." I heard the malice and the jealousy in that tone. "I'd sure like to know what happened to the other fellow," she said, looking incorrigibly saucy.

"He isn't dead," Charley said. "Don't make that mistake."

"Then bring him around, why don't you?" she challenged.

If she knew Kent Shaw was insane and unable to bear witness, we might never get the truth about the blue envelope and without that one detail. . . . Now, she'd got in her head the notion that Kent Shaw was dead and no witness, ever. No danger. So Cora was going to hang on. She had to. Guilt didn't bother her and good-looking women had got off things before. She could be very confusing. It was her only chance. In a muddle she might squeak through. She had nothing to lose by trying. She wasn't going to confess. I stopped hoping for it.

"Tell us about Pankerman," the Boss said, as if she gladly would. The suggestion of his manner didn't work.

"I've seen his name in the papers," said Cora. "Is that what you mean?" Her eyes lit with the old mischief. "Oh, go on, it's nothing but a plot," said Cora outrageously. "To save your precious John Paul Marcus from what are his just deserts, as far as I can see. I don't care what you say or do. Keep me in custody. *I dream. That's all I know.*" She sighed prettily. "More headlines," she pouted. "Will I always be the most famous woman in America?"

Several people in that room (including me) could have socked her. There she was, Cora Steffani, phony, illogical, unreasonable . . . completely beaten, and still not beaten. And what was there to do?

Darlene Hite frowned faintly and looked up at Bud Gray. Gray looked at Charley Ives. Charley turned his head, ever so slightly. Before he could turn too obviously to me, I knew I was for it. I said, deep in my throat, "Too much ham in me, after all."

They all looked at me. Ned Dancer's neck stretched.

"Most famous woman in America," I began to laugh. I arched my back, which I hoped would make the blood flow from my little wound. I put my fingers on the bandage and drew them away and looked at them, as if there were blood. "Changed my mind," I said. "I don't think I'll take this secret to the grave." I looked insolent. I felt power. (Oh, there is nothing like a Bad Girl role. It's so comparatively simple and easy.)

The doctor looked startled and moved and I said sharply, "No,

Doctor. If I want to sing a swan song, I shall do it. This is a fine audience, as good as I'd choose."

(Charley had to help me. I had to make him help me.) I glanced at Cora only briefly. "Old friend, dear friend," I said and laughed. "You'll only be the second most famous woman in America tomorrow morning."

"What are you talking about?" said Charley, almost too hopefully.

"So many men in the world," I said to him, "why did I want only you?" I sultried my eyes. (Oh, it's corny. It's easy.) And Charley was staring at me. "You should know, gentlemen," said I, "for future reference, that a woman who wants a certain man very much, and cannot get him, really has to protect herself." I looked only at Charley.

Did Cora wince?

"It's a weird triangle," said I, "that's only two parallel lines. I thought you were fond of your wife." I bit that word out, looking at Charley, for this was necessary. And he did what I wanted. He locked his gaze with mine. "Charley, my boy," said I and it wasn't teasing, "can you imagine? Cora thought you were fond of *me*? But Charley Ives isn't fond of any woman, is he? And long ago the old man," I said viciously, "didn't hold with cousins marrying."

I could feel Cora's stare.

"Women are dangerous," I said. "Aren't we, Cora?" I didn't turn my head.

"What are you raving about?" she exploded. I did *not* look at her.

Neither did Charley. He kept taut the line of attention between us two.

"It's been amusing," I said. "You thought she was using me, didn't you, Charley? When *I've* used Kent Shaw. *I've* used Ray Pankerman. *I've* used my old friend Cora. *I'm* the one with the money," I said contemptuously.

People were shocked and silent. I smiled in insolent power. "Don't you believe it? Why, how funny! How very amusing! How is it that nobody wonders why Kent Shaw went after *me* with his knife? Little man, loved his little part, he did. Couldn't even trust *me* not to tell." My eyes clung to Charley's eyes. I tried to pierce him with a look of meanness and power. His face was slowly turning red and horrified. "But now I tell because I choose," I said haughtily. "Let it smash. I'd like to have killed your ex-wife, Charley, my boy. I could do without her. Such a witty way to do it, too. With a humbug. Oh, if I had and if Kent hadn't been quite so quick. . . . But I don't mind," said I. "It would have been very dull."

I threw back my head and strangled my voice with tension and ugliness. "Two places at once! Wasn't it *fun?* And you're not very happy. You hate her, now. And me, too? Then so much for True Love, Charley, my boy." I leaned forward. "Still, now that you know what I did, in my Ivory Tower, *that I pulled all the strings,* will you call me Teacher for this lesson?"

And Charley said, in a frightened voice, "Cousin Ollie!"

So I let it all go. I let my heart break. I said, "Charley, I've been . . . hurt . . . so long. You didn't care. *Did* you? Charley?" I fell back.

Charley flew to me, knelt to me. I put my hand, my fingers spread, on the back of his head, in his hair.

Cora had her legs curled under her and was on her knees. "That's just not *so,*" she gasped childishly. "That's not *so.*" She beat her fists and howled for attention. "It wasn't her money. She hasn't got that kind of money. I can prove it was Pankerman's. Kent and I watched him put it in the safe. I think she's going crazy. Make her tell you," screamed Cora Steffani, "that she's just a liar!"

"Where is this safe?" said Bud Gray quickly, softly.

She told them where it was. She began to tell them everything.

"Get me out of here," I said in Charley's ear. So he signaled and the doctor wheeled me out.

In the corridor I got stiffly out of the chair. "You said I can go home? This isn't so bad I have to stay here?"

"No, no, go home if you want to." The doctor was looking at me with a blank expression.

Ned Dancer came out. I was standing, calm and collected. He stopped in his tracks and said sourly, "Quite an act."

"Only way I could think of," I told him. "She was going to cause too much trouble. The one thing she couldn't stand was to think *I'd* fooled her."

"Should auld acquaintance be forgot," said Ned, surprising me with such quick understanding.

Dr. Harper said with a very phony laugh, "You pretty near fooled me, I can tell you."

Charley Ives came flying out of Cora's room. He shot blue lightning at Ned, who said quickly, "I won't use it. Couldn't hope to." Then, like a male, "Dames, huh?"

"Takes a dame to fight a dame," said Charley heartily. "Cora's tied in Pankerman all right. And she says Kent Shaw gave her the title of that book in March. In a ladies' room, for gosh sakes. So we've got it!"

"That's splendid," said I stiffly.

He took me by the shoulders. "Wow!" He was grinning. (I didn't think he was fooled, somehow.)

"It was a real juicy part, and very melo," I said in my teacher's voice, "but, you see, it was sound."

"Sound?" Now Charley sounded strange.

"The feeling. I told you. It was *hers*. Her own true feeling. The meanest kind of jealousy. So she was afraid what I said *might* be so, because she recognized the *feeling*. That's about the only thing can make-believe. See Dramatics 2, Miss Hudson, Monday, Wednesday and Friday."

Charley looked queer. He let me go.

"But you mustn't worry," I said primly. "It wasn't *all* because she felt things about you. Or about me. She had several other motives mixed in."

"I . . . daresay," he drawled. "I'll try to be tough about it."

I heard myself snap, "Now, if you think you can manage, I'd like to go home."

He said wryly, "Teacher, we can always call you. . . ."

Ned Dancer was gone.

"Oh, Charley," I said, "I suppose you thought I was off my rocker. But you can't act and so I *had* to. I'm glad if it worked. I hope you understand. I bet you don't."

(I guess he understood.)

"Rest your imagination," Charley said kindly and kissed me in a fond cousinly way and sent me home.

Chapter Twenty-three

THE WHOLE THING burst with one last bang. How quickly it died away! What's duller than a burst balloon? People, on the whole, got that one word. *Hoax*. They then said, if they could, "I told you so." And if they couldn't, they said, and still say, darkly, "There's a lot more we haven't been told."

Kent Shaw went to a mental hospital. Ray Pankerman collapsed. Wept useless dollar signs. As much money as they found in that safe can't travel without leaving traces. He even asked for Marcus' mercy in confessing about the blue envelope. But the law had *him*.

The law would have to examine the murder of Ed Jones. Was Cora an accessory? Was Darlene? Then, it would all roll out under the rules and the evidence be presented exhaustively. Millions would be too bored to read every question and answer, or to reason and conclude from these, or take the pains. Yet there, in the questions and answers, would be every careful detail, the very best we could do.

Marcus' household was happier and Marcus on the phone was just the same. Vindicated as far as was humanly possible. But he has a scar.

My wound healed nicely. It wasn't much. I stayed at home and talked as freely as I could to all newsmen, all callers. Miss Reynolds had asked me back, since I now began to rank as a clever spy on the right side. The girls came by and made a fuss of me. Oh, I'd go back. When summer was over.

Meantime, I had no work. I felt empty. All my friends came to see me, but no Cora Steffani, and I missed her like an aching tooth. The pain of that was still in me, the echoes of all the years of tension between us, an occupation lost in a victory that left me empty. I was let down. I felt like a fool, besides. I was really moping. I didn't go to Washington.

A week had gone by. It was late, the night he came.

"Didn't want to run into a mob here," he told me. "Have I timed it right?"

"Everybody's gone home, Charley, my boy," said I brightly. "I was about to go to bed, myself. Tell me, how is Marcus?"

"Marcus is fine. Tough, you know." Charley sat down. My walls bulged, as ever they did when he came in. "And you?" asked he.

"Nothing left but an interesting little scar," I said and hurried on, wishing I hadn't put it quite that way. "I'm doing business at the old stand. Back to school in the fall. All is forgiven."

"Splendid," he drawled.

"Where is Darlene Hite?" I asked quickly. "Vanished again? I don't read about her."

"Bud doesn't want her read about. She's in Washington, under his wing. He's fighting to save her, says she's too valuable to be sacrificed, cites theories of modern penology, wants her free and working for him. I'll bet he's going to win. Besides being smart, she's quite a fine girl, or can be."

"Bud always was entranced by Darlene Hite," said I, amused. "I think he fell in love with her modus operandi."

Charley threw back his head and roared.

"It wasn't *that* funny," I said feebly. I was uncomfortable. I knew, whatever I did, I could put on no act for *myself* anymore. "Charley, my boy," I said, "if you will excuse me and come again another day? Us teachers retire pretty early."

"Stop that!" said Charley Ives violently.

"What?"

"I'll be damned if I'll let you pull that Teacher stuff, ever again. You've intimidated me long enough."

"I . . . ?"

"Sit still, and I mean still." (I sat still.) "I am going to tell you some things Marcus said. I— seems, I repeated your remark about you and Cora being measuring sticks. Marcus says that's *so*. He says people do that for each other. He says"—Charley looked at me nervously.

"You and I had a fight," he stated, starting all over again.

"We did, indeed. We still fight. We *may,* any minute," I said primly.

"*Exactly,*" pounced Charley. "Now, Marcus says you were once a moonstruck little girl, thin-skinned, sensitive, timid."

"I—I am."

"Marcus says you *were*. But now, he says, you have courage, you have bite and force, and a sense of duty as big as you are, because what I said, on my side of that fight, has rankled all this time."

"Oh, I don't . . ." I stammered. "I can't . . . I'm certainly not all that."

"As for me," said Charley, swelling up, "I was pretty crude. A narrow violent type, hell-bent, slam-bang, and on my way to being the kind who shoots first and asks questions, if any, afterward. But now, he says, I can see grays, and I've become sensitive and I may even grow up, someday. Because I've brooded many hours on what you said. So, Marcus says, people sometimes are each other's measuring sticks," Charley turned his eyes, "in envy and antagonism, or else in love."

I could not breathe. I sat still.

"So I think," Charley said awkwardly, "you really are my Teacher."

"Then," said I, and our eyes locked, "you are mine."

"*That's* so," said he quietly.

I trembled.

"Am I a mouse?" said Charley Ives to the wall, "or a cat to look at the queen? To hang around Cora's apartment because my cousin Ollie loyally wouldn't have anything to do with me, but she did come there. And then get struck with the notion that you and Bud Gray. . . ."

"Charley, my. . . ."

"STOP THAT!"

"Charles," I said. But, oh, I was warm and my blood was flowing and the world was alive and I was in the fray. "Are you trying to figure out whether we are in love with each other?"

"I am," he said. "And, oh, my not-so-very-much-a-cousin Ollie, my apostle of gentle kindness and wildest melodrama, my tigercat with a touchy conscience, my bold, ridiculous, adorable, terrifying little Teacher," his fingers touched my chin, "*wasn't* it true, Love?"

I told him how true it was, without a word.

The End.

Ah, finished, and with a clinch, too! What a mess I've made of it! Haven't put in that Pankerman's in jail, that Cora got off with a short sentence and is now abroad and God knows how she lives. That Kent Shaw is still in his limbo. That Darlene Hite has "vanished" although I know Bud Gray knows where she is and what she is doing. Oh, well, all this must go in somewhere.

But *I* won't do it. Haven't time. I'll look at Portugal on the ceiling and it won't be long. I can tell.

Be born, child. I am not afraid. Dr. Harper's an old fussbudget and Charley is a thousand times worse. Putting me here in the hospital weeks early! As if I, only thirty-five years old, can't quite safely bear this child! Never did it before, but Dr. Barron, when he married us, wished us a dozen.

Boy? Call him Charley? For my husband, my lover, my darling, my foe. . . .

Secretary. You, girl. Delete this. Stop where I said "The End." Mind, now!

OLIVIA HUDSON IVES

Nurse?

EDITOR TO PUBLISHER:

> How about the beginning and ending, Charley?

G.D.

PUBLISHER TO EDITOR:

> Leave it the way it is, George. I've got a daughter who'll eat it up when she gets to the romantic age. I'm bound she'll have it. Never mind what her Mama says. I'll fight for this.

C.I.

THE END